The

A Paranormal Murd

By Andrew M Stafford

To Gipsy

To the special 700th customer

Text Copyright © 2014 Andy Stafford
All Rights Reserved

All the characters in this book are fictitious, and any resemblance to actual persons living or dead is purely coincidental.

ISBN-13: 978-1506174020

For Kerry, Olivia, Sam, Mum and Sharon.
Especially for Dad.

ACKNOWLEDGMENTS

DC Rob Callaway (Retired) for his advice on matters of the law
Penny Rowe for proof reading
Ian CP Irvine and Michael Lewis for their advice and encouragement

CHAPTER ONE

Badock's Wood
Bristol
9.15pm
Sunday 6th September 2009

At Badock's Wood ghostly windmill sails turn and, like a rewound film, spin through history to remote times when this was burial place for Bronze Aged warrior in that landscape wolves prowled and nervy red deer grazed while hogs rooted among trees
John Fairfax (1930 – 2009)

Ben Walker was feeling good about life. Everything seemed to be falling into place.

He walked through the woods with Liz, not quite hand in hand, but he was hopeful that things would soon be moving up a notch.

Even at twenty-one, Ben was shy around girls, never having the 'bottle' to ask one out. He had plenty of friends who were girls, but never a real girlfriend.

He had known Liz for eight months and had met her through a group of friends. They had got on well from the start, but Liz got on well with everyone. She was the kind of girl that everyone liked, including the boys she met.

For Ben, it was love at first sight, but he had no idea how she felt towards him. She was a hard book to read and the last thing he would do was ask her how she felt about him, let alone tell her the feelings he had for her. He was simply too shy to ask.

Liz was twenty years old and attractive. She had a fair complexion which was highlighted when she wore lipstick. She was slight in build with her dark hair cut into a bob. From the first time Ben had met her, he had been drawn to her looks, but now her personality had won him over. Her confident nature and continuous good humour rubbed off on Ben. She was bursting with fun and positivity. This was why everyone liked her.

Perhaps Liz's confidence was due to achieving a second Dan in Taekwondo by the age of eighteen. She had started martial arts when she was twelve and now was an instructor, teaching students of all ages and grades.

She had mentioned to Ben that her young cousin was doing a school project on slow-worms and she had offered to find one for him to help with his assignment. Ben told her he knew the best place in Bristol to find the lizards, which was Badock's Wood in the north of the city.

Truthfully, he had no idea where to look for them, what time of the year they could be found, or whether slow-worms even lived in the woods. Minor details, as the reason for helping Liz was to spend time on his own with her and away from the others who were always around her. Where better to be with her than the beautiful woods where he grew up playing as a boy.

Ben knew every inch of the place. He had climbed many of the trees and paddled in the river that ran through the middle.

They walked next to each other taking in the beauty of the surroundings whilst ducking from the last of the summer gnats that were doing their merry evening jig. A blackbird was singing. Liz thought the song of the blackbird was one of the most wonderful sounds imaginable, epitomising the British summertime at its finest. The evening was warm and both were dressed in T-shirt and shorts.

They stopped to watch a pair of Painted Ladies flutter around a crop of purple foxglove.

"Do you know they're used in medicine to help people with heart conditions?" said Ben, breaking the silence.

Liz looked at him puzzled and with half a smile she replied, "Do you mean they use butterflies as medicine?"

Ben laughed and explained that foxgloves were used as medicine, not butterflies. Liz screeched with laughter at her own stupidity, laughing so hard that all other sounds in the woods seem to fade.

Liz's naivety was another thing he loved about her, as was the way she would crease up laughing over something that other people would not even find remotely amusing. There were no two ways about it, Ben was falling even further for her.

He loved her imperfections and found the tiny scar above her lip 'kinda cute'. The scar was due to an accident in Taekwondo when she broke a length of wood with her knuckles during a demonstration, launching a sharp splinter towards her face.

Although Ben had never said anything, Liz knew how he felt towards her. She sensed his jealousy when other boys were around and vying for her attention. She liked Ben a lot, but had not long finished with Malcolm, her last serious boyfriend and because the breakup had been awkward she had made a decision to stay single for the foreseeable future.

If it had not been for Malcolm, Ben would have been on her radar as definite boyfriend material. She loved his kind ways. He was someone who always wanted to help others, especially the underdog.

He was also very diplomatic, often breaking up arguments amongst their friends and dispelling any friction. Ben hated confrontation.

At five foot ten inches, Ben was a couple of inches taller than Liz. He was well built, had a warm smile and sandy fair hair. He was a good looking lad, and Liz saw an attraction in him that was beyond looks. But despite all of Ben's positives, Liz wanted to steer clear of any commitment, at least for the time being.

The other reason why Ben was in a happy place was because tomorrow his career was taking a step in the right direction.

When he was seventeen Ben had volunteered for the Avon and Somerset Constabulary as a Police Community Support Officer.

But since then, Ben had been getting bored of dealing with barking dogs and cars without tax discs. He really wanted to get his teeth into something meaty.

As a PCSO he had a police radio which worked on the same frequency as the radios used by police officers and he was able to listen in on the incidents that the officers were being called to investigate. Incidents he was not allowed to be involved with.

Many times over the radio he had heard of a fight breaking out in a pub, a burglary in progress and other more interesting cases. Although it was not within his remit, he would make his way over to these incidents and get involved.

Every time he'd involved himself in something he shouldn't, he'd ended up being reminded by his superiors what his duties were and that there were lines that he should not cross.

His superiors had their job to do and it was part of their duty to pull up young keen PSCOs and remind them where the boundaries lay.

On the positive side, it was noted that Ben had ambition and commitment.

When he turned nineteen he made an application for consideration as a police officer. His application was accepted. He was called to the assessment centre to be evaluated and once there did outstandingly well.

Following the assessment he attended an interview. Those on the interview panel were impressed by his professional conduct, his attention to detail and his composure.

He ticked all the boxes.

That was two years ago and it was worth the wait. Tomorrow Ben would begin his new role as PC Ben Walker.

Ben had an ultimate goal of becoming a detective.

They continued to walk and Ben thought how odd it was to see foxgloves and hear blackbirds so late in the year. This place seemed to defy the seasons.

As they took in the beauty, the sounds and the smells of the woods, they emerged from the canopy of trees into a clearing where the evening sky could be seen revealing the waning sun low in the heavens. In front of them was a small hill which was about forty feet high and one hundred and twenty feet long. This was his favourite part of the woods.

When he was young, he had spent many weekends with his Brother Michael climbing over the hill and letting it fuel their imaginations by transforming it into a make believe castle, or a mountain and even the surface of another planet.

The small hill was a Bronze Age burial mound which, when excavated many years ago, was found to contain fragments of skull and other human bones as well as Bronze Age flint tools. This made the place even more enchanting to the young boys. Just to think, they were playing upon a hill full of old dead people.

As Ben and Liz walked towards the hill, the memories came flooding back. He'd not visited the woods in years and seeing the hill took him back in time to the days he'd spent there with Michael.

Words could not explain how much he missed his brother, whose young life was wrenched from him at such an unreasonable age. Ben hated the C word with a fury. Stupid cancer.

As he stopped to look at the hill, Liz looked at him from the side, wondering what he was thinking. He was lost in his own thoughts and she was beginning to feel awkward.

"Race you to the top," she shouted as she charged up the small hill.

Ben snapped out of his stupor and chased after Liz as she giggled and scrambled her way to the top.

He was about four foot behind her when he noticed something he had not seen before. As her t-shirt rode up whilst she climbed the hill, he noticed a little tattoo of a butterfly on the base of her back, peeking out over her shorts.

Up until now, he hated tattoos and he especially hated them on women. But like the little scar above her lip, he found her little tattoo 'kinda cute'.

All of a sudden Ben heard a yelp. He looked up and saw the tattoo on Liz's back very much closer than it was a second ago. She had lost her footing and was falling back towards him. Having lost traction she rolled unceremoniously on to him and the two of them hurtled down six foot of the sloping mound and stopped at the base of the hill with Liz lying on top.

They lay there quietly for second or two until Liz let out a big huff and launched into her trademark uncontrollable giggle. Ben lay beneath her staring into her eyes with a broad smile. They were inches apart and he took the opportunity to admire her beauty.

Liz stopped giggling and looked down on Ben. No one spoke and without thinking Liz moved closer and brought her mouth down upon his and began to kiss him. Ben needed no encouragement as he closed his eyes and kissed her back. And there they were, lying together at the bottom of the hill in their first passionate embrace.

As they kissed, Ben felt as if time stood still and the moment seemed to be lasting forever. If this moment *was* to last forever then Ben would be the happiest man alive.

Ben had no way of knowing what was about to happen next.

CHAPTER TWO

Badock's Wood
Doncaster Road entrance
9.35pm

Danny 'Boy' Boyd walked into the woods accompanied by a group of young reprobates.

Boyd was trouble. He liked causing trouble, wherever he went there was some incident or another. Petty crime, fights, theft....you name it. If Boyd was around, then something was going to happen.

Earlier that night he had stolen a Toyota Previa.

The foolish owner of the vehicle had left the keys in the ignition with the engine running whilst withdrawing money from an ATM. The Previa had been only feet away from him, but he was so busy reading the screen of the ATM he hadn't noticed Boyd in the shadows slipping on his black gloves then quietly opening the driver's door and deftly climbing in. He put the people carrier into gear and released the handbrake, then letting up the clutch, the vehicle jerked forward. The owner looked around to see his Previa awkwardly lurching away. Boyd had his grey hoody up, which was how he wore it most of the time. As the man ran to the driver's door his eyes met with Boyd's. He briefly saw his spotty pale face looming from within the hoody, looking like a pitiful variant of the Grim Reaper, just as his beloved wagon disappeared from view.

Shit! Thought Boyd. *He saw me, he'll recognise me.*

Boyd awkwardly handled the vehicle through the back streets of the east of the city, hitting kerbs and cutting corners. He had no driver's license and had learnt to drive at Danny Boy's self-taught school of motoring.

He had purloined the thing on the fly, without having any idea why he was stealing it. The Previa had just been there for the taking. He had not thought it through and now was worried the owner may recognise him.

"Ah well," he sighed to himself.

He craned his neck to look to the rear of the vehicle and was impressed by how big the Previa was. It was immaculate. *The owner must have thought a lot of this thing* thought Boyd. He reckoned whoever he had taken it from must have thought more of the vehicle than his wife.

The theft of the Previa was reported to the police at 8.41pm.

Looking at the size of it he guessed he could fit maybe five or six of his mates in the back. *Why not?* he thought. *If I'm going to get caught driving this thing, I may as well have a posse with me.*

He pointed the Previa towards the centre of the city and headed off to pick up as many of his gang of under-achievers as he could.

For a Sunday evening the streets were quiet. Normally he would see many of his idiot peers with their backs against the walls of street corners looking pathetically menacing and shouting to each other across the streets. Boyd continued towards the city centre and decided to veer left in the direction of the Foundation.

By day the Foundation was a fantastic place offering opportunities to the unemployed by giving training to help them get back to work.

It was also a multiracial meeting place where many of the local residents would get together in an effort to understand and appreciate the cultural differences and changing ethnic landscape in their part of the city.

By night the Foundation was a different place altogether. After the doors had been locked and the evening hours approached the doorway transformed into a magnet, attracting the groups of reprobates to which Boyd had adhered.

This evening the Foundation had six teenagers grouped together sharing a litre bottle of cider, looking as bored as sin and most of them tapping some useless garbage into their phones, probably bleating away on Facebook about how great they were.

Boyd recognised the kids. He knew all of them with the exception of a young girl who must have been the youngest of the gang. She didn't look much older than fourteen. *Whatever*, he thought to himself.

"Oi, you lot!" he shouted from the window of the Previa, "fancy a ride?"

The kids looked up and saw Danny at the wheel of the silver Previa. They looked at each other and shrugged their shoulders in a 'why not' kind of way. Without any discussion they slipped their phones into their pockets and apathetically clambered into the vehicle with as much enthusiasm as if they were entering the offices of JobCentrePlus for one of their regular benefit reviews. The only one of the group who showed an air of nervousness was Carla, the young girl who Boyd didn't know.

"Where did you get this bus from?" shouted Mossy.

"Mind your own fuckin' business," snapped Boyd as he viewed Mossy in the driver's mirror. "You best not ask," Boyd continued with a smile upon his spotty face.

"Where are we going?" asked Greeny.

"Dunno," replied Boyd, "Don't worry, I'll find us something to do," he added.

Boyd did have a plan. He took delight in intimidating and bullying anyone he could get away with (providing he had back up from his team of no hopers). He decided to drive to north Bristol to the adventure playground on Doncaster Road. He knew that on a Sunday evening there would be a gang of young kids he could pick on. Like pulling the legs off defenceless insects. He knew that his accompanying passengers would enjoy baiting the kids at Doncaster Road.

Daniel John Boyd was twenty years old and just under six foot tall. He was as thin as a post with a dull pallor that gave his skin the appearance of clay. His hair was as black as coal and was so greasy it looked as though it was permanently wet. His sickly appearance was due to his drinking, drug taking and poor diet. He preferred the moniker Danny Boy and had been known by this name for the last three years.

Things hadn't always been like this. Daniel had come from a good family, with loving parents who had high aspirations for him. He had been doing well at school and was in the upper stream. He didn't have a large circle of friends, but he was definitely no loner.

But something happened to him shortly after he turned thirteen. Whether it was down to puberty, testosterone kicking in or something else, no one seemed to know, but Daniel had just turned bad. He gave up on his studies, he gave up on his interests and he gave up on his friends and retreated into himself. He was also prone to anger attacks.

The family doctor suggested that Daniel should attend Cognitive Behavioural Therapy, but the sessions amounted to nothing. Daniel seemed to be happy in his unhappiness.

Things went from bad to worse culminating with his expulsion from school.

By the time he was eighteen his parents had given up on him. His mother and father had almost split up due to the stress and anxiety he had caused. In June two thousand and seven he was thrown out of the family home. Emotions had been running so high, the violent clashes between Daniel and his father had resulted in Daniel knocking his father unconscious.

Since then he had careered out of control, moving from squat to park bench to the occasional friend's couch (if he was lucky). He had survived by stealing, dealing and the occasional hand outs from charitable organisations during the festive season.

Although his life had turned to one of crime, Boyd had never been charged or arrested. He had always been quick enough not to get caught. He was faster than the heavily built but unfit security guards employed by most of the shops from which he stole his food and cigarettes. Although he was unhealthy he was fast on his feet when fuelled by adrenaline.

He had been captured many times on CCTV, but the images were never good enough to identify him. They were always a fuzzy representation of a stereotypical youth which could have been one of many like him.

Although he was known by many, he was unknown to the law.

As the Previa approached Doncaster Road, Boyd shouted to Seb, who was sitting at the back of the vehicle between the two girls, "Oi! Got any Speed Seb?"

"No, Danny Boy, I'm all out".

"Well, what have you got?" Boyd demanded.

"Just a bit of crack, mate."

"Come on mate, share the wealth."

Seb knew it wasn't worth arguing with Danny as he would have beat it out of him if he didn't hand over the drug of his own free will.

Boyd had become dependent on drugs, which among other things, had increased his paranoia.

He looked at his passengers in the rear view mirror as he smoked the joint.

There was Stuart 'Mossy' Moss and Paul 'Greeny' Green, who were both sixteen and had come from similar backgrounds. Both had alcoholic parents who were never there for their boys. Both had begun to hang around with Danny for the kick. Something always happened with Danny. They enjoyed getting into trouble and looked up to him as a mentor.

Seb, like Boyd had been thrown out of the family home and spent most nights either at Greeny's or Mossy's homes.

John was in the passenger seat next to Danny. John was the quietest and most violent of the four male passengers. Nobody knew much about him. He just seemed to appear one day and latch onto them. He was good to have around if a fight broke out and was relentless in battle, not stopping, not ever. Normally a fight would finish by one of them pulling him off his unfortunate opponent in case the fight ended up in a killing.

And then there were the two girls. Charlotte and Carla. Charlotte was Greeny's girl and Carla was Charlotte's bestie.

Carla loved spending time with Charlotte, but felt uncomfortable when the boys were around. She did not have many close friends and accepted that time spent with Charlotte would ultimately mean spending time with Greeny and his mates.

John liked it when Carla was with them. He spent most of the time eyeing her up. Carla knew he fancied her and felt flattered, albeit an awkward flattery.

John was a very mixed up individual. Although he hardly spoke to Carla, he had created a world in his mind where they were a couple. He would make up scenarios that he found difficult to tell apart from reality. In his world he would enact the most depraved sexual acts with her. Acts which were fuelled by his unhealthy obsession with pornography.

As Boyd parked the Previa opposite the adventure playground in Doncaster Road he saw that it was empty. Normally there would be a gang of teenagers who he could intimidate, bully and prise cigarettes, drink, cash, drugs and anything else from their pockets.

The drugs were beginning to kick in and Boyd was desperate for some action.

He jumped out of the Previa and yelled to the others "you comin' or what?" With that, the six youngsters followed Boyd into Badock's Wood.

"What's the plan?" asked Greeny.

"The plan is, my dear boy, we go into those woods and frighten the shit out of the first person we find."

The others looked at each other and grinned, apart from Carla who didn't want to be there and wished that she had stayed at home.

The woods were dark, although the sun had not yet completely set, the canopy of trees prevented any remaining sunlight making its way through to the ground below. This gave the place an air of mystery. *Perfect* thought Boyd.

Boyd led the group followed by Seb, Greeny and Mossy. Behind the boys were the two girls who in turn were followed by John who was admiring Carla's rear.

As the motley group of youths headed towards the enclosed area of the woods they walked past a hill which was about a hundred yards to their right.

At the bottom of the hill Boyd could see a young girl on top of her boyfriend and they were kissing.

He turned to the others and put his finger over his mouth to denote "sshhhhh" and signalled them to stop.

Boyd whispered, "I'll go over and say hello to our new friends, and when things kick off, and they will kick off, you lot can come over and finish the job."

They smiled, with the exception of Carla and John. Carla was feeling increasing uneasy unlike John who never showed emotion. In fact none of the others had ever remembered him smiling.

Boyd approached the couple, who were unaware of his presence, he stopped walking when he was about twenty yards from where they were. Straining his eyes in the dimming light he suddenly realised he knew who the boy was.

Daniel Boyd and Ben Walker had been at the same school in the same year. Boyd had left before Ben when he was expelled.

They had encountered each other only once during school and it was something that Boyd would never forget. The scenario of their encounter was something that regularly repeated in Boyd's mind, like a DVD on loop in his memory.

CHAPTER THREE

Whitcroft Senior School
Bristol
February 2003

After a promising academic start, Daniel Boyd's prowess had nosedived. Once he was a bright and enthusiastic pupil who fitted in well with his peers, now he was hardly ever there and when he was in attendance he was disruptive.

He was fifteen and had achieved very little since he became a teenager.

Daniel had become a bully, a loser and somebody that the other kids would do their best to avoid. He always picked on the smallest kids and had been in detention so many times that the punishment had lost its impact.

One day he decided to pick on one exceptionally small boy called Jason, with the expectation that the kid would just crease up in tears, as did most with whom he picked a fight. This time he was taken aback by Jason's determination not to give in to Boyd's bullying. Jason gave as good as he got. Boyd's nose and lip were split and were bleeding profusely as Jason continued to battle against him. Jason began to get weary so Boyd was able to knock him to the ground and continue his assault by kicking him when he was down.

A group of kids had formed a circle and watched the fight.

Ben Walker was walking across the concourse and saw that there was a ruckus going down. He strolled over and peered over the heads of the onlookers.

He saw the fight and could not allow such a small lad to take such a beating from the other boy. Ben had no idea why the conflict was happening but decided enough was enough. He dropped his rucksack and pushed through the crowd, sending a couple of the kids to the ground. He pulled Boyd back whilst taking him by surprise. Ben was restraining him by twisting his arm behind his back and yanking it as high as he could.

They were similar in height, but Ben was heavier and found it easy to hold him back allowing Jason to get up and dust himself off.

Ben made it clear to Boyd that he would be keeping an eye on him from now on and if he was going pick on anyone he should make sure to choose someone his own size.

As Boyd struggled to get out of the arm lock, which was now becoming excruciatingly painful, he saw that the crowd who had gathered to watch the fight were laughing at him.

Many of the kids in the crowd had been his victims and were sick of his intimidation and torment. They took great delight in seeing him brought down at last. They cheered Ben.

Boyd had never experienced such humiliation and felt mortified.

Eventually Ben let him go and gave him a long hard stare. Boyd was expecting him to knock him to the ground and was gearing up for this to happen. But Ben made no further moves, for which Boyd was grateful as he had no more strength, plus his right arm was hurting far too much to be of any use.

Ben stooped down and calmly picked up his rucksack and slowly walked backwards away from Boyd without averting his gaze.

That day Ben Walker became a minor school hero, but he was not interested in admiration.

Since then Daniel Boyd's bullying had diminished but it had not stopped. He had become more selective over who he decided to bully and where it would take place.

That day sparked a hatred in Daniel Boyd towards Ben and the rancour became a bitter enemy which ate into his very being. One day he would get his revenge.

At first the need for pay Ben back ravaged him, but after his expulsion the following month he focused less on what happened that day. But deep inside a fire burned that was fuelled by a subconscious desire to severely hurt Ben Walker.

That day would happen.

CHAPTER FOUR

Badock's Wood
9.40pm

As Boyd watched Ben Walker kissing the girl he knew the time for revenge had come. The revenge that had been lurking within his muddled mind for the past five years. The drugs he had just taken were racing through his veins and were giving him a feeling of strength along with a false sense of security.

It was true he had become a better fighter since he had left school, but he was no match for Ben. But none of this was registering with Boyd. He was on a mission to right a wrong that had been bubbling under for far too long.

Boyd slowly walked up to the couple who were in a deep embrace on the ground. He stopped and stared down upon Ben whose eyes were tightly shut whilst he was in a world of his own kissing Liz.

He silently watched them whilst figuring what to do next. He had waited for this day for such a long time and had created many mental scenarios of how to deal with Ben Walker. Now the time had come and the moment of revenge was minutes away, but Boyd wasn't quite sure how to settle the score.

One thing he knew was that he wanted to see the whites of Ben Walker's eyes.

Would Ben Walker remember me? thought Boyd. He hoped he would. But perhaps Ben would not recollect their encounter back in secondary school.

Boyd took a step closer with his feet just inches from the side of Ben's head. He coughed, as if he was deliberately clearing his throat.

Ben quickly opened his eyes and stopped kissing Liz. He moved his head to one side to get a better view of the tall stranger standing over him.

Boyd had his hoody pulled over his head and Ben had no idea who it was towering over him.

"Can I help you?" asked Ben nervously.

Boyd needed no excuse to fight, but felt he could not just launch into an attack on Ben, without him knowing his motive. But Boyd was confused and didn't know what to say. What he said next just came out and it was the sort of thing he would have said back in the school yard.

"You doggin' me up?" he asked Ben in his slow east Bristol accent.

"What?" replied Ben as he climbed to his feet.

Liz got up and nervously stood to one side.

"You heard me," and he repeated, but this time with elaboration "you've been dogging me up and you want a fight."

Ben had no intention of fighting. He wasn't scared, it was just a principle thing. He hated fights and always had done.

Boyd was determined to goad Ben into throwing the first punch. He had contrived a plan many years ago which was if your opponent threw the first punch, then in the eyes of the law, should the law ever be involved, you would be seen as defending yourself and therefore innocent.

Ben and Danny were now standing eighteen inches apart. Daniel Boyd pulled the hood from his head to allow Ben to recognise him.

Ben stared at him. Recognition was not instant as he looked at Danny's sickly face. His appearance had changed since school. He looked ill, spotty, drawn and worthless. He was sporting a lame attempt at a beard which was sprouting irregularly about his face.

Ben was trying to gather his thoughts. *Who is this person and what does he want with me?*

Again Boyd repeated, "You've been doggin' me up, why are you doggin' me up?"

"I've not been doggin' you up, I've been kind of busy doing my own thing." Ben calmly replied.

When Boyd heard him speak he remembered how composed and unruffled Ben had been that day at school. And he was the same now.

Boyd's rage was escalating, and because he could not get Ben to retort, it was making the matter worse.

Ben stood facing him waiting for Boyd's next move. Ben's fists were clenched waiting in readiness.

Boyd was confused. He wasn't sure what to do next.

Without thinking Boyd moved to hit Liz. Boyd's hurried and not enormously cunning plan was that Ben would have to retaliate to protect the girl. This would give Boyd the excuse to thrash Ben.

Boyd swung around to throw a punch at Liz which was purposefully lame, as hurting her was not his plan, it was just a catalyst to provoke Ben. But before Boyd knew what was happening, Liz had effortlessly blocked his punch which caused him to lose his balance. He felt a striking jolt to his solar plexus as she landed a precise hit which brought him down. Boyd was taken off guard.

Ben quickly moved over to Boyd and sat on him using his weight to prevent him from getting back up.

It was only now that Ben Walker recognised Daniel Boyd as the school bully whose reputation he had thwarted five years earlier.

"NOW" screamed Boyd at the top of his lungs. His voice was muted because Ben was sitting across his chest.

"NOW, GET OVER HERE NOW" he screamed again.

This time the others heard him. Greeny, Seb and Mossy ran over and started attacking Ben by continuously kicking him. Ben recoiled allowing Boyd to get back up whilst holding his hand against the pain in his chest which had been inflicted by Liz.

Boyd watched as the three boys repeatedly and relentlessly kicked Ben, who had no chance of getting up and was becoming disoriented.

Liz was yelling at the top of her voice for them to stop, but they carried on.

John strolled slowly toward the fracas with a disinterested swagger.

Carla had witnessed the boys fighting before but this was different. She ran towards Liz with a vague plan that the two of them could diffuse the situation and end the fight.

Liz saw Carla running towards her screaming and when she was close enough Liz instinctively threw her to the ground.

For the first time John showed emotion. Seeing Carla being thrown like a rag doll incensed him. He walked up to Liz, who in the confusion had not seen him coming and delivered a sharp blow to the back of her head. Liz had no time to prepare and could not have reacted in time as she didn't know John was there.

Liz was on the ground and John was standing over her.

The next thing Liz heard was John yelling at her in a rage. He was ranting and raving and making no sense. He was screaming something about hurting his girlfriend. Liz was lying to one side hearing John's furious inane rage somewhere in the distance as she helplessly watched the three teenagers attack Ben. All she could see was a blur of feet kicking him. Liz and Ben's eyes met and he looked too weak and powerless to defend himself. Liz tried to get back to her feet, but was stopped by John who landed another blow to her head with the sole of his boot.

In the short space of time since Boyd had initiated the fight it seemed like so many things had happened. The memory of the school yard fight back at Whitcroft came flooding back to him. This was the second fight he'd had with Ben Walker and it was the second time that Walker had humiliated him. Not only that, he had been hit to the ground by the girl.

His mind was a disorder of confused emotions. He pulled the hoody over his head and walked around with his head down. Although the fights were continuing just behind him he had distanced himself from them. It was as if they were happening on a television programme in the background which he wasn't watching.

His head was down and as he was walking in circles with his hands in the pockets of his hoody when he noticed an angular rock on the ground. He bent down and picked it up. It was heavy. It was heavier than he had expected it to be. It was pennant stone and had probably once been part of a dry stone wall many years before.

The rock was large and he needed to hold it with both hands. Silently he inspected it, rolling it over in his palms. One side was spherical and having the rough texture of pennant it was easy to grip. The other side was sharp and jagged. He ran his fingers over the angular side of the rock sensing the sharp and irregular points. He tossed the rock around in his hands. Sensing a sudden pain, he realised that one of the points on the sharp side of the rock had sliced into the palm of his hand causing it to bleed.

Perfect, he thought, as a dry smile of anticipation spread across his face.

Boyd turned around and slowly walked with intent towards the bottom of the hill where the fights were continuing.

Lost in his own deep thoughts he had not noticed that John was now relentlessly attacking Liz, kicking her with slow powerful blows as regular as a swinging pendulum. Each time he kicked, her body lurched an inch closer to the hill. If Boyd had noticed, it would not have concerned him as he had his own score to settle.

Seb, Mossy and Greeny stood away from Ben when they saw Boyd move towards them with the rock in his hands. He was rolling it from one palm to the other letting the blood from his cut seep on to the sharp side of the rock. Loose fragments of grit irritated the wound, but this did not bother him, in fact it enhanced the moment.

Boyd positioned himself over Ben and looked into his tired eyes. Boyd's head moved from side to side as he took time to savour the moment. Ben was conscious after the beating but was too weak to do anything other than lie on the ground and look up at Boyd whose legs were now astride him. Boyd stood over Ben with his legs apart either side of Ben's chest.

Boyd raised the rock above his head and held it firmly with both hands, gripping the spherical side with the jagged side directly over Ben's head.

Ben knew what was going to happen next and there was nothing he could do about it.

Liz was only just conscious when John had stopped his attack on her to watch Danny.

Liz's bleary and tearful eyes absorbed Boyd's features. She looked at his dreadfully haggard face, his jet black hair and his dull colourless skin. She knew she would need to remember his face. As Boyd stood over Ben with the rock held above his head she knew what this boy's intention was. She was about to witness the death of a young beautiful person before she had a chance to really know him.

As hard as she tried to fight it, Liz found herself becoming less aware of her surroundings. It was becoming difficult to focus on either Boyd or Ben. They were becoming a blur and she was falling in and out of consciousness. Slowly her eyes closed as she was robbed of awareness.

Boyd dropped the rock towards Ben's head. Ben instinctively brought his left arm in front of his face, deflecting the rock as it crashed on to his wrist smashing and stopping his watch in the process.

Boyd bent forward to pick up the rock and assume the same position. This time Boyd slammed the rock into Ben's face knocking him out.

He retrieved the rock for a third and final time and held it high above his head. Then lowering the rock he moved close to Ben's bloodied face and spat in his hair. Boyd resumed his original position, holding the rock back in place. He summoned all the strength he could to deliver the final blow.

The rock crashed down upon Ben's skull like a ball launched from a cannon. The dull thud of the impact could be heard by all who were there. Ben's forehead fractured as the rock and his cranium became a fused mix of bone, blood, stone and grey matter.

The incident was followed by a deathly silence. What happened next brought all of them back to their senses.

"Run, it's the police" screamed Carla at the top of her lungs pointing towards the entrance of the woods.

What followed was a mix of confusion, fear and panic. Nobody knew which way to run.

Seb, Greeny and Mossy ran to the depths of the woods, quickly followed by the rest. Even John was running.

Above the stampede of seven pairs of feet crashing through the undergrowth could be heard their adrenaline charged heavy breathing as they gasped for breath. It had been fight or flight as soon as Carla shouted "police."

When they reached the far side of the woods everyone stopped. They stood at the gate which was the Lakewood Road entrance to the woods. Seb and Mossy had unbearable cramp and Carla vomited.

Carla hadn't seen the police. Shouting "police" was her knee jerk reaction to end what was happening. Although it was too late for Ben, she knew he was dead, her instinctive impulse would hopefully save the girl's life.

There were no police nor were there any witnesses to what happened that night other than the seven scared and confused youths.

After regrouping and discussing their options, they all agreed to leave Badock's Wood and walk home separately.

Ben's corpse lay at the bottom of the hill with Liz's cold and lifeless body nearby. Liz was barely alive. Her almost undetectable shallow breathing was the only sign of life.

Ben's broken watched had stopped working at 9.56 pm, precisely one minute before his young life had so violently and quickly ended.

CHAPTER FIVE

Bristol Maternity Hospital
9.31pm
Sunday 6th September 2009

Maria Jameson was lying on her back in the delivery suite, her cervix had dilated to seven centimetres and she was now in the active labour phase.

Although she was only admitted on Friday, when she was ten days overdue, she felt as though she had been in hospital for a week. Early this morning she had been induced.

On Friday her nerves were on edge. Over the past months she had made herself sick worrying about giving birth. Now she was just desperate to get it over and done with.

She had been given an epidural to help ease the labour pain, but the contractions were still excruciatingly torturous.

Maria's mother Claire, and her best friend Samreen, were by her side.

Maria was to be a single mum. Her long term partner Rob had left her the day she announced that she was pregnant. Maria had been devastated when Rob upped sticks. She had considered terminating the pregnancy, but was talked out of it by her friends. Claire was initially disappointed with how things had turned out for her daughter but she was now happy that Maria had decided to keep the baby.

The initial shock of Maria's announcement soon faded and Claire was looking forward to becoming a grandmother. A new baby in the family would be the perfect antidote to help fill the void left when her husband, and Maria's father, Christopher, had died the previous year.

Maria was a twenty-six year old fiery red head who had a good job with Westhouse Marketing in Bristol.

She graduated from the University of York with a first in Business Studies and was quickly picked out by Westhouse during a graduate recruitment drive.

Maria slotted into her role of business analysis manager effortlessly and enjoyed leading her team. She had made many friends since working there and enjoyed the social side of Westhouse.

This was where she met Rob, who was brought in by Westhouse as an IT consultant. Rob worked for a different team and had the unenviable job of bringing their systems up to date to stay a step ahead of the competition. It was a very cut throat market.

Rob's contract had only been for a year, although he had been offered an extension, he had decided to move on to pastures new. Rob and Maria had become an item and seemed the perfect couple and were even discussing plans to move in together.

Her boss was hoping she would return to full time work after maternity leave as she had become an invaluable member of his team.

But now her priorities had shifted and her future with Westhouse was uncertain. She knew she would have to return at some point because of the agreement tied in with Westhouse's generous maternity package, but her focus was now being a mum and not working full time.

She had given up trying to contact Rob months ago as it became apparent that he would not be part of her future. She had considered herself a good judge of character and had mentally beaten herself up over the last nine months over how wrong she had been concerning her judgement of him.

He was out of her life and even if he did return, she would prefer to make her way on her own.

Maria and her mother were exceptionally close, even more so since they had lost Christopher. Claire and Maria had become more like sisters than mother and daughter.

As well as her best friend Samreen, Maria was lucky enough to have a large network of friends, some were also young mothers and would be around to help and support her during her journey through motherhood.

The pregnancy had gone well. Maria had experienced a little morning sickness in the early stages, but this had soon faded. The baby was developing well with no signs of any health issues. Maria had decided not find out the sex of the baby. On a practical level it would be useful to know, but she wanted it to be a surprise.

The last few days pacing up and down the corridors of the maternity hospital seemed to last a lifetime, but Maria now felt everything was happening much too fast. She was excited, scared and worried as those and a dozen other emotions raced around her mind.

Her legs were now in the birthing stirrups and the obstetrician was telling her that her cervix had dilated to ten centimetres. Now was the time.

With the midwife in position and Claire and Samreen providing the obligatory encouragement, Maria pushed with all her strength.

And she pushed and she pushed. Maria held tightly to her mother's hand, squeezing it so hard it was causing Claire to flinch with pain.

"I can see the baby's head" said the midwife in her calm 'I've seen it all before' tone of voice. "Keep going darling, you're doing amazingly."

Claire and Samreen were shouting "push" in unison. Maria was moaning, joining the throng of other mothers-to-be in the delivery suites along the corridor.

All of a sudden the baby slid out, like a bar of soap slipping out of a wet hand. The midwife swiftly cut the umbilical cord, without offering the opportunity to either Claire or Samreen. The baby was quickly whisked away to the corner of the suite where all the usual medical checks were done and weight was recorded.

The midwife looked at the clock on the wall which was showing 9.58pm. She recorded the time as 10.00pm precisely. The moment Maria's baby was born was 9.57pm. Three minutes earlier than the time noted by the midwife.

Samreen slumped in a chair in the delivery suite. She was worn out. She couldn't imagine how Maria was feeling. She glanced at the clock on the wall and saw that the time was just before 10pm.

The baby was quickly returned to Maria as the midwife gently laid it on her chest. The little pink face rolled its tired blue eyes as it quickly adapted to its new world outside Maria's womb.

Maria held the baby close to her. She was in a state of emotional bliss. She had never felt so happy as tears of elation rolled down her cheeks.

"Don't you want to know what you've got?" enquired the midwife. Maria looked at her in puzzlement.

"Is it a boy or a girl?" asked her mother.

Maria pulled back the little blanket which was keeping the baby warm and looked between its legs. She looked at her mother and replied softly, "he's a little boy."

Maria already knew the name she had for him.

Maria beamed as she posed for pictures with baby Christopher and Claire, followed by pictures taken by Claire of mother, child and Samreen.

Phone calls were made as relatives and friends were told of the good news. Both Claire and Samreen's phones were pinging as text after text were being sent as the news got around.

Despite all the excitement and high emotion Maria felt a pang of emptiness because of the absence of Christopher's father. As much as she appreciated Samreen being by her side, it was Rob who should be here sharing this moment. She quickly dismissed the thought and focused her attention on her beautiful little boy.

After Maria had attempted breast feeding, the midwife suggested they should all have something to eat and ordered coffee and toast for everyone.

Christopher was sleeping in a little plastic cot alongside Maria as she, Samreen and Claire quietly ate toast. The midwife returned to the delivery ward to collect something she had left behind. She hurriedly made her way to the door to head off to the next delivery when Maria asked her a question.

"Why isn't Christopher crying?" Since he had been born just under an hour ago he had hardly made a sound, only the occasional whimper like a kitten.

"Don't worry," replied the midwife as she stood at the door, "this happens a lot." Pausing, she looked at Maria and, with a reassuring smile, told her that she was sure that Christopher would, without any uncertainty find his voice.

No one in the room could know how true her words would to turn out to be.

CHAPTER SIX

Badock's Wood
9.54pm
Sunday 6th September

Boyd dropped the rock on Ben's face, which he was able to deflect with his arm. Ben felt the pain but it failed to register. His brain was confused and muddled.

Ben could barely comprehend what was happening as Boyd stood over him with the rock held high for the second time. This time he felt no pain as it crashed onto his skull. The impact had instantly knocked him unconscious.

Boyd was not sure whether Ben was still alive, but he was taking no chances so he sent the rock crashing down for a third and final time.

At this point he knew he'd finished the job and Ben Walker was dead. His physical presence no longer had a right to exist in this world.

His body lay at the bottom of the hill, bent and twisted. His shattered skull lay in a small depression on the underside of the slope.

In the instant that Ben's life had ended, something new began to evolve.

An Awareness.

An Awareness had started to develop.

An Awareness that had no physical senses. It could not see, it could not hear, it could not smell, it could not touch and it could not taste ………..but it did exist.

The Awareness had a presence and it had a right to belong…….to exist.

The Awareness had lasted only a fraction of a second……..and then it was gone.

CHAPTER SEVEN

Badock's Wood
6.26am
Monday 7th September

The emergency services were alerted by a woman walking her dog.

When the ambulance crew arrived they assumed they were dealing with two bodies but discovered that the girl was still breathing. She was admitted to Southmead Hospital which was just minutes away from where she had been found.

It was a miracle she was still alive. She had been found on a cold September morning and during the night the unseasonable temperature had not been much more than six degrees. She was dressed only in shorts and a T-shirt. The paramedics were amazed that she had not died from exposure let alone from whatever caused the horrific bruises on her body.

The young man's cadaver made a chill run through those who had seen it. Many had seen a dead body before, but not many had seen the aftermath of an act so brutal.

The area was cordoned off and declared a crime scene.

Detective Chief Inspector Markland Garraway was assigned to the case of murder and attempted murder.

Garraway shouldn't have been assigned as his caseload was already at breaking point. Detective Inspector Tom Strawbridge should have been heading up the Walker murder, but his wife rang in earlier that morning. He wouldn't be working for the foreseeable future. It seemed that Strawbridge had experienced something akin to a mental breakdown. A couple of hours after midnight he began rocking back and forth with his head in his hands crying like a child. His wife had been so worried about him she had called the 'out of hour's' doctor who eventually arrived and prescribed a sedative to calm him down. The sedative seemed to have the opposite affect and Strawbridge became worse and had been violent towards both the doctor and Mrs Strawbridge. The doctor had called the police for assistance. Strawbridge had been admitted to hospital at just after four o'clock on Monday morning. When he awoke he had no recollection of what had happened and had no idea why he was there. He was kept in for tests over the next few days and was eventually discharged on Wednesday. The doctors were baffled by what had happened. Tom Strawbridge had a reputation as a fine Detective Inspector. He was level headed, calm and collective and had never caved in under pressure. He didn't have a particularly large caseload and was not under any stress either at work or at home. He was desperate to return to work, but the doctor had signed him off for two weeks to be certain he was fit to return to duty.

Garraway had been a detective for far too long. He had solved many cases and seen so many murders he was almost void of emotion. But there was something about this case which had struck a chord. Something about the murder seemed different. He wasn't sure whether it was two young people that made a difference. Or was it the surroundings? There was something about the place where the young man died that felt strange.

Garraway stood over the forensic scientists who were examining the rock embedded in the head of the body, he placed a foot on the base of the slope and leaned forward to get a closer look. As he did, he felt the urge to vomit. He moved away from the area and was sick behind a tree.

"Are you OK sir?" asked Sergeant Colin Matthews.

"Yes, I'm fine," replied Garraway. "I've probably eaten too much breakfast."

"If you are unwell sir, I am sure someone else can be assigned to the case," the sergeant suggested.

"No no Matthews, I'm fine, come on we've a lot of work to do."

The sickness passed, but it had left him feeling faint with an aching in his arms and legs.

Garraway and Matthews had worked together for just over eighteen months and made a good team, although at times they didn't see eye to eye and had differing approaches to work. Matthews did everything by the book whilst Garraway was more open minded, some might say maverick.

Garraway was fifty two and Matthews was a mere boy at thirty four. They both wore suits, but Garraway's broad shoulders and sturdy frame carried it off better than Matthews. Matthews' diet of microwave meals and takeaways was beginning to take its toll. He was one of those men who seemed to have an inability to keep his shirt tucked in. Perhaps if he had a good woman in his life, as did Garraway, he would care more about his appearance.

Matthews handed Garraway a tissue which he used to wipe his mouth. They returned to the body and knelt alongside the team who were busy doing their thing.

"What can you tell us?" asked Garraway.

"Not a lot" said Gillian West who was leading the forensics team. "We obviously have the murder weapon" as she pointed to the rock.

"I'm pleased to see the constabulary are getting their money's worth" he replied sarcastically.

West ignored his comment. "It's about all we do have" she continued. "We do know that there were at least three or four involved because of the multiple bruising on the body and on the girl, also the ground has been heavily disturbed."

"Do they have names?" asked Matthews.

"That's something we do know," said West. "The girl is Elizabeth Mason, and the boy was Benjamin Walker." And there's something else, she added, "he was one of ours."

"He was a police officer?" asked Garraway.

"He was a PCSO sir," she replied. Garraway looked down at the body.

"What a terrible waste of a human life." he said under his breath.

"So whoever attacked the two of them left their ID on them?" said Matthews.

"Not only their ID, they didn't take money or any valuables." she replied.

Ben had his iPhone and eighty pounds in cash on him and Liz had her credit card.

"So it wasn't a mugging gone wrong." said Matthews.

"No sir, it doesn't look that way." replied West.

"It looks like there were a few attacking the boy." she continued. "There are boot marks all over his body and they are from at least two different pairs of boots."

"And the girl?" asked Garraway.

"We don't know yet, she was rushed to Southmead before we had time to examine her." she replied. "Ahh!" exclaimed Garraway.

It was only eight thirty in the morning but Garraway was frustrated that there was so little evidence. He knew that even if the murderer or murderers weren't wearing gloves the chances of finding any prints on the rock were slim. The rock had no smooth edges where a fingerprint could be left. If the murderer had used a nice smooth piece of granite then it would be covered in prints.

An hour later the woods were teaming with police officers looking for clues. The highly trained search officers were everywhere. Random objects were bagged and recorded, but so far nothing particularly noteworthy had been found.

Matthews organised the door to door investigations. Officers where knocking on all the neighbouring houses.

Two hundred yards from where the murder took place stood a school. Garraway decided to pay a visit in case anyone had been working there the night before. He knew it was a long shot as the murder happened on Sunday night or early on Monday morning. He spoke with the deputy headmaster who told him the only one who was likely to have been there was the caretaker Doug Plummer.

He was introduced to Doug. Doug took Garraway to his little office, which was jammed full of tools, buckets, pots of paint, broken sports equipment as well as a load of other things. Garraway sat in the only chair whilst Doug leant against the wall.

"I was in school yesterday," said Doug, "I was here between about five and seven."

"Why were you in on a Sunday?" asked Garraway.

"Because the girl's showers were leaking and they needed fixing before Monday." replied Doug. "And if you didn't already know, today is the first day of the new school year............are you suspecting me, Mr Garraway?"

"No, no not at all Mr Plummer." replied Garraway. "Did you see or hear anything suspicious yesterday?"

"No, not a thing, other than the kids in the adventure playground I don't recall seeing anyone and the kids had gone by the time I left the school."

Garraway thanked Doug and gave him his card and asked him to call if he did remember anything.

"I think it's disgusting." said Doug as Garraway turned to leave the cramped office.

"I beg your pardon?" asked Garraway.

"I said I think it's disgusting that the school should open when such an awful thing has happened. The kids can see everything from their classrooms."

Garraway nodded and sighed. "As you say Mr Plummer, it is the start of the new school year."

He thanked Mr Plummer again and left the school.

The door to door investigations carried out by the police officers yielded no significant information. The locals were scared and worried that this had happened on their doorsteps. Only one person reported something which may be of use. A woman walking her dog had seen a group of youths walking away from the Lakewood Road end of the woods. She had taken little notice and wasn't able to give a good description.

Just after ten, Matthews and Garraway met up in a nearby cafe and discussed whatever information they had found. Both agreed they had nothing to go on.

"How's the girl?" asked Garraway.

"Not good, she's critical and in intensive care," said Matthews. "I doubt if she'll be much help for the time being," he added.

Garraway's phone rang. It was Gillian West calling from the forensics lab.

"I think I might have something," she said.

"We're on our way," he replied, as he and Matthews grabbed their jackets and left the cafe.

Garraway and Matthews were waiting for Gillian West in her office. West entered the room with three mugs of coffee on a tray. Garraway and Matthews were grateful for the drinks as the two they had ordered in the cafe were left there to go cold in the rush to get to her lab.

"What's the boggle?" asked Matthews. West looked at him blankly.

"He means what can you tell us?" added Garraway.

West smiled, "as you may remember, the rock found embedded in Ben Walker's head had a jagged side, which was the section of the rock that laid to rest in his skull, the other side of the rock was rounded and fairly smooth. The smooth side was the part of the rock the murderer was holding."

"Are there any fingerprints on the rock?" asked Matthews.

"No," replied West, "but there is a blood stain."

"Interesting," said Garraway.

"I'm waiting for Collins to call me with the results but I'm pretty sure that the stain on the smooth side of the rock won't be Ben Walker's blood sir."

"If you're right Gillian, it doesn't necessarily mean it's the murderer's blood, but at least it's something, as we have very little to go on just now," said Garraway.

Matthews stretched, yawned and was just about to speak when Gillian West's phone rang. She snatched the phone off of its cradle and abruptly answered it. As she spoke she scribbled some notes. She thanked the caller and put the phone down.

"That was Collins from the lab, and he has confirmed the blood stain isn't Ben Walker's."

"Good work," said Garraway, "but as I just said, it could be a blood stain belonging to anybody. Let me know when you've run it through the DNA database."

"Collins is already on it," replied West.

"Is there any news from the pathologist?" asked Matthews.

"Not yet," replied West. "We won't know the outcome of the autopsy for the next few days."

Garraway stood up. "OK, I'm off to do some thinking. Matthews you head over to Southmead Hospital and see if you can find out anything about the girl, and Gillian, I'll speak to you tomorrow, unless you have any more news this afternoon."

Markland Garraway was born in Kilchoan, a tiny village on the west coast of Scotland. When he was two his family moved to Ullapool, where his father worked as a fisherman. After eight years his father started working in the construction industry and had to go where the money was. For the next few years Markland and his parents moved around Scotland and England from one building contract to the next, eventually ending up in Bristol where his father found steady and well paid work. Because of constantly being on the move Markland found it difficult to make friends which made him somewhat a loner for the rest of his life.

He married Joan when he was twenty six, the same year he became a police officer. The couple had met at the Granary, a rock venue near the centre of Bristol. They soon started a family and were blessed with two daughters.

When he became a detective, Joan considered herself a police widow because of the long and unsociable hours, but stood by her husband like the loyal wife she was.

Markland Garraway didn't have much time for hobbies, although he did have a fascination for UFOs ever since seeing something amazing over the skies of Ullapool when he was nine. Since then he had read book after book on the subject and the fascination was still with him today. He was convinced UFOs were real because he had seen one with his own eyes. Perhaps this was the reason he was so open minded. Having an open mind had helped him solve cases which otherwise may have ended up on the 'pending' pile. Behind his back some of his colleagues referred to him as 'spooky' Garraway, but never to his face as, at six foot three inches tall, few would want to see his angry side.

Garraway made his way back to the crime scene. Often he found when investigating a murder, spending time at the scene alone cleared his mind and allowed him to concentrate.

As he made his way to the hill he saw PCs Carter and Fleming patrolling the area making sure that nothing was disturbed. The hill had been cordoned off with police tape. Garraway ducked under the tape and stood where Ben Walker's body had been lying. It was three thirty in the afternoon, but it felt a lot later.

Small talk was exchanged between Garraway and the constables. Garraway preferred them not to be there as their presence interrupted his thoughts. He scrambled his way to the top of the hill to survey the area from a higher point. For the first time he was taken in by the beauty of the woods. He listened to the sound of the trees swaying in the gentle September breeze. Birds were singing and he could hear the children in the nearby school. Perhaps Doug Plummer was right when he said the school should not have opened today.

He sat his large frame down on the top of the hill and closed his eyes. All of a sudden he was overwhelmed with a feeling of nausea. He held his head in his hands and waited for the feeling to pass. Unlike this morning, he wasn't sick. As the nausea began to fade, it was replaced by another feeling. He lay out flat on the hill, with his eyes gently closed as the feeling evolved into a sensation like something was trying to get his attention. It was the same sensation when he knew someone was watching him. It wasn't a bad feeling, but it was unsettling. The feeling slowly left him and he sat up. Opening his eyes he saw the two officers looking at him. Perhaps this was why he'd felt the sensation of someone looking at him.

"Is everything alright sir?" asked Carter.

"Everything's fine thank you," replied Garraway as he made his way down the hill.

"I was just taking a moment," he added.

"If you ask me, this place gives me the willies," added Fleming helpfully.

"Yes, I know what you mean," replied Garraway.

Walking back to the car he felt a crunching in his neck. He massaged the back of his head and thought about what just happened. Shaking his head he continued back to his black Audi A5 which was parked nearby on Doncaster Road. Garraway sat in his car and wondered what to do next. He started the engine and pulled away, carefully avoiding the badly parked Toyota Previa in front.

CHAPTER EIGHT

Southmead Hospital
1.18pm
Monday 7th September
Earlier that day

Matthews had been waiting in the reception area of the Intensive Care Unit for half an hour. He was fighting a losing battling with a vending machine. The machine had been happy enough to take his money, but was not so forthcoming with the goods. Matthews was starving and could have walked to the Café at Southmead Hospital, but he didn't want to risk the chance of missing the intensive care consultant who had been dealing with Elizabeth Mason.

Just as Matthews was about to tilt the vending machine Dr Robert Clarke entered reception.

Clarke offered his hand to Matthews. "Sergeant Matthews, sorry to keep you waiting, it's been a rather busy day," he said as they shook hands.

Clarke was a small man in his late forties, with a shock of black hair which was swept over his brow. *This man needs to see a stylist* thought Matthews.

"Can I see Elizabeth?" asked Matthews.

"I would prefer if you didn't sergeant," said Clarke. "She's not awake, so there's nothing she can help you with right now, plus her parents are at her bedside and as you can imagine they're rather upset."

"Is there anything you can tell me?" asked Matthews.

"Only about her injuries," replied Clarke. "When she was brought in she was suffering internal bleeding, she has a number of broken ribs and has taken a severe beating to her head." He paused for a second and then continued, "she is suffering an intracranial injury and so as you may appreciate sergeant, it may be sometime until she is able to talk with you."

Matthews nodded. He removed a card from his wallet and handed it to the consultant.

"I would be grateful if you could call me as soon as she comes around."

Clarke took the card, glanced at it and put it in his pocket.

"To be honest with you, after what this girl has been through, I think she would prefer to forget whatever took place last night."

Matthews thanked the consultant and turned to walk out.

"Sergeant!" called the consultant, "I almost forgot," Clarke walked behind the reception desk and came back with a neatly folded pile of clothes wrapped in polythene.

"I thought your people would be needing this," he said as he handed the package to Matthews.

"It's the clothes she was wearing when she was admitted this morning."

"That's very forward thinking of you," said Matthews as he took the clothes from the consultant and thanked him again.

"I am very surprised one of your highly paid detectives didn't think of asking me for these earlier."

Idiot thought Matthews as he walked away.

CHAPTER NINE

Avon and Somerset Police
Kenneth Steele House

The Incident Room
4.12pm
Monday 7th September

Garraway parked his car outside the newly opened building which housed the incident rooms. The red brick building was nestled amongst nondescript warehouses and other offices on a trading estate near the canal, which flowed from the east of Bristol towards the city centre. The building boasted four fully-equipped major incident rooms, briefing facilities and meeting quarters.

Garraway entered incident room number two. The large office was teeming with detectives, police officers and civilian staff. He strolled the thoroughfare between desks and chairs, at the same time stepping over files which littered the floor, *Health and Safety would have a field day* he thought, he walked up to Sally Johnson and Andy Warrington, the Major Crime Investigation Officers, who were busy collating whatever information they had.

"The board's pretty empty," said Garraway.

"We know," replied Warrington, "there's not much we have to put on it yet, it's early days" he added.

Garraway knew he was right. The crime had been reported less than 12 hours ago, but normally by now they would have found someone who had seen or heard something.

Garraway spotted an early edition of the Bristol Post on the desk. As he had expected the case had made front page news. There had been requests for him to talk on the local news but he didn't want to speak to the public just yet. It was far too early. The requests had been deftly dealt with by the

Police Department News and Information Team. He knew that before long there would be a press conference. He hated those things, but appreciated how important they were as a well written announcement to the public often yielded useful information.

He felt tired. It had been a long day and feeling sick earlier didn't help. He slumped in a chair and picked up the newspaper. The front page had a colour photograph of the crime scene. PCs Carter and Fleming were in the picture looking expressionless and the forensics team where in the rear of the image doing their thing. Dominating the image was the hill. He stared at it and thought about the strange feeling that came over him earlier.

He rubbed his face and yawned.

"You look knackered, if you don't mind me saying sir," said Warrington.

Garraway looked at him and smiled. "I'm not feeling my best."

"Why don't you head home?" suggested Johnson.

"I think maybe I will," said Garraway. "Call me if anything comes up." He stood up, looked around and then left the office to head home.

CHAPTER TEN

The Foundation
7pm
Monday 7th September

Danny had called a meeting. He'd sent texts to Seb, Greeny and Mossy and asked them to contact John, Carla and Charlotte so all would be present. Seb replied to Danny saying that no one had John's number. In fact no one had ever seen him use a phone, perhaps he didn't have one. Greeny had sent a message to Charlotte, but it had been pending delivery and eventually returned as unsent. Her phone must have been turned off. Greeny didn't have Carla's number, he had never needed to contact her.

Nobody spoke as the four of them stood in the doorway of the Foundation looking tired and scared. Eventually Mossy turned to Danny and asked him what the plan was. Danny had been thinking hard about what to do next. All he cared about was not getting caught.

"The plan is, if any of us get picked up by the Bill, then we don't grass on the each other," said Danny.

"Is that it, is that the plan?" shouted Greeny. Danny stared down at him.

"That works well for you then Danny, you're the one who bloody killed him and why the fuck did you do it any way, what's the matter with you?"

Danny pinned Greeny against the wall. "How do you know it wasn't you kicking the shit out of him that didn't kill him in the first place."

Greeny stared at Danny and said nothing.

"Look, you two need to keep your voices down, if anyone hears you shouting your mouths off, then we've all had it," said Mossy.

Danny let go of Greeny who slumped back down.

"I think Danny's right," said Seb. "We all need to look out for each other and if any of us get picked up we gotta keep schtum."

"I'm scared," said Mossy, "I mean really scared." He was the first to admit it. "I don't know how I got myself mixed up in all this shit."

"Well you seemed happy enough kicking seven bells of shit out of him last night," said Greeny.

"Look," said Seb, "the best thing to do is lose contact with each other, like we never knew each other. Delete all contacts from our phones, block each other on Facebook and never see each other again."

Seb waited for someone to say something, but no one did. "It's the only way," he added.

"What about the girls?" asked Danny.

"Well I don't think Charlotte will want anything to do with me again and I don't suppose Carla will either."

"Why did Carla shout 'police' last night, there were no police?" asked Seb.

"Dunno," said Greeny, "I guess she thought she saw them."

It seemed a simple enough plan and they had convinced each other that nothing could go wrong. They had seen no one else in the woods and the nearby adventure playground had been empty, so there had been no witnesses. If Carla had seen the police it would have been 'game over' by now. They hoped that the girls were as scared as they were and would keep quiet about the whole thing. Greeny said he would keep trying to contact Charlotte to let her know about the plan.

As for John, they just had to hope for the best.

And that was it. They walked away from each other and wouldn't see each other for another three years.

CHAPTER ELEVEN

The Incident Room
9.30am
Tuesday 8th September

Garraway answered his phone when he saw it was Gillian West calling. "What have you got for me?"

"Good morning to you too," replied West sarcastically.

Garraway apologised and West continued. "It's not great news sir. We've heard back from the lab and they can't match the DNA from the blood on the rock to anyone we have on file."

"So perhaps the rock was handled by someone before the murder, someone else who inadvertently got their blood on the rock and was nothing to do with what happened," suggested Garraway.

"I think not sir," replied West, "there's something else, I've seen the pathologist report and there aren't any great surprises about how Ben Walker died, it was definitely the rock that killed him, but the pathologist found something we didn't expect."

"Carry on," said Garraway with an inquisitive tone.

"Well sir," continued West, "the pathologist found saliva in Ben Walker's hair."

"Saliva?" replied Garraway, raising an eyebrow.

"Yes sir, saliva,"

Garraway said nothing, pressuring West to continue.

"The pathologist took it upon himself to get a DNA report on the saliva and unfortunately it doesn't match anyone we know but.......... it does match the blood found on the rock."

Garraway stood in silence and thought about what West had just told him.

"Thank you Gillian, how extremely interesting." He asked her to email the pathologist report, thanked her again and hung up.

Just as Garraway finished the conversation with West, Matthews entered the incident room with a package under his arm.

"Good morning Matthews, late night was it?" asked Garraway as he looked at the clock on the wall. Matthews ignored his remark and sat down at the desk. Garraway told him the news he'd just heard from West. "Excellent sir," said Matthews "so we definitely have DNA to match to the killer." "Yes we do," replied Garraway, "the only thing is we still don't have a killer to match the DNA."

"Well that could all change sir," said Matthews, "I've just been informed of a stolen vehicle, a Toyota Previa which was taken on Sunday night from the high street in Kingswood."

"And, how does the stolen Previa help us?" asked Garraway.

"It's been found sir, and it's been found on Doncaster Road. A resident was suspicious as she didn't recognise it and it had been badly parked."

"She's part of Neighbourhood Watch," he added.

"Thank the Lord for Neighbourhood Watch!" exclaimed Garraway with his hands in the air.

"And, the owner of the stolen Previa said he saw the thief drive off in the vehicle," continued Matthews.

"Did he get a good look?" asked Garraway.

"Apparently no, not a great look, the thief was wearing a hoody so most of his face was concealed."

Garraway nodded thoughtfully.

"Forensics are dusting it for prints and after that they'll be over the vehicle with a fine tooth comb."

"Perhaps now we're getting somewhere," said Garraway hopefully.

Matthews smiled.

Matthews put down the package given to him by Dr Robert Clarke the day before.

"It's the girl's clothes," he said as he placed the package on the desk.

"Thank you Matthews," said Garraway, "let's hope Gillian's team can find something useful."

"What's the name of the owner of the Previa?" asked Garraway.

Matthews looked in his notebook, "It's a Mr Paul Jackson, sir."

"I think we need to speak with Mr Jackson, see if there is anything else he can remember about the theft," said Garraway.

"I'm on it," replied Matthews.

Later that morning Garraway and Matthews were in Paul Jackson's office. Jackson was an accountant running a small business in Fishponds in the east of the city.

Jackson's secretary brought in coffee and biscuits as Matthews smiled at her and subconsciously 'eyed her up' as she left the office.

"So, two detectives are interested in my car, eh?" said Jackson. "I wish the police were more interested in dealing with it when I reported it stolen," he continued.

"Perhaps it wouldn't have been stolen in the first place if you hadn't left the keys in the ignition and the engine running," replied Garraway in a calm, yet smug tone.

Jackson looked embarrassed, "I was in a bit of a rush, and I wasn't thinking," he replied, knowing how stupid he had been.

"Anyway," continued Garraway, "as you have probably heard there was a murder close to where your Toyota Previa was found. This may be coincidence, or the murderer or murderers could have stolen your car and driven it to Badock's Wood."

Jackson sat in silence.

"Is there anything you remember about the person who stole your car?" asked Matthews.

"I've already been through all of this with the police officer earlier this morning," replied Jackson.

"We know," continued Matthews, "but the police officer was taking a statement because your car had been stolen, whilst we're investigating a murder and there is a possibility you saw the murderer."

"OK," said Jackson, "but I can only tell you what I told him."

Jackson went over the whole story again, trying his hardest to recall the thief's face, but his description was as vague as it was when he described Daniel Boyd to the officer earlier that day.

Garraway and Matthews had no further questions for Jackson and stood up to leave.

"When do I get my car back?" asked Jackson.

"That depends," replied Matthews, "forensics are currently checking your car for fingerprints and anything else they can find, and if it can be linked to the murder of Ben Walker, we may need to keep it for some time."

Jackson looked dispirited. "Good luck with the fingerprints," he said.

Garraway and Matthews stopped and looked at him.

"My Previa will be teeming with them, I had just returned from the New Forest with a group of Boy Scouts, their fingerprints will be everywhere."

Matthews and Garraway thanked him and went on their way.

As they left and walked to the car park behind Jackson's office, Garraway's phone rang.

"It's Gillian West," he said as he looked at his phone.

"Hello Gillian, good news I hope," said Garraway in a mock cheery voice.

"It's the girl's clothes sir, we've had a chance to check them over and the first thing we know is that whoever was kicking Ben Walker, and we know there were a few involved, were not involved in kicking Elizabeth Mason."

"How do you know this?" replied Garraway.

"The boot marks on the girl's clothes are different to the ones on the boy's, also there are only one set of marks on the girl's whilst there are at least three sets of boot marks on the boy's."

Garraway stood beside his car and took in what West was telling him.

"So it looks like the killer and the person who attacked Elizabeth are two different people," said Garraway.

"Unless, the killer's boot marks weren't on Ben's body, but for some reason he decided to 'lay the boot in' on the girl," replied Gillian.

"It doesn't add up," he replied. "Why would so many different people attack and kill one person, whilst only one person attacked the other?"

"I've no idea sir, that's your job," replied Gillian.

"Thank you for reminding me of that," said Garraway as he ended the call.

More useful information was turning up, but there was nothing concrete.

Later in the day, Garraway decided to pay a visit to the adventure playground on Doncaster Road. Doug, the caretaker in the nearby school had told him that he had left the school around seven o'clock the night of the murder. Garraway knew that the murder probably happened nearer to ten, which was the time Ben Walker's watch had stopped.

So if Doug had left the school when he did, he wouldn't have known if there were any kids in the playground at or around the time the murder happened.

He parked in the same place where he had the previous day.

It was 4pm and there were youths hanging around the adventure playground.

Garraway walked into the play area which was well equipped with climbing frames, Tarzan ropes and sandpits. It looked as though the council had pumped a lot of cash into the playground and most of the equipment looked new.

He stopped and surveyed the area. There were around 20 kids, all boys, who looked to be between 14 and 19. Some were hanging around in groups chatting, others where smoking, one or two were chugging cans of beer and one was on his own by the fence playing keepy uppy.

The youths looked at Garraway warily. The boys who were drinking put down the cans and shuffled awkwardly. Garraway had no interest in under aged drinkers.

He walked towards the largest group of youths. There were five of them who were slowly turning on the roundabout looking particularly aloof.

"I imagine you all know about the incident which took place on Sunday evening," said Garraway.

Some of them nodded, one grunted and the other two just stared at him with a look of indifference.

Garraway slightly raised his voice so he could be heard by the other groups dotted around the playground.

"Were any of you here, or near the woods on Sunday night, say between nine and ten pm?"

No one replied. Garraway stood moving his head slowly around the playground to emphasise that he was talking to all of them.

Garraway felt his authority amounted to nothing as the entire group of youngsters' perused him with little regard to his position as a detective.

"We're good boys mister, and we're all home and in bed by eight thirty," said one cocky lad with a smirk on his face.

Garraway nodded slowly. "Very well, but if any of you did see or hear anything, and I mean anything you think could help us in our investigations I would be grateful if you get in touch."

As he walked out of the playground he could hear them quietly sniggering and mocking his Scottish accent.

Little shits, he thought to himself.

As he left the playground he glanced towards the hill. The search patrol officers were still busy examining the area. The immediate vicinity where Ben and Liz had been found was still cordoned off. The public wouldn't be setting foot anywhere near the place for at least the next week.

Garraway had a great deal of confidence in his team but was impatient that nothing much was turning up.

Focussing on the hill, he slowly began to walk towards it without realising he was on the move. There was something about this place which fascinated him. He always became gripped by the vicinity of where a murder had happened, but this was different.

He found himself at the bottom of the hill which was covered in stubbly grass and a few wild flowers. He walked slowly around its perimeter with his hands in his pockets and was subconsciously disturbing the loose soil with his feet.

He sat down on the smooth slope and looked towards the autumn sky. Again, without warning, he was consumed by an overwhelming feeling of nausea. He closed his eyes and began to gag, but as quickly as the feeling came, it went.

When he opened his eyes things were totally different. He was surrounded by hundreds of figures moving silently around him. They passed through one another and none of them were distinct. As his brain processed what he was seeing, he felt no fear and instinctively knew that the figures could not harm him.

They were blurry, as if they had been photographed using a long shutter speed. They seemed to ebb and flow, backwards and forwards like the sea washing over the shore and then returning to where it came.

They were wearing clothes of varying fashions, some looked up-to-date and some looked old. The figures in old fashioned clothing were the hardest to focus on. Some were walking dogs, some were riding bicycles and a few were lying down motionless.

One thing the figures had in common was that they didn't last for more than a few seconds before fading away, only to be replaced by others.

The vision began to fade and soon everything was back to normal. The apparitions were there for less than a minute, but it seemed a lot longer.

He slowly stood up and was shaken by whatever he'd just seen.

His arms ached as if he had been carrying a hod of bricks and his legs burned like he had run a mile.

When he had composed himself he saw that he was being observed. This time it was by a real person and not an apparition.

Doug Plummer, the school caretaker who Garraway spoke with the day before, was watching him from the other side of the fence which ran around the perimeter of the school. Garraway made his way to Doug.

"You look like you've seen a ghost," said the caretaker, remarking on how shaken Garraway looked. "Perhaps I have Doug, perhaps I have," he replied.

"Tell me Doug, what you know about this place?" continued Garraway.

"What would you like to know?"

Garraway pointed to the hill behind him. "What's the story behind that thing?"

"That thing," replied Doug, "that thing is a Bronze Age burial mound, its over five thousand years old." "Is it really?" replied Garraway.

"That's what they say," he continued, "it was excavated by archaeologists about a hundred years ago or so."

"And what did they find?" asked Garraway.

"You know, the usual things, bones, stone tools, bits and pieces."

"I presume the bones were human and not animal?" asked Garraway.

"A bit of both I reckon," said Doug. "Look, I'm no expert," he continued, "if you really want to know ask an expert, or even better Google it."

"I will Doug, thanks for your advice."

"One thing I can tell you, this place has always attracted nutters," added Doug.

"How do you mean?" asked Garraway curiously, "what kind of nutters?"

"You know, all types."

Garraway shrugged his shoulders encouraging Doug to continue.

"You get couples at it on that hill."

"At it, at what?" asked Garraway.

"You know, sex, they have sex up on that hill," said Doug.

"And who exactly are 'they'?" said Garraway, in a mocking tone.

"I don't know who they are, but couples who are having problems conceiving do it on the hill because they think the place has special properties, like it's magic or something."

"Anything else?" urged Garraway.

"You get your druidy types," he replied, "you know, in their funny outfits and everything."

Garraway continued to say nothing forcing Doug to keep talking.

"I've even seen oddballs up there charging their divining rods, all very strange if you ask me."

"And what do you think Doug, what do you believe?"

"It doesn't matter what I believe," he replied, "all I know is this place can be strange and what happened here on Sunday night is only going to make things even stranger."

Garraway smiled at Doug and thanked him through the wire fence.

"Perhaps I will Google it when I get back," said Garraway.

And that's just what he intended to do.

CHAPTER TWELVE

Carla's house
7.30pm
Tuesday

Carla Price was curled up under her duvet. Her room was a mess. Her clothes were strewn across the floor and her wardrobe door was wide open with a jumble of shoes spilling out on the floor. The photograph of her mother and father in a pink heart shaped frame was face down on her bedside cabinet.

Carla had hardly left her bedroom since getting back to her house on Sunday night. The only time she ventured out of her room was to stumble across the landing to the bathroom to be sick. She had told her father that she had a stomach bug mixed with a heavy period. Any mention of the word 'period' sent her poor father, Richard, scurrying away.

Carla was in a state of emotional turmoil and she could not get the horrific images out of her head of that poor girl being so violently kicked by John and the vision of Danny slamming that rock into the boy's head. She had been crying continuously for almost two days.

Carla was fifteen and should have started her final year at school that week. Her father contacted her school and let the secretary know that she wouldn't be in today as she had a bug. Carla couldn't stay away from school forever, but she felt that she could never face the real world again.

She was scared and had no idea where to turn. She couldn't tell anyone what happened as she feared that she would be accused of murder and spend the rest of her days in prison. She wanted to disappear, where no one would know who she was.

She hadn't switched her phone on since Sunday and wanted no contact with the anyone. In her bedroom she had found temporary sanctuary. The only contact with the outside world was a small television in the corner of her bedroom. She turned it on for first time since Sunday. Regional news was reporting from the woods. Carla turned off the television and was sick again.

Until now, Carla had been a happy cheerful soul and was doing well at school. She spent most of her time with her best friend Charlotte, but lately had been seeing less of her since Charlotte had started dating Paul 'Greeny' Green. Carla had other girls to hang around with, but missed spending time with Charlotte, which is why she had started hanging around with Paul Green and his mates so she could be with her.

She never felt comfortable around the gang of older kids, but if she wanted to hang around with Charlotte, she would need to accept the others into her life.

Carla's home life had been traumatic. Her mother had left in 2007 after Richard had discovered she'd been having an affair with her boss. Before this, her family life had not been brilliant because of the tension created by the affair.

It had come as a shock to Carla's father when he found out his wife had been having an affair, but in fairness all the signs were there and he should have known something was wrong. Carla's mother had been getting in late from the office, was acting aloof and for most of the time was unapproachable. Carla and her mother were not communicating, which was upsetting and Carla felt unloved.

This had brought her closer to her father and the bond tightened after her mother had left home.

There was more trouble ahead as Richard lost his job two months after they had separated and since then he had been living on benefits.

Considering the past two years, Carla had been able to remain cheerful on the outside, only letting her emotions show to a few friends, including Charlotte.

She hadn't seen her for almost two days. Normally Charlotte would be the first friend she would turn to if she had a problem, now she never wanted to see her again. If it hadn't been for Charlotte seeing that stupid boyfriend, then none of this would have happened, or if it had, Carla would have had nothing to do with it.

But it <u>had</u> happened, and she was stuck in the middle with no idea of how to escape.

Carla was curled up on her bed with her face in her pillow, when she heard a knock on her door.

"Carla honey, can I come in for a minute?" called Richard softly from outside her room. Carla sat up in her bed and grunted an indistinguishable response, which her father took as 'yes'. He slowly entered her room and was taken aback by a stale smell as the warm air of her dark bedroom hit him.

"Are you feeling any better?" said Richard as he gently sat beside her.

"Not really daddy, I still don't feel very well," she replied.

"Perhaps I should call the doctor," he suggested.

"No daddy, please don't," she retorted.

Richard moved back slightly as Carla snapped at him. He assumed it was her hormones getting the better of her.

"OK, but let's see how you are in the morning," he replied. Carla nodded and put her face into her pillow.

"I've got some news for us, and I thought you might like to hear it," said her father.

In his hand he was holding a letter and was running his fingers over it, as to him it was something of great significance.

Carla rolled over and looked at her father.

Richard continued, "I've got some good news and some not so good news." Carla pulled herself into an upright position and looked at her father.

Richard was shocked to see how pale she looked, but put it down to her upset stomach and period pains.

"The good news is that I've got a job," he said as a beaming look of pride spanned his face. Carla smiled back, this was the first time she had smiled in two days.

"That's great news daddy, I'm really pleased for you," she half-heartedly replied.

"But there is some news which isn't so great," continued her father, "the job is in Darlington, which is too far away for me to travel to and from Bristol every day, ……..sooooo, I am afraid we are going to have to move up north."

Carla put her hand on her father's and looked into his eyes and replied with a tired and weak voice, "Don't worry daddy, that's OK. I'm just pleased you have found some work."

"When do we have to move?" asked Carla.

"I start my new job in early October, so we'll be off in about three weeks."

Richard kissed Carla on her forehead and left her room.

As he closed her bedroom door, he was pleased at how well she had taken the news, but was concerned that she would not be seeing her friends anymore. The change in school at such a crucial time in her life bothered him. He assumed if she had been feeling better she would have put up a fight over the whole thing.

Carla lay back on her bed and let out a big sigh. *Perfect* she thought. Now she had a reason to get out of Bristol. She wanted to get as far away from the place as possible.

She closed her eyes and tried to escape the memories of Sunday night, but couldn't.

CHAPTER THIRTEEN

The Incident Room
10.30am
Wednesday 9th September

Matthews's phone was ringing.
Dr Robert Clarke was calling with some bad news. Liz Mason's condition had deteriorated overnight and she was now in a coma. Clarke could not put a timescale on how long it might be until Liz would be in a position to talk. The brain injuries she had sustained were severe. Should she come round Clarke could not promise that Liz would be able to communicate. Even if her speech had not been affected by the injuries, he could not guarantee that she would remember anything about what happened.
Matthews slumped in his chair, he had a habit of slumping when things were not going to plan. Whenever he slumped, his disheveled appearance was accentuated. Three days into the investigation and he was getting frustrated. If only Liz was conscious, the whole thing could have been done and dusted by now.
It was times like these when Matthews wondered if he was cut out for this line of work.
Gillian West entered the room.
"Ah Matthews, just the fella," she said, smiling as she sat down beside him. Her smile did not last very long.
"What's the boggle?" asked Matthews.
"The boggle is, Mr Matthews, that my good friends in forensics have finished dusting Paul Jackson's Previa, and he was right, the thing was rammed with fingerprints, and as you may have guessed none of the prints match anything on police files."
Matthews grunted as he pushed a pile of files away from him.

"Colin, I can only tell you what forensics have told me. I can't polish a turd. This is what we have to work with and it's up to you and Garraway to work your way through all this crap and get a result….. It's what you do."

Matthews half-heartedly nodded and pulled the files back towards him. "Yeah, yeah, I know, it's just that sometimes, it gets a bit……."

"Frustrating?" said Gillian, completing the sentence for him.

Markland Garraway entered incident room number two and was greeted by Matthews and West. He could tell by Matthews' expression that Gillian hadn't given him any better news than she had done over the last couple of days. He looked at Matthews with the look a father would give a son who'd come last in the egg and spoon race.

"It's the Previa," said Matthews, "the prints are useless sir, just like everything else, nothing matches anything we have on file."

"Forensics haven't quite finished," added West, "We haven't yet completed the task of going over the vehicle for fibres, hairs and anything else that could help us identify anyone."

"Sorry to sound pessimistic," said Garraway, "but if the evidence we have from the scene and the prints in the vehicle are not coming up trumps, then I don't hold out much hope of there being anything of any use in the Previa."

The three of them sat in silence. Matthews was pulling at his bottom lip whilst gazing into the middle distance, Gillian thumbed through the files she had in front of her whilst Garraway let his mind wander and thought about what he had experienced yesterday on the hill.

Garraway jumped up. Breaking the silence he announced he had things to do. He moved to another desk and logged onto a computer and turned the monitor for privacy.

The previous evening he'd intended to research the history of the hill, but had felt too tired. The only thing he had felt fit for was relaxing with a glass of whisky and gazing at the television until falling asleep in the armchair.

He fired up Google and typed 'burial mound Badock's Wood'. The first results brought up news reports on the murder of Ben Walker and the attack on Liz Mason. He scrolled down until he found a result from a local archaeology website. He clicked the link which opened up a badly designed website which looked like it had not been updated in years.

There was brief mention of the burial mound which sketchily detailed an excavation which took place in 1878. Bronze Age tools and small fragments of a human skull and other human bones had been found. This wasn't what he was looking for.

He typed another search into Google, this time he entered 'burial mound Badock's Wood strange sightings', this search didn't help him find what he was looking for. He tried again, this time he decided to search using 'burial mound Badock's Wood mystical happenings', but before he finished typing it, Google finished the search for him and suggested 'burial mound Badock's Wood mysterious qualities'. Garraway clicked the link which opened up www.mythicaluk.net.

The home page of Mythical UK welcomed visitors to the site and explained how anyone who had a 'story to tell' about anywhere in Great Britain that had a paranormal history could submit a story and attach photographic evidence to accompany the submission. There was also a search bar which allowed visitors to the site to search www.mythicaluk.net. Garraway typed in 'Badock's Wood' and hit search.

The screen jumped to a section of the site which showed an image that Garraway recognised instantly. It was the hill in the woods. Alongside the image were two paragraphs of text which had been submitted by Polly Ellis from Bristol. According to Polly the burial mound had very potent qualities comparable to the Rude Man of Cerne Abbas in Dorset. What Doug Plummer had said was true, couples tried and successfully conceived on the burial mound. It mentioned that at summer solstice the burial mound was visited by a small group of druids who believed the place to be more significant than Stonehenge.

The second paragraph explained how Polly had personal experiences of the burial mound's mystical qualities. Unfortunately, Polly did not elaborate on what her experiences were. Garraway was intrigued.

The website gave those who had uploaded a story the option of providing contact details and Polly had left her email address.

Garraway bookmarked the website, noted her email address and logged off from the computer.

Matthews walked over to Garraway and put a fresh cup of coffee on his desk.

"Thank you Mr Matthews," said Garraway as he gratefully took the drink.

"I've just spoken to the guys over at News and Information and they say its show time sir," said Matthews.

Garraway disliked press conferences. He hated to see his face on TV and in the papers, but even more, he loathed the sound of his own voice. Perhaps it was hearing how different it sounded amid the West Country twang. Even though he had left Scotland many years ago, he still had a distinct accent. It wasn't as if he was embarrassed by his Scottish roots, in fact he was very proud to be a Scotsman, it was just he didn't like to stand out from the crowd - he didn't like to be seen (or heard) to be different. But as he was the senior detective he had to make an appearance.

Both Ben and Liz's family had agreed to take part in the press conference, but only Liz's father, Terry, had felt strong enough to speak and he'd agreed to say a few words on behalf of both families.

The press conference had been arranged for one fifteen and would be broadcast live. This would place it conveniently in the middle of the regional lunch time news programmes. It would also be repeated throughout the next few days, unless there were any further developments. If there were any new developments Garraway would need to make further television appearances.

The press conference was broadcast and as far as News and Information were concerned, it had been successful. Garraway had delivered the facts and appealed to anyone who had any information which could help with their enquiries to come forward, no matter how trivial the information may seem. He also asked if anybody noticed anyone returning home on Sunday night/Monday morning with bloodstains or anyone acting out of character, to please contact the police.

Liz's father had spoken next. He mirrored mostly what Garraway had just said, but his added emotion and the strain in his voice reinforced Garraway's words. As he spoke he held his arm around Liz's mother, whilst Ben's family sat beside Garraway. They were motionless and silent, looking ashen and tired.

Carla Price caught the press conference on the Wednesday evening edition of BBC Points West. She watched from the darkness of her bedroom. The curtains had not been opened since they were drawn closed on Sunday turning the room into a state of constant night. After the conference had finished her stomach began to wretch, but there was nothing else to bring up other than sour tasting bile. Her father was downstairs and had walked into the lounge just as Liz's father had finished speaking. He stood staring at the television and saw the pain in Terry Mason's face as he held his wife. As Richard Price turned off the television to concentrate on some paper work for his new job, he heard Carla retching in her room. *If she's no better tomorrow I will take her to the doctor* he thought. This had gone on long enough.

In the press conference Terry Mason had said if anybody noticed anyone acting out of character they should call the police. This did not register with Richard Price, and why should it? He would never suspect his daughter to have any association with such a crime.

She was a good girl.

CHAPTER FOURTEEN

Maria Jameson's home
7pm
Wednesday

Maria had returned home from the maternity hospital with her beautiful baby boy on Monday evening. Everything had gone smoothly. Baby Christopher was feeding well and he'd even allowed Maria four hours of uninterrupted sleep every night since they had returned home. Admittedly they had only had two nights together at home since leaving hospital, but Maria was very happy. Exhausted, physically and mentally, but very happy.

This was the first night she would be spending on her own with Christopher. Her mother had stayed on Monday and Tuesday and had slept on the couch, but had not been needed. Maria was quickly adapting to the life of a mother.

Maria couldn't take her eyes off Christopher. She watched over him as he slept in her arms. She could hear the faint sound of his tiny breaths which were occasionally punctuated by a quiet yawn or whimper. Even without Rob in her life to share this wonderful time, she felt complete. More so than at any time in her life.

She had received many visitors to her small flat that day. She was grateful for their gifts, but there were only so many blue balloons she could cope with and her mantelpiece was a muddle of congratulations cards. She knew that this would be the way of things in the short term and soon the phone calls and visitors to her door would fade allowing her to continue the journey of being a new mother.

She put Christopher in his Moses basket and covered him with his little blue blanket. Sitting beside him she found herself dozing and soon was fast asleep on her couch.

She was rudely awoken at nine thirty. Christopher was awake and crying for his feed. Maria rubbed her eyes, gently lifted the tiny bundle and began to breast feed him.

As Christopher fed, Maria stroked his down-like hair, which was so white it was as if it had been artificially dyed. She didn't expect Christopher to have such white hair. She was a red head and Rob had a thick mop of dark brown hair.

She marvelled at Christopher's little 'scrunched up face' and the way his eyes were tightly shut as he fed. She put her finger in the palm of his tiny hand which Christopher instinctively gripped.

"You're a strong little boy aren't you darling?" she whispered to him.

It was a rhetorical question and she was not expecting an answer, but as she looked down at his sweet face his eyes suddenly opened and he seemed to look right at her as he took a pause from feeding, then continued to suckle.

She smiled and said, "You've been here before little boy, haven't you!"

Christopher had begun to suckle less and his little eyes began to close. Maria rocked him gently and listened to his gentle breathing as he lay happily in her arms.

Her lounge seemed so quiet, only to be filled with the wonderful sounds Christopher was making.

Her mother had bought him a little Jelly Cat soft toy which was on the arm of the couch. Maria gently reached for it and put it under Christopher's arm. The small cuddly toy seemed huge compared to Christopher. This was his first toy and she hoped he would want to keep it for ever as she still had the same fluffy dog that her mother and father had given her the day she was born.

How she missed her father and wished so much that he could be sharing this moment with her and her mother.

A tear appeared and slowly made its way towards her soft cheek picking up momentum as it progressed down her pretty face and eventually abandoning her to finally settle upon Christopher's forehead.

She sadly wiped it away from above his eyes. More tears followed and then more until she found herself crying uncontrollably.

All the emotions which had been pent up over the last three days suddenly erupted.

Eventually she stopped crying. She felt better and was certain there would be more tears to follow over the next days and weeks.

When she had composed herself she noticed that Christopher was fast asleep. She put him back in his Moses basket and made him comfortable.

She looked at the time which was just after ten o'clock. She'd realised that she had lost all contact with the outside world since returning home on

Monday. She hadn't listened to the radio, looked at a newspaper or had even turned on the television.

She reached for the remote control and turned on her TV whilst keeping the volume low as not to wake Christopher. She punched 82 into her remote to bring up the Freeview channel for Sky News and catch up with the national headlines.

As the news channel came up she could see there was some kind of press conference with some very sad looking people who were consoling one another whilst a smartly dressed man was talking into a microphone. Beneath was some text.

She fumbled for her glasses which were next to the TV remote. The text was referring to a Bristol murder.

Maria turned up the volume a little so she could hear what was being said.

The man who had a softly spoken Scottish accent was explaining how a brutal attack which had taken place on Sunday 6th September in Badock's Wood in Bristol had left a young man dead and young woman critically ill.

Maria increased the volume and was straining to catch what the Scottish man was saying.

He explained that the police were pretty certain they knew the exact time that the young man had been killed as his watch had been smashed during the attack recording the time that the assault had happened. The murder had taken place a few minutes before ten pm.

Maria dropped the remote control on the floor, causing Christopher to stir in his Moses basket. Her jaw dropped as she considered that when Christopher was being born, the poor boy was being murdered. She remembered that her grandmother used to tell her that whenever someone dies another is born at the same time.

A shiver ran down Maria's spine. She looked down at her son who was sleeping peacefully and quickly dismissed the thought.

She slowly stood up and picked Christopher up in his basket and gently carried him into her bedroom. She undressed and got into bed. As she lay there absorbing the quietness she could not get the thought of what she had just heard out of her head. Her mind was swapping between the happy memories of giving birth to the vicious attack on that poor young man. Both were happening at exactly the same time and less than two miles apart.

She began to cry again, letting her emotions run wild and only stopping after she had cried herself to sleep.

CHAPTER FIFTEEN

Markland Garraway's home
10.38pm
Wednesday

Markland Garraway had just switched off the television. The press conference had been repeated several times and he was surprised that it was being broadcast on national as well as local TV. *It must have been a slow news day*, he thought. He'd seen and heard enough of himself on the television for one day.

He sat at his laptop. His wife Joan was in bed and now was a good time to compose an email to send to Polly Ellis, the girl who had a 'personal experience' on the hill.

He stared blankly at the screen and had no idea where to begin. Should he introduce himself as the detective in charge of the investigation of the murder that happened in the woods? Although he was about to email Polly because of personal reasons, he understood that he had a professional obligation to fulfil. *Fuck it* he thought to himself. *I've just had a scotch and I'm definitely 'off duty'.* He decided to email Polly from his Hotmail account and not his work email address, as he thought she may decide not to reply if she thought that Garraway was contacting her because of the murder. He rolled up his sleeves, closed his eyes, took a breath and began to type.

Subject: Burial mound at Badock's Wood

Dear Polly
My name is Markland. I hope you don't mind me contacting you out of the blue.

We don't know each other, but I came across something you had posted on the Mythical UK website about the burial mound at Badock's Wood.

You mentioned that you had a personal experience relating to the mystical qualities of the hill. You didn't go into very much detail and I would be grateful if you could elaborate on the experience you had.

The reason why I am interested is that recently I have been to the same place and have experienced something strange and this has happened a few times and I wondered if we were experiencing the same thing.

I fully understand if you wish not to tell me what happened and won't be offended if you decide not to reply.

Kind regards
Markland Garraway

He sat back, re-read the message and hit 'send'. He had Bcc'd himself into the email to make sure he had a copy. He watched the little 'sending icon' spin for a few seconds and then the message disappeared into the ether.

He got up, walked to the kitchen, poured another home measure of scotch and buttered some crackers. He wondered whether Polly would reply or just ignore his message. He was doubtful whether she would want to discuss her 'experience' with a total stranger. He reached into the freezer, grabbed a couple of ice cubes and plonked them into his drink. He looked at the kitchen clock. It was almost eleven o'clock, he really should be climbing the wooden hill.

He sat back down in front of the laptop and was just about to close the lid when he noticed that he had received a reply from Polly. *My god* he thought, *she must be keen.*

He felt a rush of excitement mixed with anticipation as he clicked her message which was taking a few seconds to load. Whilst the message was loading he took a sip of scotch. Eventually her reply loaded.

Re: Burial mound at Badock's Wood

Dear Markland,
I would very much like to speak with you about the thing you experienced in the woods.
I could share with you my experience.
Please message me your number and I will call you tomorrow if this is convenient.
Polly

And that was it. Brief and very much to the point. He replied, giving her his mobile number. He told her to leave a message if he could not pick up and he would get back to her.

He closed the lid of the laptop, stood up and drank the last of the scotch and was a little unsteady on his feet. The alcohol mixed with tiredness left him feeling giddy. He took his empty glass to the kitchen and left the uneaten crackers on a plate next to the glass. He removed his tie, threw it over his jacket which was hanging on the back of a chair and headed up to the bedroom.

As he lay next to Joan, listening to her sleeping peacefully, he turned to look at the orange glow of the streetlamp outside his bedroom window. He pondered over how quickly Polly had replied to his email and hoped she had something which could explain the strange thing he saw on the hill. As he began to drift away he thought about the press conference earlier in the day and how Liz's father had bravely spoken. He was determined to solve this case no matter how long it took.

His alarm woke him at six forty-five. He had slept well. Joan was still sleeping and had not heard the alarm. He decided not to disturb her and quietly got out of bed. As he stood up he felt the effects of the larger than normal glass of scotch he had consumed the night before. Rubbing his forehead he made his way to the bathroom and had a shower.

Downstairs he sat at the breakfast bar and dreamily held his coffee mug. Garraway didn't often eat breakfast. He found it got in the way and slowed him down in the morning. He definitely wasn't a morning person and the idea of preparing something to eat, no matter how basic, was too much for him. He would normally pick up something midmorning, either from the canteen, or if he was on the road, he would get a bread roll from the bakery.

As he waited for the caffeine to work its magic he flipped the lid of his laptop to see what the world had in store for him. He opened his email account and was surprised to see that there was another message from Polly. He clicked the message.

Re Re Re: Burial mound at Badock's Wood

Hi Markland,

Thanks for your phone number. I hope you don't mind if I call you on Thursday morning.
Can I call between eight and nine o'clock?
If this is not convenient please let me know.
Best,
Polly

She is keen he thought. He was surprised that she was so eager to talk to him and he wondered if the woman was some kind of nut. He didn't reply to her last message and expected to hear from her.

His original plan that morning had been to drive straight to the incident room, but he didn't want to take Polly's call with his colleagues nearby listening in. They were a nosey bunch in that room - he would be amongst half a dozen detectives, so what was he to expect! Although speaking to Polly would be police business in a way, the call would, in truth, be a personal one.

Garraway rang Matthews and left a message on his voicemail letting him know he would be at the incident room a little later than normal and to ring him if anything came up. He shouted up the stairs to Joan to let her know he was leaving. He heard no reply, *that woman could sleep for Britain*, he thought. He gently pulled the front door shut and got into his car. He decided to buy a newspaper, find a quiet café and wait for Polly's call.

He parked outside the Regency café which was halfway between his home and the incident room. As he entered the café he was viewed by the clientele with an air of suspicion. Most of those who were tucking into their 'Monster English' were unshaven with double chins and wearing baggy fitting jogging bottoms covered in paint and plaster from the previous day's work. He ordered a bacon sandwich and cup of tea. Glancing at his watch he saw it was just before eight. He sat at the only empty table and opened his newspaper. The tall thin man who had taken his order brought him his tea and told him his sandwich would be over in a few minutes. Garraway didn't often visit a café before he got to work but thought he could probably get used to it. Although he didn't often bother with breakfast at home, this was different. He dismissed the thought, as he didn't want to end up looking like 'podgy' Sergeant Matthews. He supped at his tea and skimmed the pages of the newspaper just as his bacon sandwich arrived. He was about to take his first bite when his phone rang. It displayed a number he didn't recognise.

"Is that Markland," said a female voice.

"Yes it is," he replied, "and you must be Polly." This was followed by an awkward few seconds as neither knew what to say. Garraway broke the silence.

"So I understand you've had some kind of experience to do with the burial mound in the woods".

"Yes, I have, and can I assume you also have experienced some kind of happening?"

Garraway didn't want to give too much away and neither did Polly. They didn't know each other and were only voices on the end of a phone. They both felt vulnerable, neither of them wanted to open up.

"To be honest Polly, I've been looking forward to talking with you, but now you're on the phone I'm feeling a little foolish, because some of the things about that burial mound and how they have affected me have been bothering me."

"So the reason you wanted to speak to me was nothing to do with the murder that happened the other day?" said Polly, taking him by surprise.

"No, no," he replied. "How did you know I was involved in the murder case?"

"I watched the press conference yesterday, and I don't suppose there are many other Marklands' with a Scottish accent who have an interest in that area of Badock's Wood."

Garraway sighed. "Sorry Polly, I should have remembered, I hate doing those press junkets and choose to forget them quickly".

Polly laughed. "So, if this is nothing to do with the murder, there must have been something pretty extraordinary that happened to you in the woods?"

"Maybe," he replied. She could sense his wariness.

Polly was as keen to know about what happened to him as he about her. The telephone conversation wasn't going as well as either of them had hoped. Polly suggested that it may be better if they meet up over a beer to discuss things. After a pint they would probably loosen up a little and be less inhibited. Polly suggested meeting up in a cheap and cheerful Weatherspoon's bar in Clifton the following evening.

"How will I recognise you?" asked Garraway.

"Don't worry," replied Polly, "Remember, I already know what you look like, I'll introduce myself when I see you."

CHAPTER SIXTEEN

Southmead Hospital Bristol
10.30am
Thursday

Terry and Anne Mason walked slowly to the entrance of the hospital where their daughter was being cared for. Terry's face was strained. He had hardly slept since his daughter had not come home on Sunday evening. Agonising worry beyond belief did not sum up what he and Anne went through that night. When Liz didn't answer her mobile they called Liz's friends, none of who had any idea where she was. They had also called Ben Walker, but had no answer. Liz had decided not to tell anyone about her night out with Ben, preferring to keep it a secret. She loved her friends dearly, but they did have a habit of jumping to conclusions and gossiping.

She was expected home around eleven o'clock and when she was not there by midnight her parents began calling anyone who may have known her whereabouts. By one o'clock they called the police who asked lots of questions and said they would send an officer to take some details. The officer had arrived an hour later. He took further details and a photograph of Liz.

Neither of them had slept that night. Until then it had been the worse night of their lives.

When Liz was younger Anne would always ask who she was going out with, where she was going and what time she would be home. As Liz grew older her parents enquired less and less. They had no idea where she was going on Sunday night. The last words Anne heard her daughter say was "Love you mum, see you around eleven……Bye."

There was a knock at their door at seven fifteen on Monday morning. Two police officers were standing outside their porch. Terry let them in hoping for good news. Anne was standing in the lounge looking tired and scared. Her short dark brown hair was a mess. She'd run her fingers through it so many times it was standing up. One of the officers, WPC Johnson looked at Anne. The officer's face suggested that the news was not good. Terry walked over to his wife and put his arm around her.

PC Taylor spoke first. "We have some news about your daughter."

As he explained the circumstances in which Liz had been found Anne broke down and cried into the arm of her sofa. The officers had decided now was not the right time to tell them about the murder of Ben Walker, that could wait until later. Terry asked if they could be taken to Liz. Anne went up to the bathroom to wash her face and put on some make up. If Liz was awake when Anne was at the hospital, she didn't want Liz to see her looking like she did at that moment.

The neighbour's curtains twitched as WPC Johnson guided Anne out of the house whilst Terry locked up behind them. Anne was led to the rear door of the police car and PC Taylor opened the door for her. Terry opened the rear off side door and slowly climbed in and sat next to his wife. They held hands as they were driven to the hospital. No one said a word during the twelve minute journey from the Mason's home to the hospital.

When they arrived at Southmead Hospital early on Monday morning they were taken into a small consulting room where they were introduced to Dr Robert Clarke who had been caring for Liz since she had been admitted an hour or so earlier. He asked if they could wait whilst his team worked to stabilize her condition. Terry and Anne knew that Liz wasn't conscious, so she wouldn't be aware whether they were there or not, but they wanted to be with her. Anne just wanted to put her arms around her beautiful, amazing daughter and hug her. She began to cry. This time her tears were uncontrollable. Terry put his arms around her, but found he'd lost the strength to hold his wife. He joined her in a cacophony of bawling tears. Dr Clarke left them to their grief and shut the door behind him. Both police officers stood sentry outside the room to ensure a small amount of privacy for the grief stricken parents.

Later that morning Terry and Anne were allowed to sit beside their daughter. She was attached to drips and was wearing a clear plastic mask over her mouth. Her face and head were badly bruised and cut. There were stitches visible where her hair had been shaved to deal with a severe cut to the top of her head. More tears flowed.

That was on Monday and now it was Thursday. Anne and Terry had been by Liz's side almost the entire time, leaving to go home to catch a few hours' sleep at the insistence of the hospital staff. On Tuesday they had been told of the death of Ben Walker.

They were existing in a world of numbness and monotony which was running on an endless loop of holding Liz's hand, journeys to the toilet, vending machine coffee, half eaten sandwiches and being driven home by

Terry's brother for an attempt at sleeping. The last four days felt more like four weeks.

Terry Mason was a wealthy man. He was the managing director of TM.IT. A business he created in the dot com era and one of the few to have survived and prospered. He had a good team of managers and could afford to not always be in the office all the time. He would be neither use nor ornament to his business and was grateful that his company could carry on, at least temporarily, without him.

As they entered the hospital corridors on Thursday morning they sensed a difference in the attitude of the hospital staff. Since Monday they had been greeted by cheery and encouraging smiles, today was different. Everyone seemed to have their 'heads down' in an attempt to avoid eye contact. Anne put it down to yesterday's heart wrenching press conference. Anne had been so proud of her husband and the way he'd conducted himself on television. His words had really struck a chord with those present in the room, and also the entire city of Bristol. This was why Anne thought the staff at the hospital found it difficult to engage with the two of them this morning, it was just too hard for them. She squeezed her husband's hand and in return he kissed her on her head as they continued the trek to their daughter's ward.

Dr Clarke was in reception when Anne and Terry turned the corner to enter Intensive Care. He nodded at them and they reciprocated with shallow weak smiles. Dr Clarke never wished them good morning as he knew there was nothing good about any of their days since what had happened to Liz. He was hoping that one day soon there would be a reason to wish them 'good morning' or 'good day' or 'good anything'. Since Liz had slipped into a coma, her deep state of unconsciousness was very difficult for them to accept. Where had all that boundless energy gone? Where was the girl with the infectious laugh? Where was the girl that had the gift of making everyone happy by just walking into the room? Anne was hoping she was still there somewhere.

She had asked Dr Clarke how long it would be until Liz would come round. Clarke was one of those who delivered the news as it was without dusting it with a coating of icing sugar. He believed that although it was important to remain positive, it was his duty to deliver the facts as they were and to avoid any false expectations. He had told Anne that comas generally do not last for more than a few weeks. Anne and Terry knew it would be quite a few days until they would see Liz open her eyes. They were prepared for her to recover one step at a time. Dr Clarke had advised them that her brain trauma had been so severe it was hard to tell how she would respond when she regained consciousness. Anne and Terry would be ecstatic even if they saw a flicker of an eyelid or a twitch of that beautiful nose, because right now the only movement was her chest slowly rising and falling as she gently continued to breathe. Anne had asked Dr Clarke whether Liz would be dreaming. He told her that nobody really knew. When a person comes out of a coma they usually don't remember much, but some patients do seem to recall vague memories of dreaming. He had added that she would not be experiencing any pain or discomfort.

Anne and Terry resumed their positions dutifully next to Liz as she silently lay in the hospital bed. Visitors came and went. Her friends from Taekwondo brought cards and sat with her for an hour or so before leaving to continue with the rest of their lives. The hospital usually had a limit to the amount of visitors a patient can have, but in cases like this the hospital staff exercised a level of flexibility. Terry's secretary, Sally, who was also Liz's godmother, called in on Tuesday and Wednesday. Sally had been a welcome distraction for Terry because there were things he needed to attend to in the office. Although there was no way he would be going back to work for the foreseeable future, Sally was able to help tie up a few loose ends and, with his recommendations, she was able to delegate some of his work to his senior managers. After Sally had left he and Anne returned to their quiet vigil over their uncomfortably peaceful daughter.

CHAPTER SEVENTEEN

Weatherspoon's Bar
Clifton, Bristol
9pm
Thursday

Polly Ellis sat near the doorway of the busy Clifton bar. She specifically chose this bar as she knew how busy it would be. Although she knew Markland Garraway was a detective and was probably a very decent man, she had decided not to take any chances by meeting him somewhere quiet and 'out of the way'. *Better to be safe than sorry* she thought.

Polly was an attractive girl in her late twenties. She had short blond hair and wore glasses. She had a ruddy complexion and suffered slightly from acne rosacea, which became apparent whenever she blushed or was nervous. Tonight she was glowing like a beacon.

She had posted her small feature on the Mythical UK website in an attempt to find out if anyone else had a similar experience to her when visiting the burial mound. In the eighteen months since it went up on the website, she had only had one response and that was from Markland Garraway. This would explain why she was so keen to meet him.

Polly was a lecturer in Economics and Finance and had lived in Bristol for around eight years. In the time she had lived there she had accumulated a lot of friends, but didn't feel comfortable sharing her experiences on the hill with them. She was hoping that Markland would be forthcoming when describing what had happened to him and she hoped they would be sharing similar experiences.

Polly knew about the murder of Ben Walker and thought it was odd that the senior detective on the case would want to talk to her about the hill and not the murder. She began to worry whether she was considered a suspect due to her posting on the Mythical UK website. Anyway, she had plenty of friends who could confirm her whereabouts on Sunday night.

Whilst nursing a gin and tonic she watched everyone who entered the bar. The windows were huge which gave her a good view of everyone passing by. Outside the main window she noticed a tall man, wearing a grey suit and a red tie. He stopped and peered through the large window raising his hand above his eyes to reduce the glare of the spotlights illuminating the glass to get a clearer view of who was in there. She recognised him from the press conference. Polly and Garraway were about eight foot apart and separated by the window. He looked right over her head as he tried to focus towards the back of the bar. He walked in and stopped just by the doorway and viewed the middle distance of the bar. Polly sat at her table just six foot away from him.

"Mr Garraway!" called Polly, raising her hand above her head.

"Polly, hello!" he said stepping over to her table. He offered his hand and as her palm touched his they flinched as a blue electric spark jumped from his hand to hers which made an audible crackle.

"Yow," said Polly as she quickly snapped her hand away from his.

"What on earth was that?" she asked.

"I'm not sure, but I felt it too," said Garraway. "It felt like a static shock, the sort you get sometimes when you touch a car door," he continued as he rubbed his palm with the thumb of his other hand.

"Would you like a drink Polly?" she pointed to her three quarter full glass of gin and tonic and shook her head.

"No, I'm OK thank you." He nodded and headed to the bar and quickly returned with a pint of lager.

For a moment they said nothing until Garraway broke the silence.

"OK, then......where do we begin?"

"Do you mean if you show me yours then I'll show you mine?" she replied smiling. This brought a smile to his face.

"Well if you put it like that I suppose I do."

She had broken the ice and Garraway was now grinning from ear to ear.

He told her about the first couple of times he was at the burial mound, how the first time he was sick, and how the second time he'd felt nauseous and dizzy and he went into detail when he described what had happened the third time he'd had a strange experience on the hill.

"It was all very strange Polly," he said pausing for a sip of his pint. "I lay on that hill and just phased out, I mean I really phased out".

"Tell me what happened when you 'phased out," asked Polly eager to hear more.

"Well, this is when it started to become really odd. I had put the first two episodes down to feeling tired, or a jippy stomach, but this time Polly, I swear to you, I could see the most vivid things around me". Polly was all ears and was staring at him intently, waiting for him to continue.

"What happened next, seems unbelievable, so please bear with me. What I saw next I shall never forget. I was surrounded by thousands of figures all walking around the burial mound. None of them were with me on the mound, they were walking around the mound."

"Were they Bronze Age characters?" asked Polly.

"I don't think so," he replied. "There were just so many people going about their day to day business, you know, walking their dogs, strolling along, some with children and some on their own".

"What were they wearing, what style of clothes did they have on?"

"I do remember what they were wearing varied in style, it's hard to say though as the characters were very clear on one hand, but on the other they were not, and they had what I can only describe as ghost like qualities". Polly stared at him and he continued.

"The characters who were the clearest and who I could easily see what they were wearing, just seemed like you and me, but the ones which were harder for me to focus on seemed to be wearing older style clothes, you know the sort of suits men would wear in the fifties". He paused for reflection, as he stared into his pint glass.

"And there were some very, very soft focus characters who seemed to be wearing even older styles of clothing and these were the ones on which I was having difficulty focusing."

"What happened next?" asked Polly.

"What happened next was…….. it all just stopped."

Polly looked at him for a second, resting her chin on the palm of her hand.

"Wow!" she said, "that's nothing like what happened to me."

"So you mean I've just spent the past couple of minutes sounding like a fool?" he said.

"No, not at all," she replied, "it's just so very different to what I see. Did anyone see you on the hill, did you speak to anyone?"

"Well, there were a couple of officers there, but I don't really think they noticed me," he paused as he remembered what happened next.

"The next thing I remember was chatting to a guy called Doug Plummer. He seemed to know about the area. He was the one that told me that the hill attracted nutters, his words, not mine, I hasten to add".

"Who's Doug Plummer?"

"Oh, sorry, he's the caretaker at the school a couple of hundred yards behind the hill. Do you know him?"

"No, but I think I know of him. I've seen a man working in the school when the kids have gone home, and I think I may be one of the nutters to which he likes to refer."

"How do you mean?" asked Garraway.

"Well, like you, I've sat on that hill and have been a million miles away in my thoughts and I have come around back to the 'real world' only to find his face scrunched up against the fence staring at me. We've never spoken and, to be honest, I think he's a bit creepy."

"I know what you mean," he replied and added, "I think he's harmless enough."

Garraway stood up and finished the rest of his beer.

"I'll tell you what, I need the little boy's room, but when I come back I'll buy us another drink and then you can tell me all about what happened to you".

Polly nodded and smiled and Garraway went about his business.

When he returned to the table with their drinks she had gone. *Typical* he thought. He sat alone at the table feeling stupid after opening his heart to a complete stranger, only to find that she hadn't kept her side of the deal. He wondered what to do next. If he went now he could get a bus home. He'd decided not to drive as he wasn't certain how many 'stiff drinks' he may have needed before he told Polly what had happened to him. He was expecting to stay out late and get a taxi home. He looked out on to the pavement. It was dark outside and the lights of the traffic illuminated the street, punctuating the sulphurous glow of the street lamps. He pulled his phone from his pocket and checked for any messages. He considered ringing her, but thought better of it, she probably wouldn't pick up anyway. Just as he was considering leaving his untouched pint and head off home, Polly came bounding back in through the doors.

"Sorry about that," she said, "fag break, I really must give these things up."

Garraway smiled.

"No problem," he replied, "right, it's time you showed me yours." He noticed her face turn bright red as she picked up a beer mat and fanned her face. "It's hot in here," she said.

"Don't worry, take your time."

"OK," she paused and took a breath. "What happens to me, and it happens whenever I go to those woods, is different to what you see and the difference is that I see and I speak to one person." Polly stopped and looked down at the table avoiding his eyes.

"And do you know this person?" he asked. Polly lifted her head up and looked at Garraway. He could see that her eyes were beginning to water.

"As I said, take your time." She opened her mouth to speak, but nothing came out. She tried again and her voice was shaky.

"I do know the person," she paused again and looked him directly in the eye.

"Her name is Sarah."

"And who is Sarah?" he asked.

"Sarah is, sorry, Sarah was, my partner."

"Your partner?" said Garraway, suddenly realising how dated he sounded.

"Yes Mr Garraway, Sarah Greenfield was my partner, my girlfriend and we loved each other very much."

"I am so sorry." Garraway didn't quite know what to say.

"Do you mind if I ask where Sarah is now?" he asked, anticipating what the answer would be.

"She's dead," said Polly. "She died just over two years ago in an accident." Polly began to cry. He reached for her hand, but she withdrew, reaching into her pocket for a tissue. Garraway said nothing, giving her time to compose herself.

Polly fanned herself with the beer mat and looked at Garraway and feigned a smile.

"Sarah was killed on Doncaster Road, not far from the woods." She continued to dry her eyes, which was punctuated by blowing her nose.

"She was killed in a hit and run, they, I mean, you, never found who did it." Garraway sat back in his chair and looked up at the ornate ceiling of the bar. He cast his mind back and as he did so he shut his eyes.

"Sarah Greenfield," he said. "Yes, I remember that case." My colleague Sergeant Brock was involved in solving it.

"That case, THAT CASE," she said as she raised her voice, "that case was not just a case, it was my partner and my best friend and you can tell Mr Brock that he didn't try very hard at solving 'that case!'"

He apologised for being insensitive. Polly took a gulp of her gin and tonic. "Sorry, I didn't mean to lose my temper, but you must understand how frustrated I feel. To be robbed of somebody you love and to know that there is someone out there who is responsible for her death, probably enjoying life, whilst my Sarah has gone."

Garraway nodded.

"I'll understand if you don't wish to continue, perhaps we should do this some other time," he suggested.

"I'll be fine, just give me a few moments."

"I think it's my turn now, would you mind if I powdered my nose?" said Polly as Garraway smiled and nodded.

"And if you don't mind, I'd love another G and T."

Garraway returned to their table with a gin and tonic for Polly and half a shandy for him. This time Polly didn't disappear, she came back to the table and was looking better after her visit to the ladies.

"Shall I continue?" said Polly. Garraway nodded.

"Well you can probably guess what I am going to say next, and yes it's true. When I sit on that hill and close my eyes I can see Sarah as clear as I can see you. It used to take a while, but now she appears as clear as day and I see her immediately. It's almost as if she is there waiting for me."

"Is the burial mound the only place you see her?" he asked.

"Yes it is, although I do see her in my mind's eye wherever I am, but it's different when I'm there." She paused for a second and then continued, "Mr Garraway, would you mind if we referred to it as 'The Hill' instead of the burial mound, it's just that......" her voice trailed off.

"No, I agree, let's just call it the hill from now on, it's much nicer." Polly smiled, "thank you," she replied.

"It's not that I just see Sarah," she continued. "We have conversations, and I mean full on conversations. I don't mean talking out loud, it's as if I leave my body and join her wherever it is she has gone and we just talk, but I never have to open my mouth, does that make sense to you?"

Garraway nodded. "I think so."

"I'm telling you Mr Garraway, that hill has something special about it. It's a good place and I'm sure I'm not the only one who experiences the things I do." She looked at him and added "well you've seen things so you must know what I mean."

"Yes, I definitely have seen things, but not with as much clarity as you have."

"I know, but perhaps the hill is trying get your attention, perhaps it wants to tell you something," said Polly.

"To tell me what?"

"I don't know, have you lost anyone close to you"? asked Polly. Garraway shook his head. Even his parents were still alive, they were getting on, but were still very much alive and kicking.

"I'll tell you what," she said, "why don't we go to the hill together and see what happens?"

"We can't do that just yet, it's still a murder scene and the general public aren't allowed there just yet. Our people are still looking for clues," he paused, "I'll tell you what, as soon as our people have finished with the hill, you and I will be the first to go there, and as you say, 'see what happens'."

They clinked their glasses to seal the agreement.

"And if you don't mind Polly, I must be on my way, I have long day ahead of me." She smiled, "yes, we'll speak soon, and thank you for my drink."

He turned to walk out, stopped and turned back to her. "I'm so sorry, where are my manners, would you like me to see you home?" he asked. She shook her head.

"No, but thank you for your kind offer, I only live around the corner." Garraway nodded, smiled and walked out of the bar.

CHAPTER EIGHTEEN

The Incident Room
during the next few weeks

Garraway, Matthews and the rest of the team had worked tirelessly over the past few weeks. The search officers had gone over every inch of Badock's Wood carrying out a fingertip search. The officers had taken away over eight hundred items which may have given a clue to who the killer or killers were. There had been extensive door to door enquiries which took place in all the domestic and business premises surrounding the woods. Every teacher who worked at the nearby school was interviewed. The press conference had resulted in a few members of the public coming forward with what they thought could be useful information and even Paul Jackson was allowed his beloved Toyota Previa back.

So far, all the work had amounted to very little. The best evidence the police had was found on the morning Ben and Liz had been discovered and that evidence wasn't allowing them to move forward as they had hoped. The woods were now completely reopened and the general public were allowed full access.

Even the most decent people have a macabre side to them and this was evident by the greater than average amount of people who decided to walk their dogs, ride their bikes, and push their babies in prams in the area where Ben and Liz had been attacked. Some people subtly viewed the area by slowing down as they walked past the now famous location. Others confidently marched and stood directly where poor Ben's body had been found and took photographs and disturbed the area. Perhaps they thought they would find missing evidence that the police had overlooked?

Many people had left flowers and cards. There was a huge card which had been placed by the Taekwondo Association of Great Britain wishing Liz a speedy recovery and Ben's colleagues in the constabulary had left flowers and cards. Over the coming week the hill became a mass of colour as more and more beautiful flowers arrived. A photograph of the hill with a thumbnail of Ben appeared on the front page of the Bristol Post with the headline – **In Memory of Ben** - . This headline upset many people as it hadn't mentioned Liz, although the story which accompanied the headline didn't forget her and gave a glowing story of what a wonderful person she is. Many of their friends had jumped to the conclusion that they had be 'secretly' dating.

The team who had responsibility for the forensic post-mortem agreed that Ben's body could be released. A date for the funeral could now be arranged. This would allow Sophie and James Walker to slowly accept that their son was not coming back. The past weeks had been an absolute hell on earth. After losing their first son, Michael, to cancer many years ago and having to go through bereavement a second time was unbearable. Both of them had been prescribed anti-depressants and tablets to help them sleep. James had been allowed long term leave from work to help him cope with the death of his son. Together they had intended to visit the woods to lay flowers and were driven there by Sophie's brother. When the car parked near the entrance of the woods they couldn't even confront stepping out of the car, let alone standing at the spot where their young son's life had been taken.

They received enormous support from their friends, workmates and the church to which Sophie belonged. Every day had been spent bumbling around with no sense of purpose and on some days James could not find the strength to get out of bed.

As hard as it was for them to lose Michael, they did have time to prepare for the loss as the cancer had taken just over a year to take his life. Ben was different. One day he was here and the next he was gone. They had such high hopes for him and were so proud of what he had achieved in his short life.

Although the investigation was still on going, it would be scaled down. There was a limit to the staff available at the constabulary which meant detectives were investigating several crimes at one time and both Garraway's and Matthew's case load was stretching them to the limits. Unless new evidence was forthcoming it would seem that whoever had beaten Liz and whoever had murdered Ben would be free to come and go as they pleased and possibly commit more crime.

CHAPTER NINETEEN

All Saints Church
Bristol
Wednesday 30th September

The crowd who turned up for Ben Walker's funeral on that last day of September was vast. Over four hundred people were there to pay their respects. It was anticipated that there would be a large congregation but not at this level. Luckily the church had arranged for loud speakers to be placed in the gardens so those who weren't able to fit into the place of worship could hear the service from outside.

The congregation slowly filed into the church and quietly found somewhere to sit. The building could safely hold one hundred and fifty people so there were over two hundred and fifty people waiting outside.

The hearse pulled up at ten fifteen as the service was to commence at ten thirty. Behind were two cars carrying Ben's family. His coffin was unloaded and carried with great solemnity by six pallbearers. Sophie and James Walker followed behind looking weak and vulnerable. Walking behind them were other members of the Walker family.

Sergeant Matthews and Detective Chief Inspector Garraway sat at the rear of the church to pay their respects. Matthews had expected to see Terry and Anne Mason, Elizabeth's parents at the funeral. He looked around the church but could not see them.

Considering the circumstances the service had gone well. The vicar, who was a close friend of Sophie Walker, conducted a moving service, reading a dedication to Ben's life which had been written by his parents. Ben's father had been strong enough to get up and say a few words. There were many tears from the congregation which was made up by a majority of young people. Ben had clearly been a very popular young man.

The Walker family were no strangers to All Saints Church. Michael's funeral was held here, Sophie and James were married here, James' grandparents and father were buried here and now Ben's funeral was taking place here. James never wanted to set foot in the place again. Apart from getting married, every other reason for attending a service had been miserable.

After the church service, Ben's body was taken to a crematorium three miles away. A long slow procession of cars followed the hearse to get there.

The crematorium was smaller than the church so there were even fewer inside to hear the short service. Unfortunately there were no loud speakers this time, so a couple of hundred people waited outside in silence.

Garraway and Matthews decided not to attend the service. As they left All Saints neither of them noticed the young girl walking away from the church on the other side of the road. Had either of them seen her they may have considered talking to her. It wasn't unheard of for a murderer to turn up at a victim's funeral and watch from a safe distance.

Carla Price had known that Ben's funeral was today because of the announcement in the Bristol Post. She knew that she wouldn't be able to attend the funeral as people would have been suspicious of why a stranger who had no connection with either Ben or Liz would want to be at the funeral. She needn't have worried as many of the congregation were strangers who just wanted to be there to show their respect.

She felt partly responsible for what happened to Ben, although the murder probably would have taken place whether she had been there or not. Carla's quick thinking probably saved Liz's life when she called out 'police' and put an end to John's attack on her.

She knew she should turn herself over the police to put an end to all of this, but was terrified.

Next week she would be moving up to Darlington to escape what was happening in Bristol and start a new life.

She used to love living in Bristol and enjoyed hanging around with her friends, but since the murder things had changed so much. Now she hardly ever left the house, stopped seeing her friends and had little interest in anything. The only thing that occupied her enough to take her mind off the murder was art. She was a talented young artist and could turn her hand to drawing anything. Her favourite thing was pencil portraits and she had drawn many of her school friends. The pictures were so good they hung on the bedroom walls of her friends. But her drawings were different since the murder. They were dark and sinister. Last night she flicked thought her sketch book and saw some pictures she couldn't remember drawing. She was completely different to the person she was a few weeks earlier.

She had returned to school at the end of the first week of the new term and although she had become introvert and kept herself to herself she'd found the distraction of school had taken her mind off what had happened.

She had been dreading seeing Charlotte and was relieved to see that she had not returned to school. Presumably Charlotte was experiencing the same trauma as she was. Some of Charlotte's friends presumed Carla would know why she wasn't at school. Carla just shrugged her shoulders whenever anyone asked.

Arrangements had been made for Carla to join her new school in Darlington in October. Carla's and her father's belongings were packed and her father had sold a lot of his things as they were downsizing to a two bedroom house.

Carla walked slowly home, contemplating how her life had turned upside down. The image of Ben Walker's parents was fresh in her mind. How sad they looked as they walked behind their son's coffin. Carla cried as she walked home.

After the service at the crematorium the congregation returned to the hall next to All Saints Church to attend the wake. Normally wakes are a mix of emotions. Some are there to celebrate life, some are there to seek the comfort of others and some are there to give comfort.

Ben's wake was different. Everyone was numb and no one knew what to say to one another. The food was left untouched and only a few had a drink in their hand.

One of Ben's fellow PCSOs had spent a long time putting together a photo slide show made up of pictures of Ben doing all the things he'd loved. There were pictures of him with Liz, with his friends, and with his family. There were pictures of him in his police uniform and lots of him growing up. One of the pictures had been taken at Whitcroft School and if anyone looked closely enough at the blurred image of the lone school boy behind the crowd scene, they would have seen his murderer.

When the slide show began on the forty seven inch flat screen television not a word was spoken and all eyes were on the screen. Quietly people started to weep. The tears created a chain reaction as more and more people started sobbing. The crying was getting louder until it became a crescendo of wailing. The slide show was set to repeat, but was turned off after it had finished the first loop. It was too sad for anyone to endure.

The wake lasted for ninety minutes and all who were there stayed until the end. As the hall emptied, those who knew James and Sophie Walker well enough briefly spoke with them and promised to be in touch. All Sophie could take in was a blur of familiar faces whose names she could barely remember saying the same thing, "If there's anything you need just call." She feigned a weak smile and in auto mode thanked them for coming.

James stood next to his wife half-heartedly shaking hands with the men and accepting a kiss on the cheek from the women.

The hall was empty, other than James, Sophie, her brother Martin and the catering staff who were putting the uneaten buffet food in black dustbin liners. The caterers left the hall to take the food away and Sophie's brother left them whilst he went to get his car to drive them home. James and Sophie were left alone. Silently they looked at one another, too dazed to talk and too tired to reach out to hold hands. Neither could cry anymore. So many tears had been shed there were no more left.

Martin drove them home just after two o'clock in the afternoon. They were left alone in their empty house with the challenging business of rebuilding their lives.

CHAPTER TWENTY

Badock's Wood
8pm

Thursday 8th October 2009

As arranged, Markland Garraway and Polly Ellis had agreed to meet a second time, this time at the woods. Understandably, Polly had been reluctant to wait there alone for Garraway so he had offered to pick her up from her flat. The journey from her place to the woods had taken around twenty minutes during which neither of them said very much. There was a bit of small talk here and there, but mostly there was an air of awkward silence. Evidently the alcohol consumed at their last meeting had dispelled the nervousness they felt. But now was different. No drinks, anyway Garraway was driving, and Polly had decided to go with a clear head. She had considered a crafty joint before Garraway turned up to collect her, but decided against it.

It was a cool evening in early October, and even though the clocks were yet to go back, it seemed darker than it had the last few evenings. He parked his car on Doncaster Road. It was a five minute walk to the entrance and the hill was another few minutes from there to where the woods became a more arboreal landscape. The area where the hill was situated was known as Milltut Field. It had been recorded centuries before that a windmill had stood on the hill, hence the name Milltut.

Garraway had not told his wife he was seeing Polly this evening. He hadn't even told her about his experiences at the hill. Joan had no time for this sort of thing and had laughed when he had told her about his encounter with a UFO when he was a boy. This evening he felt as if he was seeing someone behind Joan's back, which he was and he wasn't. It was true that Joan thought her husband was out on police business, but even if Garraway had intentions of making a move on Polly, he definitely wasn't her type, so that would have put the end to any inappropriateness. It was just better that Joan didn't know.

As they walked from the car to the woods they discussed the hill and how best they should use their time together. Polly suggested that they should just climb to the top, sit down and see what happened. Garraway was starting to feel awkward about the whole thing. If Joan knew what he was up to she would have had a field day, sat on top of a hill, in the woods and with another woman!

"So Polly, do you have any idea why this hill affects you and me the way it does?" asked Garraway.

"No I don't, all I know is that over the years others have come here for different mysterious reasons."

"You mean the witches, wizards and bonking couples?" smiled Garraway.

"I can't say that I am a believer in that kind of thing, but it does seem to be very coincidental. I had no idea about the properties of this place until I experienced them for myself. And then it was only after I had done some research, spoke to a few of the locals, searched the internet which then led me to discover what I now know about the burial mound."

They arrived at the bottom of the hill and stood in silence, momentarily lost in their own thoughts.

"Shall we do it?" said Garraway. Polly smiled.

"OK, you first." As Garraway started to climb the slope, he turned to offer his hand to Polly. "I'm fine thank you."

The grass on the top of the hill was wet from an earlier rain shower so Garraway, always the gentleman took off his coat for Polly to sit on.

"What about you? You'll get a wet arse," laughed Polly.

"Don't worry about me," he replied.

"Don't be so soft Markland, sit next to me, I won't bite, I promise."

The two of them sat on his coat waiting for something to happen, but nothing did. They sat there for about five minutes both expecting the visions they'd seen before.

"Well, it's not happening for me," said Garraway.

"What's different, why can't I see Sarah?" Polly huffed, "I've seen her every time I've come here."

"Do you always sit here on your own?" he suggested.

"You're right, I am always on my own, how about you?"

"No, I've always had others nearby," he replied, "but no one has ever been on the hill with me, they've been milling around at the bottom of the slope, right over there," pointing to an area in the near distance.

"The first time I was here, when I was sick, I didn't even climb the hill. I was standing with Sergeant Matthews at the bottom."

"Perhaps that's it," she said, "perhaps we need to be up here alone."

"Do you mind if I have a ciggy," said Polly, "I could do with calming my nerves".

They made their way down the hill whilst Polly walked to a nearby bench. She felt a bit disrespectful and a little odd smoking on the hill, almost like she would be upsetting someone or something. Then she remembered how Sarah hated her smoking. *That was probably it* she thought as she lit her cigarette smiling to herself. Garraway sat next to her.

"So, when did you start to come here and begin to see the visions of Sarah?" he asked.

"It was the month following her death. I'd turned up to the place where she'd been killed on Doncaster Road to lay some fresh flowers. At that time there were lots of flowers and cards, she had a lot of friends. These days it's just me and her parents who leave flowers".

She paused for a second and Garraway could see a tear welling in her eye. She wiped her eye and continued.

"This time I decided to take a stroll to the woods. This place looked peaceful and I thought I should spend a bit of time on my own and think of her."

She paused again, wiping another tear from her eye. She inhaled on her cigarette and withheld the smoke as she thought of what to tell him next.

She let out the smoke and pointed to the hill.

"And then I saw that thing." Garraway didn't look to where she was pointing, he continued to look at her, hanging on to her words.

"Did you have an urge, or a calling to climb it?" he asked.

"No, not really, well, not at all actually, I just decided to climb, there was nothing to it, I didn't really think about it, I just went up the hill, just as thousands of people who walk these woods probably do."

"And is that when you had your vision of Sarah?"

"Yes" she replied, "but you must understand, she's never been a vague vision, I can see her as clearly as I can see you".

"What about her voice, can you hear her talking to you?" he asked.

"We've discussed this before, I can hear her, but it's strange, I can't explain exactly how I hear her, but I do".

They sat in silence as Polly finished her cigarette.

"OK," said Polly, "how about this. We try it again, but this time we'll do it one at a time?" Garraway nodded. They stood up as she put out her cigarette. Polly said that she would go first. Garraway sat down as she walked to the hill. As he watched her climb, he remembered his coat.

"You don't want a wet arse do you?" Polly looked back and smiled as Garraway walked over and passed her his coat which she took with her to the top of the hill.

Garraway sat on the bench and watched Polly on the hill, adjusting herself to get comfortable. He watched as she sat quietly. Listening to the sounds of the wood, it was not until now that he'd realised how noisy it was here. Birds were singing, dogs were barking in the distance and he could hear the sounds of children playing in a nearby sports field. He looked back to Polly and watched as she sat there with her eyes closed, almost as if she were meditating. She was rocking ever so slightly back and forth. At first she looked content. He thought he could make out a smile on her face. Then her contented look changed. She now had a look of irritation and appeared to be shaking her head. Polly had been sat at the hill for around five minutes when she quickly stood up and scuttled down the slope, almost losing her footing as she hurried down.

Garraway got up from the bench and walked over to her at the bottom of the hill.

"Is everything OK?" he asked, sensing things clearly were not.

"Yes Mr Garraway, everything is OK," she replied, in the tone of voice he had heard many times before from his wife when she couldn't hide her disapproval.

"Did you speak to Sarah?" He asked as she lit another cigarette.

"Yes, I spoke to Sarah, or rather, she spoke to me," she replied bluntly.

"Is there anything wrong?" he asked, sensing that there was.

"No, no everything is fine," which clearly it wasn't.

"OK," said Garraway walking away from her. He had learnt enough about women to know when it was best to keep his distance.

Near the bench was a monument which was about six feet tall. It was like a stainless steel menhir. On it was an inscription which he'd never noticed before. He read the inscription quietly to himself whilst Polly smoked her cigarette and sat alone.

"At Badock's Wood ghostly windmill sails turn and, like a rewound film, spin through history to remote times when this was burial place for Bronze Aged warrior in that landscape wolves prowled and nervy red deer grazed while hogs rooted among trees"

He pondered over the words. How apt they sounded *'windmill sails turn and, like a rewound film, spin'* It was almost like the words were meant for him. It made him think of the figures he saw the last time he'd sat on the hill. Like rewinding time, he had been watching those who'd walked past the hill, so many figures over the years.

Polly was finishing her cigarette as Garraway walked over to her.

"Do you want to continue or have you had enough?" As she looked up at him he could see there were more tears in her eyes. *This place really has an emotional impact on this* girl thought Garraway.

"I'm OK, let's carry on," she replied.

"Do you want to talk about it?" he asked, softening his voice. His Scottish accent appealed to her. She liked the way he sounded. He had the voice of someone she could trust.

"The cow," said Polly as she looked at Garraway.

"I'm sorry?"

"Sarah, the bloody cow," she said, as she rested her chin on the palm of her hand and stared into the distance.

"I've been coming here for almost two years and we've always talked about us, our friends, her parents," she paused and looked at Garraway.

"Guess who she wanted to talk about this time?" Garraway shrugged his shoulders.

"You," she continued, "she wanted to talk about you?"

Garraway didn't speak, he looked puzzled.

"What did she say?" he asked.

"She said that they had chosen you," continued Polly.

"Who are 'they', and what have I been chosen for, did she tell you what that meant?"

Polly shook her head.

"She said something about you needing to be here and they also mentioned another man's name and that he wasn't the one."

"What other man?" asked Garraway.

"I'm trying remember," said Polly.

She sat for a second trying to recall what Sarah had said.

"Strawfield, or Strawman or Straw........." Garraway interrupted her. "Strawbridge," he said, not asking her, but telling her. "Strawbridge, is that the name she said?"

"Yes," she replied, "I think she said John Strawbridge."

Garraway couldn't believe what he was hearing.

"Does this mean something?" she asked.

"Yes, it does," he replied, "it's not John Strawbridge, she's trying to tell you about, it's Tom Strawbridge. He was supposed to be heading up the Walker murder investigation, but he wasn't able to do it. He was ill at the last minute and the case was assigned to me".

They sat silently and weighed up what they had just discussed.

"Was that all she told you?"

Polly nodded her head.

"It's your turn," said Polly.

Garraway felt an air of anticipation as he made his way to the hill leaving Polly behind to watch from the bench.

With his damp coat under his arm he took half a dozen large strides and made his way to the top. He arranged his coat just where Polly had put it when she had been sitting there. As he sat down he began to feel nausea just as before, but this time it wasn't as acute. The feeling quickly went and he was able to relax. He let his mind unwind as he slowly closed his eyes and waited.

Markland Garraway was on the beach at Ullapool. He was nine years old. It was an evening in early March and the sun was just setting. He was with his dog Bonnie, a Border Collie and they were both resting after playing on the sand. All of sudden Bonnie began to bark. She jumped up and tried to stand on her hind legs as she continued to bark and whine.

"What is it Bonnie, what's the matter?"

Markland looked to the sky to where Bonnie was barking and he saw something magnificent.

Above him was a large black triangular shaped object silhouetted against the half-light of the Ullapool sky. It had faint lights twinkling like colourful stars around the perimeter of whatever it was.

It made no sound as it hovered in the sky.

He lay back in the sand and stared at the thing. Bonnie had stopped barking and was now whimpering and trying to bury herself into Markland's side.

He didn't feel scared, only fascinated by what he was watching. He found it hard to judge how close it was.

He looked up and down the beach to see if there was anyone else watching it, but other than Bonnie, he was alone. As he looked back to the thing hovering above him it was no longer there. It had gone, just like that.

Markland jumped to his feet and strained his eyes as he looked up to the sky. The thing had definitely gone. Without a sound the thing came and went and had been there for less than a minute.

His heart was pounding and he was breathing heavily as if he had just run the length of the beach.

Bonnie had stopped barking and whining and had bolted away. Markland ran after her.

"Bonnie come back, come back now!" he shouted as he chased after her.

Bonnie was making her own way home with Markland trying to keep up.

When he reached his front door Bonnie was there waiting for him, panting with her tongue hanging out. Markland started banging furiously at the door for his parents to let him in. He had a key, but his mind was in such turmoil he didn't think to use it.

As Markland waited for the door to open the vision started to fade, the number on the door became blurred, but he could still hear his dog by his side.

Markland Garraway was back in 2009 as he came to on the hill. He instinctively went to stroke Bonnie, who was still panting by his side. As he became aware of his surroundings the dog he could hear wasn't Bonnie, but a Golden Retriever who was next to him on the hill.

The owner called her dog and apologised for bothering him, whilst giving him an odd glance as he sat alone on the hill.

"It's OK, he's with me," shouted Polly as she made her way to Markland atop the hill.

The dog walker smiled and walked off with the Retriever bounding behind.

Garraway rubbed his forehead as he tried to comprehend what had just happened.

"Well?" demanded Polly, "what happened?"

"I'm not too sure," he replied in a shaky voice. "Can I have one of your cigarettes please?"

"I didn't think you smoked," said Polly.

"I don't, I used to. I could really do with one now, please."

She handed him a cigarette and her lighter.

They made their way back to the bench and sat down.

He coughed as he drew in the smoke. He hadn't smoked in ten years. Spluttering, he put the thing out.

"Ughh, now I remember why I gave those things up!" Polly smiled at him.

"Are you OK?"

He looked at her and nodded.

"I'm OK," he replied flexing his arms and legs whilst rolling his head from side to side.

"Are you aching like an old man?" asked Polly.

He nodded again.

"It's something you get used to," she said reassuringly.

Garraway told Polly everything that had just happened. He explained how clear everything was. How he could even smell his pet dog Bonnie and hear the sound of the soft waves lapping Ullapool beach.

He couldn't understand the relevance of the UFO memory and why he hadn't seen a repeat of the shadowy figures he saw last time. Why was it that Polly saw the same image of Sarah every time and he had seen two completely different things?

"Perhaps they're sounding you out, you know, seeing how open your mind is?" suggested Polly.

"It's got to be to do with the murder case you're dealing with, perhaps it's planning to tell you who the murderer is and it's preparing you?"

Garraway laughed. "So you're trying to tell me that the hill is just going to rock on up and tell me Colonel Mustard did it with a length of rope?"

"I thought it was a rock to the skull," said Polly in a serious tone of voice.

"Look," she added, "my Sarah seemed to know thing or two about you and your Strawbridge mate, explain that!"

Garraway shook his head and looked at his watch. They had been there for well over an hour.

"I can't explain it," he said. Wearily he added, "I'm tired and I need to go home."

His body ached as they walked back to his car.

CHAPTER TWENTY ONE

The Awareness

At the same time Garraway experienced his latest 'episode', something else, somewhere very different began to stir.

The Awareness that lasted no longer than a blink of an eye at the time Ben lost his life had begun to develop again. Just as before the Awareness had no senses, it could not see, speak, hear, touch or taste, but it did have a life force which was very strong. It was fighting to change, to develop and mature. It had a story to tell.

And again, just as before, as soon as the Awareness began, it stopped.

CHAPTER TWENTY TWO

Darlington
9.15pm
Thursday October 8th 2009

It had been a long drive from Bristol to Darlington. What should have been a four hour journey ended up taking almost six. An accident on the M5, a punctured tyre on their hired transit van and Richard getting lost as he approached Darlington had all added to the longer than anticipated journey.

"We're here," said Richard softly as Carla began to open her eyes.

Carla had been sleeping for the last hour. Still tormented by visions of what happened in those woods, her dreams were no longer nice ones. She sat up and looked out of the window of the white van.

"Which one's ours?" she asked, wondering which house she would be setting up her new life in. She had seen a picture of the house on the internet, but in the leafy street in Darlington all houses looked much the same.

"It's that one there," said her father pointing to the red brick Victorian building in front of them.

"I like it daddy," Carla smiled. It was the first time Richard had seen her smile in weeks. He smiled at her as he swept her hair away from her sleepy eyes.

Richard had no idea why Carla had been so unhappy since the start of last month. In the following weeks he put it down to the move to Darlington as it had happened at such an important time in a vulnerable young girl's life. He knew she'd have preferred to stay with her friends, especially with her final year at senior school, it would be a massive upheaval for her.

He had convinced her to visit the doctor as he was concerned about the huge change in her character. The busy doctor had confirmed Richard's diagnoses. When she returned from the surgery she hadn't been given a prescription but was told to accept her situation and deal with it. She had been told that her hormones were affecting her, she was already pining for her friends and she wasn't accepting the move to Darlington. Carla knew the real reason for her low mood and character change, but preferred to accept what the doctor had told her in order to satisfy her father. Richard felt awful to think all of this was down to him. But he desperately needed the work and he couldn't leave Carla in Bristol. He had no choice.

As they stepped out of the van and approached the door of their new home Carla felt a huge relief to be there. It was true that she felt like a stranger in a strange land, but it was better than being a loser in a lost land, which is what she had become in Bristol.

Inside the house the rooms were small but cosy and finished in magnolia, which was the standard 'blank canvas' colour that most houses were painted when they were prepared for sale. Carla went upstairs and found the room which was her bedroom. She looked out of her window to the street below and could see her father unloading things from the back of the van. Her temporary 'inflatable' bed was still in the back and was yet to be unloaded. Across the street she could see curtains twitch as the locals viewed their new neighbours arriving late in the evening. Carla ran downstairs and into the street to help her father unload their belongings into the house. Richard was beginning to see a change in his daughter. For the first time since he could remember there was a look of enthusiasm about her.

She got to bed around eleven o'clock. As she lay on her inflatable mattress she began to drift away and for the first time in what seemed like a lifetime she had a restful and dreamless sleep. No nightmares of that awful September evening. She slept well because she felt safe. Safe that she had escaped the torturous time she was experiencing in Bristol.

But she wouldn't be safe there forever. Even with Bristol 250 miles away. No matter how far she escaped from what happened on that Sunday in early September, it would never leave her. In fact it would eventually become closer than ever before.

CHAPTER TWENTY THREE

Markland Garraway's house
11am
Friday 9th October 2009

Garraway had booked the day off as annual leave. He had slept well, in fact he had slept a little too well and was surprised when he awoke at such a late hour. He was normally an early bird and was always up before seven, even on a day off. Today he would treat himself to breakfast as he was unusually hungry. Joan was already up and out of the house. He relished the thought of a bit of time home alone. He made himself a bacon sandwich, a pot of tea and poured a large glass of fresh orange juice.

As he sat in his armchair and ate his sandwich he thought about the night before. It must have taken it out of him as he'd slept like a log. He recalled the clarity of how he'd flashed back to the beach at Ullapool. He had thought about that UFO many times since he was a boy, but the older he got the more distant the memory had become. But last night it was different. He remembered it with pinpoint accuracy. It wasn't just the memory of what he saw that night which intrigued him, it was how he remembered the sounds and the smells and everything around him. If he'd taken the time to concentrate he probably would have memorised the number plates of the cars which were parked outside his old house.

Perhaps Polly had been right about what Sarah had told her, maybe he had been selected by some strange supernatural force to take on Ben Walker's case. It was certainly odd how Tom Strawbridge had been taken unexpectedly unwell that Monday morning after the murder leaving yours truly to head up the case, and it was equally odd how Tom made such a quick recovery and was able to return to work later that month.

He had so many questions but didn't know where to turn. Should he keep returning to the hill to see what happened next? Or should he seek a medium to interpret what was going on? He was confused. For the first time in his life Markland Garraway didn't know what to do. It was true that the case had hit a standstill. It would take a miracle to make any headway. *Perhaps the hill could produce a miracle?* He sighed as he finished the rest of his breakfast.

He spent the rest of his day off being particularly inactive, which wasn't like him. Normally a day off would be a blank canvas for Garraway to fill. There were so many things around the house he should be doing. Joan had been complaining about a few DIY jobs he'd never finished. He should be using this day productively and get at least a few things done, but he was squandering his time.

By two o'clock he was still lounging around the house, phasing in and out of drowsiness. Despite the marathon thirteen hour sleep, he was still tired. Just as he was about to slip back into another half sleep his phone rang. He picked it up and viewed the number. It was Polly.

"Hello Polly, how are you?"

"I'm OK, but you sound knackered," she replied.

"I know, and I feel knackered, it's my day off and all I want to do is sleep."

"I used to get like that every time I'd spoken to Sarah on the hill, the following day I would be so dopey I could sleep for England. I don't get it any more now, I suppose you get used to it," she replied.

"Perhaps that's it," he replied. "Anyway Polly, what can I do for you?"

"It's more like what I can do for you."

"I went back to the hill again today, I've just got back. Last night in bed I was thinking about Sarah and the fact that she had little to say about me and her, and that it was more about you. I was selfish and I got off the hill before she had finished talking," she continued.

"So are you getting jealous about me and Sarah?" joked Garraway, immediately sensing he'd just said the wrong thing.

"Yes, I suppose I am, or at least I was yesterday evening" she paused. "As I was saying, I cut Sarah off last night and now that I've thought about it I was sure she wanted to say something about the murder."

"So you went back to the hill?"

"Yes, and I don't think she was happy with me, at least not at first."

"Why's that?"

"Because it took a long time for me to connect with her." Garraway could hear her voice wavering.

"Normally I sit on that hill and it's like broadband, she's there instantly, this time it was like dial up. I was just about to give up and all of a sudden she was there."

Garraway was amazed by the way she calmly referred to her supernatural conversations with Sarah as if they were as normal as picking up the phone. He assumed she'd just become accustomed to it all by now. He heard sadness in her voice.

"What did you and Sarah talk about today?"

"You again, she wanted to talk about you," said Polly.

"She told me that 'they' felt you were better placed to help solve Ben's murder than Strawbridge".

"Did she say why 'they' felt I was better placed?" asked Garraway.

"She wasn't specific," said Polly, "only that you were better placed because your mind is more open than Strawbridge's".

It was true that Detective Inspector Strawbridge did everything by the book and suffered fools lightly, whilst Garraway had always taken on a case and dealt with it with an open mind. All the years he had been a detective he reminded himself of the famous Sherlock Holmes quote:

'Eliminate all other factors, and the one which remains must be the truth.'

This had helped him close some rather difficult cases over the years, which other detectives may not have solved so quickly.

"I don't think the message was that 'they' would be giving you clues, it was more advice to be open minded," said Polly.

"Who do you think 'they' are?" he asked.

"I've absolutely no idea. I've tried to find out, but Sarah seems to phase out as soon as I ask heavy questions".

Garraway held his phone away from his ear as he was suddenly struck by a thought.

"Changing the subject," he said, "has Sarah ever told you anything about when she died, any names or anything about the hit and run?"

"She's told me lots," answered Polly, "and I've volunteered the information to Sergeant Brock and a lot of good that did".

"I presume Brock said he couldn't use it?"

"It wasn't so much that he couldn't use it, he clearly thought I was insane, or that I had been *so* affected by Sarah's death I had been hallucinating," she paused, "I suppose I can't really blame him, it must have seemed very farfetched." Garraway nodded, as if Polly could see him.

"Mr Garraway, perhaps if you had been investigating Sarah's death more would have been done?"

He decided not to comment.

"Thank you Polly, I'll let you know if anything comes up which may require your, or Sarah's, assistance."

As he ended the call, he deliberated whether Polly would ever move on with her life, or spend the rest of her time having a 'long distance' relationship with a ghost. She was spending too much time on the hill and he thought how sad she sounded today.

He thought about what to do next. He was in no mood for pottering around the house. With Polly's words still fresh in his mind he decided to go back to the hill, just to see if anything might happen.

He drove to the woods and became mesmerised by the little pine air freshener hanging from the rear view mirror. The thing was rocking to and fro as he drove towards Doncaster Road and it was almost sending him to sleep. Suddenly he snapped out of the stupor just as he came to a zebra crossing with a mother and her small child slowly trying to get across the road. He slammed the brakes as the woman gave him a vile stare. He was still dead tired after the previous evening's event on the hill.

He locked his car and walked over to the hill. A group of children were kicking a ball. He looked at his watch and saw it was time for the school to empty out. There was no way he could concentrate with a few hundred kids making their way home, screaming and shouting. He decided to explore the woods whilst they made their way home. He hoped in fifteen minutes or so the place would be quiet again, and hopefully Doug Plummer, the school caretaker, wouldn't be hanging around either.

As he walked through the depths of the woods he took time to appreciate how beautiful the place was. Over the past few weeks he'd been through every square foot over and over again, but until now hadn't noticed the intricate wonder of the woodlands. This was the first time he'd taken a step back and appreciated it. It occurred to him how he took for granted the beauty that was on his doorstep. From the interviews with Ben and Liz's friends and family no one knew they were dating, so the day Ben died could have been their first get-together. Garraway could appreciate why Ben would have taken Liz here. It's the sort of place he used to take Joan way back in their courting days.

Twenty minutes later he was back at the hill. The school kids had gone and, apart from the occasional dog walker and jogger, the place was quiet. He scrambled his way to the top and sat in the same place as the previous evening. This time the ground was dry. He switched his phone to vibrate and sat and waited, and waited, and waited. But nothing was happening. He glanced at his watch, three forty five. He decided to give it another few minutes. The jogger went past again, paying him no attention. He lay back and looked up at the cloudy sky. He was feeling drowsy as a breeze blew gently, which kept him from falling asleep. As the breeze died down Garraway began to drift. Pleasant dreams drifted through his mind as he lay.

Whilst he was in a light slumber, something else, somewhere very different began to stir. The Awareness was evolving within its own dimension and it was developing with more urgency than before. It was still void of senses, but this time its need to be known, to be accepted and to be heard was greater than ever. It needed to develop a voice. It had no physical body but it did have an essence which took a virtual form, floating in a void of darkness. As it floated it kicked and it wriggled, it struggled and it fought like a newly conceived blastocyst determined to break through to a dimension where it could flourish and have a resolve to thrive.

As the Awareness battled like an upstream swimmer it developed its first perception of emotion. It felt like it had been fired from a cannon and blasted out of its dimension and pulled into another. As it soared out and through to the other side its need to be heard multiplied a thousand times. The Awareness had a determination to release four simple words which had been pent up and were now boiling under pressure like a volcano ready to erupt.

Garraway was lightly sleeping when he was awoken by such a force it almost knocked him from the hill. He sat bolt upright. Beads of perspiration where on his brow as four words were ringing in his ears. Four simple, basic, pleading words. Four words which sounded as if they were being shouted by an innocent but condemned man.

PLEASE – HEAR – MY – VOICE.

He jumped up and looked around. There was no one. The words were still ringing as if someone had crept up and shouted into his ear.

His whole body ached. He slowly climbed to his feet and walked around the hill to make sure there was definitely no one around and as he moved his body hurt badly. It felt as if there was sand in his joints. He sat back down to digest what had just happened.

Maria Jameson's home
3.47pm
Friday 10th October

Maria was in her favourite chair holding Christopher closely while he gently slept. After five weeks he had developed so much and she could see changes in him every day. There was an unconditional love that only exists between mother and child.

She gently rocked him and smiled contentedly.

Christopher suddenly awoke and with penetrating blue eyes stared at his mother. He jerked his head to one side and let out a blood curdling scream as if a firecracker had exploded next to his ear. Maria jolted forward and instinctively held him closer. He cried an agonising wail which quickly ebbed to a soft whimper and then he went back to sleep.

Maria stared at him and wondered what on earth had happened.

Southmead Hospital
Liz Mason's ward
3.47pm
Friday 10th October

Liz hadn't moved for four weeks. She had shown no signs of life other than her chest rising and falling as she gently drew in and exhaled breath.

Her mother Anne was sitting beside Liz, drowsily reading a copy of Closer magazine. Anne was in a state of permanent jet lag. One day was morphing into the next and she had little idea of which day was which. Time had lost its purpose.

Had she been more alert, instead of half reading a story about Jordan's latest Botox treatment, she would have seen Liz's eyes impulsively open. They darted from left to right as if she was consciously panicking, then they settled as she stared at the light in the ceiling above her bed. Slowly her lids closed as she returned to the state she had been in for the last four weeks.

As Anne turned the page of her magazine she reached for a glass of water.

The ten second occurrence had gone unnoticed.

CHAPTER TWENTY FOUR

Badock's Wood
3.54pm
Friday 10th October

Garraway wearily made his way down the hill. The pain in his joints was now subsiding. His phone in his shirt pocket was vibrating, he fumbled for it and saw it was Matthews. He welcomed the interruption as it brought him back to the real world.

"Good afternoon Sergeant Matthews, to what do I owe the pleasure of your dulcet tones?"

Matthews could hear Garraway's voice was shaky.

"There's been a suicide sir and we've been called in, so I'm afraid your day off has been cancelled."

"For a suicide, on my day off?" snapped Garraway. "Why can't a uniform PC and a uniform Sergeant deal with it?"

"Because it's got your name all over it sir, and it may not be a suicide."

"Can you give me forty five minutes?" requested Garraway.

"Yes sir, I'll pick you up at your place and I'll explain on the way."

Garraway returned home, had a quick shower and changed his clothes. Although he was feeling a little better, the pain in his joints was still there and he was still feeling extremely tired. He made a strong coffee whilst he waited for Matthews.

Joan wasn't back and the house was quiet. He took the time to think about what had happened on the hill. He called Polly to let her know about the voice he had heard. Her phone went to voicemail so he left a message for her to call him back.

He could hear Matthews sounding his horn outside. He finished his coffee, grabbed his keys and left the house.

Garraway got in the front passenger seat and Matthews sped off.

"What's this about?" asked Garraway.

"The suicide of Polly Ellis," said Matthews.

Garraway did a double take and then his heart sank as he stared at Matthews without talking. He thought about how sad she'd sounded when they last spoke, but not to the degree of taking her life.

"Her flatmate found her in the bathroom, he called 999, but it was too late" Matthews continued.

"Did she leave a note?" asked Garraway.

"She did, and this is why we're involved."

Garraway stared blankly out of the window.

"You need to read the note sir." Garraway nodded.

Garraway was feeling uncomfortable about the suicide, not just because he liked Polly, but because she had somehow become tangled up in his enquiries. None of what they had discussed had been reported by Garraway as he didn't feel it would be relevant to the case or even accepted as evidence. Mentioning voices from the dead via Polly wouldn't make him look good. He knew he already had a reputation of being a maverick.

Polly's road was teeming with police and paramedics. Matthews parked as close as he could. They got out, walked to her flat and climbed the stairs to the first floor where she'd lived. Garraway followed slowly behind Matthews. He walked like an old man. His arms and legs still ached.

Her upstairs hallway was busy with uniformed police constables.

"She's in there sir," said the WPC. Matthews and Garraway took it in turns to look around the bathroom door. Matthews had already seen her body and Garraway decided there was no need for him to go into the bathroom. He'd seen enough from the door. He walked across the hall and into Polly's lounge and sat on the arm of her sofa. Garraway looked shocked and insipid.

"Are you OK sir?" asked Matthews

"Yes, I'm fine," he replied.

"What's in the note?"

Matthews handed it to him, sealed in a clear police evidence bag. Garraway squinted his eyes and read the note.

To my dear mum, dad and all my wonderful friends. Please don't think badly of me for what I have done. I know my Sarah is waiting for me because she has told me.

I cannot live without her.

I will be happy again when I am with her and hopefully you will eventually find happiness in your hearts despite what I have done.

I love you all so much but have been so sad these last couple of years since Sarah died and I would rather be with Sarah in her world than without her in mine.

Polly

Please tell Markland Garraway not to give up on Ben Walker. Accept the evidence you find no matter how it is presented.

Garraway read the note three times. He wondered why Polly would have thought to mention him in her note. He looked at Matthews and shook his head.

"What a waste of a young life," he sighed. He looked at the note again, then turned it over and looked on the other side. It was blank.

"What's so important about this letter?" he asked Matthews.

"It's the bit which mentions your name sir, can't you see it?"

Garraway looked again and cast his eyes over the last section, this time he read it out loud.

"Please tell Markland Garraway not to give up on Ben Walker. Accept the evidence you find no matter how it is presented."

He looked back at Matthews shaking his head. He felt tired and weary and was clearly missing something.

"It's not the words sir," said Matthews, "it's the writing".

Garraway looked again. He looked at the first four lines of the note and Polly's signature and then he looked at the last line.

"It's different handwriting," he said.

"That's right," said Matthews, "so there must have been someone with her when she died, or just after."

"Unless, her state of mind caused her to write that last line differently. You don't know what must have been going through her head," said Garraway.

"But the writing is so different," said Matthews, "look at the first few lines, her writing is small and spidery and the last line is large and, well, loopy."

Garraway stood up and looked around her flat holding her note. He walked into her kitchen and rustled through her drawers. He closed them and continued to look around. He walked over to the far wall where Polly had hung her calendar. He and looked at the note made against Thursday tenth of September. He squinted his eyes to read the small spidery writing.

Markland Garraway, Weatherspoon's 9pm

He looked at the first four lines on the suicide note and compared it to the writing on the calendar. It was identical.

Matthews walked into the kitchen and watched Garraway as he looked from the suicide note to the calendar and back to the note.

"I will get the forensic handwriting guys to check it out, but I think there's no doubt someone else had got their hands on the note," said Matthews.

"It just doesn't make sense. Why would someone turn up, presumably after Polly had killed herself and leave a note for me?………It's almost as if whoever wrote this wanted it to be found, as a way of getting a message to me." Matthews agreed.

Garraway looked at his watch. It was half past five.

"Sorry to be a pain Colin, but would you mind running me home?"

Matthews looked up. Garraway never referred to him by his first name, unless he needed a favour.

"It's been a long day and although it's been a day off, I feel totally knackered and not in the best frame of mind."

Matthews nodded and smiled, "No problem sir."

Matthews drove Garraway home and no one spoke during the journey. Matthews stopped the car outside Garraway's drive. Garraway got out and thanked Matthews for the lift.

"Do you think Polly Ellis could have been involved with the murder?" asked Matthews as Garraway was about to shut the car door.

"I think that's highly unlikely. I'll see you tomorrow bright and breezy," said Garraway as he went to close the car door.

"And I'll get this note over to handwriting now so hopefully we'll have some news in the morning," replied Matthews.

Garraway smiled and shut the car door.

He opened the front door and threw his keys on the table in the hall. He called out to Joan, but there was no reply. He walked into the kitchen and saw a note on the dining table. He picked it up. She had left a note to say she was at her sister's and would be back around ten. Garraway opened the fridge and saw a lone microwave curry on the middle shelf. He pulled it out of the fridge, looked the curry over, tutted, threw it in the microwave and punched four minutes thirty seconds into the timer.

He had intended to wait up for Joan, but after half finishing the curry he decided to have a very early night. He took off his jacket and tie, slung them over the back of the kitchen chair and went up to bed. It was only six thirty, but he fell asleep as soon as his head hit the pillow.

He suddenly woke up at three fifteen in the morning. He sat upright and saw Joan in the half-light sleeping soundly beside him. He felt wide awake and was thinking about the suicide note. A thought crossed his mind which he immediately dismissed. Shaking his head he bedded back down, stared at the ceiling and thought about the strange day. Polly's death, the voices on the hill and the note. He was sure there was a link. Tiredness returned and he fell back into a deep sleep until his alarm woke him just over three hours later.

CHAPTER TWENTY FIVE

The Incident Room
9am
Saturday 11th October

Matthews was already in the incident room when Garraway arrived. Garraway helped himself to fresh coffee and sat next to Matthews.

"Are you feeling better today?" asked Matthews.

"Yes, I am. Thank you for asking."

"I've spoken to Handwriting this morning and they've confirmed what we had suspected. There are two different sets of writing on the suicide note," said Matthews.

Garraway nodded as he leant back in his chair with the back of his head resting in his hands.

"I would like to speak to my friend Sergeant Brock," he said as he gazed towards the ceiling.

"What's Brock got to do with the price of bread?" asked Matthews.

"I don't know, maybe something, maybe nothing," he answered in an intriguing tone of voice. He had a look in his eye which Matthews knew meant he was having one of his 'out there' ideas.

"I'll start getting handwriting samples from those who knew Polly," said Matthews,

"Yes, good idea Matthews, you do that," answered Garraway in a nonchalant manner.

As Matthews left the room Garraway picked up the phone and dialled Brock's number.

"Sergeant Brock, how the devil are you?" said Garraway. "I wonder if you could do me a favour?"

Later that afternoon Matthews returned to the incident room and was looking pleased with himself. Garraway was also there and was looking even more pleased.

"I've got the uniforms doing the rounds taking handwriting samples from those who knew Polly sir," said Matthews.

"Good work," replied Garraway. "Be a good lad and run this over to your friends in Handwriting".

He handed Matthews a shopping list in a sealed police evidence bag. He had put masking tape over the 'victim', 'suspect' and 'case number' section of the bag so Matthews couldn't see to whose case the evidence related.

"What is it?" asked Matthews.

"I'll tell you after Handwriting confirm whether it's written by the same person who wrote on Polly's note."

Matthews looked at the list again. The writing did look similar, with its big loopy flowing style.

"Run along," said Garraway.

Matthews hated it when Garraway had that smug patronising attitude about him, but whenever he did, he was usually proved right.

CHAPTER TWENTY SIX

Darlington
2.15pm
Saturday 11th October

Carla Price was unpacking the last of her belongings and was arranging her bedroom. Her new bed had arrived the day before and her temporary bed was up in the loft along with fifty boxes of bits and pieces that she and her dad were going to sort through over the coming weeks. Since she'd moved away from Bristol she'd almost become her old self. Her father was happy to see her back to normal. Whatever it was that had upset his daughter seemed to have passed. Although, she could still be abrupt and snappy, which he put down to teenage hormones and thought nothing else of it.

Carla and her father had new starts after the weekend. It was to be Carla's first day at Hurworth School and Richard would be starting his new job as an Analytical Chemist for CKT, a Waste Management organisation. This would be the first time in two years that he would be employed, since things had gone wrong when his wife had left him.

They were both looking forward to the new directions in their lives. Especially Carla, who saw Hurworth as a blank canvas to re-start her life, where no one would know anything about her past.

News of Ben Walker's murder had made the middle pages of some the national newspapers and was mentioned on Sky News, but in general the incident had gone unnoticed in Darlington, which is why she felt a weight had been lifted and she could hold her head up and begin to smile again.

She smiled to herself as she placed her CDs in their rack, neatly filed in alphabetical order. She had put her Linkin Park and Flo Rida posters on the wall. Her bedroom was beginning to take shape. The photograph of her mother and father in the pink heart shaped frame was given pride of place on her bedside cabinet. She loved her father and appreciated everything he had done as a single parent, but she missed her mother and wished her parents were still together.

She kissed the photograph and lay on her bed holding it close to her chest.

CHAPTER TWENTY SEVEN

The Incident Room
3.45pm
Saturday 11th October

Matthews returned to the incident room to find Garraway beavering over a pile of paperwork. Matthews strode over to him and abruptly stopped.

"How do you do it sir?"

"How do I do what, Sergeant Matthews?"

"This," he said as he threw down the two evidence bags, one with Polly's note and the other with the shopping list.

"I assume that the forensic handwriting analysis bods are telling us that the handwriting samples match?" asked Garraway smugly.

"They're 97 percent certain that the last line on Polly's letter was written by the same person who wrote the shopping list".

Matthews stood over and watched Garraway as he held both evidence bags and looked from one to the other. He saw a look of incredulity in his eyes. Matthews waited silently for Garraway to speak. He knew that silence would eventually urge Garraway to say something……….. but couldn't wait any longer.

"Would you mind sharing what you know sir?" he asked impatiently.

Garraway sighed. He wasn't quite sure how to explain what he had proved. He drew in a breath and decided to tell Matthews the facts.

"Sergeant Matthews, the handwriting on the shopping list and the handwriting at the bottom of Polly's suicide note were both in Sarah

Greenfield's handwriting." He waited for Matthews to contemplate what he had just been told.

"Do you mean the same Sarah Greenfield who was killed in the hit and run over two years ago?" asked Matthews.

"The very same."

Matthews face contorted as he tried to work out the scenario. As he deliberated on how this could have happened he grimaced comically.

Matthews cleared his throat and suggested that perhaps Polly had found some paper on which Sarah had already written those words before she died and Polly used it to write her suicide note. Garraway shook his head.

"How would Sarah Greenfield known over two years ago that I would be investigating Ben Walker's murder, which happened last month?"

"Well it makes more sense than what you're suggesting," replied Matthews in an agitated voice.

"What am I suggesting?" Garraway calmly replied.

"It sounds like you are telling me Sarah Greenfield was in Polly's flat when Polly killed herself and then added her own words to the suicide note," Matthews snapped back sounding tense.

"No, Sergeant Matthews I don't think dead people can do that."

"Well, what do you mean?" asked Matthews impatiently.

"I'm not entirely sure, I need to mull this one over and I will let you know," he replied with a telling smile. And then he added.

"I may have indicated that it was Sarah Greenfield's handwriting, but I haven't suggested it was Sarah who wrote it."

Matthew raised his hands in the air, turned round, said he was giving up and left the room.

Garraway smiled.

Garraway knew he could be patronising. He didn't do it on purpose, it just happened, and he knew how much it annoyed Matthews. He knew that Matthews was aware that the hill had been having an effect on him, but he had never told him to what extent. Neither had he told him about Polly's visions of Sarah. It was time he came clean.

Garraway followed Matthews and found him in the corridor at the water cooler. Matthews looked annoyed, he couldn't hide it.

"If you expect us to work together you've got to stop playing stupid games," said Matthews holding a cup of water.

"I'm sorry," replied Garraway in an empathetic tone.

"There are some things I've not told you," he continued.

"About the case?" asked Matthews.

"Not exactly," said Garraway, "but I suppose there is a connection, but it's more about me".

Matthews looked concerned.

"Are you OK sir?" he enquired.

"Yes, well, at least I think so," replied Garraway.

"Shall we find an empty meeting room, and you can tell me what's going on?" suggested Matthews. Garraway nodded.

Garraway sat down at the table in meeting room two. Matthews changed the sign on the door to 'meeting in progress' and shut the door behind him.

"Shoot!" said Matthews as he sat opposite Garraway.

Markland Garraway looked around the small office as if searching for the right words.

He started from the very beginning. From the first time he had been to the place where Ben Walker had been found and how he was sick, how he'd had strange visions when sitting on the hill to how he recalled every detail of the UFO encounter and the strange voice that he heard.

Matthews listened silently.

"What about Polly?" asked Matthews. "You mentioned just now that you went to the woods with her." This was the part that Garraway was feeling most awkward about, especially since her suicide, and now the strange note she had left.

Garraway explained how he had made contact with her after finding her post on the Mythical UK website about the burial mound, or 'the hill' as he now preferred to call it. He told him about their telephone conversation, their meeting in the bar, their visit to the hill together, how Polly would sit on the hill and talk with her dead girlfriend, and how Sarah had told Polly that he should keep an open mind about Ben Walker's murder.

"So you didn't think to mention in our investigation that Polly had some kind of interest in the case?" asked Matthews.

Garraway shrugged his shoulders.

"I didn't think it was relevant," he replied, "and if I had mentioned that she had been given hints from beyond the grave, no one would have believed her, or me, and the evidence wouldn't have been of any use."

"That's not the point sir, and I think you know it. The point is that she had an interest in the case and I think we should have brought her in for an interview, if only to eliminate her from our enquiries."

Garraway knew Matthews was right.

Matthews stood up and looked out of the office window. He turned around to Garraway and cleared his throat.

"To be frank sir, I don't think you should be on this case."

Garraway sat upright and stared at Matthews.

"I beg your pardon?" he calmly replied.

"I'm worried about you sir, what you are telling me is all very odd."

Garraway viewed Matthews suspiciously.

"Keep going," said Garraway.

"Let's consider the evidence sir, you're seeing things, you've been off colour, you admitted that on your day off you slept for most of it, which is very unlike you and you've been keeping back information which could help with our enquiry." Matthews paused to consider what to say next.

"And, you believe that Polly was communicating with her dead girlfriend about the case."

"Well I was right about the handwriting wasn't I?" snapped Garraway, his voice rising in anger.

"It would seem so," replied Matthews.

"Can I ask you something sir?" said Matthews in a compassionate tone, which could be construed as patronising.

"What?" retorted Garraway.

"Is everything OK at home, you know, between you and Mrs Garraway?"

"I would like to remind you to mind your own business about my home life, it's got nothing to do with you," shouted Garraway so loud that the staff outside the meeting room could hear his voice.

"It does have something to do with me if it's affecting our work," replied Matthews calmly.

"I think I need to speak with Detective Superintendent Munroe, sir," he continued.

"Well that's your prerogative Colin," snapped Garraway as he stood up, walked out of the room and slammed the door behind him.

Matthews stayed in the meeting room and let out one hell of a big sigh. He didn't like what he'd just done, but he was worried about his colleague.

CHAPTER TWENTY EIGHT

The Incident Room
9am
Monday 13th October

When Garraway returned to work on Monday he was told to report to Munroe. He huffed, and slowly made his way to Munroe's office on the fourth floor. He knocked on the door and heard Munroe's gruff voice.

"Enter."

Garraway felt like a school boy about to see the headmaster. He pushed the door open and walked into the office.

Munroe was a short rotund man in his late fifties. He had been in the force for over thirty five years. He rarely smiled, and Garraway made no effort to hide his dislike for him.

"Sit down, please," barked Munroe.

"I think you know why you're here," said the Detective Superintendent.

"I assume you've been speaking with Colin Matthews sir."

"Mmmmm, yes" he replied nonchalantly as he thumbed through some notes.

"Matthews is concerned about you, and I think he's every right to be," he said, as he took off his glasses and focused on Garraway's face.

"I would have to say you've been acting out of character since you've been involved in the Walker investigation."

"I'm no expert Mr Garraway, but I would say you are heading for some kind of nervous breakdown."

Garraway opened his mouth, but was thwarted from speaking by Munroe raising his hand.

"I want you to make an appointment with Occupational Health."

Garraway tried to talk again, but Munroe spoke first.

"I think you should take some time off, let Matthews carry on with the Walker investigation, he's a good policeman and he's got plenty of support."

"Honestly, I'm fine," said Garraway.

"You're not fine, sometimes you can be brilliant, but you're not fine, at least not now," replied Munroe.

"Are you suggesting that I am off this case for good?" he asked.

"I'll reserve judgement until after I've read the report from Occupational Health."

Garraway knew there was no point in protesting. He could appeal, but not until the report from Occupational Health had been submitted.

"I recommend you go home Mr Garraway and rest up. Occupational Health will be in touch with you soon."

"Sometimes, the best decisions are not the easiest ones to make," he added sympathetically.

Garraway nodded and turned to leave.

"There is one thing," said Munroe as Garraway opened the door.

"I'm intrigued," he said, holding a sheet of A4 and pointing at the paper, "How did you work out that the handwriting on Polly Ellis' suicide note would match Sarah Greenfield's?" He paused as he skim read the paper in his hand, "and how do you think her handwriting appeared on the note over two years after she died?"

"It's all about having an open mind sir," replied Garraway as he left the office closing the door behind him.

CHAPTER TWENTY NINE

Markland Garraway's home
3.45pm
Friday 17th October

Garraway had been assessed by Tim Westlake of Occupational Health and had been told to see his GP. He had been honest with Westlake and told him everything that had happened since early September. On the recommendation of Westlake and Garraway's GP, he had been signed off work for four weeks due to stress.

Garraway was not happy. He was more stressed at home attempting to recover, than when working.

Joan hadn't been particularly supportive and told him not to sit around the house and get under her feet. She had given him a list of things that needed doing.

He had considered booking a cottage somewhere for a short break with Joan, but didn't have the motivation.

He had been told by Westlake not to return to the woods and, in no uncertain terms, he should not go to the hill. Hearing this was like a red rag to a bull. It was the only place he wanted to be. The hill had become an obsession. Since being signed off work, it was about the only thing he could think of.

He jumped up, grabbed his coat and car keys and headed back to the hill, despite implicit instructions not to.

Fifteen minutes later he was there. It was a cold afternoon, the sky was covered in heavy clouds and it was getting dark. He didn't notice how cold it was and left his coat in the car. He climbed the hill and sat down. He'd not been here since Polly died and now the place had a sinister air. He lay back and waited for the nausea to return. As it did he became drowsy and was soon in a state of semi-consciousness.

The Awareness started to wake and was developing quicker than before. With less effort, it was finding it easier to reach out from its dimension to another place. The Awareness was not alone this time. There were other consciousnesses contending to be heard.

Garraway sensed several consciousnesses simultaneously vying for his attention, like lots of radio stations fighting to be broadcast on the same wavelength. At first he was hearing unidentifiable psychobabble but as he lay on the hill with his eyes closed in a hypnagogic state of half sleep, half-awake, he was able to focus on what he was sensing.

He was tuning into a distinct cerebral transmission. As he focused, his face contorted as if he was experiencing a low long drawn out electric current. A distant voice was materialising in his mind. The more he concentrated and fixated on what he was hearing, the clearer the voice became. It was the voice of a woman, gently calling his name. Instantly he knew who it was.

He could hear Polly Ellis.

His closed lids agitated as his eyes darted in all directions. Now he could see her face, smiling as if reaching out to greet him, but her smile was not a happy one, it was one which reflected guilt. He tried to speak, but didn't know how. All he could do was listen.

Polly was apologising for what she had done and the trouble that she had caused.

She was saying sorry on behalf of Sarah for writing on the note and told him that she was with her when she had taken her life.

Polly was telling Garraway that someone else wanted to speak with him, but was having difficulty being understood and she had promised that she would help the 'someone else' to be heard.

As he was hearing and seeing Polly a second face was taking shape beside her. It was that of a girl, with dark hair. She had a pretty face with smooth olive skin. She opened her mouth and spoke, but he could not hear her words. His focus on her intensified but still no words could be heard. She looked troubled as she could not be comprehended.

Polly's face came back into focus and she told him that it was Sarah who he could see and that she wanted to thank him. Sarah ceased trying to talk and smiled.

Polly told him that the 'someone else' was ready to speak, but like when Sarah spoke, he would not be able to hear the words or even see the face. The 'someone else' wasn't yet able to be seen and heard as plainly as Polly.

Polly would speak on behalf of the 'someone else'.

Garraway watched Polly's face as she concentrated. Her head was slowly nodding. Sarah was still next to her, but her clarity was waning. He lay on the hill waiting for what was to come next.

Polly closed her eyes as she began to relay the message and as she did her voice was so clear and distinct it was as if she was still alive and sitting beside him.

"Do not give up on me as I will help you. You may not know my voice when you hear me speak, but when you hear my words you will know they are mine."

Garraway opened his eyes and sat up. Polly and Sarah had gone but the words Polly relayed were ringing in his ears.

He sat on the hill and knew he had been hearing the words of Ben Walker. He climbed down the hill and tolerated the pain in his joints to which he was becoming accustomed. He made his way back to his car, walking like a man who was twenty five years older.

Uncertain if he would be allowed to 'officially' investigate Ben Walker's murder, or even if he would continue to be a detective, he knew that he would not give up until Ben's killers were brought to justice.

He didn't know quite how he would do this, but felt sure that with Ben's help, the work he had started would be finished.

It was early evening when he returned home and the house was empty. As always, Joan was conspicuous by her absence. Feeling tired was something he was becoming used to. He climbed the stairs one step at a time whilst holding on to the bannister. He turned to walk into the bedroom, desperate to sleep, but stopped as he reached the bedroom door. He ached and felt tired to the core and decided to sleep in the spare room so not to be woken by Joan when she came to bed. He dropped like a stone onto the single bed and stared at the ceiling and wondered how he was going to solve this case with which he was becoming so unhealthily obsessed.

    He closed his eyes and fell into a dreamless sleep.

CHAPTER THIRTY

The Awareness

One of the many things the Awareness had no concept of, was time. It had no idea of the length of time that had passed since it evolved.

It had developed basic emotions, urges and senses, although the senses did not allow it to see, hear, touch, taste or smell.

It recognised that it was in a safe place and it was in an environment where there was unconditional love. It sensed happiness and that it was not alone.

It had started to remember things. Although it could not see or hear, it could perceive images and sounds like memories recalled in a vague dream.

It knew what it had been like to be happy, sad, loved and scared.

The awareness was learning and it was learning fast.

CHAPTER THIRTY ONE

Maria Jameson's home
7.30am
Tuesday August 3rd 2010
10 months later

Christopher was waking up. Maria could hear him crying over the baby monitor. He had been sleeping in his own room since he was six months old.

Just five more minutes please! She thought as she lay in her bed. She rubbed the sleep from her eyes and sat up. Pulling back the curtain she saw it was a fine August morning. Smiling, she listened to Christopher cooing in his room. She walked along her hallway whilst tying the belt on her dressing gown, then gently opening the door to her son's room she was greeted by his beaming cheery face.

"Hello my baby boy," she said as she lifted him from his cot. His little legs kicked with delight when he saw his mother. Christopher replied with giggles and gurgles. Every morning was a wonder for Maria to see her son.

In the past eleven months he had changed so much. His once white hair had darkened to fair brown, his once tiny body was filling out nicely and he was crawling around the flat. Last week she found him pulling himself up and teetering against the sofa. He still had the same piercing blue eyes as he did when he was born. Maria was pleased that his eyes hadn't changed colour as he'd got older.

Since he was born, every day had been a good one. He slept well, fed well and was a happy little chap and had got off lightly with the ailments that her friend's children had been through like colic, eczema, coughs and colds.

Soon Maria would be returning to work and this was something she was dreading. She had agreed with Westhouse to return three days a week starting next month. Her mother Claire was to look after Christopher when Maria was at work. This was something Claire was looking forward to.

Maria carried Christopher into the lounge and placed him in his rocker while she went to the kitchen to make up his baby rice. Christopher had become attached to the Jelly Cat cuddly toy which Claire had bought him when he was born. It was a little grey cat which went with him everywhere. Claire had named the cuddly cat Misty and the name had stuck.

Maria could hear him crying from the lounge. She was getting to understand the different cries he made. He wasn't crying because he wanted his breakfast, she recognised this as one when he wanted something else.

She walked into the lounge with his feed and saw that he was upset because he had dropped Misty. Maria picked up the toy and gave it back to Christopher. As she tucked the cat under his arm he smiled at her and gurgled. The gurgle sounded different, as if he was saying something. As he gurgled and cooed he was making a 'mmmm' sound. Maria listened closely as he continued 'mmmm'. He dropped the toy cat again and started crying. She handed the cat to him and clearly heard him say "Meee."

Is this his first word, was he trying to say mummy? thought Maria.

Christopher held Misty close to him and smiled as he repeated "Meee, Meee, Meee." Maria listened carefully. He wasn't trying to say mummy or mama, he was trying to say Misty.

He had said his first word and Maria was elated. Looking around her empty lounge, she found it lonely having no one to share the special moment with.

She called her mother who was over the moon, and a little smug that Christopher's first word was the name she chose for his favourite toy.

Maria wanted to tell the world, but settled on calling Claire and her best friend Samreen as they had both been present when Christopher was born. Samreen was so happy for Maria and suggested a girl's morning chilling in Coaster's with coffee and a Danish pastry.

She placed Christopher in his door bouncer whilst she had a quick wash and change. Gone were the days of long relaxing baths as she daren't leave him alone too long without knowing he was safe. As she dressed she could hear him cooing, gurgling and saying "mee, mee" as he bounced up and down in the bedroom doorway.

CHAPTER THIRTY TWO

Coaster's Coffee Shop
10.54am

Samreen was waiting at the coffee shop when Maria arrived just before eleven o'clock. It was her day off and she had nothing planned, so time spent with Maria and her gorgeous Godson would be perfect. The best friends hugged and Samreen picked Christopher out of his buggy and gave him a cuddle. His face beamed.

"Who's a clever boy?" said Samreen as she bounced him on her lap. Christopher smiled and gurgled with delight. Maria put him in a highchair and gave him a rusk to suck on.

"Watch this," said Maria as she took Misty from Christopher and hid the toy behind her back. "Meee, mee, mee," said Christopher as if on cue. "That is too cute," said Samreen as she grabbed Misty from Maria and gave the toy back to him. Christopher beamed and cooed.

"You are so lucky Maria, he's gorgeous."

Maria smiled.

Maria went to the counter to order coffee and something to eat. She was served by a good looking dark haired man in his thirties. *Hello*, she thought to herself *He's new*. She ordered a cappuccino for Samreen and an espresso for herself. She needed a jump start as she was feeling tired. She sat down with Samreen and waited for their coffees.

"Who's the new guy?" asked Maria.

"I've no idea, he must have only just started," replied Samreen. They giggled like school girls.

Their order was brought by the waiter and Maria took note of his name badge. He put their drinks and food on the table, turned to Christopher and remarked what a handsome boy he was. He made a fuss of Christopher who wriggled and chuckled in his highchair.

Maria watched the waiter and thought about Rob. She wondered where he was and what he was doing.

"Your little boy's a proper Bobby Dazzler," said the waiter. "You must be very proud of him?"

"Thank you Campbell," said Maria.

The waiter looked a little embarrassed when she'd said his name. He smiled at her and the two women giggled again.

Christopher was getting tired and crotchety.

"That's not like him," said Samreen.

"He's a little tired, I'll put him in his buggy."

Maria covered him with his blanket and made him comfortable. He was still crying so Maria reached for his dummy and popped it into his mouth.

"I don't like those things, but sometimes they're a life saver," she said as he stopped crying.

Maria and Samreen chatted, read the papers and relaxed. Maria took a few crafty peeks at Campbell when he wasn't looking. Samreen watched her and smiled.

"I bet you'd like to get your hands on Campbell's meatballs," whispered Samreen.

Maria gave her a playful punch.

Samreen worried about Maria being a single mum and wondered how her life would pan out. She hoped she would find someone to replace that rat Rob.

Campbell looked across the shop and smiled at the pair of them and Maria smiled back. The two women giggled again like a pair of seventeen year olds.

Christopher was crying again. His dummy had fallen out of his mouth and landed on his blanket. Maria took a sip of espresso, put down her cup and reached for the dummy which was covered in fluff. She popped it in her mouth and sucked off the bits of fluff.

"Ewe!" remarked Samreen.

"I know, the things I do," said Maria.

She put the dummy back in his mouth. As Christopher tasted the bitter espresso his mother had inadvertently passed to his dummy, his faced scrunched up and he spat the thing out and continued to cry.

Maria picked him up and cuddled him until he settled. Gently rocking him until he went back to sleep. She put him back in his buggy.

The miniscule amount of caffeine from the dummy was ingested and entered his blood stream. It made its way around his tiny system as it was shunted with every beat of his heart. The caffeine molecules started to counteract Adenosine when it reached his brain which caused his heart to beat a little faster and his breathing became a little heavier.

The tiny amount of caffeine passed through his pineal gland and triggered a reaction which had an instant and profound effect on Christopher and would shape his formative years of development.

As he lay asleep in his cot he started to rock from side to side. Maria and Samreen were engrossed in conversation and didn't notice.

Campbell came over to take away their empty plates and saw Christopher rolling from side to side.

"I used to do that when I was a nipper," he said pointing to Christopher.

Maria turned to Christopher and looked horrified.

"What are you doing Christopher?" she instinctively said.

"Does he normally do that?" asked Campbell.

"No, I've never seen him to this before, what's he doing?"

"He's a little head banger," he replied. "I did that in my sleep until I was about three. My mum took me to the doctor who told her I would just grow out of it," he added.

"What do you mean, a head banger?" she asked Campbell crossly.

"When I was sleeping, I would roll from side to side and, when I was a little older, I would bang my head up and down on the pillow. Lot's of kids do it, it's nothing to worry about and he'll grow out of it."

"He's never done this before." She said picking him out of the buggy and holding him close. Christopher stopped rocking and cooed happily in his sleep.

"See, he's fine," said Campbell.

CHAPTER THIRTY THREE

The Awareness

At the same time Christopher ingested the caffeine the Awareness started to rouse after a long period of inactivity.

It was acclimatising to a new level of wakefulness. It had a clearer understanding of what it was and what it had been. Memories were returning faster than before. Images were connecting with sounds. Voices had familiarity. Faces and places were beginning to mean something.

The Awareness was starting to understand who it had once been. Although it had no knowledge of where it was, it was starting to comprehend that it existed for a reason. It knew it had something to achieve, which was to be heard and understood, but the awareness had no idea what it needed to say.

In its present incarnation it was lasting longer than before, as hundreds of connections were being made like little lights coming on one by one. A catalyst had happened which allowed it an increased longevity.

As Christopher's brain was processing what was happening, he was rocking from side to side. The more the Awareness was evolving the more Christopher reacted by rocking in his sleep.

When Maria picked him up and held him close, the Awareness blinked off like a light going out when a circuit is broken.

Although the Awareness was again latent it wouldn't be long before it would reawaken. From now on, the catalyst, that molecule of caffeine, would ensure its development and with each incarnation it would build and remodel itself. Each time it would draw upon its memories which would become clearer and more meaningful.

The Awareness was a soul which had found Christopher. In Christopher the soul had a body where it could flourish and thrive like a hermit crab finding a shell in which to live.

CHAPTER THIRTY FOUR

Liz Mason's home
Wednesday August 5th

Liz was at home. She'd left Southmead hospital early in July. She was lying in bed when Anne came into her room to see her. She sat beside her daughter, moved her hair away from her eyes and kissed her on her forehead.

Liz had been in a vegetative state of coma for almost a year. Her father's good financial position had allowed his daughter to be cared for at home thanks to a team of medical helpers who were with her at all times. Since Liz had left hospital her parents had begun to accept their daughter's situation and felt better that she was at home in her room. It was a small step but it felt like progress.

Terry had returned to work, which was a good thing, as the distraction of the daily grind of running one of Bristol's most successful IT businesses helped him take his mind off what was happening with Liz. Although images of his daughter peppered his mind every few minutes, being at work was structuring his life allowing him to move forward.

The medical staff who looked after Liz were amazing. They fed her, turned her in her bed, changed her and managed muscle tone along with countless other daily tasks to ensure she was as comfortable as possible. They truly were amazing and they came at a truly amazing price.

Terry had planned on taking Anne on an eight week cruise that summer, but all that had changed after what happened to Liz. Although the cost of the cruise would hardly cover the cost of Liz's treatment for a couple of months, he had decided to put the money he had saved towards her medical care. He was a rich man, but didn't know how long it would take for Liz to recover and as his money pot wasn't bottomless he had to be sensible. The private medical insurances he'd taken out did not cover all of the cost, in fact he was taken aback by how little the insurance pay-outs were, considering the premiums he had paid over the years. He would do whatever was necessary to provide round-the-clock care for his daughter, even if this meant selling his company.

Liz had shown little improvement since she was found in September. She had opened her eyes in November which was amazing. Terry and Liz could not believe what they were seeing and were convinced Liz would soon be sat up in bed and talking.

Sergeant Matthews had been informed and was geared up to visit her as soon as she was ready to talk. She was the only key to unlock the evidence needed to capture Ben Walker's killers.

Unfortunately things had not improved since the day she opened her eyes. She appeared awake but showed no signs of awareness.

Whilst Liz lay in her bed, Terry and Anne would sit with her. Looking into her wide open eyes was like looking into the face of a Victorian porcelain doll. She showed no emotion and was not aware there were people around her. At times Anne wished Liz's eyes were closed as she appeared more peaceful, as if she was sleeping normally. Now she had the appearance of a dead person who was alive. Her chest would rise and fall, but her face and eyes remained motionless.

Liz received very few visitors these days. When she was brought home in July there was an influx of callers who had been expecting more from her. Those who called to her home hoped for a smile or a flicker of movement in her eyes. But she remained virtually motionless apart from the occasional twitch or fidget.

Every week a fresh bouquet of flowers arrived and was put on her bedside cabinet. Her friends from Taekwondo had not forgotten her and would make sure every Monday someone from the association would bring the flowers to her home. Anne had insisted that each new bouquet would never include lilies as she associated them with death.

CHAPTER THIRTY FIVE

Darlington
August 2010

Moving to Darlington was the best thing to happen to Carla. She was rebuilding her life. Her new school welcomed her and she quickly made friends. A few pupils and teachers noticed how shy she was at times. The teachers put this down to the move away from Bristol which happened at an awkward time in her life.

Her school friends loved her West Country accent. They'd never heard anything like it, other than on television. Some of the school boys said she sounded like a pirate and would call "argh" as she walked passed. This made her laugh. She didn't mind, as it reminded her how different she was in Darlington, which confirmed how far away from Bristol she had escaped.

She finished school at the end of term and was enjoying the summer break. Her plan was to return to sixth form and study for A levels. Her goal was to study art at university. Right now she was waiting on tenterhooks for her GCSE results, which would determine whether or not she would be attending sixth form.

She had found a summer job working in a café and was saving money to go on holiday at the end of the month with Sarah, who had become her best friend at Hurworth School.

Carla had told no one at Hurworth anything about what happened in Bristol. The memory returned to her regularly, especially as she lay in bed. She would love to tell someone, but it just wasn't possible. Had she witnessed a mugging, or a car accident, things might have been different, but to have witnessed a murder which had not been solved was too much. She had to keep everything to herself. The only ones who knew what happened were those who were there.

She often thought about Charlotte and wondered what had happened to her. As Carla had never received a visit from the police she had assumed that she, and everyone else involved, had kept quiet and got away with it.

Her father was doing well in his new job. Richard had only been at CKT for eleven months and had already been promoted. He was happy about his career and he was even happier because Carla had settled in so well. He was surprised that she didn't seem to be bothered about staying in contact with her old friends. Especially with Facebook making it so easy to stay in contact these days.

He was elated when she told him about her plans to go to university.

There was something Carla hated, and it was something from which she could not escape. She hated night time.

Lying in her bed her thoughts would return to Badock's Wood and that terrible night. She would drift off to sleep, then suddenly wake and sit up sweating and shaking as she was haunted by the memory of the rock crashing onto Ben's skull and that poor girl being attacked. Sometimes she reminded herself that it was her that ended the fight when she called 'police' and how everyone ran. She was sure this is what saved the girl.

Every night, as she closed her eyes, she prayed that morning would come soon.

CHAPTER THIRTY SIX

Bristol
August 2010

Daniel Boyd had cleaned up his act. He'd had to. He'd needed to break away from his life of crime. He knew that if he was caught doing anything illegal his finger prints would be on file along with his DNA and this could link him to the murder. He'd broken contact with the others and moved on from his old social circles.

He had been living on benefits for years and was about to lose them as he hardly ever attended reviews and half-heartedly attended job interviews. Now he was different. He had taken a job in a builder's merchant and found he'd liked it.

One night, seven months earlier he sat alone in his bedsit and thought about who he was and what he'd become. It was the first time he'd taken stock of his life.

There was a persona that had run its course. He needed to get his priorities straight and his head screwed on. Instead of always running away, ducking and diving he needed to do something different and achieve something good. That night for the first time in a long time he was sober and he was figuring out who he was and working out if he wanted to keep living the way he'd been. He'd become a terrible addict. He was addicted to drugs, drink, violence and crime. But he was lucky as he'd never been caught. He knew his run of luck wouldn't last forever. He needed to get his life together and figure out how he'd ended up the way he had.

Every time the sun rose, he knew it could be the day his luck ran out.

The next morning he left his flat with a spark of ambition as he made his way to attend a meeting at JobCentre Plus. He was a mess but he was willing to change.

Brian, who was Daniel's careers advisor, sat opposite him in the cramped interview room. For the first time ever he had arrived for his appointment on time which had caught Brian out. He was hoping to have time for a crafty cigarette in the car park as he knew that Daniel would either be late or not turn up at all. But at half past nine on the dot Daniel was waiting to see Brian.

Brian had told him of some vacancies and one was at Jarrett's Builders Merchant which involved picking orders and packing boxes. Daniel agreed to go to the interview and even bought a suit from a charity shop to make a good impression. He tried it on in the dressing room and looked at himself in the mirror and liked what he saw. He decided to wear it out of the shop with his other clothes in a carrier bag under his arm. "Interview?" asked the shopkeeper. Daniel smiled as he handed over seven pounds for the suit. The interview hadn't gone particularly well as Daniel wasn't good at selling himself, but there was something about him that day which was different and he'd impressed the manager of the business enough to give him a chance. Daniel started work the following week.

His first day was awful. He'd found it difficult to get out of bed and was scared of the new direction his life was taking. Perhaps he should forget the job and continue the way he was. He sat at the end of his bed and smoked a cigarette. As he looked around his tiny dark damp room it reminded him why he needed to change.

Being told what to do was something he was not familiar with. He was used to ordering others around, bullying people to do what he wanted. Now he was on the receiving end and he would need to get used to it.

That was seven months ago and he was still working. Slowly he was changing. He still drank, but had stopped taking drugs. He bought food and cigarettes instead of stealing. Sometimes he thought it would be easier just to take things out of the shop without paying, after all it had been the way he'd lived since leaving home. He felt frustrated just waiting in a queue to be served and at times was ready to walk out without paying, but a voice in his head reminded him to do the right thing.

He went out with his workmates for drinks on payday, but didn't have any close friends.

When asked about his past he did his best to avoid specifics and told his colleagues he had been unemployed for a long time and this normally did the trick, no further questions were asked.

He was always one step ahead. He worried about saying the wrong thing to the wrong person which could link him with the murder of Ben Walker. He wanted to improve and be a better person, but there was no way he would give himself up to the police willingly. He was, and always would be, a coward.

As far as he was concerned, if the police had anything on him, he would have been arrested and charged by now. The murder happened almost a year ago, and unless any of the others confessed, he would remain a free man.

He was sure that Greeny, Mossy, Seb and John would keep quiet and he was almost certain Charlotte would. The only one he couldn't depend on was the other girl. He couldn't even remember her name. She bothered him, but he was hanging on to the hope that if she was going to turn herself in, she would have done it by now.

CHAPTER THIRTY SEVEN

Markland Garraway's home
7.30am
Monday 10th August 2010

Markland Garraway was getting ready for work. He'd returned the previous week for the first time since he had been signed off sick last October, which was a lot longer than the four weeks for which he was initially signed off. It was a long road to recovery after his mental breakdown but he was getting there. He walked using sticks due to the arthritis which started about the same time as he began having mental health problems.

He was seeing a consultant about the arthritis who was taken aback by how quickly, and without warning, it had appeared. Until last October he had been a fit man who enjoyed playing sports, especially cricket and had no history of the illness in his family. Now he could hardly walk. The pain wasn't just in his legs, it was in his back, arms and wrists. He even found it difficult to hold a pen.

His consultant couldn't find a reason for the sudden onset of the illness. Garraway didn't smoke, he had no previous injury that could have brought it on, his job wasn't physically demanding enough to be the reason and he had no underlying illnesses which could have triggered it. It seemed that it had just been the element of chance.

After his breakdown he felt he'd got as well as he could at home and wanted to continue getting better whilst back at work. He needed routine and normality. Garraway consulted with his GP, occupational health and bosses at work, and it was agreed that over the following months he could slowly increase his hours. The initial reduced hours were non-negotiable. It was a condition he had to accept in order to take the first step of getting back to work.

That first day returning to work was scary for Markland Garraway, but he just wanted to get that moment of walking through the door on the first day back, over and done with.

When he returned he felt like the elephant in the room and he didn't mean his weight gain either. That was another effect of the depression, weight gain. A year of downing vast quantities of whisky whilst eating lard and doing absolutely no exercise meant he was now packing a fair bit of extra timber.

But what to say to other people! Should I say something? Should I not? What do they think has happened to me? What do they know? He thought the first day back.

In the end he decided not to make any big announcement, just crack on with his work. Slowly, over the weeks, he was hoping it would all just come out naturally, just by chatting to people around the coffee machine about how he'd been over the last year.

He was to keep the rank as Detective Chief Inspector, but would be office based and had been given a choice to train other detectives or to work in intelligence, and had chosen training. Office based work was as much as he would be able to manage until his arthritis improved.

At the end of his first week he bumped into Sergeant Colin Matthews in the staff canteen. It was an awkward moment. After small talk they went their separate ways.

Garraway had never stopped thinking about Ben Walker and was determined that sometime in the future he would be able to solve the case. He had decided he would never return to the hill as he knew that the strange Bronze Age burial mound was the cause of all his problems.

CHAPTER THIRTY EIGHT

Maria's home
9.35pm
Monday 10th August 2010

Maria was reading a book in her lounge. She had turned the lights down low and was planning on reading just one last chapter before going to bed. Next to her was Christopher's baby monitor. She turned a page in her book and was just about to read it when she heard a creaking noise coming from the monitor. She put down her book and quietly crept along her small hall to Christopher's bedroom. He was facedown and rocking from side to side in his cot, like he had been in the coffee shop earlier in the week. She stroked his head and made him comfortable. He had become uncovered and, although it was a warm August evening, Maria covered him up in case he was rocking from side to side because he was cold. The rocking stopped. She went back to the lounge and continued with the book.

Five minutes later he started again, this time there was no creaking noise, instead there was a dull repetitive thud accompanied by Christopher making an "ughh" sound every time there was a thud. "Ughh ughh ughh ughh ughh ughh ughh ughh ughh," he went over and over again. Maria closed her book and listened to the monitor. "Ughh ughh ughh ughh ughh ughh ughh ughh ughh." She had never heard him do it before and she was worried. She crept back into his room, put his light on low and knelt down to his level while he lay in his cot.

He was lying on his front banging his head on his pillow making the strange "Ughh" sound. She looked at him closely and saw he was fast asleep.

"Ughh ughh ughh ughh ughh ughh ughh ughh," he continued with his strange mantra like chant. She picked him up and held him close with her head against his. As soon as she picked him up he stopped. He was fast asleep. As she held him she rocked him from side to side. After laying him back down she watched him whilst he slept.

Feeling tired she decided to turn in for the night. She took his monitor to her bedroom and got changed for bed. She was just about to lie down when it started again. "Ughh ughh ughh ughh ughh ughh ughh ughh," along with the thudding of his head against the pillow. Maria was worried and didn't know what was happening. Was he ill, was he having some kind of fit? He was clearly not distressed as he was sleeping so soundly. She went back to the lounge, turned on her computer, brought up Google and typed 'head banging babies'. As soon as she typed in the search lots of websites came up, all with the same thing. Head banging in childhood seemed extremely common and up to twenty percent of children do it. The websites were all saying the same things. Boys were three times more likely to do it than girls. Most children stop by the time they are three. She closed the lid on her computer and thought about what Campbell had told her the other day. She felt a little more relieved now that she'd done a little research courtesy of Doctor Google. She thought about asking Campbell about it next time she was in the coffee shop. He said that he'd done it when he was a child and had grown out of it.

She went back to her bedroom and got into bed. "Ughh ughh ughh ughh ughh ughh ughh ughh ughh," he continued. Maria thought it would be best to let him carry on and decided to take him to the doctor tomorrow.

As Christopher continued his strange rhythmic head banging the Awareness was waking up. Was Christopher waking the Awareness by head banging, or was it the Awareness causing him to bang his head? Either way they were working together. The Awareness was recalling new and different memories, faces, voices, places and sounds. They meant nothing but were being stored somewhere for the Awareness to pool later. Christopher had no idea he was banging his head, or that there was something very strange going on in his brain. He knew nothing of the Awareness and sensed nothing of the memories the Awareness recalled. Eventually Christopher stopped as the Awareness drifted back from where it came. The rest of the night went without incident.

The next morning Maria was woken by Christopher's usual cooing and gurgling. He was calling for Misty as the toy cat had fallen out of the cot. "Meee, meee, meee" he called as Maria opened his door. She handed him the toy and smiled at him. He smiled back with his beaming grin.

As soon as her doctors' surgery opened she was on the phone to book an appointment. From what she had read on the computer his head banging didn't seem to be harmful. Her surgery would only see patients on the same day if it was an emergency. She told the receptionist that she needed to see a doctor today as her son had been acting very strangely in the night, banging his head and moaning. This was enough to convince the woman on the other end of the phone that Christopher should see a doctor straight away and booked an appointment for eleven that morning.

Maria called her mother and told her about Christopher's head banging. Claire tried not to sound alarmed, she had never heard of anything like it before and told Maria she was right to take him to see a doctor.

She put down the phone and watched her son happily crawling around the floor and pulling himself up onto the side of the sofa. Teetering as he went, he was able to walk the length of the sofa by holding on to it. He made his way over to his mother who scooped him up into her arms. "You'll be walking like a big boy soon," she told him as he beamed at her looking very pleased with himself.

11.20am. The Saint John Fisher Health Centre.

Maria sat in the waiting room of her doctor's surgery. She bounced Christopher on her lap as she waited for his name to be called over the surgery's intercom. They had got to the surgery before eleven o'clock and it was now twenty minutes past. Christopher was getting restless. She let him crawl around the waiting room floor and pull himself up using chairs, much to the amusement of the others waiting to see their doctor.

At last Christopher's name was called. Maria entered the consulting room and sat opposite Dr Marsh with Christopher on her lap and explained what Christopher had been doing the previous night.

Dr Marsh was young, Maria thought she didn't look much older than twenty five, but realistically she must be closer to thirty. Maria felt more relaxed when doctors was at least in their forties, or else how on earth would they have had time to learn all the different illnesses a person could have.

The doctor gave Christopher a thorough examination and found nothing wrong with him. He had no sign of an ear infection, respiratory problems, throat infection and she went through an extensive list of all the other things he didn't have wrong with him. Dr Marsh had no idea why Maria's son had behaved as he had, and suggested that as last night had been a particularly warm one Christopher was just having trouble sleeping. There was nothing else the doctor could suggest and sent Maria and Christopher on their way and told her she should contact the surgery again should he have more episodes.

Maria strapped Christopher in the car and wasn't satisfied with the diagnosis. A mother knows when something isn't right, and something certainly hadn't been right with Christopher last night. She thought back to what Campbell had said in the coffee shop when he called her son a little head banger. She hated his description, but it summed up exactly what Christopher had been doing. He had told her that head banging was something he used to do when he was young and had grown out of it when he was three.

She thought another trip to Coaster's was in order. It was lunch time. She could have a snack, feed Christopher and if Campbell was there she could ask him about his head banging.

She got to the coffee shop at one o'clock, just as Campbell was taking off his apron and getting ready to leave. She stood at the counter whist Christopher slept in his buggy. The girl serving asked for her order.

"Actually, before I order, could I have a quick word with Campbell before he leaves?"

The young girl called Campbell, who walked over to Maria and gave her a warm smile. Campbell told her that he was starting his lunch break. Maria didn't want to take up his time and told him it was nothing. Campbell bent down and looked at Christopher silently sleeping in his buggy.

"I see he's stopped that head banging business," he said, looking up at Maria.

"Well, that's what I wanted to speak to you about."

Campbell listened as she told him about Christopher's unsettled night and how she remembered him saying that he used to do the same thing when he was young. Campbell listened and smiled. Maria liked his smile, he had a kind face.

"Look, I'm just off for a bite to eat and you and Christopher are welcome to join me, we can chat about all this head banging stuff at the same time."

Maria briefly thought about it and didn't take long to accept his invitation.

Campbell Broderick was thirty three years old, five foot eleven inches with black hair and tanned skin. His father was from County Cork and his mother was from Indonesia. The mix race of his parents had resulted in an aesthetically pleasing son. He reminded Maria of Keanu Reeves.

She followed him across the road and into a bakery. Campbell ordered himself a baguette, a sandwich for Maria and a cappuccino for both of them. They sat at a small table at the far end of the bakery. The smell of freshly baked bread and cakes was wonderful and Maria wondered why she'd never eaten here before.

"So how come you work in a coffee shop and don't have your lunch there?" she asked.

"You've tasted that stuff we serve up, it's horrible, much too bitter, I prefer to come here."

Maria laughed. *He's funny* she thought.

"So what did you want to ask me about my head banging days?"

Maria was embarrassed, she didn't know the man and here they were talking about his childhood.

"You know that my son has started banging his head, and he kept me awake for most of the night doing it. I took him to see the doctor this morning and a fat lot of good she was."

"What did the doctor say?" he asked.

"Not a lot, she said it had been warm last night and it was probably what disturbed Christopher,..........I've seen him warm at night before, we've just had a hot couple of weeks and he was fine. Yesterday was different, he was chanting, banging his head and rocking from side to side and I was really concerned."

Campbell smiled. "I don't want to sound like your doctor, but I am sure that he will be fine. It might just last a few weeks or a few years. It took me until I was three to stop and my parents were convinced I was some kind of nutcase and look at me now." He smiled as he held his hands up as an invitation for Maria to inspect him.

"I don't know why I did it, but when I was little my mother was told by the doctor it was something to do with my brain developing and it was my way of dealing with it all. It was obviously down to my extreme intelligence as a child." He winked at her to show he was joking.

She smiled, but looked concerned. "But the chanting thing, did you chant when you banged your head?"

He shook his head. "I don't remember my mother saying I chanted, I just banged my head."

He could tell by her face that she was concerned about her son. "Look, if he carries on doing it and this chanting doesn't stop, I suggest you ask your doctor to arrange a health visitor to drop by."

Maria smiled at him and nodded.

"Why don't you film him on your phone?" he added.

Maria looked puzzled.

"You can bet your bottom dollar if the health visitor calls round he won't be asleep banging his head and chanting, so at least you'll have something to show."

"Good idea," she said as she took another sip of coffee.

They spent the next twenty minutes making small talk and enjoying each other's company, Campbell looked at his watch.

"I'm going to have to head back to work," he said as he stood up to put his jacket on. Pausing as he had one arm in his sleeve, he added, "I enjoyed having lunch with you, perhaps we could do it again?"

Maria blushed. "Maybe," she said as he ran her fingers through her red hair trying to hide her embarrassment.

He smiled and nodded as he left the bakery.

The next few weeks were fairly peaceful for Christopher and Maria. Although he was still occasionally banging his head and moaning, it was nothing like that strange night in early August.

During the nights when Christopher was sleeping well, the Awareness which nested deep within him was dormant, but was preparing for its biggest advancement yet.

CHAPTER THIRTY NINE

Markland Garraway's home
6.27pm
Monday 6th September 2010
One year since the death of Ben Walker

Markland Garraway struggled to get out of his car. Today his arthritis had been bad. He slowly made his way to the front door, awkwardly put the key in the lock and let the door swing open. Dropping onto the settee he let his two walking sticks fall to the floor.

It had been a hard day for him. A year since Ben Walker had been murdered and what had resulted in being the worst twelve months of his life. Joan was finding it hard dealing with his mood swings since his breakdown and had struggled to come to terms with the physical changes of her once tall standing husband. Now he was bent forward with the pain of his illness and she was left to do many of the jobs around the house that once they would share.

One thing he did enjoy was his work. After returning last month his role had completely changed. Although he still held the rank of Detective Chief Inspector he was not actively working on any cases. Detective Superintendent Munroe and Occupational Health said he needed more time before returning to his old role. Instead of solving cases he was now training others how to do it and found he actually quite liked it. He was putting the past twenty seven years of experience to good use.

But today had been particularly difficult. Whether it was the anniversary of Ben's murder having a subconscious effect on him or just the damp September day making his joints hurt more than usual. The case had been on his mind the whole day. He had tried his best to distance himself from it since he'd returned to work but today it had become an obsession, like it had been when he was at home suffering his breakdown. Never had his work affected him so much. He'd seen worse over the years. Children beaten to death by parents, women killed and mutilated by husbands and so many other gruesome things, but Ben's murder had really got to him. Deep down he knew exactly why he was so ill. All this had been brought on by the hill in the woods. Something about it had made all these things come together. From the first time he was there he knew the place was strange. If not for that place Polly Ellis may not have taken her life and instead been able to move on and find her future without Sarah.

He was certain that the key to his future wellbeing and mental health would be closure on Ben Walker's case. To find Ben's murderer had been, and still was, his obsession. Being off the case wouldn't mean that he couldn't be the one to solve the murder, it would just be a hell of a lot harder not having the support of his old team.

He knew Sergeant Matthews wasn't actively working on the case which was now residing in the unsolved pile. Matthews was not the sort of policeman who expected the unexpected and had no interest in embracing the mysteries of nature and forces that weren't fully understood. Witnessing that UFO in Ullapool forty three years ago is what shaped Markland Garraway into the man he had become.

He instinctively reached for his whisky but remembered that Joan had thrown it out on Saturday. She was sick of his dependence on the stuff. He knew she was right. He didn't consider himself an alcoholic, but sometimes he really needed a drink and this just happened to be one of those times.

He went to bed early and was endeavouring to read a challenging Fyodor Dostoevsky novel. By nine forty five his heavy eyelids closed and he slumped onto his pillow with the book in his hand. He began dreaming immediately.

This dream was different. It captured the moment Daniel Boyd crashed the rock into Ben Walker's head. He could see there were others standing around watching Boyd murdering Ben. His dream allowed him to pan around the scene. He could see the hill and the school behind. As he turned back the rock was resting in Ben's forehead, just as he'd seen it the morning Ben's body had been found. He panned further to his left where Liz Mason was lying unconscious on the ground. There was a young girl who looked to be fourteen or fifteen. She turned and pointed directly at Garraway. He could see her face as clear as day. Then, as if in slow motion she shouted something whilst pointing at him. He could read her lips as she yelled "Run, it's the police." All of them took off and ran to the depths of the woods leaving Ben and Liz alone. The images were very clear, but there was no sound in his detailed dream.

Then he was awake. His sheets were soaked through with sweat. He checked the clock to see how long he'd been sleeping and was surprised that it was a matter of minutes. It felt as if he'd been sleeping for hours. It was just minutes before ten o'clock. He recalled the time captured on Ben's watched the moment he died. Had Garraway witnessed a detailed vision of what happened a year ago to the minute? Had he just witnessed the murder of Ben as it happened? Were the youths in his dream the actual ones who were there? And what about that shouting girl, did she shout to make them all run to the woods? He knew there were no police on the scene so unless she thought she'd seen something, she must have being trying to stop the attack and had probably saved Liz's life.

What was he thinking? It had only been a dream. But the more he thought about it he was convinced the hill was working its magic again. He remembered the line on Polly's suicide note, the one which had been written by Sarah.

Please tell Markland Garraway not to give up on Ben Walker. Accept the evidence you find no matter how it is presented.

He was now certain he had witnessed the murder first hand. But what could he do? He couldn't make out any of the attackers, other than the girl who had shouted. For some reason she was the only one who he clearly saw. Anyway, who in the force would accept what he had just seen as evidence? He knew the answer was nobody, especially Sergeant Matthews.

Garraway picked up the novel which had fallen to the floor, grabbed a pen and scribbled what he had dreamt on the back inside cover. He jotted a detailed description of the girl's face before it faded. He wrote the date and his initials beneath the notes.

Then he fell into a proper sleep.

CHAPTER FORTY

Maria's home
Christopher's first birthday
7.05pm
Monday 6th September 2010

"Little man you've had a busy day" sang Maria as she tucked her son in for the night.

It had been a busy day for Christopher. Maria made sure that his first birthday would be one that she would remember, even if Christopher didn't. She had arranged a little party. Samreen and Claire were there along with a group of mums and their babies she had made friends with at Joe Jingles. Maria's small flat had been trashed. There was cake and crisps trodden into the carpet, juice had been spilt over the furniture, and the kitchen bin stank of soiled nappies. All in all it had been a great day and she had loved every minute of it.

He had so many birthday presents there was not enough room for them all. Maria could see a visit to the charity shop looming up as there was no way he could play with all the things he had been given.

She kissed him on the head as he slept soundly.

Returning to the lounge she started to clear away wrapping paper, cardboard boxes and the remains of burst balloons.

It had been an excellent year and he was growing so well. He'd learnt to walk while holding her hand. She would let go of him and watch him attempt to balance, only to fall with a soft thud. His speech was improving. He still said "Meee", but was also saying mummy and Nana. He was trying to grasp some other words which Maria couldn't work out.

By half past nine she was done in and was craving a glass of wine. Five minutes later she was relaxing on her sofa, nursing a large glass of Sauvignon Blanc and watching Bridget Jones's Diary for the umpteenth time.

She was fifteen minutes into the film when she heard "Ughh ughh ughh ughh ughh ughh ughh ughh ughh." Maria put down her wine, paused the DVD and turned the volume up on the baby monitor. "Ughh ughh ughh ughh ughh ughh ughh ughh ughh." *Oh no, he's at it again*, she thought. She waited for a moment and hoped he would stop. He didn't and she could hear his head banging against the pillow.

Maria opened his bedroom door and waited for her eyes to become accustomed to the orange glow of the nightlight which illuminated his room. She watched as he lay face down banging his head as regular as clockwork up and down on his pillow. He would stop for a few seconds and then start rocking from side to side still chanting his strange mantra "ughh ughh ughh ughh ughh ughh ughh ughh ughh." She picked him up and held him with his head against her shoulder. He continued to rock backward and forward and chant into her ear. "Ughh ughh ughh ughh ughh ughh ughh ughh ughh." She rocked him, but he wouldn't stop, so she began to gently shake him but he carried on. He was in a deep sleep from which she couldn't wake him. She didn't know what to do. Carrying him in her arms she took him into the lounge and sat with him trying to hold his head still as it rocked from side to side and backwards and forwards. The chanting continued "ughh ughh ughh ughh ughh ughh ughh ughh."

Maria started to sob. She was alone and had no one to turn to for help. She sobbed and rocked Christopher hoping that he would soon tire himself and stop.

CHAPTER FORTY ONE

The Awareness
9.45pm
Monday 6th September

Christopher was chanting while rocking and banging his head because the Awareness had awoken again. It had been evolving for exactly twelve months and was about to flourish and grow faster than before. It was sorting images and memories into order and was working out who was who and what went where. It didn't know the names of faces, but it was able to sort them into categories. Categories of who was good, who was bad, who it had loved and who it had disliked. It was identifying places as well as faces. Places which were important, places which were good and places which were bad.

Then it remembered the burial mound. It paused and held onto the image of the grassy hill. The Awareness was experiencing confusion. It couldn't work out what to do with this image. It was both good and evil. Now that the Awareness had learnt to access and recall memories it was visualising good things about the hill. It could see a young boy playing there. The boy was laughing and smiling as he played. The Awareness felt love for the boy and knew that the boy loved him in return. This was why it was a good place. The Awareness was accessing more memories of the hill and they were also happy ones. All of the memories were with the boy. The Awareness was experiencing happiness. It was remembering how it had felt to be happy and loved.

The Awareness was visualising the hill again. This time the image was different. The young boy had gone and it was now seeing an image of a young woman, who was laughing and smiling. It was recalling more good memories. She was running up the hill and the view was from beneath her looking up. She fell backwards and as she did the Awareness saw she had a small tattoo of a butterfly on her back. Next there was confusion and a lot of scrabbling around at the bottom of the hill. The image of the girls face was very near and she was smiling. The Awareness was feeling a strong emotion of love for her and it was the happiest memories it had experienced since its formation.

The image of the young woman's face had become so close it could not make out her features. It was confused and did not understand what was happening. The emotion of love intensified and was merging into a new feeling. It felt warm and the Awareness found its level of happiness was increasing. Her face was so close it was blocking everything else. It could not see the hill behind her or the sky above and then for the first time it became conscious of two of the five senses. It was experiencing the sense of touch as it could feel her lips and it was experiencing the sense of taste from her lipstick. The emotion of love, the warmth of happiness and the senses of touch and taste had taken the Awareness to a higher level. It wanted to hold on to these new sensations as they felt so good.

Next there was confusion again. The feelings of good were replaced with feelings of bad. The young woman was still in the image but she was lying on the floor. There were new figures all around, figures it didn't recognise but sensed they meant harm. Then one of the figures was attacking the young woman and kicking her over and over. The Awareness then became conscious of a variation of the sense of touch it had experienced with the young woman. The feeling was more acute. The Awareness was trying to register what was happening. It concentrated on this new experience whilst seeing that the harmful figures were very close. The acute sense of touch was repetitive as it started and stopped over and over again. It was feeling pain. It was remembering the pain that night as it was set upon by the bad figures. The Awareness could still see the young woman but now she looked different. Her eyes were closing and she was not smiling. The Awareness looked up to the sky and saw a figure standing above with something in its hands. It could not work out what was happening. Why had such a happy memory turned into something so bad?

The figure standing above him was holding a rock. The Awareness concentrated on the figure's face. It was trying to match the face with other memories but couldn't recall where it had seen the face before. Again, the awareness recalled a memory of acute pain. It looked up and saw the figure was standing above him but without the rock. The Awareness was regrouping its thoughts and was attempting to work out what had just happened, when another image of the figure returned holding the rock high above his head. Again, the Awareness focused on the figure's face but it still couldn't work out who it was. This time the Awareness saw the rock falling and was followed by another sensation of acute pain.

This time the feeling of pain stopped as soon as it had started. The Awareness was trying to work out what all of this meant.

Whilst the Awareness was recalling the memories, Christopher was in his cot rocking, chanting and banging his head over and over. Maria was crying as she could not stop him. He wouldn't wake up and his chanting was getting louder and more disturbing.

The Awareness replayed the last sequence again and again, which was causing Christopher's head banging and chanting to intensify.

Finally the Awareness comprehended what had happened. The last memories, which were the most recent ones, were of the moments it had stopped being what it once was. It placed what it had just experienced in chronological order and filed it with the other images and memories and contemplated what it meant.

The Awareness had no real concept of time, but now it was alert to how long it was taking to work out what all of this meant. It was conscious that it was taking time to piece together the jigsaw of memories. It was replaying the memories of the girl, the hill, the figures, the falling rock and the acute pain. All of these were the last things it had experienced before it had become what it was now.

Then it made sense. The Awareness had finally worked out what all of this meant. It knew it had once been alive and had been spending happy times with people it had loved. It had many images to support this. So if it had once been alive, now it must be dead.

The Awareness was experiencing something new. It was a new emotional sensation which was fear. It was scared as it knew that it was dead and may never again experience happiness.

So if it was dead, where was it now? Once it thought it was in a safe place and surrounded by love, but now it felt as if it was imprisoned in solitary confinement.

When it first evolved it instinctively knew it had to be heard and as it flourished it understood it had something it had to say. It had a message. Now things were making sense. It understood that once it had been alive and its life had ended abruptly and violently. It thought about the memory of the girl. Who was she? She had clearly meant something.

The Awareness wondered about what it had been when it was alive. It had seen no memories of itself. Had it been young or old? Had it been male or female? What had been its home and where did it live?

It recalled memories with new purpose. It needed to learn more about itself.

As memories were replayed the Awareness was honing its ability to stop, pause, rewind and replay them. It was learning to scrutinise and analyse them. It revisited memories and was able to make use of its new sense of touch and its enhanced emotions of love and hate.

It played specific memories over again, whilst skipping ones of little significance. One memory kept resurfacing. It was an image of a smartly dressed young man looking very proud and who was wearing a uniform. It was a black jacket, blue shirt and a peaked cap. The Awareness had skipped over this image several times at it seemed insignificant. This time it examined the image in more detail. In other memories people had been moving around and interacting with others. This memory was an image of a solitary figure and there was something about it that made it different from the rest. The Awareness played it over again and was trying to work out why it was different and why it now seemed significant?

The young man was standing still but would move to adjust his hat and his jacket. He would turn to his side and look over his shoulder whilst craning his neck as if he was trying to view something before returning to his original standing position.

What bothered the Awareness was the young man's eyes. They were staring directly at the Awareness as though the young man could see it, and the Awareness felt it was staring back. The Awareness kept replaying the memory until it understood what was happening.

It was the memory of someone looking at themself in a mirror. The memory of the young man was the reflection of the Awareness when it had been alive.

The image in the mirror confirmed that the Awareness had been male and that he'd lived until he was at least in his early twenties.

He knew that he'd been killed, but he didn't know who he had been or what his name was. Hopefully he could piece these things together as he continued to develop.

He thought about the message that he had to get across and knew what it was he needed to say. He had to let it be known that he still existed and he had to get a message out about his killer.

He had to find a way to be heard and he could only think of one way and that was to shout. He was starting to fade. He'd achieved more and had learnt more about who he had been than ever before. But it had drained him of his energy. He faded until he was no more. But he would return.

Whilst the Awareness had been recalling its memories and working out who it had once been, Christopher had been reacting violently by banging his head against the wooden slats of his cot, chanting louder than ever before and rolling from side to side.

Maria was helpless, she had picked him up, put him down and tried to wake him repetitively, but he wouldn't stop or wake up. Then suddenly after about half an hour he stopped and slept. Gently snoring as if nothing had happened.

Maria was exhausted and her eyes were red with tiredness. In the commotion she had forgotten to video Christopher as Campbell had suggested. She decided to get Christopher back to the doctor tomorrow and insist on a visit from the Child Health Visitor. It was five past ten, the whole episode had lasted only thirty five minutes but had seemed a lot longer.

She was tired and needed to sleep, but didn't want to leave him on his own. Eventually she went to her room with his baby monitor and turned the volume up to ten.

The rest of the night passed without incident.

CHAPTER FORTY TWO

Darlington
9.15pm
Monday 6th September 2010

Carla had been dreading this day. Twelve months since the murder. Considering all the things that had happened during the last year she was doing pretty well. But today had not been a good one. Her stomach had been churning all day long. She should have started sixth form, but she didn't feel up for it.

She had done well in her GCSE exams and was pleased to be going back to school for A levels. Hopefully she would be well enough for school tomorrow but today had been a bad day just as she knew that it would be.

She felt awful guilt. Her life was moving forward and she had a future. Ben Walker could have had a future. She had read his obituary and knew that he'd been a policeman. She had great respect for the police and knew he would have been a good person. Although she had respect for the police, she didn't have the guts to stand up and turn herself in. She hated herself for it and considered herself a coward.

She had no idea what had happened to Liz. She had tried to find out whether she had recovered, or died. She had trawled the internet many times and, other than the news reports of Ben's murder which mentioned Liz, she found nothing.

She was tired and needed to sleep. It was nine thirty five but she wanted to stay up until ten, which was about the time Ben died. She wanted to be awake out of respect for him. She lay in her bed forcing herself to stay awake, but her eyelids were heavy and she was drifting. She pushed herself to get out of bed and walked across the landing to the bathroom. Running the cold tap, she splashed her face in an attempt to wake up. She didn't dry her face as she wanted her cold wet skin to keep her awake. As she lay on her bed she was still tired and was struggling to stay awake. She was more tired than she was five minutes earlier. She was drifting off and there was nothing that could be done.

She started dreaming of the same thing she dreamt about most nights. The murder. Over the past twelve months her memory of that night and her dreams were still detailed, but lately her memories had lost their clarity and she had forgotten small aspects of what happened that night. She was starting to forget some of the things the others had said, what they were wearing and other small details. One thing she would never forget was the dull thud as the rock crashed into Ben Walker's skull and the mess it had made of his head. Her dreams and memories always included her shouting 'Run, it's the police.' She always dreamt this as it was a way to separate her from the others. It was a way to prove she was a good person and had been able to stop the attack on Liz.

Tonight her dream was more vivid than ever. It included more detail than others she'd had before. The dream included smells, sounds and she could hear Liz wheezing after John had been kicking her. She could hear Boyd grunt as he smashed the rock into Ben's head, not once but all three times with such detail it was as if she was there in the woods.

This time there was something different about her dream. As she called 'Run, it's the police' and pointed to the entrance of the woods she saw someone looking at her. A smartly dressed man in a suit.

She awoke with the image of the man fresh in her mind. He looked familiar. She sat up in her bed and was shaking. She was sure what she had seen meant something. While the face was still clear she grabbed a pencil and pad and sketched the man. Carla didn't have any coloured pencils nearby, they were downstairs in her school bag so she made notes about the colour of his eyes, his hair and what he was wearing. There was something about the man which was so real and it seemed he had been looking at her and she had been looking at him. She had a feeling that the man was somewhere else dreaming the same dream as her.

Carla put her sketch pad down and thought about the dream and the familiar face. Lying in bed all she could see was his face going round and around in her head. She picked up the sketch book and looked at her drawing again. Where had she seen him before?

Suddenly she remembered. Jumping out of bed she bounded to the other side of her room and flipped up the lid of her laptop. Impatiently she waited for it to start. Eventually the computer was working. She typed into Google 'Ben Walker Murder Bristol' and instantly she was presented with a screen full of different websites which were mostly news sites. Scrolling through the choices she saw one which took her eye. Carla clicked on the link which opened up the BBC News archive site which had a report on the murder at Badock's Wood. It included the press conference which had been broadcast a few days after Ben had been killed. She clicked the play icon and nervously waited for the video to start. The broadcast started by showing the place where Ben had died with the BBC announcer describing what had happened. Carla was shaking as she watched. Then the news conference started. A man was talking on behalf of the police and his name was on the screen as he spoke. She paused the video and stared at him in disbelief. She walked to her bed, picked up the sketch pad, brought it over to the laptop and compared her drawing with the man on the video. It was the same person. She had dreamt of the man in the news report. As she read his name she whispered it, "Detective Chief Inspector Markland Garraway".

She cleared the history on her computer, closed the browser and shut off the power. What had just happened? She had such a vivid dream of the man, a man she had never really seen before. She had seen snippets of the press conference, but found it to upsetting to watch all the way through. She had remembered listening to Liz's father, but had paid little attention to the policeman who was leading the press conference.

She got back into bed and couldn't get the man's face out of her mind. Perhaps she had subconsciously remembered him from the news conference. The more she tried to convince herself, the less she believed it.

CHAPTER FORTY THREE

Bristol
Daniel Boyd's Flat
9.55pm
Monday 6th September

Daniel Boyd had moved out of the bedsit three weeks ago and now had a small one bedroom flat which he rented for two hundred pounds a month.

He sat alone on his couch watching one of his favourite DVDs. He loved Alien and had a thing for Sigourney Weaver. Slumped deep into his couch with his feet on a footstool and a can of Stella Artois in his hand, he had no idea of the significance of the day. Many people were remembering the life of Ben Walker and laying flowers at the place where he died, but not Daniel Boyd. As his watch ticked round to 9.56 pm he lit a cigarette and took another mouthful of beer oblivious to what had happened a year ago to the minute. He yawned and belched as his watch moved to 9.57.

CHAPTER FORTY FOUR

Maria Jameson's flat
6.42am
Tuesday 7th September

Christopher woke Maria a little later than usual. He had slept through the night without waking. The previous night's episode had worn him out and he'd needed to recharge his batteries. Maria had a terrible night's sleep. She had spent the night worrying about her son. His chanting and head banging was as if he'd been possessed by the devil. It was like something from a B movie horror film.

She was so tired it was difficult for her to lift him from his cot. He was pleased to see his mother, but he didn't welcome her with his normal beaming smile and cheery gurgle. The past few mornings he had greeted her by saying mummy, this morning he said nothing.

She prepared his breakfast and made herself strong coffee.

Christopher happily sat in his highchair and ate bread and jam. Maria watched him and thought about the night before. She hoped the doctor would be able to provide the answer and she would be on the phone to the surgery as the clock struck nine to book an early appointment.

He left most of his breakfast and became crotchety. Maria felt his forehead and he was warm. She decided not to give him Calpol because if he was going to see the doctor it would be better that he was showing symptoms of any illness he may have. She hated it when he was ill, as he had been lucky until now. He'd hardly had a cough or cold and now he had this strange head banging going on. Maria was not used to him being unwell. At times like this she wished she wasn't a single mother and could do with the support of his father, or if not his father then a good, kind and supportive man. She sipped her coffee and thought about Campbell.

Christopher and Maria were washed and ready to go by quarter to nine and he seemed a little brighter after having a bath. She had got through to the surgery just after nine and had managed to book a morning appointment. Again she was seeing Dr Marsh. She would have preferred to see another, more mature doctor, but she would have to have waited until the next day for an appointment with someone else.

She spent the next hour tidying her flat after his birthday party the day before. She took the black bags full of wrapping paper and cardboard and dumped them into the black wheelie bin. She was down on her hands and knees removing a chocolate stain from the carpet when her phone rang.

"How's the party animal?" asked Samreen cheerily.

"He's not so jolly this morning."

Samreen sensed that Maria was unhappy.

"Is everything OK, Maria?"

She told Samreen about the previous night and how strange Christopher's head banging had been.

"You're doing the best thing, I'm sure the doctor will work out what's wrong with him," said Samreen in a reassuring voice.

"I have something to tell you," added Samreen.

"Mmmm?" replied Maria sounding disinterested.

"It doesn't matter, I'll tell you another time." Samreen felt it wasn't a good time to tell Maria trivial things as she was worrying about Christopher.

"No, no, I'm sorry, what did you want to tell me."

"You have an admirer."

"Do I?" replied Maria sounding a little cheerier.

"Yes. I went to Coaster's this morning for an early coffee and guess who served me?"

"Campbell?" replied Maria expectantly.

"Yes, Campbell. He was asking after you. He definitely likes you."

Maria smiled as she held the phone to her ear. At any other time she would have been excited by the prospect of someone showing an interest in her, especially handsome Campbell, but right now her mind was focused on Christopher.

"That's nice, perhaps I'll call into the coffee shop to see him."

Samreen said she would be thinking of her and Christopher when they were at the doctors and ended the call.

An hour later Maria and Christopher were back in Dr Marsh's consulting room. The young doctor seemed stern and unforgiving as she gave him another thorough examination.

"Perforated eardrum" said the doctor as she put down her otoscope. She had delivered the diagnosis without a hint of compassion. The doctor's eyes didn't make contact with Maria's as she entered notes on her computer.

After what she'd been through last night with Christopher, she could feel her anger welling up.

"Sorry Doctor, but would this have affected him so badly last night, I mean it was like he was possessed by the devil?"

"Miss Jameson, your son was clearly in a lot of pain last night. Children have different ways of dealing with pain and Christopher finds that banging his head and moaning is his way of coping."

"But he slept through it all, he was banging his head when he was sleeping, surely that can't be right?"

"As I said, children have different ways of dealing with different things. Believe me, it will pass. All you can do is give him paracetamol and he will get better." Dr Marsh attempted to smile as she tried to reassure Maria.

Maria remembered the advice given to her by Campbell.

"I would like to have a health visitor come and see Christopher please."

The doctor was getting irritated.

"Why?"

"Because I would like someone else to see what Christopher is doing."

"OK, if Christopher continues with his head banging after his ear gets better then I will arrange for our child health visitor to see him." She paused and looked Maria in the eye.

"But I can assure you, it's just your son's way of dealing with the pain."

Maria couldn't argue. The doctor had won.

She walked along the high street pushing Christopher in his buggy. He seemed happier since she'd given him a spoonful of paracetamol. She walked past Coaster's and slowed as she considered calling in for coffee, especially since Samreen told her about Campbell. She was looking through the window and was about to walk on past when she saw Campbell waving at her from behind the counter. She smiled at him. She had to go in now, it would be rude not to.

She pushed the buggy awkwardly through the door, getting the front wheels jammed. She struggled to free the buggy and looked up to see Campbell opening the door for her. She smiled again and thanked him. He showed her to an empty table.

"Cappuccino and a Danish?" he asked.

"Oh, just coffee please," she replied sounding tired.

"Are you OK?"

She told him about last night and the visit to the doctor. Campbell seemed to be genuinely concerned.

A few minutes later he was back with her drink. He lowered himself to Christopher's level, smiled and held his little hand whilst shaking it backwards and forwards. This made Christopher smile. His big beaming grin was back.

"He likes you," said Maria.

"I think your son likes everyone, he's a lovely lad."

Maria watched as the two of them interacted and thought about what Samreen had told her. Did Campbell have a thing for her, or was it Samreen attempting matchmaking?

"I need to get back to the counter, but I'll pop back and see you before you go."

Campbell walked back to the counter as Maria admired him.

The coffee shop became busier as lunch time approached. Campbell was rushed off his feet and Maria needed to get going, but she would like to see him again before she headed off.

She made Christopher comfortable and got up to leave. Before she had made it to the door Campbell was already there, opening it for her.

"Thank you, you're a gentleman."

"Look, I know it may not be the best time to ask and I know that last night was tough for you, but I'm going to ask you anyway."

Maria waited without speaking.

"Would you like to go out one night?"

There, he'd said it. Campbell could be shy at times, especially around pretty ladies, but he just had to blurt it out.

Maria said nothing at first and then looked him in the eye and smiled.

"I would love to."

Campbell let out a sigh. He hadn't noticed he'd been holding his breath.

They exchanged numbers and he promised to call.

Despite what Christopher had been through, Maria was a little happier as she made her way home.

CHAPTER FORTY FIVE

Darlington
5.15pm
Tuesday 7th September

Carla had spent her first day at sixth form. She'd found it hard to concentrate as her mind had been occupied by the image of Markland Garraway in her dream the night before. It bothered her why an image so clear and detailed of a man she'd hardly seen before would have entered her dream. She'd muddled through the day but her heart wasn't in the right place for school.

She was home by four o'clock and went straight to her laptop to discover more about Markland Garraway. She hoped to find something which would explain why she had dreamt such a vivid image of him.

She dropped her school bag on her bedroom floor and lifted the lid of her laptop. As she opened the lid there was a note written on a yellow Post It from her father. *'Don't forget to cook our meal'.*

They'd agreed, or rather her father had, that in return for generous pocket money, she would cook the evening meal. Her father was not home from work until five thirty most evenings and after a busy day he didn't fancy cooking. This new arrangement was to start when Carla began sixth form. She was let off the chore yesterday as she'd been feeling unwell.

Carla sighed as she made her way back downstairs to the kitchen where she peeled potatoes and carrots before bringing them to the boil and had an oven ready chicken cooking away nicely in its own juices.

After she'd brought the veg to simmer she disappeared back to her room and fired up the laptop. Cranking up Google she feverishly typed 'Detective Chief Inspector Markland Garraway'. There were fourteen pages of results which mentioned Markland Garraway's name.

Carla read each entry one by one and scrutinised every page. Most of them linked to reports of cases he had worked on over the past few years.

She jotted down details in her notebook by the side of her laptop, including the address of the websites. Most of them were the BBC news site covering the Bristol region. She'd been hard at work for about forty five minutes when she was hit by an awful smell. She stopped what she was doing and looked around her room. A smoky haze filled the landing outside her bedroom door.

"Oh shit!"

She charged down the stairs and almost carried on in the direction of the front door. Skidding on the rug as she turned towards the kitchen as fast as her legs would allow her.

Thick smoke was bellowing from the kitchen as the water had boiled dry which left carrots and potatoes smouldering at the bottom of the burnt saucepan. After turning off the gas she grabbed the handle of the pan and swore as it burnt her skin. Dropping it back on the hob she used a tea towel to move the hot saucepan to the sink and ran the cold water. The water hissed and bubbled like a geyser as it splashed over the pan creating a cloud of steam.

The saucepan and the vegetables were ruined. Carla opened the windows to let the steam, smoke and smell out. Then she remembered the chicken. She opened the door and luckily it didn't look too bad. After turning off the oven she placed the chicken in its tin foil tray on the kitchen worktop.

Sitting on a kitchen stool, resting her head in her hands she began to cry.

She heard her father opening the front door. She looked at the clock on the wall and couldn't believe it was almost half past five. She knew she was in trouble. The first day she'd been left in charge of her new chores and she'd messed up.

Her father wasn't as hard on her as she'd expected. He was disappointed that she'd not been able to carry out such a basic task, but was more annoyed with the putrid smell drifting through the entire house and the waste of an expensive saucepan. Her punishment was to take a trip to the local Indian takeaway and bring back a meal which was to be deducted from her weekly allowance.

Something about Carla was still bothering Richard. Although she was brighter and seemed happier since their move to Darlington, she wasn't the girl she used to be. He found it hard to communicate with her and she had become introvert. He'd discussed her mood change with his friends at work and was told it was completely normal. Everyone he'd spoken to with a teenage daughter had said their girls were exactly the same. Locking themselves in their rooms, only coming down to raid the fridge, shouting at their parents over the most trivial things and showing total apathy towards life. This made Richard feel better, but only a little. With most girls it was a gradual change. Some girls would slowly become grumpier as their hormones kicked in and the transition took several months. Most of them started to change well before they'd hit their teenage years. But Carla was different. When she was twelve he'd noticed a few subtle changes in her character which he put down to puberty, but in the last year she'd changed dramatically. He could almost pinpoint the day she changed. It was the day he'd announced they were moving to Darlington. This was what confused him. If it had been the move away from Bristol and away from her friends that had upset her, why had she never protested? She'd gone along with the move without complaining. Almost as if she'd welcomed it.

Carla cleared the dishes and cleaned up the mess. The saucepan was in the bin but the acrid smell of burned metal and food would hang around for days.

Richard listened to her tidying up and was about to ask whether she was OK, but decided against it. She was a good girl and to think his daughter was unhappy broke his heart. Some nights he'd gone to bed and cried over her.

After she'd finished clearing away she kissed her dad goodnight and told him she wanted an early night because school had tired her out.

She shut her bedroom door and carried on where she left off, searching for anything she could find about Markland Garraway.

She wasn't surprised to find most of the reports were referring to Ben Walker's murder, but what did surprise her was that, since early October 2009, there had been no further mention of him on news, police, or any other websites. It was as if he'd vanished from the face of the planet. She checked online obituaries and websites that may have referred to his passing and tried searching 'Markland Garraway Dead' in Google. Other than a man of the same name who died in Portland, Oregon in 2004 and a boy who'd been killed in a hit and run on the Isle of Wight on Christmas day 2007, there were no other reports of anyone who could have been the detective and had died.

If he was still alive, where had he gone? She searched 'Markland Garraway retired', which also came up with nothing.

She sat back in her chair and considered why it was concerning her? Her dream and vision of the man were so clear it must have meant something. She wondered whether he was dead and was trying to contact her from beyond the grave. She scorned herself for being ridiculous.

She carried on looking into some of the older reports of cases with which he'd been involved. Glancing at her watch it was half past nine and she'd been searching the net for over an hour and a half and was getting tired. She decided to give it another fifteen minutes before turning in for the night.

Reading an archived news report from The Bristol Post she found something interesting. It was a report of a young woman who had been murdered in Bristol in 2006. Markland Garraway had been involved in the investigation. The story gave details of there being very little evidence to find the murderer. The report went on to explain that interviews had been conducted with friends, family and neighbours. Garraway had interviewed an elderly lady who lived in the flat above where the murder had taken place, and although she saw or heard nothing at the time of the murder, she told Garraway of a detailed dream she'd had earlier in the week and had made notes of what she had dreamt. She had called the police and told them. The police were grateful for the information and were very nice to her, but she knew that they would do nothing, but she felt she'd needed to tell someone.

The murder that had taken place in the flat below was almost identical to what she had dreamt, almost as if she'd had a preminition. The report explained that Garraway had noted the details of her dream and had taken her description of what the murderer was wearing and that he had a tattoo of a spider on his right forearm.

Garraway had searched the police database and found a known criminal with a tattoo which matched the description from the lady's dream. Against the advice of his seniors he pursued his investigations using the information he'd received from the lady, which eventually led him to the killer, who had been a jealous ex-lover of the girl.

Additional evidence was found and the killer was convicted. Although the information from the dream alone was not enough to find the killer, Garraway's open mindedness had compelled him to consider the lady's detailed dream. He had checked police telephone records and found a recording of the call she had made earlier in the week before the murder had taken place. She had an alibi which placed her at a rehearsal with an amateur dramatics club at the time of the murder so could be ruled out as being the killer.

Carla read and re-read the website wondering if there was any connection with Garraway's openness when it came to using information and his presence in her dream.

She cleared the history on her browser as she didn't want anyone knowing she'd been looking at websites which could connect her to Ben's murder.

The notes she made about Garraway were placed in a folder along with the portrait she'd sketched of him the night before. She was just about to lock them in her drawer when she heard her father calling. She dropped the folder next to her laptop and called downstairs to him. The folder slid onto the floor and lay hidden behind her wastepaper basket.

Her father had lost his key fob, which had his car, house and office keys on it and wondered if she'd seen them. This was a usual thing for Richard as he was always losing things. Carla knew exactly where to look for them.

She calmly made her way along the hall and opened the front door and pulled them from the lock on the outside of the door. She took the bunch of keys and dropped them in front of her father.

"You really need to be more careful dad." He smiled sheepishly and thanked her.

Carla went back to her room, got dressed for bed, cleaned her teeth, and settled down for the night.

The folder was hidden between the waste paper basket and the bedroom wall.

Morning came too soon and she could hear her father calling her. It was eight o'clock and she needed to be up for sixth form. She sluggishly rolled out of bed and headed to the bathroom. She skipped breakfast and grabbed an apple from the fruit bowl to eat on the walk to school.

Richard didn't need to be in work until nine thirty and spent time at home doing a few household chores.

Recycling collection was due that morning and he had forgotten to put the bins out the night before due to the commotion with the burnt evening meal. He hurried around the house emptying bins into black plastic bags. He didn't have time to sort card, tins and plastic bottles so he was dumping everything into general waste. He opened Carla's door, bent down and picked up her wastepaper basket when he noticed the cardboard folder wedged behind it. He was about to put it in the black bag but gave it a second thought in case it was something she needed to keep. He didn't like going through her stuff, after all, she was a young lady and there were things he was sure that she didn't want him to see. He made up his mind that he should check the folder, just to be on the safe side. He looked inside and found one of her drawings. He was impressed by the quality of the portrait she'd sketched. He was fascinated by the level of detail in her work. The intricate pencil work amazed him. He was useless at art and she had inherited it from her mother's side. Just by using a graphite pencil she was able to capture light and shade and even had light reflecting from the pupils of his eyes. He was proud of her work and was certain she would get a job utilising her skills. He had no idea who the man in her picture was. Turning the sheet of A4 paper over he saw a name written on the other side. Her drawing may be brilliant, but her handwriting left a lot to be desired. He squinted as he tried to read her spidery scribble. He could make out a surname.

"Garraway," he said holding the sheet of paper a foot from his face. He attempted to read the first name but was having problems deciphering her scrawl.

"Marland, Marklane?"

"Markland," he finally said. He repeated the full name out loud.

"Markland Garraway."

Who the hell is Markland Garraway? he thought.

Putting down the sketch he flipped through the other sheets of paper in the folder. Again he was having difficulty in working out her writing, but they seemed to be notes taken from websites. There were scribbles which were almost like some kind of shorthand or code, as if she didn't want her words to be understood and were only for her to read. Alongside each of her scribbly paragraphs was a URL. A few of them were bbc.co.uk addresses and others were from bristolpost.co.uk. He had no reason to be curious other than for the sake of curiosity. He put everything back in the folder and placed it just as he had found it behind her waste paper bin.

After taking out the rubbish and washing his hands he decided there was just enough time for coffee before he left for work. *Markland Garraway, who on earth is Markland Garraway?* he thought as he held his mug.

Was he someone on whom she had a crush? He hoped not as the man in her drawing looked older than he did. Perhaps it was one of her teachers at sixth form? He knew most of the teachers by name and was sure he would have remembered a name like Markland Garraway. Perhaps this man was the reason why she'd been acting so strange lately? His mind was creating scenario after scenario until he could take it no more. He fired up the computer in the lounge. He looked at his watch and saw it was time he should be on his way to the office. Going on-line would definitely make him late for work. His elderly computer took such a long time to crank up he wouldn't be leaving for at least another fifteen minutes, even if he did find what he was looking for straight away.

He picked up his mobile and called his office. A lady with a soft Welsh accent answered.

"Pam, hi, it's Richard Price, I'm sorry but I'm going to be a little late this morning, can you pass a message on to Art Brooks for me please?"

"Sure, I can, but why don't you speak to him yourself?"

"I would Pam, but I'm up to my armpits in battery charger. The car has a flat battery and I'm struggling to get the thing started."

"OK Richard, I'll tell him. Anyone would think you were scared to speak to him. What time do you think you'll be here?"

"I reckon I'll be there in about forty five minutes'."

"OK, I'll tell him and if Art wants you I'll get him to call your mobile."

He thanked her and ended the call.

The truth was that he didn't like Art Brooks an awful lot. He was a fair boss, but he was the sort of person that made Richard nervous. Plus, he could sniff out a lie at thirty paces.

The computer was up and running. He fired up Google and waited for what seemed like an eternity as the little hour glass signified the thing was thinking about what to do next. He drummed his fingers impatiently on the side of the table.

"Bingo!" he said as the browser finally started to work.

He remembered that a few of the website addresses Carla had made notes of were from the Bristol Post site, so it was pretty clear to Richard that Markland Garraway would have some connection with where he and Carla used to live. He typed into the browser 'Markland Garraway Bristol'.

He skim read through the results that came up and there were lots to read. He scrolled through and quickly ascertained that Markland Garraway was a policeman. Reading one particular entry he saw him referred to as DCI Garraway. "Detective Chief Inspector" he said out loud. There were plenty of things for him to read, but he didn't have the time, he needed to leave for work.

Now his curiosity was running wild. Why on earth would Carla be making notes and sketches of a detective from Bristol? He promised himself he would click just one more link and that would be the end of it. Randomly he clicked a BBC news website which mentioned a murder which had taken place in Bristol. He didn't have time to read the news report and saw there was a video link. He clicked it and waited......and waited......and eventually the video played. It was a press conference and Markland Garraway was talking about a murder in Badock's Wood in Bristol. Richard watched the report and was taken aback by how well Carla's sketch resembled the man who it was supposed to be. Suddenly he remembered the murder. He recalled how sad Elizabeth Mason's father had appeared when he appealed for anyone to come forward who may have evidence to catch the killer. *But why would Carla be interested in any of this?* Richard saw the date the press conference had been originally broadcast. Wednesday 9th September 2009.

He sat back in his chair with his mouth open. He clearly remembered the day as it was when he received the news that he'd been offered the job in Darlington. It was also the week that his daughter had started acting very strangely. His mind was racing. He was putting two and two together, but was he making four? Did Carla have anything to do with the incident in the woods? He was tense and uneasy.

His phone rang which made him jump.

"Richard? It's Brooks. Have you sorted your car yet? There's a meeting starting in fifteen minutes and I need you here."

"Hi Art, I was about to ring you. I've just got the car started and I'll be there in a jiffy."

He shut down the computer, ran to the garage and wiped his hands in an oily rag in an attempt to prove he'd been tinkering under the bonnet and then drove like a fool to the office. He would need to think about what to say to Carla. But what? He had absolutely no idea.

CHAPTER FORTY SIX

Westhouse
Bristol
2.30pm
Tuesday 28th September

Maria Jameson was putting on her jacket and was ready to head home after her first day back at work in over a year. It had been a strange morning. Her body may have been there, but her head and heart were definitely not.

It had been a struggle since the moment she'd sat at her desk. She had been greeted by an office full of cheery expectant faces who hadn't seen her since she left for maternity leave the previous year. Her chair was festooned with balloons and welcome back cards were lodged in the keyboard of her computer.

To be fair, the day had been fairly light as far as work was concerned. She had a couple of meetings to bring her up to speed with what been happening over the past twelve months and she was introduced to a couple of new members of staff who'd started since she'd been on leave.

She sounded like a stuck record. If she'd answered the question "How's your little boy?" once, she'd answered it a hundred times that morning and the irritation was showing in her voice. Maria had a reputation of being fiery and her colleagues knew when not to push her.

"Post natal stuff," she heard one of the male workers whisper to another. She chose to ignore it.

She left the building and headed to the car park with a box full of paperwork to read when she got home. She headed to her mother's house to collect Christopher. She'd not stopped thinking of him all morning. He'd been left with his grandmother many times to let Maria have a bit of *me time* or allow her to do the weekly shop, but this morning had been different and she was desperate to see him.

Claire stood at the door waiting for Maria as she was getting out of her car. Christopher was bouncing up and down in his grandmother's arms. As soon as he saw Maria he was giggling and saying, "ma ma, ma ma".

Claire passed the little boy to his mother who gave him a hug like she'd not seen him in weeks.

After spending half an hour with her mother discussing her first morning back at work over coffee, she strapped Christopher into his baby seat and drove home.

It had been three weeks since she'd exchanged numbers with Campbell and she'd not heard from him. She was waiting for his call and was looking forward to spending some time with him. Although she had his number, she had no intention of making the first move. She didn't want to appear too keen. Deep down she was angry. She'd learnt from her mistake with Rob and now doubted her ability to judge characters.

It was four o'clock by the time she got home and she was exhausted. Christopher's perforated ear drum was better and he was sleeping well at night. Maria had also been sleeping well, which was good as the rush of getting Christopher to his grandmother's house and then the journey across the city to the office followed by the return trip had done her in. She was ready for bed and it wasn't even five pm.

The new routine of juggling work and Christopher would take the young single mother time to adapt to. Until now, apart from the occasional health hiccups with Christopher she'd had an easy and leisurely ride. Her days had consisted of meeting up with other mums with their children, seeing her family and spending time with her best friend Samreen, and she'd loved every moment of it. But now the party was over. The maternity pay had stopped and she needed to earn money.

Before she had become pregnant, work had been her life. She'd loved the hustle and bustle of managing a busy office. She'd considered herself a fair boss who gave credit when credit was due but didn't suffer fools gladly. Now things had changed. The office seemed alien to her and she wished that Rob had been the right man in her life and was here with her now so she could stay at home and spend time with Christopher, whilst Rob brought home the bacon. She knew how old fashioned it sounded, but this was how she felt, preferring to stay home for the next four years until Christopher was ready to start school.

She stretched and yawned as she made her way to the kitchen to get Christopher's food ready. Her son was having a nap and now was a good time to fix a snack for him. She was mashing a banana when her phone rang. When she saw who it was she said his name under her breath, "Campbell."

"Hi Campbell, how are you, how are you doing?"

"Hi Maria, things aren't so good I'm afraid, which is why I've not called. I'm in Cork."

Campbell explained that his father had suffered a heart attack two weeks ago and he'd flown to Ireland to be with him. His father had died on Saturday. Campbell had been able to spend time with him, for which he was grateful, but now was bereft with grief and would need to spend time in Ireland to be with his mother and sisters. He promised to call her when he was back and assured her that their date would still happen. He told Maria that he needed something to look forward to and an evening with her would be ideal.

Maria put the phone down and felt awful because of the things she had conjured up about him in her mind over the past few weeks. Now she was sure Campbell was a good person and wanted to be there for him when he returned. Even though she hardly knew the man there was a definite connection between them. She called Samreen to tell her about Campbell. Samreen could hear sadness in Maria's voice.

"I'm sure a night out with you will be the tonic he needs," said Samreen reassuringly.

Maria woke Christopher to feed him. He sat in his chair slurping on mashed banana and custard whilst getting it everywhere. He looked at Maria and made her smile. He had food in his hair, up his nose and even in his eyes.

"You need a bath young man."

Christopher clapped his hands, splatting more banana and custard everywhere.

After his bath she put him in his cot and tucked him in for the night. She cleared away the dishes, tidied the kitchen and then sat down in the lounge with the box full of paperwork she had brought home from the office.

She sighed as she began the task of prioritising what should be dealt with first. Then it started again.

"Ughh ughh ughh ughh ughh ughh ughh ughh ughh."

"Oh no," she said as she made her way to Christopher's room.

She opened his door and there he was again, banging his head and then rocking from side to side.

"Ughh ughh ughh ughh ughh ughh ughh ughh."

She picked him up and cuddled him and he stopped straight away, but as soon as she put him down he was banging and rocking again.

"Ughh ughh ughh ughh ughh ughh ughh ughh ughh."

She grabbed a thermometer from the first aid box and took his temperature. 37 degrees.

"Well you've got no temperature this time," she muttered to herself.

He had shown no sign of cold or cough or anything else to make him uncomfortable. She rang her mother to check how he'd been. Claire told her that he'd been 'fine and dandy' all day.

CHAPTER FORTY SEVEN

The Awareness
7.12pm
Tuesday 28th September

As Christopher was starting his latest bout of head banging and chanting, the Awareness was waking. It had been lying dormant for almost three weeks.

It was recalling what it had discovered last time it had been awake. It was focusing on the fact that it had been alive, that it had been killed and when it was alive it had been male.

More than ever it needed to be heard.

If it was to be heard, who would listen? It had no idea where it was. Was this heaven, hell or some kind of strange nirvana state? If this was heaven or hell it seemed a very lonely place.

It concentrated on its cache of memories and it started with the young woman. The young woman who was there when it died. Recalling the time she tumbled down the hill and how beautiful she was. The Awareness paused the memory and focused on her features. It admired what it saw and noticed the scar above her top lip. The Awareness let the memory play on to when they began to kiss. The kiss was one of the most intense memories it had. It was the one which heightened its emotions. It was the memory that reminded him that when he was alive he had been a man.

He needed to know more about who he once was. He was desperate to remember his family, his life and most of all his name. All he had was a selection of memories which he'd been able to store in order of how they'd happened. Memories of his childhood were at one end and the memory of dying was at the other. He needed to work through them and piece together their significance.

As he had developed over the past year his intelligence had improved. At first he was an Awareness and that was all he was. Something void of senses, emotion and intellect. Now he possessed these things and more, and was able to utilise them.

The emotion of love drove him and the emotion was strongest when he recalled time spent with the girl. Who was she? But before he could answer, he needed to focus on who he had once been.

He recalled the image of his reflection in the mirror. This was all he had to work with. He knew what he had looked like but very little else. He scrutinised the image of his reflection to see if there were any clues to his identity. The clothes he was wearing looked familiar and he knew they were significant. He looked at the peaked cap which was black with a blue band. He wore a blue shirt with short sleeves. He looked at his arms which were muscly. On top of the shirt he was wearing a black jacket which had no sleeves. There was writing across the front of the jacket. Words were something he was struggling with. His memories included lots of them, but they made no sense. He was like a four year old and needed pictures to accompany words to help him understand. The writing on the jacket was long and complicated. He knew he needed to fathom out what it meant.

Letting the memory of his reflection fade he hunted for different ones. He was searching for memories which had words. Written words and not spoken words. Working from the most recent first he scoured his cache.

One particular memory caught his attention. It was an image of a car speeding around a bend. It must have been viewed from the pavement. The car had flashing blue lights and a siren. He immediately recognised it as a police vehicle. He saw a word on the side of the car and the word looked familiar. He flipped back to the image of his reflection and back again to the car. He paused the image of the car to concentrate on what was written on it. Flipping back and forth between the two images he compared the two words. The word on the car looked similar to one of the words in the reflection, but he couldn't work out what was different about them. They looked identical but at the same time completely opposite.

He was struggling to fathom out the difference when suddenly he understood. He found this was something that happened frequently. At first a memory would make no sense and then it would become crystal clear. The same thing had happened when he first recalled memories of speech. At first, the spoken word was difficult to understand, it was like hearing a foreign language, but once he'd found a key he could work out the meaning of the words he heard in his memories.

And now the same was happening when working out these two written words. They were one and the same. The only difference was that the word in the reflection was back to front because he was seeing its reflection while the one on the car was the right way round.

He flipped back to the memory of the car and understood that P-O-L-I-C-E must spell police. Flipping back to the memory of his reflection he worked out he was wearing a uniform with the word Police written across the front. He'd been a policeman.

He continued to trawl through memories and search for more which had images of words. Now he'd learnt one word which had proved to be such a valuable asset he was hungry to learn more. He scanned memory after memory until he had amassed enough of them to begin relearning words.

Like a child he started with basics. He recalled memories of advertisements which had a key word relating to the picture alongside. He studied a memory of a picture of a cat eating from a bowl. The wording below the image was 'Your cat deserves the best'. As he analysed the words he was quickly able to link the word cat to the image of the animal eating from the bowl.

He did the same with other images which included key words. He recalled a memory of a dog and then a car and then a building. Quickly he was linking words to images. His ability to relearn skills was extraordinary. Once he had grasped the basics it all came back. He was able to recall memories which included written words and then read and understand them as he'd been able when he was alive.

He recalled the image of himself in the mirror and read what was written on his jacket. Although the words were mirror image he worked out what they spelt.

Police Community Support Officer

He'd been a Community Support Officer. He admired the image of his reflection.

The memory he'd recalled was his first day as a PCSO. He had just changed into his uniform and was standing with his back to the clothes locker whilst looking at his reflection. His civvy clothes were in the locker and the grey metal door was slightly open.

He continued to take in the detail of the memory and at the same time he recalled an emotion which he'd not felt since he'd been alive. It was different to love and fear and hate, which were three he'd experienced since he'd died. This new emotion was pride. Seeing himself in the reflection of the mirror made him feel proud.

He continued to admire his reflection when something caught his attention. Behind him something was written on the locker door. Two words had been jotted down in pen on a small piece of white paper which had been slipped into a little holder on the locker door. The words were very small and hard to make out. He focused his attention on the piece of paper which was about the size of two postage stamps. He concentrated on the two words. The first one was short and the second one was longer. The small word was written above the larger word. With his attention fully focused on the small word it became clearer, but still he couldn't decipher what it said. It wasn't because it was a word he didn't know, it was just far too small to read.

So, if he'd opened the locker door, there must be a memory in his cache of the door, not seen as a reflection, but as seen first-hand. His accumulation of memoires had now become huge and he'd been able to archive significant memories and recall them with ease. But he wasn't so adept at recalling ones which were less substantial. He had an inkling that these two words were important. He sorted through his hoard of memories as quickly as he could. His attention was beginning to wane as recalling and disregarding memories was draining his energy. He was getting nowhere.

He flipped back to the memory of his reflection and slowly ran it in reverse, which was another thing he'd learnt. With all his strength he played the memory backwards and in slow motion. Slowly his reflection and the mirror were moving to the right. He changed the aspect of the image until he was recalling a memory of when he had been facing the locker door.

The door was slightly ajar. He now had a clear view of the two words on the piece of paper. He could make out the first word. It was made up of three letters and neatly written. With all his strength focused on the one small word he was struggling to remain cognisant. Suddenly, as if a light had been switched on he found renewed energy and worked hard to make sense of the small three letter word. And then it became clear.

B-E-N

The small word spelt Ben. Ben instantly meant something. It was such a small word but it was so significant. Now that he'd worked out the small word he toiled on the larger word beneath. This word was made up of six letters. Although the second word was twice as long, he found it easier to understand. The six letters were laid in front of him in the memory.

W-A-L-K-E-R

The second word spelt Walker. He put the two together. Ben Walker. He focused on them over and over. Ben Walker - Ben Walker - Ben Walker - Ben Walker - Ben Walker - Ben Walker - Ben Walker.

This was when the penny dropped. He now knew his name. Now that he could remember it he wondered how he ever could have forgotten.

Ben Walker began to fade. He felt his strength ebbing away. A feeling he was becoming used to. Luckily for Ben, he still had no concept of time, so the next time he would wake from the dormant state he would be unaware of how long he'd been inactive and would be able to carry on from where he left off.

CHAPTER FORTY EIGHT

Maria Jameson's flat
8.45pm
Tuesday 28th September

Christopher had been head banging and chanting nonstop for over an hour and a half. This was the longest he'd ever done this without a break. It was also the most intense his head banging had been. His pillow was soaked in saliva and splattered with blood as the chanting was forcing him to dribble furiously and had caused his nose to bleed. Maria was crying. She could not get him to stop. She'd picked him up, carried him in her arms around her flat, but still he continued. Worn out, she placed him back in his cot and watched him through teary eyes feeling totally helpless. She grabbed her phone to call her mother.

She remembered what Campbell had suggested. She selected the movie app on her phone and filmed Christopher head banging, rolling from side to side and chanting "Ughh ughh ughh ughh ughh ughh ughh ughh." She filmed him for three minutes until the camera on her phone automatically stopped.

She called her mother who stopped what she was doing and made her way over to Maria's.

Claire had never seen Christopher's head banging as it had always happened when she wasn't around. Ten minutes later she was at Maria's flat.

Maria opened the door and Claire saw her tired and bloodshot eyes. What was left of her mascara had run and smudged down her cheeks. Her hair was a mess and she was distraught.

Claire hung her coat on a peg near the door and could hear Christopher chanting, even though his bedroom was at the other side of the flat.

"Is that Christopher?"

Maria nodded and threw her arms around her mother and cried onto her shoulder.

They stood together in his room. Claire had not seen or heard anything like it. Christopher was face down in his cot and banging his head so violently that his body from his waist up arched upward and crashed back down onto his mattress. Each time his head hit the pillow he let out an "ughh" which accompanied the dull thud as his head crashed down. He would briefly stop and then roll from side to side crashing into the wooden bars of the cot. After another brief pause he went back to banging his head along with his strange chanting. "Ughh ughh ughh ughh ughh ughh ughh ughh."

Claire looked at her daughter and was lost for words.

Eventually Claire spoke.

"He's fast asleep, he doesn't even know he's doing it."

Maria nodded, "I've tried to wake him, but I can't."

They stood in silence as he continued to crash and bang in his cot.

His banging began to slow and his chanting became quieter and after a few minutes he stopped and was sleeping normally.

Maria went to the airing cupboard in the corner of his room and took out a clean pillow. She gently lifted his head, pulled out the blood and saliva soaked pillow and replaced it with the fresh one. Tomorrow she would replace his sheets and covers, but right now she just wanted him to sleep and didn't want to risk the chance of waking him.

They watched him without speaking and then quietly crept out of his room shutting the door behind them.

"What do you think it is?" asked Claire.

Maria shook her head as she sat on the arm of her sofa.

"I'll take him back to the doctor, but that stupid Doctor Marsh will only say he has a cold, or a temperature or something trivial."

"Not this time she won't as I'll be coming with you, that's if you don't mind."

Maria looked at her mother and reached for her hand.

"I would like you to be there mum, thank you."

"Why don't you ask to see a different doctor?"

"Yes, I will. Dr Marsh isn't even my regular doctor, I think it's just bad luck I've seen her both times."

Claire put her arm around Maria. "Would you like me to stay tonight?"

Maria nodded and smiled weakly. "Thank you mum."

Claire slept on the sofa and the rest of the night was uneventful. Apart from gently snoring, Christopher made no noise.

Claire was the first to wake up. She made herself coffee and crept back to the lounge as quietly as possible. It was six thirty and she felt tired after an awkward night on the sofa. Ten minutes later Maria popped her head around the door and smiled at her mother. Maria's face was smudged with mascara and her eyes were red.

"Sit down and I'll make you coffee."

Maria sat on the sofa and Claire went to the kitchen.

Claire returned with the coffee.

"How is he now?" asked Claire.

"He's sound asleep. I've never known him go this long without waking up, he must be exhausted."

They discussed what had happened the night before and drank their coffee.

"Listen, he's awake," said Maria.

They listened as Christopher was cooing and chatting to himself as if nothing had happened. Claire and Maria went into his room together and as soon as he saw them his face lit up with a washing line smile.

Maria picked him up. His little baby grow was spattered with dry blood from his nose and his face was dirty.

She carried him into the lounge, placed him in his baby walker and gave him Misty. He seemed his normal happy self. Claire couldn't believe how normal he was compared to last night.

Maria was getting ready for her second day back at work when Claire spoke.

"You're not going in today are you?"

Claire was nervous about looking after Christopher after what she'd seen last night.

"I'm sure he'll be absolutely fine mum."

Claire was concerned.

"Look, if there're any problems call me and I'll come home."

Maria went to her room to get changed.

"What if you're in a meeting or something and I can't get you?" called her mother.

"My mobile will be on and I'll warn people I may get a call."

Claire sat on the settee.

"Please don't worry mum, he'll be fine. I'll ring the surgery from work and let you know when the appointment is."

After kisses and cuddles for Christopher and hugs with Claire, Maria left her flat leaving her mother in charge. She felt bad leaving Christopher with her, but she had to work. Christopher was showing no signs of being ill and whatever had upset him last night seemed to have passed.

Maria was at her desk by eight thirty and was looking through the box of paperwork she didn't get the chance to read the night before.

She was watching the clock, waiting for the surgery to open and was desperate to get a same day appointment and was adamant she wouldn't see Dr Marsh this time.

Whilst she was waiting she replayed the video of Christopher on her phone. Watching it on the small screen didn't make what he did any less bizarre. In fact seeing it played back made it seem weirder than it did last night. His little voice sounded thin and tinny over the small speaker in her phone as he chanted.

Nine o'clock eventually came and she was talking to the receptionist. A same day appointment was available with Dr Marsh. Maria said that she wished to see a different doctor without explaining why. The tone of the receptionist's voice gave her the feeling that she'd not been the only one who'd preferred not to see Marsh. An appointment for the following morning was made with Dr Sullivan. She'd seen Sullivan before. He was in his fifties and what she considered to be a stereotypical doctor. Unlike Marsh, Sullivan had the gift of compassion. An appointment for the next day was ideal as she didn't work on Thursday.

She made a quick call to her mother to tell her what time Christopher's appointment was and checked that he was OK.

Claire told her that Christopher was fine. He was washed and ready for the day and she was planning on taking him to the park as it was a dry and sunny day, followed by a journey to the shops.

Maria's day at work was arduous and she struggled to stay awake. She tried not to think about Christopher banging his head whilst spluttering and speckling blood over his pillow, but the image wouldn't go away.

She was desperate to get back to him and the day dragged on. At four thirty she was out of there. Being a manager she would be expected to stay late from time to time, but having a child and being a single parent gave her the excuse to be out of the building and heading home bang on time.

Christopher was excited to see his mother. He was grinning and chuckling and calling 'mum, mum'.

Claire's nervousness had been unfounded, Christopher had been absolutely fine as if nothing had happened. Maria had just enough time for coffee with her mother before she headed home.

The rest of the day and night passed without incident.

Both Christopher and Maria slept well. She felt better in the morning and was less tired than yesterday. She'd found getting out of bed easier than it had been in weeks. *A day off* she thought and smiled.

Her appointment with the doctor was at ten, which gave her a few hours to potter around her flat and attend to Christopher. The chocolate stain on her carpet was still there from his birthday party. She considered having another attempt at removing it but couldn't be bothered. Depending on the outcome of the doctor's appointment she was hoping to meet with Samreen. She'd not seen her for a while and they had some catching up to do.

Just over an hour later she was waiting for her mother outside the surgery. Appointments were running on time and they were in Dr Sullivan's consulting room by ten o'clock.

Maria told the doctor about Christopher's head banging which had got worse. She was more comfortable with Dr Sullivan than Marsh. He was older, more experienced and a nicer person.

He gave Christopher another thorough examination and declared that her son was in 'rude health'. He bounced Christopher on his knee and tickled him making the little boy giggle and laughed along with him. He looked to Maria with a serious face and declared it was hard to know what was causing Christopher to head bang.

"And you are sure he is sleeping while all this is going on?"

Maria nodded and shrugged her shoulders.

"Show him your phone," said Claire, who until now hadn't spoken.

Maria looked puzzled and then remembered the video she'd taken. She pulled the phone from her bag and brought up the clip. She handed her phone to the doctor who silently watched it with Christopher on his lap. He wore a frown as the video played. Fumbling with the phone he played it again. Maria watched his expression as he viewed the clip and listened to Christopher's chanting.

He handed the phone back and subconsciously continued to bounce Christopher on his knee. He turned to write some notes and realised the little boy was still on his lap.

"I almost forgot," as he turned and handed Christopher back to Maria.

He turned back to his desk and made some notes. Maria and Claire waited silently while Christopher cooed and chattered.

"I will arrange for the child health visitor to call to your home," he said, as he continued to write.

"I'll be honest with you, I don't know why he's doing it. I know some children gently bang their head to get to sleep and it's quite normal, but what your son is doing seems, well, it seems extreme."

Maria nodded. She was relieved he had suggested that the health visitor should be involved as it was next on Maria's mental list.

Doctor Sullivan told Maria to expect a call from Esther Hall over the next few days. Esther was the Child Health Visitor for Maria's area and had been in the business for over fifteen years. The doctor told her that Esther had a wealth of experience and she was also fantastic with children.

Maria and Claire left the surgery with Christopher chattering happily in his buggy. Maria was feeling happier as now she was getting somewhere. She hugged her mother and headed to Coaster's to meet with Samreen.

CHAPTER FORTY NINE

Darlington
7.15pm
Thursday 29th September

Richard and Carla were eating the meal she'd prepared. Lately, her cooking had been pretty good, but compared to her first attempt and the awful burnt offering earlier in the month, it couldn't have been much worse. Neither of them were speaking as they worked their way through spaghetti bolognaise. Carla was expecting a comment from her father. She'd cooked a nice meal and he hadn't said a word.

There had been a frosty tension in the air for the past few weeks and Carla had no idea why. Had she done something wrong or had her father been having a bad time at the office?

Richard had been quiet since he'd found her sketch of Markland Garraway. It had been eating away at him. Why would she have such an interest in this man? He'd dismissed the idea that she had anything to do with the murder in the woods. There was no way she could've been involved, she just wasn't that kind of girl. He and his ex-wife had brought her up well and even when they were going through the divorce, he did his utmost to not let it affect his daughter.

He had resorted to the other option that Carla and the man in the sketch had been in some kind of relationship. He found it hard to understand that his daughter would be stupid enough to do such a thing, plus Markland Garraway was a detective, surely high ranking police wouldn't be involved with teenage girls? Although sickeningly inappropriate, he knew things like that did happen.

Had Garraway abused her or were they having an affair? Carla had certainly become a different girl in the past year. Maybe she was holding a torch for the man.

These thoughts and others like it were poisoning Richard and had been eating at him for weeks.

He looked at Carla as she quietly ate her food and considered how innocent she looked. Had she lost her innocence?

"Is everything OK dad? you seem very quiet."

"What, oh, I'm fine," he stuttered.

Carla knew something was wrong. She knew he was lying and was worried about him.

"You know you can tell me if there's a problem."

He shook his head and continued to eat.

"I'm fine OK!" was his sharp retort.

Carla pushed her half empty plate away and said she wasn't hungry. She walked out of the dining room and headed up to her room, closing the door with a thud.

Richard left the rest of his food and sat with his head in his hands.

His problem was that he had no idea how to approach her. What should he say?

It was Carla's job to clear away the dishes as well as cooking the meal, but Richard decided he would do it. He found it easier to think if he was doing menial tasks. Also, he didn't think there was much chance of Carla clearing up tonight. She was clearly upset.

As he loaded the dishwasher his mind worked overtime thinking about what to say. Wiping down the kitchen worktop he'd made his decision. He would just ask her outright and he would do it tonight.

He threw the kitchen cloth into the sink and walked into the hall and stopped at the bottom of the stairs. He could hear music coming from her bedroom. He strode the stairs two steps at time and stopped when he got to the landing. Holding his breath he stood outside her door.

He gently knocked. The music was still playing and she didn't come to the door. He knocked again, wrapping his knuckles on her door to be heard. The music stopped and the door slowly opened.

Carla put her head around the door.

"Hello daddy, is everything OK?"

"Can I come in please? There's something I need to ask."

Carla nervously opened her door wide enough to let him in. He looked around her room which was a mess.

"If it's about my room dad, I promise I'll clear it up, I'll do it tomorrow."

Richard wished it was something as trivial as her room.

"It's not about your room."

She anxiously looked at her father and was trying to work out what she'd done wrong.

Richard paused, which made the tension unbearable, and then he spoke.

"Carla, who is Markland Garraway?"
The colour drained from her face.

CHAPTER FIFTY

Maria's flat
8.07pm

Thursday 29th September

Maria returned home at six, after a relaxing day with Samreen. They'd spent a few hours shopping after meeting for lunch at Coaster's. Campbell was still away in Cork. The coffee shop wasn't the same without him.

Maria had put Christopher in his cot, had finished tidying her flat and was sitting down enjoying the quietness of the early evening. Something from the corner of her eye caught her attention. Her mobile phone was on the table and it was flashing. She'd missed a call. Earlier in the day she'd turned her phone to mute when she was with Doctor Sullivan and had forgotten to turn the volume back up.

She had a voicemail message. It was a call from Esther Hall, the Child Health Visitor and she had left a message to say she was in the area on Friday morning and could call over to see Christopher at ten o'clock. Esther ended the message by saying if she'd heard nothing by six o'clock she would assume Maria would be home with Christopher.

Maria sighed. She should be working tomorrow but she really needed Christopher to be seen by Esther. She called her boss, Maxwell Hart, to see if he would allow her to swap Friday for the following Monday.

Max Hart couldn't have had a more inappropriate name. He was the most uncompassionate boss she could have wished for. Although he thought a lot of Maria and valued her as manager, he had little time for people's problems and was angered by his staff when they rang in sick or had an appointment with the doctor when they should be at work.

She called Max on his mobile which diverted to voicemail.

"Hi Max, this is Maria. My son Christopher has been unwell and the Child Health Visitor has arranged to come over in the morning. I would be grateful if I could swap Friday for Monday. As far as I know there are no meetings planned tomorrow, so hope that you will be OK with this."

She ended the call and expected the worse.

A few minutes later she was watching television with a glass of wine, waiting expectantly for her phone to ring.

Her phone didn't ring, instead she heard the bleep of a text message arriving. She picked it up and read the text which was from Max Hart.

'OK. C U Monday. dnt b late'.

And that was it. His message was short, blunt and straight to the point. She was pleased he'd not called, as otherwise she'd have been trying to justify how ill Christopher was and why he needed to see the health visitor tomorrow.

She relaxed for the rest of the evening with her beloved Sauvignon Blanc.

CHAPTER FIFTY ONE

Darlington
7.37pm
Thursday 29th September

Carla was taken by surprise. How on earth would her father know about Markland Garraway?

"I don't know anyone called Markland Garraway."

He could tell by the tone of her voice that she was lying.

"I've seen the sketch Carla, so don't lie."

"You've been going through my things?" she replied with a sharp accusing snap.

Now Richard was feeling guilty. He knew not to go through her things.

"I found it by accident. It was in a folder by your waste paper basket and I thought it was to be thrown out. I only looked to make sure it was rubbish……..and then I found the picture you drew of him."

Carla was silent. Her mind was racing to come up with something to tell her father, other than the truth.

Richard swallowed hard as he paused to ask another question.

"Have you been having some sort of an affair with this man?"

Carla fell face down on her bed and sobbed. Her pent up emotions were released in one go. Her sobbing turned into howling and crying.

Richard knelt down next to her bed, put his arm around her and began to cry with her. After a few minutes Richard got up and left her room. He closed her bedroom door and stood on the landing before slumping to the floor with his head in his hands.

Carla lay on her bed. Through her tears she was struggling to think what to say to her father. Should she tell him the truth about the murder, or should she go along with the assumption that her father had made and tell him she'd been having an affair with an older man? It was the lesser of two evils and she decided to weave some kind of lie about an affair.

She knew she had to be careful about what she said. She didn't want her father contacting the police and accusing Markland Garraway of an affair with a teenaged girl that had never happened. She sat on the edge of her bed, wiped her face with a tissue and hastily put together a story.

She opened her bedroom door and saw her father sitting outside her room with his back to the wall. His eyes were red and teary. She sat alongside him and held his hand and after a brief pause she started to speak.

"I've not been having an affair with that man daddy and that's the truth."

Richard looked up at the ceiling and said nothing. He took his hand away from hers and pushed his fingers through his hair.

"Why don't you just tell me what's going on?" he replied, in a weary voice.

"I've not been having an affair, it's more of a, well……it's more of a crush."

"A crush…..why on earth would you be having a crush on a fifty something policeman who is over two hundred miles away?"

Carla struggled to find a reply and as she thought about what to say she began to spin the web of lies and hoped for the best.

"He came to my old school in Bristol, just before the start of the summer holidays." Carla took a breath and thought what to say next.

"He came to our school with some other policemen and policewomen and they gave a talk about safety and things like that."

It was true that in the June of her last year at her school in Bristol the police did turn up and gave a talk about general safety, but Markland Garraway hadn't been there.

"Me, and a few of my friends, we kind of, you know, had a crush on him." She continued as her father listened without speaking.

"He just seemed so cool and I thought he was lovely. I spoke to him afterwards and he was such a nice man and………" Her voice trailed off and she put her head in her hands.

"So you've never done anything with him?"

"No daddy, I promise, and that's the truth."

Richard was not sure whether he believed her. Why would she be sketching pictures of him, checking him out on the internet and getting so upset over him if it was only a crush which happened over a year ago?

"When did you sketch the picture of him?"

"I did it after I saw him on TV. He was doing a press conference about a murder in Bristol and I got all gooey over him again and did the sketch."

"So you sketched this picture a year ago?"

"Yes daddy. I kept it and found it the other day in the folder."

"And what about the notes on the back of the sketch?"

"I don't know, I was just Googling him and trying to find out what he was up to."

Richard thought about what Carla had just told him. It did seem to make sense. She was a young impressionable girl who had a crush on an older man. And because he was a Detective Chief Inspector she was probably attracted by his senior position.

"Why don't you find a boyfriend of your own age and forget about this man?"

"I know daddy, I will. I'm stupid, it's just a stupid crush….I'm sorry."

Richard put his arm around his daughter and hugged her.

After their talk things became easier between Carla and her father and as time went on he'd put what had happened to one side.

Carla felt awful. She had put him off the scent for the time being, but was feeling guilty about lying to her father on top of everything else. She accepted it was something she had to do and couldn't tell him the truth about what had really happened.

It would only be a matter of time before what happened that September evening in the woods in Bristol would return to haunt Carla in a way she could never imagine possible.

CHAPTER FIFTY TWO

Maria's flat
10am
Friday 30th September

Esther Hall arrived at Maria's flat bang on ten o'clock. Esther was a rotund lady in her mid-forties, with a rosy face and a beaming smile.

They shook hands and Maria liked her straight away. She invited Esther into the lounge where Christopher was in his high chair. Esther said hello to Christopher and he responded with his normal chatter and cooing.

"He's a beautiful boy," said Esther as she gave him a tickle under his chin.

"Thank you, he's my pride and joy."

Esther sat on the settee and looked serious.

"I've read the notes on Christopher so I am familiar with his situation, but I would be grateful if you could tell me in your own words about his head banging."

Maria explained in detail how it had recently started and had got worse over the past few weeks. Then she remembered the video clip on her phone. She pulled the phone from her bag and gave it to Esther to watch.

Maria watched Esther's face as she played the video of Christopher. Her serious face looked even more sombre as she got to the part of the clip which showed his bleeding nose. She replayed it twice before handing the phone back to Maria.

"What your son suffers from is called Rhythmic Movement Disorder or RMD, and believe it or not, it is fairly common, especially amongst toddlers and small children."

"Rhythmic Movement Disorder," repeated Maria

"Yes RMD. It's worse for you than it is for Christopher. He probably has no idea he's doing it".

Maria listened intently as Esther continued.

"He's doing it when he's sleeping so he won't be aware of what's going on."

"What causes it to happen?"

"Doctors aren't one hundred percent sure why it happens, but one theory is that it is a self-stimulating behaviour to alleviate tension and induce relaxation, a bit like thumb sucking."

Maria nodded her head as she listened.

"Another theory is that rhythmic movements help develop the vestibular system in young children."

"Vestibular system? Sorry I don't know what that is," said Maria.

"Sorry, it's the system that deals with motion and balance."

Maria stood up, walked over to Christopher and picked him up. She hugged and kissed him and held him close.

She turned to Esther with Christopher in her arms.

"So all of this is normal?"

"It's not unheard of, about six percent of young children develop it."

"Is there a cure for RMD?"

"No cure, he should grow out of it by the time he's three."

"So I will have to put up with another two years of bang, bang, bang?"

"Well there are some things you could try."

Maria went to the kitchen and came back with a notepad and pen.

"There won't be much for you to write down, but here are two suggestions you may like to try."

Maria put the notepad down while Esther continued.

"You could try playing continuous music on loop quietly in his bedroom, or, and this seems to be the more successful option, letting a loud clock or a metronome tick away in his room at night. It seems the rhythmic sound helps some children settle without banging their head."

Maria looked despondent. She had hoped for much more than this. At least there seemed to be nothing particularly wrong with Christopher, it was just one of those things that he was unlucky to have, and as Esther pointed out, it is worse for the parents than it is for the children who have RMD.

They continued to discuss Christopher for a while longer, when Esther brought something up.

"There is one thing I should mention, and I don't mean to worry you."

"What's that?" asked Maria, obviously looking worried.

"I've been dealing with children's health issues for over fifteen years and in that time I've seen lots of children with RMD, but I've never seen a child react in such a way as your son does."

Esther was referring to the video clip Maria had shown her.

"The children I have encountered over the years gently rock from side to side, or nod their head onto the pillow, but what Christopher is doing is extreme."

"So do you think he may have something other than RMD?" asked Maria.

"I am pretty certain it's RMD and nothing else, but with your permission I would be grateful if I could show the video clip you have on your phone to a colleague of mine in London. He is an expert and has being doing a lot of research into Rhythmic Movement Disorder and I would like his opinion."

Maria agreed to email the video clip and said she would look out for a metronome for Christopher to help him sleep.

She saw Esther to the door and thanked her for her time.

Maria sat in her lounge feeling low and helpless. She had really expected Esther Hall to have an instant answer.

At least Maria could put a name to what was affecting Christopher. Rhythmic Movement Disorder. It sounded horrible.

She looked at Christopher who was standing up and holding onto the book case whilst trying to pull out a wad of envelopes Maria had stuffed between two books. He looked at his mother and smiled. She picked him up, held him close and kissed his head again.

Maria called her mother who was desperate to know the outcome of the health visitor's appointment.

"He's got what?"

"I know mum, it sounds strange doesn't it? Rhythmic Movement Disorder."

"I've never heard of such a thing. Is she sure she knows what she's talking about?"

Maria explained that Esther was going to pass the video clip to her colleague in London for a second opinion.

They agreed to meet over the weekend and Maria ended the call.

By now it was eleven fifteen and Christopher was ready for a nap. Maria placed him in his cot and returned to the lounge. She switched on her computer, loaded the video clip from her phone onto her computer and emailed it to Esther.

She spent the next hour, while Christopher was taking his nap, searching for information on Rhythmic Movement Disorder. There was lots available and all of it backed up what Esther had told her.

There were even videos on Youtube of children in their cots and beds banging their heads just like her son. This made her feel better. She no longer felt alone, or that she was the only parent going through this.

She found five video clips which had been uploaded to the internet of children with RMD and although they were all doing the same as Christopher, none were as violent or as noisy as him. The children on her computer were almost graceful in their movements and made little 'huffing' noises as they banged their heads or rocked from side to side. None of them were making the 'ughh ughh ughh ughh ughh' grunt that Christopher did.

Maria was deep in thought when her phone rang. She quickly grabbed it from the table and looked to see who was calling. It was Campbell.

"Hi Campbell, how are you?" asked Maria, she immediately regretted asking the question considering he'd only just lost his father.

"I'm not too bad, thanks for asking."

Maria found it difficult to talk to him on the phone. She hardly knew him and felt awkward asking questions about the recent bereavement. Campbell sensed her apprehension.

"My father's funeral is next Tuesday and I am planning on returning to Bristol the following weekend, which means I'll be home on Saturday 8th October. I'll call you again when I'm back and perhaps we can arrange that date?"

Maria agreed and said she was looking forward to seeing him. They wished each other well and ended the call.

Maria's thoughts returned to Christopher. He was quietly sleeping in his cot. What she'd read about RMD seemed to indicate that children would bang their heads every time when put to bed. It was something they did regularly which had resulted in a habitual thing. Christopher wasn't like that. He would go weeks without showing any signs of RMD and then have the most violent outburst. This was something that troubled her.

The more Maria thought about things, the more she knew there was something else causing her son to act the way he did. She didn't know what it could be, it was just mother's intuition.

CHAPTER FIFTY THREE

Jarrett's Builders Merchant
9am
Monday 3rd October

Daniel Boyd was busy loading the Hiab lorry at the Builders Merchant where he had been working since January.

Colin Jarrett, the sales director, had secured a profitable order to provide building blocks to a house in the stylish Sneyd Park area of Bristol. The owner of the house was having a downstairs extension built to make life more comfortable for his daughter who had been unwell for a long time.

Daniel had been trained to use the crane attached to the back of the lorry to carefully load breezeblocks on and off the vehicle. It was tough work but he enjoyed it. His days of living outside the law and drug taking were behind him.

He was working with an older man called Stanley. Stanley was in his sixties and was close to retirement. He hated the job, but was hanging in there until it was time to give up work, sit back and watch the flowers grow. He'd paid into a pension all of his working life and was looking forward to a comfortable and well-earned retirement.

Boyd looked up to Stanley as if he was a second father. He hadn't seen or spoken to his own parents in years and found a friendship in Stanley which had flourished over the past months. Stanley didn't know much about Boyd other than he had a chequered past and had recently stopped taking drugs. He was willing to put up with Boyd's odd ways and in doing so had developed an unlikely friendship. Stanley had encouraged Boyd to work hard and aim high. He told Boyd that he was a young man with the rest of his life ahead of him and there was plenty of time for him to do well and achieve something with his life.

Stanley drove the Hiab full of breezeblocks out of the yard and headed to Sneyd Park. Sitting between Stanley and Boyd was Geoff Perks. It would take all three of them to unload the lorry and three deliveries would be needed to complete the day's work.

Twenty minutes later the Hiab pulled into the driveway of the large house. The drive was long and was surrounded by immaculately kept lawns and trees.

"Look at the size of this place, rich bastards," exclaimed Boyd.

"If you work hard enough Daniel perhaps one day you'll have a place like this, in fact my son, if you work really hard you can have whatever you want. It's up to you choose your own destiny," replied Stanley.

Stanley steered the Hiab around to the side of the house where a man in his early fifties, wearing a blue shirt and jeans, was waiting for them.

Stanley jumped out of the cab and walked over to the man.

"Mr Mason I presume?" said Stanley as he approached the man.

Mr Mason walked around the side of the Hiab and examined the load of breezeblocks.

"Don't worry, there's another two deliveries on the way. It's a big order sir and we're grateful for your business."

Mr Mason smiled. He was a business man and appreciated that the driver of the Hiab was thanking him for the order. Few people seemed to do that these days.

Mr Mason told Stanley where to put the blocks. Boyd, Geoff and Stanley started to unload the delivery which took forty five minutes.

By three o'clock the final delivery was being unloaded and Stanley was preparing the paperwork for Mr Mason to sign.

Mr Mason checked the delivery note and counted every block that had been unloaded. Once he was happy he signed.

"Are you building anything nice sir?" asked Stanley.

"A downstairs bedroom for my daughter."

Boyd and Geoff were securing the Hiab's crane. Boyd was doing an impression of Mr Mason behind his back and Stanley was doing his best to ignore him.

"That's nice, I hope your daughter will like her new bedroom, don't tell me she's already outgrown her old one?" said Stanley attempting to be humorous.

"I only wish she had," replied Mr Mason sounding serious.

Stanley knew he had said the wrong thing and looked sheepish.

Mr Mason felt bad for the old man as he knew that he was only trying to be pleasant.

"Unfortunately my daughter is not very well and she requires around the clock care, so this new extension will include sleeping quarters for the medical staff who look after her."

"I'm sorry to hear that sir, I hadn't realised," replied Stanley in a soft voice.

"Do you mind me asking what's wrong with your daughter?"

"She's in a coma and has been for over a year."

"Was she in some kind of accident?" asked Stanley.

"You could say that. She was badly beaten up by a group of thugs last autumn, you may have heard about it, she was all over the news last year."

"Sorry sir, I can't say I remember," replied Stanley.

"If you don't remember my daughter, you would probably remember her friend who was there. Unfortunately for him he came off worse than my Liz. He was murdered. It happened in the woods near Southmead."

Stanley cast his mind back.

"Yes I do remember, Badock's Wood and if I remember they never found who did it. I am sorry sir, I had no idea."

Boyd had heard the last bit of the conversation and had turned white. He started to feel queasy and dizzy. All of a sudden he was sick over Terry Mason's drive and could hardly stand up.

Stanley ran over to Boyd to see what the matter was and saw that he was barely conscious.

Stanley turned to Terry Mason and apologised for what had happened and offered to clear up the mess on the drive.

Terry Mason waved them on saying that he would take care of it, and suggested he took the boy straight home.

Stanley parked the Hiab at the end of Boyd's road. The lorry was too wide to negotiate the narrow road where he lived.

"What's wrong with you Daniel, you look awful. You're not back on those stupid drugs are you?"

Daniel shook his head and rubbed his eyes. He was a pale looking boy at the best of times but now he looked positively ghost-like.

He was reeling with shock after finding out who Mr Mason was. For the first time the gravity of what he had instigated hit him. Over the past year he had put the murder of Ben Walker to the dark depths of the back of his mind and he'd not given the girl a second thought. But now things were different. He could see how sad her father was and the trouble he was going through to make life for his daughter bearable. For the first time Boyd felt ridden with guilt.

Stanley was concerned for him. He couldn't work out why one minute Daniel was fit and well and the next minute he was retching all over Mr Mason's immaculate driveway like a sick dog.

"Was it something you ate?" asked Stanley.

"Probably," murmured Boyd in a faint reply.

Boyd was having difficulty finding the strength to open the door of the cab. Geoff sat perfectly still between Boyd and Stanley. He was petrified that Boyd was going to be sick again. Stanley climbed down from the cab, walked round to the passenger side and opened the door for Boyd. His legs were shaking and he could hardly stand. Stanley helped him slowly climb down the step of the cab and walked him to his flat.

Boyd struggled to find his keys and eventually opened the door. Stanley helped him in and dropped him down onto his settee. He watched Boyd land like a sack of potatoes.

"You look ghastly, why don't I call the doctor?"

Boyd shook his head and said nothing, Stanley was reluctant to leave him but needed to get back to work, there were more deliveries to be made and with his wing man down it would be just him and Geoff taking care of things for the rest of the day.

"OK Daniel, I'll make you a sugary mug of tea and then I'm going to have to get back to work."

Boyd nodded as Stanley went to the kitchen and made a brew.

He returned a few minutes later with the milky sweet drink and handed it to Boyd.

Stanley waited until Boyd had finished the mug, and saw that some colour had returned to his face. Boyd seemed a little brighter.

"I suggest you get yourself to bed and see how you are in the morning. I'll warn Mr Jarrett that you may not be in work tomorrow."

Boyd nodded and made his way to his bedroom.

Stanley left Boyd to sleep and made his way back to the Hiab. He wondered what had come over the young man. He'd not made the connection between Terry Mason's mention of the murder in the woods and Boyd's sudden and violent reaction.

The past was beginning to catch up with Daniel Boyd.

CHAPTER FIFTY FOUR

Maria's flat
7.15pm
Sunday 9th October

Maria had enjoyed a relaxing weekend. She'd spent time with a few of her new mum friends she'd made at Joe Jingles. Christopher had played with his little mates and was interacting well with other children.

He was picking up new words quickly and Maria was surprised how much he could say. It was far too early for him to string words together to make any sense, but he was learning the names of his friends, he had words for some of his toys, plus half a dozen other things

He had shown no signs of RMD for over a week.

Maria had bought a second hand metronome and set it ticking every night when Christopher slept. It seemed to be doing the trick.

Christopher was asleep in his cot and Maria could hear the ticking of the metronome over his baby monitor. There was something about the rhythmic 'tick – tick – tick' that she found comforting and could appreciate how it could help him get a good night's sleep.

The gentle ticking was beginning to make her feel sleepy, almost as if she was being hypnotised. She was tired after a busy weekend and the 'tick – tick – tick' was so relaxing. Her eyelids were becoming heavy, her thoughts were drifting elsewhere and she began to dream.

In her dream she could hear a drilling noise. The noise was getting louder and was becoming shrill. Suddenly she woke up to the sound of her phone which was ringing and vibrating on the lounge table. The vibration of the ringing phone was amplified as it resonated through the wooden table.

She awkwardly lurched for her phone and dropped it on the floor. It stopped ringing as it nestled into the carpet.

Maria scooped the phone from the floor and checked to see who had called.

Her heart skipped a beat as she saw that it had been Campbell. She assumed that he would leave a message and patiently waited for her messaging service to bleep to tell her she had voicemail.

But there was no message.

Why didn't he leave me a message? she thought.

Maria waited for him to call again, but he didn't.

"Bollocks, this is the twenty first century, what am I doing?" she said to herself and called him back.

"Hi Maria!"

She smiled as she heard his voice.

"Hi Campbell, sorry I couldn't pick up just now, where are you?"

"I'm back in Bristol, I landed yesterday afternoon."

They exchanged small talk for several minutes until Campbell posed the question that Maria had been hoping for.

"So Maria, I was wondering, when would be good for us to meet up?"

Maria felt like a teenager, she wanted to speak but her lips seem to be separated from her face and were beyond her control.

Eventually she spurted out "when's good for you?"

"I'm free this Friday, I was thinking we could get a bite to eat, I know a nice Italian restaurant, do you like Italian food?"

"Yes that sounds lovely, and Friday should be fine."

"Great, well that's a date, well not a date, but you know what I mean."

Maria giggled. She knew he was as nervous and tongue-tied as she.

He said he would call over at eight on Friday to pick her up.

Maria got straight on the phone to Samreen who was over the moon and offered to babysit Christopher.

Maria had the rest of the night to relax. She poured a large glass of Sauvignon Blanc and opened her laptop.

It had been a busy weekend and she'd not had time to check Facebook since Friday. She opened the browser and logged into her account to see what had been going on in the world during the past two days.

As the distinctive blue and white social media site opened she saw that she'd had a friend request. Ignoring it, she scrolled through the various posts and status updates. It was the usual stuff.

'Share if you love your daughter'

'Share if you miss someone who was close to you'

She hated the gooey aspect of Facebook.

She scrolled through various pictures of her friends' Sunday lunches and enough selfies to sink a ship.

Maria yawned as she was about to close the lid on her laptop before she remembered that she had received a friend request.

She clicked the little icon at the top of the screen and felt a chill run through her body when she saw who had sent it.

It was from Rob. The man who was the father of her son.

Frozen, she sat in front of her computer screen.

CHAPTER FIFTY FIVE

Jarrett's Builders Merchant
8.30am
Monday 10th October

Daniel Boyd returned to work for the first time since his sickness episode the previous Monday. He didn't need to see a doctor as he knew very well what had made him ill.

He'd spent the last week moping around his flat and feeling sorry for himself.

At one point, the guilt which was eating into his soul almost pushed him into turning himself over to the police, but that notion didn't last very long.

He'd spent the week alone. He'd had no visitors and, other than Stanley, he'd had no phone calls. Stanley was the only person who showed any concern for him. Boyd liked him. Although they were not friends in the true manner of the word, Stanley was the closest thing to a friend.

Boyd had resisted the urge to go out and score drugs and, other than a bottle of cheap wine he had at home, he'd not had a drink.

What occurred to him during that past week was that he was entirely on his own. He had no one to turn to and no one, other than Stanley, cared about him.

He'd spent the last six day's wallowing in self-pity and considering the implications of what he'd done.

Coming face to face with Liz Mason's father had been the catalyst which sparked the first embers of guilt that were slowly burning inside him.

Before now he'd never felt remorse for any of his actions.

All the people he'd fought, stolen from, abused, angered and ridiculed, had never left him with a pang of guilt. But now he was different, and he didn't know whether he liked the new Daniel Boyd.

The guilt he was feeling was because of what had happened to Liz and not the death of Ben. This was peculiar as he had not laid a finger on the girl, she'd happened to be in the wrong place at the wrong time. But with Ben, there had been a motive for his murder and he'd gone out of his way to end Ben's life, and because of that he felt no remorse.

As he walked around the builders merchant that morning, no one asked him how he was feeling. Colin Jarrett nodded at him and handed him a clipboard of orders that needed to be packed for delivery. Stanley had the day off and Geoff hardly said a word to him.

He wandered around in auto pilot mode, packing orders and loading lorries until it was time to go home for another lonely night in front of the television.

CHAPTER FIFTY SIX

Maria's flat
7.15pm
Wednesday 12th October

Maria had taken a few days to consider Rob's friend request on Facebook. She hadn't yet responded and wasn't sure why he wanted to befriend her.

She had written him out of her life and didn't want him to have anything to do with Christopher. She'd done alright up until now without him and had been pretty certain she could continue without him in her life.

But since he'd sent her the request, and seeing the little thumbnail picture of him, it had made her think about him.

She logged onto Facebook and ignored the request that was still hanging at the top of the page.

There was a new notification. She'd received a message from someone. She clicked the link and gulped as her heart skipped a beat. It was from Rob. She read the message.

Hi Maria, this is Rob. I hope you and our baby are OK and I hope you don't mind me sending you this message.

I've been thinking about you recently and regret what I've done. I shouldn't have left you and looking back, I don't know what I was thinking. I hope you can forgive me.

I bumped into Sean from Westhouse last week and he said that you were looking good and that I should say hello, so here I am saying hello.

Could we meet up at some point as I would love to see the baby and catch up with you?

You never know, we may get things going again?

Look forward to hearing from you,

Love Rob

And that was his message.

Maria read it, and read it again.

She was confused and didn't know what to do. She had made her mind up a long time ago to make her way in life without him and that was based upon the assumption that he wouldn't resurface. But now he was back her mind was changing.

She needed time to think about what to do, and what she really needed was to talk it over with someone.

She copied the message and dropped it into an email and sent it to Samreen to see what she thought and then called her mother.

Claire's response was exactly as Maria had expected.

"Don't go anywhere near the pig," was Claire's reaction.

Maria knew her mother was right as she'd only end up with a broken heart, for a second time from the same man.

Samreen was quick to reply to Maria's email and her response was much the same as her mother's.

,

Think with your head and not with your heart. The man's a rat and he always will be.

Why don't you reply and make out how rosy life isn't now you have a child. Tell him about all the hard work you have to do, tell him about the end of your social life and mention Christopher's head banging.

Then see how keen he is to be back in your life with the responsibility of looking after a young child.

Take care
Samreen
xxxx

Maria could always rely on her best friend for sound advice. She decided to reply to Rob's email and spin a few white lies to test the man's mettle.

She sat at her computer and composed a reply.

Rob,
I must admit I am surprised to hear from you after such a long time.

I'm a bit too busy to consider meeting up at the moment, but would not rule it out altogether.

The baby, my little boy doing OK(ish). My life has turned upside down since he was born and it is a struggle to balance everything to fit around him. Being a single 'working' mum is very demanding and I don't get very much time for socialising.

He is currently seeing a paediatrician in London as he suffers badly from RMD, but I am hopeful he will be OK.

Anyway, enough about me, what have you been doing for the last two years?
Maria

She hit send and closed her laptop.

CHAPTER FIFTY SEVEN

Bottelinos Italian Restaurant
Bristol
7.30pm
Friday 14th October

Campbell picked Maria up by taxi at seven thirty. He'd decided not to drive. He had been a little anxious about his evening with her and he knew he would need a wine or two to ease his nerves.

He was wearing jeans, an open necked shirt and a waist coat. This was the first time she had seen him wearing something other than the Coaster's uniform and noticed how handsome he looked when casually dressed.

She wore a green flowing floral dress down to her knees and a small sage green cropped cardigan. Her tousled red hair fell over her shoulders. Campbell thought she looked stunning.

Campbell passed her the wine list and was surprised when her favourite wine was the same as his. He ordered a bottle of Sauvignon Blanc.

They enjoyed each other's company and got on well. She helped him briefly forget the horrible few weeks he'd been through since the death of his father.

She asked him about his past. He'd recently finished a three year PhD in Computer Science and was working at Coaster's temporarily until a job in software engineering came up.

He'd been in a long term relationship when he was a student, but unfortunately the intensity of his studies made the couple become distant, both by location and in love and their relationship had eventually fizzled out.

He asked about her. She told him about her childhood, her job, her ex Rob and why she was a single parent. She didn't tell him that Rob had recently been back in touch.

He was a good listener and Maria felt at ease in his company. She found it hard to keep her eyes off him. There was a definite spark between them.

Campbell asked about Christopher, and Maria told him about his head banging and how it had got worse. She told him about Rhythmic Motion Disorder. He listened intently as she told him about her visit to the doctor and Esther Hall.

By the time they had finished their meal it was nine forty five and the evening had flown by. They enjoyed each other's company.

Samreen was babysitting and Maria promised her that she would be home by ten. Samreen had to be up early for work the next day so didn't want to stay up too late. This suited Maria as she had no idea how her evening would turn out, and if it had been a disaster then she had a good excuse for getting out of there. Fortunately the night had gone well, and Maria would've loved to have spent more time with Campbell.

Campbell called for a taxi as Maria finished the last of her wine. She hoped he had enjoyed the evening as much as she, as she would love spend more time with him. Who knows where it could lead?

The taxi pulled up outside Maria's flat followed by an awkward moment. Campbell was shy and wasn't sure whether he should kiss her goodnight, whilst she sat in silence waiting for something to happen. She couldn't stand waiting any longer and punctuated the uncomfortable moment by asking him in for coffee.

She hadn't planned on it, it just happened. However well the evening had gone her intention was to have the meal, go home and decide whether she would like to see him again. She didn't expect to ask him back to her flat.

"If you don't mind, I would love to."

Maria caught the eye of the taxi driver in the rear view mirror and he quickly looked the other way. Even though she couldn't see his face, she could tell that he was smiling.

Campbell paid the fare and the taxi pulled away.

Maria fumbled for her keys and dropped her purse spilling loose change onto the pavement. Her nervous excitement was getting the better of her.

He knelt down and helped her pick up the coins. Her hair brushed against his face and he could smell her shampoo. She smiled at him and he smiled back.

And then he kissed her.

It wasn't a long embracing kiss, not like in the movies, it was more of a clumsy peck, which ended up half on her lips and half on the side of her face.

It didn't matter, Maria's heart fluttered, no matter how awkward his attempt to kiss her had been.

She stood up and opened the door. Samreen was standing in the hall waiting for Maria. She had heard the sound of the door opening and was desperate to find out how the evening had gone. She was surprised to see Campbell, as Maria had told Samreen that no matter how well the evening went she wouldn't be bringing him home for the night.

The night must have gone very well thought Samreen.

"Would you like me to make coffee?" offered Campbell. He knew the girls would want a few minutes to chat together.

"That would be great," said Maria. She asked Samreen if she would like to join them for a drink.

Samreen shook her head with a cheeky grin.

"No thanks, I'll leave you guys to it. I need to be up early in the morning."

Campbell brought two mugs of coffee into the lounge. He had made two cappuccinos.

"How did you know I'd like a cappuccino?" said Maria.

"Duh," said Samreen, "he does work in your favourite coffee shop."

Maria walked with Samreen to the front door. They stood on the step and chatted for a few minutes before Samreen kissed her on the cheek and whispered in her ear "You dirty hussy." Maria gave her a look as if she was offended, then giggled.

"I'll call you tomorrow."

"You'd better do," said Samreen as she walked to her car.

Maria closed the door and nervously turned and walked to the lounge where she found Campbell perched on the edge of the settee.

It had been a long time since she'd been on her own with a man and she'd never invited someone back to her house after a first date. She had no idea what should happen next. As much as she liked him, she wasn't going to start rolling around on the floor with him like a desperate teenager. Their conversation had flowed in the restaurant but now things were different and neither of them knew what to say.

"Nice cappuccino," she said.

"Thanks, I've had a bit of practice."

Maria had a little cappuccino making device in her kitchen and he had struggled with it as it was very different to the one he used at Coaster's.

As the conversation began to flow, they both felt more comfortable. They sat back on the settee and her arm brushed against his.

They were talking about 'things' when a familiar sound returned over Christopher's baby monitor.

"Ughh ughh ughh ughh ughh ughh ughh ughh," and then a pause.

"Ughh ughh ughh ughh ughh ughh ughh ughh," and then another pause.

"Ughh ughh ughh ughh ughh ughh ughh ughh," and then a pause.

Christopher had started again. It had been a few weeks since he'd banged his head and he sure chose a bad night to start up again.

Campbell looked at Maria awkwardly as he listened to Christopher chant and bang his head.

"Would you like me to stay, or would you rather be on your own?"

Maria hardly knew him but she didn't want to be on her own right now. She knew how bad Christopher could get and would appreciate someone being with her, and Campbell was that someone.

"I'll go and see him, you wait here for a minute and hopefully I can get him to stop."

But she couldn't. He was fast asleep and totally unaware of what he was doing. Banging and crashing around in his cot, chanting and grunting.

But this time his chanting sounded different.

CHAPTER FIFTY EIGHT

The Awareness

The Awareness stirred after several weeks of inactivity. It had been building its strength after its last awakening which had drained it.

Still having no concept of time, it carried on from where it had left off.

It had learnt so much. It knew its name, it knew when it was alive it had been male, he even knew he had been a policeman and the important thing he knew was that he'd been murdered.

But where was he now? Was he in some kind of limbo? If it was heaven or hell it was certainly a let down.

Memories were all he had. He concentrated on his memories of Liz and remembered how much he'd loved her when he was alive and how he still loved her now.

Every time he remembered their kiss, the memory segued seamlessly to when he had been killed. The memory intrigued and saddened him. He had recalled the memory of the boy holding the rock many times before, but he was unable to work out who he was.

By now he was able to recall the names of those who had been close to him. He remembered the names of his parents, his brother Michael, many of his friends and of course Liz. But the name of the boy who had dropped the rock eluded him.

Whoever his killer had been was most likely still alive. Perhaps he'd been caught and was imprisoned for what he had done, or he could still be free and killing others.

The more he thought about the killer and the others who had attacked Liz, the more he thought he was in limbo. He didn't imagine eternity to be like this. He was trapped in solitary confinement. He considered himself to be a good person and didn't understand why he'd ended up in a place like this to spend eternity. It didn't make sense.

Perhaps he was in limbo for a reason. If his killer had never been caught then his memories could be the only evidence.

Maybe there was a way he could get a message out about his death? But how? He was frustrated and had no way of communicating.

It was as if he was on a conveyor belt, going round and round unable to get anywhere. He was angry. He only wanted to be heard, he had to get his message across and the more he thought about it the angrier he became. The anger felt real, just as if he were alive. It bubbled and stewed and was poisoning his soul. The anger was creating energy. It was a new energy he'd not sensed before. As anger consumed him the new energy force became stronger and stronger until he could bear it no longer. Whatever this new energy was, it was hurting and he could feel real pain.

The energy force reached a climax and he did something he thought was impossible.

He screamed at the top of his voice.

CHAPTER FIFTY NINE

Maria's flat
10.45pm
Friday 14th October

Campbell sat alone in the lounge sipping his coffee. He could hear Maria over the baby monitor trying to settle Christopher.

Maria placed him back in his cot and Christopher lay still for a few seconds. Slowly he opened his mouth, screwed up his tired eyes and let out a most hideous scream. The scream went on and on.

Maria covered her ears as she helplessly watched her son screaming at the very top of his voice.

He was screaming until the last of the air in his lungs had gone.

Afterwards he lay in his cot, silent and still.

Campbell ran into Christopher's room.

"What's happening?" he asked as he came through the door.

"I don't know sobbed Maria, my son's just not normal." She threw her arms around Campbell, buried her head into his shoulder and cried.

Campbell had never heard a noise like it from a child. It sounded like a primal scream which went on and on.

Maria turned to Christopher. He lay quietly and slept. He looked peaceful. Other than his chest rising and dropping he was perfectly still.

"What on earth *was* that?" said Maria.

Campbell had no idea and decided it was best not to answer.

Maria stroked Christopher's head, covered him and made him comfortable.

His scream was ringing in her ears and she couldn't get it out of her head. It sounded as if it had come from someone else, not her baby boy. How on earth could her son have created such a blood curdling sound? It didn't seem possible that a thirteen month old child would have had the ability to do such a thing. It sounded so 'grown up'.

Campbell thought about what he'd just heard. Christopher's scream sounded like someone yelling as they fell to their death from the top of a building.

Both of them stood over his cot and watched him sleep without saying a word.

Maria tapped Campbell on the shoulder and indicated that they should leave Christopher on his own.

They sat together in the lounge without talking.

Then the head banging started again. But this time it was different. Much different.

CHAPTER SIXTY

The Awareness

He was shocked at what he'd just done and felt better for doing it. He had just screamed at the top of his voice. But how could this be as he had no voice? But even so, it had seemed so real that he was certain he could hear it. And the pain, he had felt pain when he could no longer sustain the scream.

He thought about what he'd just done and wondered if he could do it again. His energy was fading and he didn't have the strength to try.

He was sure that what he'd just learnt to do was important. It had allowed him to vent his anger and this made him feel better.

He recalled the last memory of him and Liz kissing at the bottom of the hill and again the memory seamlessly carried on until his life ended.

He needed to be heard. He wanted someone, anyone, to hear his voice. He started a little four word mantra with his thoughts. Slowly, one by one each word appeared in his mind.

Please – Hear – My – Voice.

And again,

Please – Hear – My – Voice.

And again,

Please – Hear – My – Voice.

And again,

Please – Hear – My – Voice.

Repeating the four words over and over in his thoughts made him feel good. It almost made him happy.

As he repeated the words he visualised the last seconds before he died. The happy feeling instantly changed to anger again. The same anger he'd felt when he screamed.

He recalled the memory of his death and recited the four words in his thoughts. The more he repeated them, the angrier he became.

Again the anger was creating energy, the same energy as when he screamed.

Just as before, the anger developed into a bitter poison which burnt like acid. The angrier he was the more intense the four words became.

Please – Hear – My – Voice, Please – Hear – My – Voice, Please – Hear – My – Voice, Please – Hear – My – Voice, Please – Hear – My – Voice.

Now he couldn't stop. The anger felt good and repeating the four words felt even better. It was almost joyous.

Please – Hear – My – Voice, Please – Hear – My – Voice, Please – Hear – My – Voice, Please – Hear – My – Voice, Please – Hear – My – Voice. Please – Hear – My – Voice, Please – Hear – My – Voice, Please – Hear – My – Voice, Please – Hear – My – Voice, Please – Hear – My – Voice.

CHAPTER SIXTY ONE

Maria's flat
11.02pm

"I think it might be best if I go," said Campbell with a solemn voice.

"Please don't," replied Maria with an air of desperation.

"Would you mind staying a little longer? I'm a bit shaken after what has happened and I wouldn't mind your company."

Campbell nodded and put his hand on hers.

And then it started. Christopher was banging his head and chanting. But this time it was different. His tone was different and he wasn't chanting the usual 'ughh ughh ughh ughh ughh ughh ughh ughh'.

He was repeating a rhythmic four beat chant and it sounded completely different to 'ughh'. Each bit of the chant sounded different.

Maria stared at the monitor as if she was looking at her son.

"This isn't the same, he's never made this noise before."

Campbell didn't answer. He strained as he listened.

Over the monitor his voice sounded thin and tinny. Maria quietly stood up and motioned to Campbell to follow.

They crept out to the hall and across to his room. Maria slowly pushed his door open and watched from the edge of the room. Campbell stood behind her in the hall.

It was as if he was singing a little monosyllabic song as he banged his head.

"Get your phone, film him before he stops," whispered Campbell, "You may need to play this to the health visitor."

Maria nodded and crept back to the lounge and returned with her phone.

Christopher's room was dark and the little lens on her phone wasn't picking up a very clear image. Maria turned the bedroom light up a little.

The video may not be picking up a very clear image, but it was recording the sound of his chanting.

Maria put her phone down so she could pick him up. She tried to wake him, but he continued to chant as he banged his head against her shoulder.

"What should I do?" whispered Maria.

Campbell was stuck for words.

"Perhaps you should let him sleep, he doesn't seem bothered by what he's doing."

Campbell was right, although Christopher was banging his head and chanting, he didn't seem distressed, not like he'd been when he was screaming.

She lay him back in his cot and let him carry on.

They returned to the lounge. Maria glanced at Campbell. He looked tired. This was the last thing he'd expected and, after the death of his father, it was probably the last thing he wanted.

"You can go if you want," she whispered.

"Not if you don't want me to."

She smiled and squeezed his hand.

They sat together in silence for over an hour and listened to Christopher as they held hands.

"Listen," whispered Campbell.

"What?"

Campbell put his finger to his lips and made a quick shushing sound.

He strained as he listened to Christopher's voice over the monitor. Campbell stood up and tiptoed to Christopher's room. Maria followed.

Campbell opened the door, walked over to cot and knelt down close to the little boy.

"What is it?" whispered Maria.

Again, Campbell signalled for her to be quiet.

"Listen," he whispered.

Maria listened, but she didn't know what she was supposed to be hearing.

"It's as if he's saying something."

Maria concentrated.

The four rhythmic noises he was repeating had begun to sound distinct. Together they crouched down and listened closely.

Maria grabbed her phone which she'd left by his cot and filmed him again.

After she'd turned her phone off she knelt even closer to her son.

"You're right, he's saying four words over and over."

Campbell nodded.

"He's barely a year old, what on earth can he be doing?"

Campbell shushed her again.

"That third bit of the chant, it sounds like he's saying meee."

"That's what he calls his favourite toy Misty," said Maria.

"Hang on, it's different to what he calls Misty, he's not saying 'meee', it sounds more like 'my'."

Campbell nodded.

"You're right, it does sound like 'my'."

They sat in silence for a few more minutes and were gobsmacked by the regularity and precise way he was chanting. Every third sound was definitely 'my'.

"That first noise he's making, it starts with a popping sound," said Maria.

"It sounds like 'p' or 'puu'."

Campbell nodded.

"And it's ending with a kind of 'eese' sound."

Maria closed her eyes and cleared her mind to concentrate on what she was hearing.

"He's saying 'peas'."

Campbell shook his head.

"I don't think he's saying peas, listen again."

They sat together on the bedroom floor focusing on the first noise of the sequence.

"There's a 'lu' in there, listen carefully" whispered Campbell.

"Where?"

"It's really faint, but it's right after the 'puu'."

And then Maria could hear it. A very faint 'lu' sound which came right after the 'puu'.

"It sounds like he's saying 'please'," she whispered.

Campbell nodded.

The more Christopher repeated, the clearer it became. It was like an aural version of a magic eye picture. The more they concentrated the clearer things became.

"That's two words we can hear, 'please' and 'my'," said Maria as she pushed her hair away from her face.

She was right. They could both hear 'please' followed by a less distinguished sound, followed by a crystal clear 'my' followed by another less distinguished sound. He repeated over and over without a break. He'd been chanting for over half an hour.

"How many words are in his vocabulary?" asked Campbell.

"I'm not sure, a good twenty or so."

"Let's go back to the lounge and have a chat."

Maria followed Campbell back to the lounge. Campbell shut the door and sat next to her on the settee.

"Tell me the words he can say."

Maria began to reel off the words in his vocabulary, "mee, that was his first word and it's what he calls his favourite toy."

Campbell nodded.

Maria looked towards the ceiling in an effort to remember.

"And he can say 'mama' and 'nana' and 'duck' and 'Sam'."

"Sam, who is Sam?" interrupted Campbell.

"Oh he's trying to say 'Samreen'."

Campbell nodded and Maria continued.

Maria recalled around twenty basic words. Most of them weren't proper words, but were more like attempts at words. He had tried to say the names of his friends from Joe Jingles, but could not pronounce any of them correctly.

"So he hasn't said 'please' or 'my' before?"

Maria shook her head.

"Nor strung together any words to make a sentence?"

Maria looked at him incredulously.

"Sentences? He's only thirteen months old."

Campbell shrugged his shoulders.

Christopher was still banging his head and chanting. They stopped talking and continued to listen.

"Would you like another coffee?" asked Campbell.

Maria smiled and nodded. Hers had gone cold.

Campbell disappeared into the kitchen and shut the door behind him. Maria listened to Christopher and wondered what on earth was going on. Sitting on her own, his odd repeating chant sounded haunting. It didn't even sound like his voice, it was as if it was from another child and although it sounded childlike, there was maturity in the intonation.

She paid attention to the fourth sound, or word, as she was certain he was saying words instead of a random chant. It sounded almost European, perhaps German or Austrian. Maria focused on his fourth word by blocking out the other three. It sounded like 'edelweiss'. There was no way he would be saying edelweiss, it was such a complicated word for a thirteen month old child who couldn't even properly say the name of his favourite toy.

Campbell came in with coffee.

"Listen," said Maria, "listen to the fourth word."

He placed the mugs on the table and put his ear to the monitor.

He closed his eyes and concentrated.

"What does that sound like?" said Maria.

"I'm not sure, it does sound like something."

"It sounds like he's saying edelweiss."

"Edelweiss?" asked Campbell, in a quizzical tone.

"That's what I think it sounds like".

Campbell listened again.

"I know what you mean, but I don't think he's saying edelweiss."

They listened together in silence.

"The first bit isn't a word," said Campbell. "It's the noise he's making as his head thumps the pillow."

Maria listened again and realised he was right.

"So, it sounds like he's saying 'weiss' or 'vice'?"

"Or 'voice'," added Campbell.

"Yes, voice, he could be saying 'voice'."

Maria was feeling tired. She was irritable and wished it would all just go away. She lay on the settee and closed her eyes.

Campbell let Maria sleep on the settee while he sat at the table in the lounge. It had been a strange evening. He knew Maria had appreciated his company and he was glad to be there for her.

Tiredness was enveloping him. He put his head in his arms and shut his eyes.

He woke to the sound of a radio. He was befuddled and didn't know where he was. Sitting up he rubbed his aching neck. He wasn't hearing a radio, it was Christopher and he was still head banging and chanting the same four words. He looked at his watch, it was just after one thirty in the morning. He had dozed off for a couple of hours.

Maria was sleeping on the settee with her back away from him. He debated what to do. He could call a taxi and be home in in half an hour, or he could wake her up so she could sleep in her bed and he could stretch out on the settee.

He was thinking about what to do when he noticed that Christopher's chant was different. The three words he and Maria had heard earlier in the evening were clearer and more pronounced. He was still repeating 'please', 'my' and 'voice', but there was a new word. The second sound, which at first had been a grunt had now become another clear and defined word. Christopher was saying 'ear' or 'hear'. Campbell put the four words together.

'Please', 'ear' or 'hear', 'my' and 'voice'.

Campbell's tired mind was making sense of what he was hearing.

'Please', 'Hear', 'My' and 'Voice'.

"Please hear my voice," Campbell quietly whispered the words.

"Please hear my voice." He repeated, but louder this time.

Christopher was repeating 'please hear my voice' and had been all night. Campbell gently woke Maria, doing his best not to alarm her.

"Maria, wake up," as he nudged her shoulder.

She was fast asleep and it was difficult to rouse her. He nudged her again and she stirred.

"Maria, wake up."

She rolled over, opened her eyes and looked at him.

She was confused and it took a few seconds to remember what had happened earlier that night.

"What's the time, what's happening?"

"It's OK, take your time."

He offered his hand to help her up from the settee. She swivelled her body and sat up.

"Listen to him."

Maria put her ear to the monitor, put her hand over her mouth and looked Campbell.

"Oh my God."

She looked towards the monitor and back to Campbell.

"What's happening? He's really talking."

In the few hours she'd been sleeping Christopher's chant had developed from something indistinct to four unmistakable words. When put together they made an understandable sentence.

He was thirteen months old and putting sentences together in his sleep. She listened to the tone of his voice, it didn't even sound like him. The voice sounded like someone who'd been here before.

A tear rolled down her cheek as the significance of what was happening hit her.

"My son is talking like a grown up."

Her bottom lip was quivering as she spoke.

"This isn't normal Campbell, what the hell is wrong with my son?"

She turned and threw her arms around him and he held her tightly and let her cry onto his shoulder. Without thinking he ran his fingers through her tousled hair.

"This can't just be Rhythmic Movement Disorder," said Maria in a weak voice.

"It must be something else."

Campbell didn't answer, he held her and said nothing.

Maria pulled away from Campbell and crept to Christopher's room.

She knew that trying to wake him would be pointless. Campbell came in and stood next to her. They watched in awe.

He ticked like a grandfather clock. His head lifted from the pillow and thudded down as he said 'please'. His head lifted again and briefly poised, hovering six inches over the pillow before it came to rest as he said the second word 'hear'. He repeated the same actions as he said the next two words, 'my' 'voice'.

As he finished each sequence he briefly rested as if he was regrouping to build up strength before starting the sequence again. He'd been doing it for over two hours.

"Film him again," said Campbell in a hushed but urgent tone.

"This isn't a fucking freak show," snapped Maria.

"Film him for the consultant in London you'd told me about, you need to let him see it."

Maria apologised for snapping. She was tired and very emotional.

Campbell was right. This needed to be documented.

"Turn up his light please."

Campbell turned the dimmer switch on the wall until the ceiling light was as bright as it could be.

Maria stood over the cot and videoed her son. She knelt down and filmed him through the slats of his cot. She filmed him banging his head and chanting from all angles until the video on her phone automatically stopped and saved the file.

A very strange bond had formed between Christopher Jameson and the deceased Ben Walker.

The instant Ben lost his life something happened.

When his physical body ceased to live and breathe his spiritual body transcended, but something prevented it from completing the journey.

Ben's spirit was captured within baby Christopher the second the child took his first breath, just before the umbilical cord had been severed. From that point, Ben had developed within Christopher, unknowingly drawing upon Christopher's resources to flourish and grow.

Two disparate souls living as one.

During the last year Ben had thrived within baby Christopher with nothing to draw on but the memories of his short life. At first, Ben's memories where brief snapshots, but over time they had developed and now he was able to recall them at will. He could rewind, pause and forward them. In the beginning the memories were vague, but now they were never faded or blurred. He had a chronological pictorial reference of almost all of his life.

Now he was using his influence upon the small boy who was his host.

Ben was becoming weak. He had been causing Christopher to bang his head and repeat those four words for such a long time his force was ebbing and he was slipping away, giving the child the break he desperately needed and the opportunity for proper uninterrupted sleep.

Ben would soon be back to continue where he had left off.

Campbell lowered the light and walked over to Maria.

She turned and looked at him through bloodshot eyes.

"Campbell, there's something terribly wrong with my son. This isn't normal."

1.58am

It was almost two o'clock in the morning and Christopher was lying still. Maria rolled him over and put her hand on his chest. His heart was beating fast and his breathing was laboured.

Within a few minutes his breathing and heartbeat settled and he was gently snoring.

He looked peaceful as if nothing had happened.

She stayed with him until it was almost three o'clock, holding his hand and keeping a watchful eye over him. Overcome by tiredness she let go of his hand and left him to sleep.

Campbell was sleeping on the settee. She took a blanket and a pillow from her room and made him comfortable, kissed him on his forehead and touched his face.

Leaving him in the lounge she trudged to her bedroom, took off her floral dress and fell face down on her bed.

At ten past eight Maria was woken by a gentle knock on her bedroom door. Campbell had woken to the sound of Christopher chatting over the baby monitor which Maria had forgotten to take to her room.

He decided not to go into Christopher's room as the sight of a stranger would probably frighten him.

He slowly opened Maria's door and gently called her.

Maria quickly sat up and pulled her duvet up to her neck.

"Sorry to call you, but Christopher's awake."

It took a few seconds for Maria to remember what had happened during the night.

"Is he OK?"

"He sounds OK, but I've not been into his room, I thought I'd leave that to you."

Maria smiled and Campbell left her bedroom and shut the door behind him.

A minute later Maria emerged from her room wearing jeans and a sweatshirt. Campbell noticed that first thing in the morning even after a terrible night's sleep, she still looked great.

"I'll go and get him, would you like to make yourself some breakfast?"

Campbell nodded.

"Would you like something from the kitchen?"

"Coffee and toast would be great."

Campbell disappeared into the kitchen and Maria went to get her son.

Christopher was smiling and happy to see his mum. She picked him up and hugged him.

He seemed to be showing no ill effects from the previous night's ordeal, he was bonnier and more awake than both his mother and Campbell.

She carried him into the lounge and sat him next to her on the settee. The smell of toast wafted in from the kitchen.

Christopher looked perplexed and called for Misty.

"Meee, meee, meee."

Campbell came in with coffee and toast for the two of them and put the tray on the lounge table.

"Campbell, could you pop into his bedroom and get his little grey cat from the cot please?"

Campbell nodded, came back with Misty and handed it to Christopher.

Christopher smiled and started chattering to himself.

Campbell remembered how clear and distinct those four words had become during the night and how different he was now. Christopher was chattering the early words you would expect from a thirteen month old child. 'Mama, Nana' and the rest. Surely there was no way he could have been repeating that chant last night, he didn't have the vocabulary.

Maria handed Christopher to Campbell.

"Would you mind staying with Christopher? I just need to warm some milk for him."

Christopher happily bounced on Campbell's knee and tried to reach for his hair.

One word Christopher hadn't yet learnt was 'dada'. He didn't need to know it, at least not for now.

The microwave pinged and Maria came back with his milk.

"Would you like to feed him?"

Campbell smiled and took the bottle. He'd never fed a baby before, but he slipped into the role effortlessly. Christopher lay with the back of his head against Campbell's arm and happily drank the milk.

"You're a natural," said Maria.

Maria thought about Rob. He'd not responded to the email she'd sent him a couple of days earlier. It didn't surprise her. She knew that just the mention of life being less than a walk in the park would scare him off.

Campbell was gentle with Christopher. The two of them looked perfect together.

She dismissed the thought. Last night had been their first date, and it was never a real date, just a meal. But already she was getting gooey about him. She'd been getting gooey ever since she first saw him in the coffee shop.

Christopher finished his milk.

"Do I need to wind him or anything?"

"No, just put him down, he'll be OK."

Campbell propped him up with a cushion on the corner of the settee and held his hands either side of him in case he toppled over.

"He's fine," said Maria, "he's thirteen months old and not a baby, and you'd be surprised how tough he is."

Christopher happily sat next to Campbell on the settee clutching Mee.

Maria looked serious as she turned to Campbell.

"So what did you make of last night?"

He assumed she was referring to Christopher and not their night out.

"I really don't know."

"You said that you banged your head when you were little, did you do anything like that, I mean the chanting and what not?"

"Not that I know of. I'm calling my mum this afternoon, I'll ask her. See what she remembers."

Maria picked up her phone and played the video clip.

They both felt goosebumps as Christopher's voice crackled over the tiny speaker.

"Please hear my voice - Please hear my voice - Please hear my voice - Please hear my voice."

Maria stopped the clip and put down her phone. The horror of last night came rushing back. Discussing it was one thing, but seeing and hearing it again, was another.

"What are you going to do?" asked Campbell.

Maria shook her head as she pushed the phone away from her.

"I don't know. The doctors have proved useless."

"What about the child health visitor, what was her name?"

"Esther, her name is Esther Hall."

"Doesn't she know some hot shot in London?"

Maria was impressed with how much Campbell had remembered about their conversation in the restaurant.

"I think you should send her that clip and see what she says. I reckon she'd want to forward it to the hot shot."

He was right. Maria decided that she would email the video to Esther later in the morning.

She turned to him and asked what he was doing for the rest of the day. Campbell had a shift at the coffee shop starting at one and had a few things to do before he started work.

"I'll tell you what. Have a shower, sort yourself out and I'll drop you home."

"No need for that, I can get a bus."

"Forget that, I'll drive you home, unless you're nervous about lady drivers?"

Campbell accepted her offer and made his way to her bathroom.

Fifteen minutes later he came back looking fresher. Maria asked if he could keep an eye on Christopher whilst she took a shower.

She was drying off in her bedroom with her door slightly opened. She stopped and listened to the two of them playing in the lounge. Quickly she slipped her clothes on and peeked through the open door.

Campbell was oblivious and didn't know she was watching. He was lying on the floor, at Christopher's level and was teasing him with the toy cat. Christopher was giggling with delight. Christopher looked up and saw Maria by the door.

"Mama!"

He sat up with his arms out. Campbell was embarrassed by being caught playing with Christopher. Maria smiled.

"I'm sorry to break up the party, but this little man needs a bath."

Campbell sat on his own and read yesterday's paper. He could hear Maria and Christopher in the bathroom. His delightful giggle made Campbell smile.

Despite the strange twist at the end of the night, he felt relaxed in Maria's company. Something about her put him at ease. He hoped she felt the same about him.

Maria came into the lounge with Christopher to find Campbell with his feet up, reading the paper and listening to the radio.

"I see someone's made them self at home."

Campbell dropped the paper and sat up. She had a knack of catching him out.

"Would you mind entertaining him again? I would like to fire off an email to the child health visitor and attach the video clip I made last night."

Campbell gladly took Christopher and they played happily on the settee.

Maria switched on her computer, connected her phone and loaded the clip.

She had already sent one clip of Christopher head banging a couple of days earlier. She'd had one reply from Esther saying she'd forward it to her consultant colleague but had heard nothing since.

Maria composed a brief message explaining the events of the previous night, attached the video file and pressed send.

She closed the lid, turned to Campbell and said it was time for him to go home.

"Come on, chop chop, let's get you in the car."

Campbell wondered whether he'd overstayed his welcome.

Maria had a busy day ahead and needed to get a move on. She wasn't used to visitors staying and he had been the first man to spend the night since Rob. It broke her routine and she was finding it hard to get motivated.

She stopped outside his flat and left the engine running to signify she wouldn't be coming in. He was about to say something but stopped, as she put her finger over his lips to shush him. Leaning toward him she made the first move and kissed him on the lips. Christopher giggled from the back of the car. They stopped kissing and smiled.

"I guess that's my cue to leave."

Maria nodded.

Campbell climbed out of the car and closed the door.

Maria wound down the window and leant over to the passenger side.

"Despite what happened last night, I did enjoy it."

Campbell was about to speak, but Maria stopped him.

"Before you say anything, I would like to see you again, but I'll call you if you don't mind. I'm worried about my son and I need to put him first."

Campbell nodded. He understood. He knew if he was to see her again, he would need to be patient.

Luckily for Campbell, he wouldn't need to wait very long.

CHAPTER SIXTY TWO

Esther Hall's home
10.50am
Saturday 15th October

Esther was a terrible workaholic. Today was her first Saturday off in three months and she'd promised her husband that there would be no talk of work, or anything related to it for the whole weekend. She'd agreed they'd spend the day shopping for a new kitchen. Something her husband was keen to get on with, but couldn't do much about unless she was present.

However, she did have to send a very quick email to her boss, and assured him she'd be off the computer in five minutes.

"Go and get the car out of the garage and I'll be with you before you know it."

Bob sighed and went out to unlock the garage door.

Esther logged into her email account and saw the new message from Maria. She hesitated, but her curiosity was getting the better of her. She noticed the message had an attachment.

"Oh bollocks," she whispered as she clicked the message.

She skim read the message, which said something about Christopher's head banging getting worse before clicking the attachment.

The file was large and it was taking time to download.

She stuck her head around the front door and indicated to Bob, who was waiting in the car, that she would be two minutes. He rolled his eyes and tapped his watch.

Esther sat at her computer and impatiently waited for the file to download. Eventually the clip started to play. The images where grainy, but she could clearly see it was Maria's little boy banging his head. She wondered why Maria had sent the email. The head banging was less violent than it was in the earlier clip.

Esther was watching it with the sound on mute. She pulled the slider icon on her computer back to the start so the clip played again from the beginning and this time had the audio turned up to seventy five percent.

And then she heard it. At first she thought it must be something else. As she watched the footage the more it became apparent that the little boy was talking. But it wasn't like baby talk, it was proper adult talk. It didn't sound like a child's voice.

"Please hear my voice - Please hear my voice - Please hear my voice - Please hear my voice - Please hear my voice - Please hear my voice - Please hear my voice - Please hear my voice - Please hear my voice - Please hear my voice - Please hear my voice - Please hear my voice."

Esther closed the lid on computer. She was totally shocked. In all the years she had been working with children, she'd never seen, or heard, anything like it.

She left the house and got in the car with her husband.

"Are you OK love?"

Esther nodded. Because of confidentiality she could not disclose to Bob what she'd just seen.

"You look very pale, are you sure?"

"I'm fine, just drive."

Bob reversed the car onto the road and was just about to pull away when he noticed Esther had left the front door of their house wide open.

He pulled over onto the pavement, got out and locked the house. He got back in, looked at his wife and shook his head.

They spent the day looking around kitchen showrooms, but Esther couldn't concentrate on anything other than what she'd watched on her computer. Surely that wasn't for real? Was Christopher really saying those words?

Bob pulled over at a garage for petrol, filled up and walked to the kiosk to pay. Esther could see there was a large queue at the till. She had just enough time to make a quick call to Maria. She was desperate to speak with her.

She reached for her mobile and called Maria. She was diverted to voicemail. Esther sighed and left a message.

'Hello Maria, this is Esther, Esther Hall. I've watched the video clip and would like to have a word. Please call me as soon as you get this message.' She flipped the lid on her phone and slipped it into her handbag, just as Bob returned to the car.

"Who were you talking to?"

"Oh, no one, it was one of those stupid sales calls."

"Good, as long as it wasn't work."

They returned home after a fruitless day of window shopping and picking up brochures. Bob was grumpy. He wanted to have come home with a deposit down on a new kitchen, but it wasn't to be, and he knew why. It was Esther, she had work on her mind…..again.

She'd felt guilty about spoiling their first weekend together in months. He was sitting in the lounge with a face as long as a fiddle. She came in with a peace offering and handed him a glass of beer and kissed him on his receding hair line. Bob tried his best attempt at smiling, but failed. Instead he lifted his glass to signify gratitude. Esther switched on the television for him and left him alone while she prepared a light tea.

She was busying herself in the kitchen when she heard her phone ring. The phone was in her bag, which was hanging at the bottom of the stairs.

"Phone's ringing," she heard Bob call from the front room.

She grabbed it from her bag and saw it was Maria.

"Hi Maria, thanks for calling back, I can't speak for long."

They spoke in depth about what had happened during the night. The call lasted almost an hour.

Esther brought in their food and placed it on the coffee table.

"I've been waiting so long my sandwiches are cold," joked Bob, but Esther didn't smile and he knew it was to do with work and he also knew it must be something serious.

Esther had asked Maria for permission to forward the video to her consultant colleague in London. She needed Dr Peter Phelps' opinion on what was happening with Christopher as it was out of her league. She hoped that he would want to be involved.

The first video she forwarded to him probably wouldn't have interested him too much. It was pretty much standard Rhythmic Movement Disorder, albeit very severe. But this second clip was different, completely different.

Many children talk in their sleep. It was something she'd come across many times, but she needed advice on what was happening with Christopher, and she needed specialist advice. She was grateful to be acquainted with Phelps, even though he wasn't always the easiest of people to get on with.

Phelps was Britain's leading researcher in Paediatric Sleep Disorders and had been for over ten years. He'd spent his time researching sleep terrors, sleep paralysis and somnambulism but was particularly keen on advancing research on both Rhythmic Movement Disorder and sleep talking.

Esther hoped that Christopher's case would interest Phelps enough to be involved.

Esther and Bob cleared away the dishes. She was happy for her husband to be sucked into the vortex of Saturday night, brain numbing television. He was easily drawn in by the myriad of talent, quiz and family entertainment shows which she hated.

She left him to vegetate in front of the TV while she disappeared to the study to compose an email to send to Peter Phelps.

She needn't have worried about what to write. The video clip was enough to get his attention. It didn't take long for Phelps to spring into action.

CHAPTER SIXTY THREE

Hampstead, London
10.09am
Sunday 16th October

Peter Phelps climbed out of the bath, grabbed a towel and dried off. He caught sight of himself in the full length bathroom mirror and hated what he saw.

Phelps was fifty one years old, short and round. He had an equally round balding head. He could be grumpy, evasive and short-tempered but on the other hand he had a compassionate and understanding nature. He was born in Australia and even though he moved to England when he was fifteen, he had never lost his accent.

He put on his 'slouching around Sunday' clothes and went downstairs to the kitchen. His wife, Jean, was sitting in the kitchen diner reading the Sunday papers and eating cereal. He kissed her and poured a glass of orange juice.

He considered himself a lucky man to have Jean. Even after twenty five years of marriage and knowing her for more than thirty, she still looked as gorgeous as the day he'd first set eyes on her. He had no idea why she was ever interested in him, but had stopped questioning it years ago and accepted that she must be mad.

He was a man with little self-esteem but one who excelled in his work.

They had not been able to have a family due to Peter being diagnosed with testicular cancer in his early twenties. He had been successfully treated, but had been left infertile.

They had adopted two boys shortly after they were married. The boys were now young men. Andrew lived with them whilst Colin was at university studying Medicine.

Because Peter couldn't have kids of his own he'd wanted a career helping children. He always believed that children were the future and wanted to be involved with their development. At the age of twenty four he graduated as a doctor. His medical career quickly led him down the path to become a paediatric doctor which eventually introduced him to working with children with sleep disorders.

His research over the past ten years had made new discoveries into why children suffered sleep deprivation and what could be done to help them.

He joined his wife for breakfast. She passed him the newspaper while she read the entertainment section of the Sunday supplements.

Peter Phelps worked seven days a week, fifty two weeks a year and that's the way he liked it. Jean knew that any holiday spent with her husband would include him bringing a briefcase full of non-confidential paperwork and making at least three phone calls a day.

She was used to it. In return, his hard work had bought them a more than modest five bedroom home in Hampstead Village, two Mercedes and a holiday home in Dorset. Not that the two of them spent much time there, he was too busy working. Jean enjoyed spending time with her sister at the holiday home in the Canford Cliffs area of Poole.

After breakfast Peter checked his email. He deleted the ever increasing spam that was filling up his inbox and filtered out the wheat from the chaff.

He saw the email from Esther. He didn't know her very well, but had been grateful for the information she had provide over the past few years which had helped with his research. He had met her at a conference the previous year and had been impressed by her dedication to work.

He'd already received an email from her a few days earlier and watched the video clip of the young boy violently head banging during his sleep. It was something he'd seen several times during his research into Rhythmic Movement Disorder. He appreciated her sending it, but it wasn't earth shattering. He'd filed the video on his computer in a folder called 'rmd standard stuff'.

He opened the email and read her single line of text.

Peter, please watch. I've never seen anything like it. Esther.

Peter opened the attachment and waited for it to load.

The server was slow that morning and it was taking an age to open. He strolled to the kitchen to refill his coffee and slowly walked back with a cold slice of toast in his other hand. He put down the coffee just as the file had downloaded.

He pressed the play icon and sat back.

He watched the entire three minute video clip whilst holding the toast to his mouth. He put the toast back on the plate and played the clip again, and again, and again.

Over the years he'd seen children talk in their sleep and he'd seen them make strange grunts and groans associated with Rhythmic Movement Disorder, but never had he heard a child as young as this talking in such a way during sleep.

The little boy's voice was not only saying things that were way beyond his age, it was the tone of his voice that was so strange. Peter did not believe in reincarnation but it sounded like this boy was speaking as an adult, or if not an adult, someone at least ten years older than the child appeared to be.

He brought up Esther's email form earlier in the week, where she had given a detailed description of the little boy and his circumstances.

The boy was Christopher Jameson, he was born on 6th September 2009. His mother had been concerned about symptoms similar to RMD for the past few weeks.

The boy's barely a year old he thought. He grabbed his notebook and hurriedly began writing.

He replied to Esther telling her to expect a call from him first thing in the morning.

CHAPTER SIXTY FOUR

The Saint John Fisher Health Centre
Bristol
7am
Monday 17th October

Esther Hall struggled to find the key to her office door. She was holding two box files under one arm, a dripping umbrella under the other while searching the pockets of her wet jacket. The two files fell to the ground and the contents spilled onto the floor. Esther cursed as paperwork fell on to her wet foot prints smudging the ink.

Her office door swung open and the light automatically came on.

Scooping up the paperwork, she placed it on the spare desk and cursed again.

She had got to work extra early. She'd read Peter Phelps' reply to her email. When he said he was going to do something 'first thing', he really meant first thing.

At seven fifteen the phone on her desk was ringing. It was Phelps.

"Morning Esther, how are you?" asked Phelps in his harsh Australian drawl even before she had a chance to say hello.

"I'm good Peter, how about you?"

"Yeah, can't complain, can't complain. Listen, I would like to know more about young Christopher Jameson, what can you tell me?"

Esther told Phelps what she knew, which really wasn't that much, since his strange sleep talking had only started on Friday night.

"Do you think the mother would say yes to seeing me?"

"I'm sure she would, she's desperate for an answer."

"Well, I don't think we will have any answers for her just yet. I've not seen anything like this before."

"To be honest with you Peter, it's scary, god only knows what it must be like for the boy's poor mother."

"Look Esther, I'm going to think about things at my end and I would be grateful if you could set up a visit for me. I'm coming to the West Country next week and could slot in a visit to Bristol. I'm pretty flexible so I should be able to work around everyone's timetables."

Esther agreed and they ended the call.

Esther called Maria just after nine and told her about the conversation with Phelps. Maria was bothered that her son was attracting the attention of Britain's top researcher into RMD, but was grateful that he was willing to meet with her.

A meeting was arranged for the following week.

Esther spoke with Phelps again just before she took lunch. He agreed to come to Bristol on Monday 24th and that they should both be present. Phelps suggested that the meeting should take place at the boy's home and not at the surgery.

"Can you drop by her place with an actigraph monitor?" asked Phelps.

"I could do with a week's worth of the boy's sleep patterns before I get to meet him."

Esther agreed and made time in her diary to visit Maria later in the day to drop off the monitor and run through what to do with it.

CHAPTER SIXTY FIVE

Daniel Boyd's flat
1.30pm
Monday 17th October

Daniel Boyd was on annual leave. He'd planned nothing and wasn't really bothered about taking time off. His boss had been on his back for weeks about taking holiday. Apart from the few sick days the previous week he hadn't had a day off since he started working in January and if he didn't take time off soon he'd lose his holiday for the year.

Daniel's life revolved around his job. It was a distraction from the miserable existence that was between five pm and eight am.

He had no friends, no hobbies and did little else than mope around his flat when he wasn't at the builders merchant.

Since he'd met Liz Mason's father he'd been fretting over the possibility of getting caught. It was a close call. He had been standing face to face with the father of a girl, who because of Boyd, was now in a coma.

He had become paranoid about being caught for the past few months, which is why he hardly ever left his flat, but since the chance meeting the other week, Boyd's paranoia had become worse.

He had considered seeing a doctor to get something to calm his nerves, but he was even anxious about doing that.

He lay in bed and smoked a cigarette as the thoughts of being caught, arrested, charged and finally locked away, buzzed around in his head.

He'd become too nervous to talk to anyone and only spoke when it was necessary. This made his colleagues at work very wary of him. Other than Stanley, most of them kept away from him. This was the way Boyd preferred it, but what sort of life was it? His existence certainly had no quality.

He lived only miles away from where he'd murdered Ben Walker, surely sometime soon his time would be up.

It would only take a slip of the tongue from Mossy, Seb, Greeny or any of the others who'd been there that night and the game was over.

He imagined what it would be like to be a prisoner. Perhaps it wouldn't be all that bad. Life in prison surely couldn't be much worse than it was for him as a free man?

Life in prison would probably be structured and perhaps he could learn a skill?

What was he thinking of? He was not going to prison, not if he had anything to do with it and that was final.

He chain lit another cigarette and felt the knot in his stomach tighten. The knot which had been there since he'd met Terry Mason.

He groaned as he got out of bed and pulled on his trousers with the cigarette hanging out of his mouth. He looked in the mirror and loathed what he saw. He was pathetic.

He'd hoped that having a job would improve his life. It failed to register that now he had a flat, money and a purpose to get up in the morning. He didn't appreciate any of these things.

He made a mug of tea and turned on the television and watched a re-run of a property programme. The presenter was helping a wealthy couple buy a holiday home in Cornwall.

Cornwall was where he spent his holidays as a kid with his mother and father, back when he was happy. The programme was filmed in Newquay. He watched it longingly, remembering the beach he played on when he was young. It had been filmed in summer time and the place looked wonderful.

The programme ended and he sat watching the closing credits.

He remembered happy times in his life and those brilliant summer holidays in Cornwall. His favourite place was St Ives and when he was a little boy he wanted to grow up and be a fisherman and live near the beach. He would spend hours on Smeaton's Pier watching the fishermen unload the day's catch and he'd laugh as they dodged the dive bombing seagulls as they came swooping down to steal the fish.

The fishermen had an exciting life. Out to sea in all winds and weathers. The idea of what they did appealed to him.

That was a long time ago and things hadn't quite worked out the way he'd planned. Most of his friends wanted to be train drivers or firemen and he doubted if they ended up doing what they wanted either.

What was it that Stanley had said the day they pulled into Terry Mason's driveway? 'It's up to you choose your own destiny'.

Then the penny dropped. He'd made a decision. He was going to leave. Just disappear and tell no one where he was going. Not Stanley nor anyone else.

He went to his bedroom and pulled a backpack from under his bed. Inside was a plastic bag sealed with sticky tape. He ripped the bag open and emptied the contents onto his bed. A pile of five, ten and twenty pound notes where scattered on the duvet. He counted the notes and laid them neatly on his pillow. One thousand four hundred and eighty pounds.

Since he'd started work he had put aside twenty five pounds every week and this, added to money he'd acquired before he started gainful employment, amounted to what was in front of him now.

He reckoned that he had enough cash to get to Cornwall, stay in a B&B until he found a labouring job, or perhaps seasonal work in the spring, and eventually find someone to let him work on their boat. He'd even do it for free to begin with, so he could learn the trade.

The underlying reason for going to Cornwall was to get out of Bristol. Just like Carla Price, the further away the better. He couldn't leave the country, he didn't have a passport. Cornwall sounded ideal.

He'd made his mind up and he was leaving today. He grabbed a pile of clothes from a drawer and shoved them into the backpack with the cash. He put on a hoody, slipped on a pair of trainers, grabbed his cigarettes and lighter and pushed them into the back pocket of his jeans.

Boyd quickly looked around the flat and saw his phone on the floor. He bent down to pick it up but stopped before he could reach it. Did he really need it? No one ever called him. He kicked it under a chair, grabbed his coat and pulled the door behind him leaving the keys swinging in the lock on the inside.

He waited at the bus stop, and for the first time in years he felt excited. He had a plan and he was going to make it work.

Twenty minutes later he was at the coach station near the city centre working out which coach would get him to Cornwall. There didn't seem to be one. Surely his plan couldn't be over before it had even started. There were loads of other places he could go. London, Leeds, Birmingham, Cardiff and even places in Scotland. Boyd didn't want to go anywhere other than Cornwall. He'd been to London once and didn't like it, and the other places he knew nothing about.

He turned to the attendant in the ticket office and asked whether he could get a coach to Cornwall.

"Plymouth's as far as we can take you love," replied the lady behind the window. She wore so much makeup she looked like she was lightly caked in mud.

"But I need to get to Cornwall."

"Which bit of Cornwall are you trying to get to my love?"

"Uh, I don't know, St Ives, no, Newquay."

He decided that there was more chance of finding work in Newquay, It was much bigger than St, Ives and would be busy, even though the holiday season had ended.

"You want to go to Newquay, do you my love?"

Boyd nodded.

"Get the coach to Plymouth and when you get there you can get a bus to Newquay my love."

Boyd nodded again and handed over the money. The woman eyed the large wad of cash in his ruck sack and quickly looked the other way as he handed her the fare.

"The next bus leaves at four."

He looked at his watch. It was two fifteen.

Boyd could have waited at the station but instead he spent an hour looking around the city centre. This would be the last time he'd see the place and wanted a little bit of time to look around before he left for good.

He was back at the station by ten to four. He bought a packet of cigarettes, a newspaper and something to eat and drink for the journey.

He boarded the coach and made his way to the back, sat down and pulled his hoody over his head. He huddled against the window and closed his eyes as the coach left the bay. He was on his way and, other than the lady in the ticket office, no one knew where he was going.

CHAPTER SIXTY SIX

Maria's flat
4.30pm
Monday 17th October

Maria brought a tray of coffee and digestive biscuits from the kitchen and placed it on the table in the lounge.

"Help yourself," said Maria as she offered the plate to Esther.

"Ooh, digestives, my favourite," said Esther, as she eagerly grabbed a couple.

"So what's this monitor for?" asked Maria as she turned the small plastic device over and viewed it suspiciously.

"It's to monitor Christopher's sleep patterns".

Maria said nothing and continued to look at the monitor.

"It will provide us with information about your son's real world sleep behavior and rest-activity rhythms."

"Sorry Esther, you've lost me."

"No, it's my fault. Basically the data information captured on that little thing will help Dr Phelps make appropriate diagnostic and treatment decisions."

"So when you say treatment decisions, do you think that Dr Phelps will be able to cure Christopher's Rhythmic Movement Disorder?"

"No, he won't be able to cure RMD, there's no cure for that. He's hoping to find out more about your son's sleep talking."

Maria seemed disappointed.

"As we've discussed before, RMD will just stop, Christopher is very likely to just grow out of it,………Do you still use the metronome to settle Christopher?"

Maria nodded.

"And was it switched on last Friday night when he started sleep talking?"

Maria nodded again.

"Dr Phelps is interested in what is causing Christopher to talk like he does when he's sleeping. He's researched sleep behavior in children for years but until now he's not come across anything like this."

Maria looked serious, which was something she was doing more and more recently. Her face was showing signs of stress.

"Dr Phelps will go into more detail with you when you see him next week, but I know he's interested in understanding why your son is saying words that are beyond his vocabulary."

"So Christopher's going to be his special guinea pig?"

"Yes, if you put it like that, but hopefully if he can find out more about what's happening with your son, he may find a way of stopping him from doing it."

Christopher was sleeping in his cot and Maria and Esther went to see him.

"Does he only bang his head when he sleeps at night?" whispered Esther.

"I've never known him do it during the day and my mum hasn't mentioned seeing him do it either, it's just a night time thing."

Maria stroked Christopher's face and he wriggled in his cot.

"He doesn't head bang every night and there's a chance he may not do it before Dr Phelps visits me next week so this monitor thingy may not pick up any information."

"Perhaps, but there's not much we can do about that."

Christopher was waking up. Esther left the bedroom so Maria could get him out of his cot on her own.

She brought him into the lounge as Esther was packing her notes into her bag. She put the actigraph monitor back in its box and placed it on the table.

"I need to get going," said Esther as she put on her coat.

"I'll see you on Monday with Dr Phelps, but if you need to speak to me, just give me a call."

Maria thanked her and walked her to the door.

She closed the door and heard her phone ringing from the lounge. As the phone was ringing Maria could hear Christopher.

"Eyo, eyo, eyo."

He was trying to say hello. He was copying Maria because 'hello' was always the first thing she said when she picked up the phone. He had been doing this for about a week and it made Maria smile. She checked who was calling. It was Campbell.

"Hello Campbell, how are you?"

They had a fifteen minute conversation. Campbell knew that Maria was hesitant about going out on another date just yet, but he was desperate to know how Christopher was. Maria told him what had happened over the last few days and about the appointment with Dr Phelps.

She was missing Campbell. They'd only been out once, but it seemed like she had known him for years.

She didn't want to go out with him again just yet because she didn't want to leave Christopher with a baby sitter. She was worried that his strange behaviour would start and she wouldn't be there for him.

"I've got an idea" said Maria, "how would you like to come over one night this week and I can cook us a meal?"

"I'd like that," said Campbell.

A date was made for Thursday and they ended the call.

Maria smiled. Campbell was selfless. He hadn't made the call so he could see her again, he'd done it because he was concerned about her son.

Later in the evening Maria struggled to attach the actigraph monitor. The thing was meant to be worn like a wristwatch, but Christopher's chubby wrists were too small for the strap to fit.

Maria took the thing into the kitchen, opened a drawer, the one with all the batteries, phone chargers and keys to unknown things. She pulled out a small Phillips screwdriver and used it to make a new hole in the plastic strap. She took it back to Christopher who was lying in his cot. Eventually she made it fit. She tucked him in and kissed him goodnight.

Within a few minutes he was sleeping, and within a few more minutes he was head banging.

CHAPTER SIXTY SEVEN

The Awareness
7.27pm

Ben Walker's spirit began to stir and, as always, he carried on from where he left off.

Please – Hear – My – Voice.

He briefly continued to chant the four words and then stopped.

He had a sense that he was getting somewhere. He didn't know why, but it just felt that someplace else, he was being noticed. It was the same perception as the time he screamed. He'd screamed so loud he was sure he could hear his own voice.

It was like sending out a mayday call and hoping to be heard. But who or what had heard him, and would they return his call?

Ben was frustrated and the frustration was turning to anger and the anger was turning into energy and the energy had to be released.

Please – Hear – My – Voice... Please – Hear – My – Voice... Please – Hear – My – Voice... Please – Hear – My – Voice... Please – Hear – My – Voice... Please – Hear – My – Voice.

After lying dormant for a few days Ben was recharged and ready to be heard.

Please – Hear – My – Voice... Please – Hear – My – Voice... Please – Hear – My – Voice... Please – Hear – My – Voice... Please – Hear – My – Voice... Please – Hear – My – Voice.

He could feel the four words resonate as he chanted them over and over.

CHAPTER SIXTY EIGHT

Maria's flat
7.48pm

Christopher started head banging shortly after Maria had closed his door.

He started with a few gentle thuds against his pillow, followed by a few minutes of rolling from side to side before he started to chant.

He was chanting the same four words as before, but this time his voice sounded different. It had a different tone, a different timbre.

"Please – Hear – My – Voice… Please – Hear – My – Voice… Please – Hear – My – Voice… Please – Hear – My – Voice… Please – Hear – My – Voice… Please – Hear – My – Voice."

Maria's heart sank. She went back to his room to try to wake him. Although he'd got to sleep only minutes earlier he was in a deep slumber from which he wouldn't wake.

She had given up trying to wake him and was on the floor with her back against the wall and her head in her hands.

Maria had learnt from experience there wasn't much point in trying to wake him. Once he started there was no stopping him. She'd just have to let him do his thing.

She went back to the lounge and turned on the computer. She searched 'children sleep talking'.

There were lots to choose from. She spent half an hour trawling through the various sites trying to find something that could explain what was happening. She read that more than one in ten young children talk in their sleep more than a few nights a week, and that half of all kids between the ages of three and four years old talk while asleep.

Three and four? she thought to herself, *but Christopher's barely one year old.*

Maria changed her search to 'one year old sleep talking'.

She found a forum website and one worried mum posted a question about her child.

'My one year old child talks when she's sleeping. The other night, she pointed and said "what are you doing?" She was fast asleep when she said it. Usually it is real words she blurts out in her sleep (what are you doing, duck, cow, daddy, mummy, etc.), it's not just baby babble. Is this something I should be worrying about? Should I take her to the doctor? Or do I worry too much? I must admit, it's cute and I quite like it'.

Maria read the posting. "Cute? What my son does certainly isn't cute," she whispered as she listened to his chant crackle over the baby monitor.

She read the responses to the mother's question.

The replies were all much the same. She came to the last of the six responses

'She sounds just precious!!! It is very common and absolutely normal. You should record it so you can always remember her sweet night time babble. I'm sure she would love to listen to it when she's all grown up.

Make the most of these precious times, they go so fast.'

Maria slammed down the lid of her laptop. Searching the internet didn't help her, it had made things worse. She'd found nothing useful. Other than drippy mothers getting soppy over their precious kids, there was nothing that suggested that any other one year olds spoke in their sleep like an adult.

She felt lost and alone.

Christopher was banging and chanting away in his room, but it wasn't the same. His rhythm was changing and his chant was different.

CHAPTER SIXTY NINE

The Awareness
8.29pm

Please – Hear – My – Voice… Please – Hear – My – Voice… Please – Hear – My – Voice… Please – Hear – My – Voice… Please – Hear – My – Voice… Please – Hear – My – Voice.

Ben was repeating the words in his thoughts and was wondering if there was any point in carrying on?

In his strange little prison he still had no concept of time. Each time he faded into his dormant state and then awoke, he had no idea he'd been away. As far as he was aware he was permanently conscious.

Ben felt he'd been chanting the same four words continuously for an eternity and they didn't seem to be getting him anywhere. What he needed to know was whether anyone was listening, and if there was, he needed a sign. He needed to know that he'd been heard. He'd been reaching out and now it was someone's turn to reach back to him.

He stopped repeating the four word mantra and started a different one.

Please – Let – Me – Know – You're – There….. Please – Let – Me – Know – You're – There….. Please – Let – Me – Know – You're – There….. Please – Let – Me – Know – You're – There….. Please – Let – Me – Know – You're – There….. Please – Let – Me – Know – You're – There….. Please – Let – Me – Know – You're – There….. Please – Let – Me – Know – You're – There…..

This was his new message. He wasn't going to stop until he had a response. He had no idea what kind of response to look out for. Would he hear someone's voice? Would he see a picture? Would he stand face to face with god?

Please – Let – Me – Know – You're – There….. Please – Let – Me – Know – You're – There….. Please – Let – Me – Know – You're – There….. Please – Let – Me – Know – You're – There….. Please – Let –

Me – Know – You're – There….. Please – Let – Me – Know – You're – There….. Please – Let – Me – Know – You're – There….. Please – Let – Me – Know – You're – There…..

CHAPTER SEVENTY

Maria's flat
8.35pm

Maria listened as Christopher's chanting changed. The first thing she noticed was the difference in the rhythm. He had stopped the four beat measure and had increased it to six. Six times his head thudded against his pillow and each time his head came down he grunted a word. After the sixth beat he would stop and take a brief pause and then start the sequence again.

The six new words were immediately distinct. Unlike before, when he was chanting 'please hear my voice', when it had taken her and Campbell hours to work out what he was saying, these words were as clear as a bell.

She jumped up from her seat and ran to his room. Standing in front of him the six words sounded even clearer.

"Please – Let – Me – Know – You're – There….. Please – Let – Me – Know – You're – There….. Please – Let – Me – Know – You're – There….. Please – Let – Me – Know – You're – There"

Maria grabbed her phone. She needed to call someone. Her impulse was to call her mother. She was about to make the call but changed her mind.

She scrolled through the contact list on her phone and stopped at Esther's number. She looked at her watch and wondered if it was too late to call her. She held the phone tightly in her shaking hand and pressed the call button.

"Hello, Esther?"

"Maria, is everything OK?"

"Listen to this."

Maria held the phone next to Christopher so Esther could hear him. She kept the phone above his head for thirty seconds which gave Esther enough time to take in what was happening.

"How long has he been doing that?"

"He's been chanting 'please hear my voice' for about forty five minutes, but it's just changed in the last few minutes."

Maria's voice was unsteady and she was close to tears.

"Esther, I'm sorry to call you, but I don't know what to do."

"Don't you worry, I'm on my way over."

Maria sighed, put her hand to her forehead and turned away from Christopher.

"Thank you."

"Maria, after you finish this call start filming him and I'll make sure Peter Phelps gets to see what's happening."

Maria ended the call and filmed her son.

Twenty minutes later Esther arrived and went straight to Christopher's room.

He was chanting the same six words.

"Please – Let – Me – Know – You're – There…... Please – Let – Me – Know – You're – There."

Esther watched in disbelief.

"Have you tried to wake him?"

"I have but……" Maria didn't finish her sentence, she just shrugged shoulders.

They stood in silence over his cot and watched.

Esther tried to take his temperature and measure his pulse which was impossible because he wouldn't stay still for long enough.

Esther felt useless. All her years of experience had not prepared her for this. She thought it would be better to not wake him. Christopher didn't appear to be in any discomfort or danger, so there was no reason to take him to Accident and Emergency.

Esther was there for Maria more than Christopher, and Maria needed someone to be there for her.

"I don't think there is anything I can do, but I am willing to stay with you if you like," said Esther as she held Maria's hand.

Maria wiped a tear from her eye and squeezed Esther's hand.

"Thank you Esther, I appreciate you being here."

Maria went to the kitchen to make coffee. They could have a long stretch ahead of them and caffeine would be the order of the night.

Esther pulled her phone from her bag.

"I'm going to call Peter Phelps, perhaps he can suggest something."

Esther was redirected to his voicemail.

"Hi Peter, its Esther. I'm at Maria Jameson's house, the lady you're coming to see next week. Sorry to call you out of hours, but I would appreciate your advice. Listen to this."

Esther walked to Christopher's room and held her phone next to him.

"I hope you could hear that, it's Christopher Jameson, he's chanting something new."

She walked out of his room with the phone to her ear.

"I would appreciate some advice, please call me, thanks."

She ended the call and turned to Maria who was back in the lounge with two mugs of coffee.

"Hopefully he'll call."

They sat in awkward silence. It wasn't easy to make small talk when a thirteen month old child was speaking like an adult in the room next door.

Maria opened her mouth to say something in an attempt to break the difficult moment, but stopped as Esther's phone rang.

"Peter, thank you for calling."

Maria listened to Esther's side of the conversation which was mainly made up of a series of 'yes' and 'I understand' and lots of 'OKs'. Maria tried to work out how the conversation was going, but gave up and waited patiently for Esther to finish the call.

"I'll ask her and get back to you ASAP, thanks Peter."

Esther ended the call, and turned to Maria who was perched on the edge of the settee.

"First of all Peter has confirmed that we shouldn't wake him. Just let him carry on. The likelihood is high that Christopher is oblivious to what is going on and waking him is very likely to cause unnecessary upset."

Maria nodded.

"Peter wishes he could be here to see firsthand what is happening. He's extremely keen to be involved and wants to find out what's causing Christopher to do this."

Esther paused as she wrote notes in her pocketbook.

"Maria, could you and Christopher spend a week in London next week?"

"London?"

"Yes, London. Peter doesn't think his visit next week will be particularly useful and wants to know if you could come to London instead so he can arrange some tests."

"Tests, what kind of tests?"

Maria wasn't happy with the thought of Christopher undergoing tests.

"Don't worry, he's not talking about invasive tests, he's talking about a brain scan."

Maria was agitated.

"A brain scan? I'm not sure."

Esther explained that the process would take place when Christopher was sleeping, so he probably wouldn't know the tests were happening. She continued to describe what would happen during the test, which would involve Christopher wearing little sensors on his head.

"Why would it take a whole week?" asked Maria.

"Only because Christopher doesn't seem to head bang and talk every night. If he stayed over for a few days then the chances of Peter getting some useful results would be much better."

Maria slowly nodded and Esther continued.

"If Christopher chants and bangs his head during the first night, I would imagine Peter would be happy for you to go home the next day."

"Oh, and Peter said he would cover your expenses."

Maria thought about what Esther had just told her. She knew it made sense and she should accept Peter's offer.

"Peter has some very important business in the West Country next week and he is willing to rearrange everything in order to help you."

"OK, let's do it," said Maria.

Esther smiled.

"I'm going to have to arrange a week away from work at very short notice and my boss won't be pleased."

"I can call him if it will help," suggested Esther.

"Thanks, but I'm sure I can talk to him on my own, I'm a big girl now."

Esther smiled again.

Eventually the small talk flowed and they happily chatted until they noticed that Christopher had stopped chanting.

Christopher was lying peacefully in his cot. Esther took the opportunity to take his temperature and pulse which were perfectly normal.

"Are you sure you'll be OK?" asked Esther, as she zipped up her fleece jacket.

"Honestly, I'll be fine. You need to get home."

Esther put her arms around Maria and hugged her.

"Call me after you've spoken with your boss and we'll get the London thing going."

Maria nodded, said goodnight and then shut and deadlocked the door.

CHAPTER SEVENTY ONE

Newquay, Cornwall
11.37am
Thursday 20th October

Daniel Boyd walked across Fistral Beach. Even out of season the place was busy. Surfers were taking on the big waves, dogs were chasing balls and rolling in the sand and families were flying kites and enjoying the sea air.

Daniel pulled up the collar of his coat to keep the wind from whistling around his ears.

It was a brisk October morning and the wind was blowing a sand devil towards the shore. The sky was blue and cloudless and the sun was bright. It was thirteen degrees, but the wind made it if feel less than ten.

The smell of the coast had hit him the moment he stepped off the bus on Monday. It instantly took him back to his childhood, and to times when he was happier.

As soon as he arrived he had booked into a cheap bed and breakfast and paid to stay for two weeks.

His polythene bag of money was depleting faster than he'd thought. The bed and breakfast had cost him over £250, even with a discount for paying with cash. He'd bought a warm coat, waterproof shoes and fresh underwear. Although he was living off sandwiches he seemed to be spending a fortune on food.

He found a sheltered spot by some rocks and counted his money. He had just over one thousand pounds. A strong gust blew, and even though he was sheltered by the rocks, the wind picked up a wad of notes. He had been counting his money in wads of fifties and he'd placed each pile of fifty on the sand with a pebble on top to stop the notes from blowing away. He'd almost finished packing the cash back into his rucksack when the strong gust of wind whipped the last pile of notes from under the pebble and into the air and across the beach. He zipped his ruck sack and raced across the beach in a hopeless effort to grab the money. The notes blew high into the air and twirled towards the sea. The wind dropped and he watched them flutter into the water, to be enveloped by a breaking wave. He patrolled the shoreline for half an hour hoping to retrieve the soggy cash but eventually gave up, admitting defeat. He cursed at the top of his lungs, but no one heard him as the wind carried his words out to sea.

He trudged back to the town. He needed to find work and soon.

He knew he could only work for cash. He didn't want anyone to know where he was and didn't want to be located by his National Insurance number. He avoided the Jobcentreplus. He hated the place because he'd spent most of his adult life there back in Bristol. Instead, he knocked on doors of pubs and restaurants, looking for washing up work. He asked builders if they had any labouring jobs. There were plenty of coffee vending huts near the beach, but most of them were boarded up for the winter, and the ones which were open were struggling for business and weren't looking to take on new staff.

By Friday he'd walked around the town ten times over looking for work and had found nothing. Boyd wasn't the most appealing looking potential employee. He trudged around Newquay wearing dirty trousers, his new coat was already looking disheveled and his spotty white skin contrasted against his greasy unkempt black hair. His personal hygiene wasn't good and he stank of cigarettes.

He walked past a boarded up petrol station where two men were having an argument. One man was Cornish and his loud drawl was echoing around the forecourt. The other man was foreign. Boyd was useless at recognising accents. The man sounded European, but he definitely wasn't French or German.

He watched from the other side of road as the foreign man took off his high visibility jacket, threw it to the floor and marched away towards Boyd.

"Fuck off back to Bulgaria!" shouted the Cornish man.

The Bulgarian pushed passed Boyd and cursed in his own language.

The Cornish man walked across the forecourt and disappeared into a temporary building. On the side of the little grey office was a badly painted sign.

'Wash and Go' - Hand Car Wash from £5.

Boyd straightened his coat, pushed his hands through his hair and with an air of confidence, marched to the shabby office building. He knocked on the door and entered.

The sparse ten by eight office was a mess. The desk was covered in paperwork and newspapers. A recently boiled kettle was steaming in the corner next to a carton of milk and tray of dirty mugs. A Pirelli calendar was hanging from a nail on the wall.

The Cornish man was sitting in a shabby office chair with a phone to his ear. Hearing Boyd knocking he spun around in his chair and ended the call.

"Can I help you son?"

"Yeah, I'm looking for a job."

"Can you wash a car?"

Boyd nodded.

"When can you start?"

"Whenever you want me."

The man pointed to the high visibility jacket lying on the forecourt.

"Put on the jacket, you start today."

Boyd nodded, walked over to the bright yellow waterproof coat, picked it up and put it on.

"Oh, and by the way. I pay cash only. It's up to you to pay your taxes."

Boyd smiled.

"Perfect," he said under his breath.

"My name's Mudge, what's yours?" asked the Cornish man, holding out his hand.

Boyd was failing at the first hurdle. He didn't want to give his real name and hadn't considered what he should call himself.

A combination of first names and surnames buzzed around his head and then he thought of Stanley, the only person who seemed to care about him.

After what seemed like an eternity Boyd shook Mudge's hand.

"I'm Stanley," said Boyd in an unconvincing tone.

"Do you have another name?" asked Mudge.

"What do you mean, another name?" asked Boyd warily.

"Do you have a surname?"

Boyd had another blank moment. He'd never known Stanley's surname and was stumped as to what to say.

"Jarrett," he eventually blurted out.

"I'm Stanley Jarrett."

Mudge told Boyd what the job involved, which was basically cleaning cars by hand. Even Boyd couldn't get that wrong.

"I'll pay you thirty pounds a day and you'll work six days a week. I close on Sunday."

Boyd's tiny mind was trying to compute how much he'd be paid for the whole week, luckily Mudge helped him out.

"When you finish work on Saturday night, I'll give you a little brown envelope with thirty pounds and a pay slip for every day you've worked, so if you're here all week you'll get £180 and if you're not you won't."

Boyd nodded.

"I'll need an invoice from you."

"An invoice, for what?"

"Listen, I run a legitimate business and you're self-employed, I want an invoice from you each week to balance my books. As I said, it's up to you to pay your own taxes."

Boyd was trying to work out how much he'd have left after he'd paid for bed and breakfast each week.

"Where are you staying son? I guess from your accent you're not from around here."

"I'm staying at a B&B up the hill."

"Jesus Stanley! That's gonna cost you a fortune."

"It's not cheap."

"I'll tell you what son, see that building there."

Mudge pointed to another temporary building which looked shabbier than the office.

"You can stay there if you like. It's another office, but I don't use it. There's a bed, a sink and a little cooker and there are public toilets just around the corner."

Mudge unlocked the door and Boyd looked inside. The building was cold and smelt damp.

"How much do you want?" asked Boyd.

"Thirty pounds a week and I'll knock it off your wages."

"If this is your spare office, why's there a bed?"

"I used to kip here sometimes if I'd had a row with the wife."

"Where are you going to go if you have a row with your wife and I'm there?" asked Boyd.

"I'm not married any more. Best decision I ever made."

Boyd smiled.

"I'll take it."

They shook hands on the agreement.

Don Mudge was a big man in his early fifties. His strong Cornish accent was sometimes hard even for other Cornish people to understand. He'd tried his hand at a multitude of failed businesses including an antiques dealer, which failed as he knew nothing about antiques.

He'd had a building company which lost so much money he'd almost lost his own house.

He'd also run a driving school, but his tolerance of nervous drivers was so low and his temper was so volatile, word soon got around to avoid learning to drive with 'Don's Modern School of Motoring'.

So here he was. Scraping a living washing cars.

To be fair, during the summer he was flat out. From May to September cars were queuing to be cleaned. But now, the season was over and it was quieter, but still busy enough to need a helping hand.

"What happened to the foreign guy?"

"Who, Toma?" replied Mudge.

Boyd nodded.

"I had to get rid of him. He was flakey, you know, turned up late, wanted to leave early. He had to go. Anyway Stanley, his loss, your gain."

Boyd liked Mudge. There was something about his abrupt no nonsense style that he admired.

"Come on son, let's have a brew while it's quiet."

Boyd followed Mudge back to the office and shut the door behind him.

"So what's your story?"

Boyd shrugged his shoulders.

"Where are you from, you sound Bristolian?"

Boyd nodded.

"I just wanted to go somewhere different, you know, see something new."

"So, out of all the places you could have gone, you came to Newquay." Mudge laughed as he poured the tea.

"Well, I suppose it could be worse, you could have ended up in Bodmin."

They chatted for a while and Boyd told him he'd split from his girlfriend and just wanted to disappear for a while.

"It's your choice son, just as long as you haven't murdered anyone," laughed Mudge as he dunked a biscuit into his dirty mug of tea.

Boyd said nothing.

A car pulled onto the forecourt and the driver sounded the horn.

"Come on son, put down your drink, here's your first customer."

Boyd followed Mudge onto the forecourt.

Bristol seemed a million miles away. For the first time since he could remember he was feeling untroubled, almost happy.

CHAPTER SEVENTY TWO

The Portland Hospital
London
4.50pm
Monday 24th October

Maria sat in the reception of the plush private hospital waiting for Peter Phelps to arrive.

Phelps had rescheduled his diary to spend the week with Christopher Jameson.

Christopher was bumbling around the reception area and had found a corner where there was a selection of toys. He'd been enticed by a large yellow plastic dumper truck and was happily pushing it backwards and forwards.

Maria had one eye on Christopher whilst watching the flat screen television on the wall, when a short round man with a bald head marched confidently up to the reception desk.

Maria watched as the man spoke with the receptionist, signed a form and was given an ID badge. The receptionist pointed the man in the direction of Maria.

The short bald-headed man walked up to Maria and held out his hand.

"Hello Maria, I'm Peter, Peter Phelps."

Maria nervously shook his hand.

"Hello Dr Phelps, thank you for seeing us."

"Oh, drop the doctor nonsense, just call me Peter."

Maria smiled.

"Anyway Maria, it should be me thanking you. You've come a long way to see me."

Phelps looked around.

"Where's Christopher?"

Christopher had somehow wedged himself under a red plastic child's table and was happily fumbling with a wooden building block. He attempted to crawl from under the table and ended up dragging it across the floor, which made him look like a tortoise with his smiley face beaming out from its shell.

Christopher made his way slowly towards Maria and Phelps, hauling the table which was firmly stuck to his back. The selection of plastic toys which had been on the table were strewn behind and left in his wake.

This was the perfect icebreaker. Phelps and Maria laughed as Christopher stopped at their feet, looked up from beneath the table and smiled.

Phelps gracelessly got down to Christopher's level.

"Hello little man, how are you?"

Christopher chatted and gurgled.

Maria lifted the plastic table from his back and picked him up from the floor.

Phelps awkwardly climbed to his feet.

"Christopher, say hello to Peter."

"Ayo, ayo, ayo."

Phelps smiled as Christopher attempted to speak.

"You've got a happy little boy," he said as he held Christopher's hand.

"He is happy, very happy. You wouldn't think any of this night time stuff was happening."

Maria paused as she kissed Christopher on the top of his head.

"He becomes a different boy when he's sleeping."

Christopher reached out to Phelps and Maria passed her son to him. Phelps walked to a chair and sat down with Christopher on his lap.

Maria watched him bobbing her son on his knee. Phelps was a funny character. When she looked at him she saw Danny Devito, but when he spoke she heard Crocodile Dundee.

He handed Christopher back to Maria.

"Follow me, I'll take you to your room".

Phelps had received a generous grant to fund his research in child sleep disorders and the grant was paying for a week in the prestigious private hospital and for the equipment required to carry out a week of polysomnography tests on Christopher.

The grant also covered Maria's out of pocket expenses.

Maria followed as she pushed Christopher in his buggy. She was in awe of the building. It was nothing like any hospital she'd ever seen. The floors were carpeted and the walls were covered in beautiful paintings. It was like a hotel. If it wasn't for the occasional doctor passing her in the corridor she could have been visiting The Ritz.

Phelps was carrying a black shoulder bag and was pulling Maria's overnight case behind him.

He stopped outside a door and used his ID pass to open it. The door swung open to reveal a hive of activity taking place in the room.

A woman wearing a white coat was working on a keypad which was at the top of a three tiered desk next to a cot. On the middle tier was a printer and the bottom tier was a computer and some complicated looking equipment.

On the other side of the cot was a stand, which looked like a stainless steel lampstand with another complicated piece of equipment attached to the top. A man, who was also wearing a white coat, was busy plugging in wires which were attached to sensors.

They stopped what they were doing when Phelps entered the room followed by Maria and Christopher.

"May I introduce you to Maria Jameson and her son, Christopher" said Phelps, as Maria closed the door behind her.

Maria smiled at the busy white coated workers.

"And may I introduce technicians Mike Prince and June Hudson."

Maria walked up to Mike Prince and shook his hand and then turned to Hudson who eagerly had her hand ready for Maria to shake.

"Mike and June will be helping me over the next few days."

The room was large. It had a flat screen television on the wall opposite the cot, a table with a kettle and a choice of different teas and coffees from around the world. On the wall was a large framed picture of Winnie the Pooh and there was a large couch in the corner. To the right of the entrance of the room was door leading to a smaller room which had an adult sized single bed. In this room was a door which led to a bathroom, where there was a toilet, shower and a sink.

Phelps carried Maria's case into the room with the bed and gestured for her follow.

"This is where you will be sleeping, so make yourself at home."

Her room also had a flat screen television, a bedside cabinet and a phone. On the shelf below the phone was a Gideon's Bible. There was a wardrobe where she could hang her clothes. It really was more like a hotel than a hospital.

Phelps left her to unpack whilst he spoke with Hudson and Prince. Christopher was sleeping in his buggy. The journey to London had worn him out.

Maria opened the blinds and peered from the window in her room which overlooked Great Portland Street. She watched traffic mill along the busy road and the mass of pedestrians making their way home. The triple glazed windows kept the noise out and it was like watching a movie with the volume turned down.

She unpacked her clothes and hung them in the wardrobe and laid Christopher's in a neat pile on a shelf at the bottom.

Maria went back to the room with the cot just as the two technicians were leaving. Phelps was sitting on the couch with a large pile of paperwork and a pair of reading glasses perched on the end of his nose.

"Sit down Maria, we need to have a talk and you need to sign some forms. It's a good idea to do it now while Christopher is sleeping."

Phelps explained that when Christopher is sleeping, Hudson and Prince will attach sensors at various points on his body to record information during the night.

"Is there any chance that this could be harmful?"

"Not at all, because what we will be doing is non-invasive."

"So you won't be blasting him with microwaves or x-rays or photons?"

Phelps laughed. "No, all we will be doing is taking measurements and hopefully the information picked up on the polysomnography recorder will teach us more about what is happening," Phelps paused for a few seconds, "of course, all of this is dependent upon whether Christopher head bangs and talks tonight."

Maria was confident that he would. He had been head banging and chanting the same six words for the past week.

Maria pointed to the computer,

"I still want to know more about the polysomwhatsit machine before I sign the forms."

Phelps nodded.

"We will place sensors around his body and record brain electrical activity, eye and jaw muscle movement, leg muscle movement, airflow, respiratory effort, EKG and oxygen saturation."

For the most part Maria was none the wiser.

"But the most important information is likely to come from electrical activity in his brain."

Maria shuddered.

"I suggest you wake him and bring him to the restaurant so we can all have a bite eat. Keep him up as late as possible so he sleeps well tonight."

The restaurant was huge and the food looked fantastic. Maria was still having difficulty comprehending that she was in a hospital. It was more like a five star holiday complex.

Maria settled on a modest baked potato while Phelps had a plateful of tagliatelle.

They discussed Christopher, and Phelps knew she was nervous and did his best to make light of the whole thing. He was both concerned and fascinated by the boy. In all the years he'd been working in the medical profession he had never seen anything like it.

Later, Hudson and Prince joined them as Maria fed Christopher.

Christopher was enjoying the attention and having great fun as the four adults took it in turns to pick him up and fuss over him.

By seven o'clock Christopher was yawning and getting crotchety.

"That's his tired head," said Maria.

"Well I guess it's time to get the show on the road," said Phelps standing up and rubbing his hands.

Maria, Hudson and Prince walked behind Phelps as they made their way back to the room. Maria carried Christopher in her arms.

By the time they were back in the room Christopher was almost asleep. Maria changed him and dressed him in his white towelling sleep suit. She gently placed him in the cot and tucked Misty under his arm. He was asleep within minutes.

Prince and Hudson placed the sensors on him, making sure they didn't wake him.

Six electrodes were attached to the top of his head. One electrode was placed above and to the outside of his right eye, and another was placed below and to the outside of his left.

"These sensors record the movements of the eyes during sleep and serve to help determine sleep stages," said Phelps as the two doctors continued to wire Christopher to the machine.

It was too much for Maria and she rushed into the other room and sat on the bed.

June Hudson stopped what she was doing and turned to walk into Maria's room. Phelps held up his hand and gestured to leave Maria alone.

"Give her some time, she'll be OK."

Two minutes later Maria returned and apologised.

"Just do what you're doing and spare me the details," she said wiping her eyes.

By eight fifteen Christopher was wired up and fast asleep. None of the sensors and wires seemed to bother him. Prince made sure the wires were slack. Phelps had warned him that his head banging could become violent and he didn't want any of the wires to come loose.

Hudson stood on a chair and adjusted a camera which was fixed to the wall. Christopher's image popped up on a little television monitor in the corner of the room, which Maria hadn't noticed before.

Prince typed at the computer keyboard and the printer began to slowly churn out a role of paper as little pens zigzagged across the page, recording the activity in his brain.

Maria took the kettle into her room, filled it with water from the sink and prepared a hot drink for her, Phelps and the two technicians.

Over the hissing of the kettle she could hear the familiar sound of Christopher banging his head. She put her head around the door and watched her son doing what she'd seen him do many times before. But wired up to the machine he looked different. He looked like a little freak. She watched the pens on the printer whizz over the paper recording what was happening in his brain. And then the chanting began.

"Please – Let – Me – Know – You're – There….. Please – Let – Me – Know – You're – There….. Please – Let – Me – Know – You're – There….. Please – Let – Me – Know – You're – There."

Phelps knew what to expect, he'd already seen it on the video clip. But to see it with his own eyes and to hear the words coming from Christopher's mouth was a different thing.

Phelps and the technicians stood in silence and June Hudson found it hard not to show her emotions.

Christopher had been chanting the same six words for a week and although Maria was getting used to it, she hated it more every time he did it.

After a minute everyone jumped into action. Prince was typing at the computer while Hudson and Phelps were making notes.

The pens recording Christopher's electrical brain activity were frantically whipping across the paper and Maria thought the machine was going to break.

Then everything stopped.

Christopher ceased head banging and instead of chanting he was gently breathing.

The pens on the printer stopped their frenzied jig and were slightly twitching and recording a gentle wave of lines.

But it was the calm before the storm. Like a receding sea before a tsunami, what Christopher did next took everyone by surprise.

CHAPTER SEVENTY THREE

The Awareness
8.35pm

Not long after Christopher had started to sleep, Ben began to stir and as always, he carried on from where he had left off, repeating his desperate plea.

"Please – Let – Me – Know – You're – There….. Please – Let – Me – Know – You're – There….. Please – Let – Me – Know – You're – There….. Please – Let – Me – Know – You're – There."

As Ben repeated the chant he felt different. He didn't know what he was sensing, but something had changed. He was experiencing a tingling feeling. Although he had no physical body to truly feel the sensation of touch, somehow he was aware of this strange new sensation.

Each time he chanted the words, he heard an echo. It wasn't loud, but it was clear and distinct. He could hear his words and his own voice bouncing back to him. It was eerie and it caught him completely off guard.

He didn't stop, he continued with the mantra.

"Please – Let – Me – Know – You're – There….. Please – Let – Me – Know – You're – There….. Please – Let – Me – Know – You're – There….. Please – Let – Me – Know – You're – There."

Every word had an echo and the tingling was becoming more intense. It reminded him of pins and needles.

Then it occurred to him. Perhaps someone was letting him know they were there. As if, in some way, bouncing his words back to him was a way of saying 'yes, I can hear you'.

The electrodes attached Christopher's head were picking up the electrical activity created by Ben's thoughts. The tiny electrical current was enough to register on the polysomnography recorder and as the electrodes sensed the miniscule flow of electrical charge, an even smaller current rebounded off the electrodes and passed back through the pineal gland, where Ben's essence had been existing since the instant he'd died.

The tiny electrical charge which was bouncing back to Ben created an echo effect and even though the current which returned to Ben travelled at one-hundredth of the speed of light, his heightened level of perception was able to detect it.

Ben stopped chanting and considered what was happening. Someone, or something somewhere had heard his voice and had let him know. His hard work had paid off. The relentless chant had resulted in someone saying 'OK Ben, we're letting you know we're here, what's next'.

It was up to Ben to make the next move. He had to choose his next words carefully. He knew there was a limit to what he could say and whatever he said could make all the difference.

Ben considered the ramifications of what was happening. If the next words he chose were to make a difference, what would that difference be? If he was set free from this strange prison-like existence then where would he go? Heaven, hell or perhaps back to where he came? What if he could be taken back to the time just before he died and be given another chance to fight back and protect Liz?

Or perhaps he would end up standing face to face with god? He'd never spent much time attending church but that didn't mean that he wasn't a believer. He worried whether he'd been a good enough person in his life to deserve entry into heaven.

He wondered about who it was that was listening to him. If it was god, then it was an odd way of communicating.

He needed to know what to do next. So he asked the question.

He tried to speak again.

"What – happens – next?"...... "What – happens – next?"...... "What – happens – next?"...... "What – happens – next?"...... "What – happens – next?"...... "What – happens – next?"......

But something was wrong. He knew his words weren't being heard. Instead of shouting he was whispering. He tried again.

"What – happens – next?"...... "What – happens – next?"...... "What – happens – next?"...... "What – happens – next?"...... "What – happens – next?"...... "What – happens – next?"......

His thoughts had no power. He had lost whatever it was he'd had before to make himself heard.

He became frustrated. It was like a dream in which no matter how fast he ran he remained in the same place. His frustration increased as he tried again to be heard.

"What – happens – next?"...... "What – happens – next?"...... "What – happens – next?"...... "What – happens – next?"...... "What – happens – next?"...... "What – happens – next?"......

But still nothing. The frustration turned to anger. He thought of Liz being attacked and the last time he saw her and the memory of the rock crashing into his head.

As quickly as his frustration turned to anger his anger turned to rage. He had another chance to be heard and he was letting it slip away.

Perhaps this was the last opportunity to be heard and if he lost it he could be stuck like this for ever.

The idea of a lonely eternity made him bitter. This shouldn't be happening to him. He had to get out.

He felt claustrophobic, trapped in this strange place with nothing to keep him company other than his memories.

This and the other thoughts were mixing and turning into a melting pot of anger and hatred.

Then the energy returned.

The words he said next were not planned and they had so much spit and bile that they took him by surprise.

"Free – me – from – this – hell"…. "Free – me – from – this – hell"…. "Free – me – from – this – hell"…. "Free – me – from – this – hell"…. "Free – me – from – this – hell"…. "Free – me – from – this – hell"…. "Free – me – from – this – hell"…. "Free – me – from – this – hell"

His words echoed and the strange tingling sensation returned.

He wasn't going to stop until he was free from his lonely cell.

"Free – me – from – this – hell"…. "Free – me – from – this – hell"…. "Free – me – from – this – hell"…. "Free – me – from – this – hell"…. "Free – me – from – this – hell"…. "Free – me – from – this – hell"…. "Free – me – from – this – hell"…. "Free – me – from – this – hell"

CHAPTER SEVENTY FOUR

The Portland Hospital
London
8.42pm

Christopher's respite from head banging and chanting didn't last long. According to the reading from the printer he had been sleeping gently and without incident for seven minutes.

Then, just like a steam locomotive gradually gaining traction as it pulled out of its station, he gently banged his head against the soft hospital pillow. Each time he thudded his head he let out an 'ughh'. He slowly thumped his head on the pillow then stopped. After two or three seconds he started again.

"Ughh Ughh Ughh Ughh Ughh."

And then another break, followed by, "Ughh Ughh Ughh Ughh Ughh," and another break followed by, "Ughh Ughh Ughh Ughh Ughh."

The pens on the printer were swiveling across the paper recording his brain activity.

"He's chanting in cycles of five," whispered Hudson.

All eyes were on Christopher. His head banging and chanting picked up pace and within a couple of minutes he was banging his head at the speed he was doing earlier.

"Listen," said Maria holding up her hand as if she was stopping oncoming traffic.

The four of them stood perfectly still and no one spoke as he chanted.

Eventually Phelps spoke in his Australian drawl.

"He's saying something."

Christopher's five cycle chant was forming into words. As the words were forming the character of his voice changed. He was moving away from the baby-like 'ughh' and his voice, although still childlike, took on a mature tone.

A few minutes later the 'ughh' had completely changed and five new words were repeating each time his head thumped against the pillow.

"Are we getting this?" asked Phelps, as Hudson typed at the keyboard.

Hudson nodded.

Prince checked that the camera was picking up the images.

The five new words sounded eerie as well as clinical and were underpinned by the whirring of the electrical equipment.

Maria dropped face down on the couch and began to sob, Hudson walked over and sat beside her without taking her eyes off Christopher.

No one spoke as he chanted his five new words. The pens on the printer were scratching away at the paper, recording a strange phenomenon that neither Phelps nor the technicians had ever witnessed before nor understood.

"Free – me – from – this – hell".... "Free – me – from – this – hell".... "Free – me – from – this – hell".... "Free – me – from – this – hell".... "Free – me – from – this – hell".... "Free – me – from – this – hell".... "Free – me – from – this – hell".... "Free – me – from – this – hell"

Maria staggered up from the couch, drunkenly lurched across the room and into the bathroom where she was trying her best not to throw up. Hudson followed behind but stopped short of the toilet door where she could hear Maria coughing and heaving.

She stumbled out of the bathroom wiping her mouth. Propping herself up against the wall she lifted her head and looked at Hudson.

"I can't take this anymore, make it go away, please make it go away."

She dropped onto the bed in the corner of the room.

"Please leave me alone."

Hudson stepped out of the room and closed the door behind her.

Maria lay in the dark. With the door shut she couldn't hear his chanting. She pulled the pillow over her face and cried.

The others could hear her sobs through the door.

"Let her be," whispered Phelps, "She'll come round when she's ready."

But she didn't. The exhaustion of the tiring journey and long day had taken every ounce of strength she'd had. And now that Christopher was acting more bizarrely than ever, it was just too much for her.

At eleven fifteen Christopher stopped and the pens on the printer slowed to a steady rhythm recording a natural sleep pattern.

Phelps left the room whilst Hudson and Prince watched over Christopher in two hour shifts. When one was watching, the other was catnapping on the couch.

The rest of the night continued without any further events.

CHAPTER SEVENTY FIVE

The Portland Hospital
7.06am
Tuesday 25th October

Maria woke at just after seven and emerged from her room looking disheveled and wearing the same clothes she had on when she fell face down onto the bed.

Her mouth tasted bitter and her eyes were stinging. Her son's chanting was ringing in her ears.

"I'm sorry." She said as she emerged from her room.

Prince, who was standing over Christopher, turned to her and smiled.

"It's OK, take it easy."

He guided her to the chair in the corner of the room and sat her down.

Maria saw Hudson sleeping on the couch.

"The two of us have been with Christopher all night. We've been taking it in shifts. It's June's turn to sleep now."

Maria nodded.

Christopher was beginning to wake. Prince slowly removed the sensors from the little boy's body. The sensors left little round marks where the sticky pads had been attached to his skin.

He opened his eyes and looked around the unfamiliar hospital room. Maria stood up, straightened her T-shirt and ran her fingers through her messy hair in a subconscious attempt at making herself presentable for her son.

His little face screwed up and his bottom lip stuck out as he was about to cry, but before the tears rolled he spotted his mother and his sad face switched to one of happiness.

Maria picked him out of the cot, carried him tightly in her arms and took him to her room shutting the door behind her.

Prince woke Hudson and passed her a fresh cup of coffee.

Both technicians were tired and Hudson had confused her dreams with reality.

"Did that really happen last night?"

Prince nodded.

"What the hell's happening with that little boy?"

Prince shook his head.

"I've no idea, but I know one thing, no damned polysomnography test is going to get to the bottom of this, I think that boy needs to see a priest."

Hudson 'shushed' him and pointed to the closed door.

"Be quiet, she'll hear you."

"So what do you think, and be honest?" asked Prince,

"I don't know, but there must be a logical explanation for the whole thing," replied Hudson.

Maria opened her door. She looked brighter. She'd thrown water over her face, applied a little makeup and tied her hair back.

"I know what you think about Christopher, my son's a freak."

The technicians didn't answer.

Maria was about to speak, but stopped when she heard a knock at the door. Prince stood up, walked over and opened it. Peter Phelps was waiting outside.

"Good morning!"

Hudson and Prince quietly responded and Maria said nothing.

Phelps could sense the tension in the room and motioned for the technicians to leave.

"How are you?"

"I've been better," replied Maria.

Over the years Phelps had dealt with hundreds of medical issues and had the difficult job of delivering bad news to parents. He'd been the one to tell parents that their child had hideous illnesses such as leukemia and other worst case scenario conditions. He'd been the one to announce that a child may have months or weeks to live.

He was a professional and was able to talk to parents in a rehearsed but compassionate manner, giving time for the awful news he'd delivered to sink in before moving on to the practicalities that came next. He'd done this so many times over the years he'd become quite proficient and was able to detach himself from the news he was conveying.

But this was different. He had no idea what to say to Maria. He didn't know what was happening to the boy and why he was talking in his sleep in such a strange way.

Phelps wondered whether the boy was repeating things he'd heard on television or that he'd overheard from adults. If so, it still wouldn't explain the transformation in his voice.

Phelps was a practical man and had no time for anything unnatural. Everything had a reasonable explanation, unfortunately he had no idea what this explanation could possibly be.

He knew it wasn't wise to speculate about what was happening to Christopher so he avoided any conversation with Maria regarding what could be happening with her son.

"So what do you think is happening to Christopher?"

"I'm afraid I can't answer that, at least not at the moment."

Phelps paused and considered his words carefully.

"With your permission I would like to keep Christopher here until Thursday, which would enable us to carry out further tests on your son, none of which would not cause him any harm."

Phelps stood up, walked to the sink and filled a glass with water.

"It will take me some time to review the data from the polysomnography test and I don't want to jump to conclusions until I have had time to analyse the results."

Maria nodded and hugged her son.

Maria reluctantly agreed to Christopher spending the next three nights at the hospital, even though she was anxious to get out of the place. She knew she may never have an opportunity like this again and she was desperate to find out what was happening to her son.

She missed home, she missed her mother and she missed her friends, but most of all she was missing Campbell. Although they'd had just one night together she was longing to see him again. She'd promised to cook for him last Thursday, but with everything that was going on, the date slipped her mind. She'd called him several times over the last week to keep him updated with what was happening, but hadn't seen him in over ten days.

She was worrying whether he'd go off the boil and lose interest in her.

Dr Phelps didn't need Maria or Christopher during the day, so she had until six o'clock in the evening to herself. She wasn't much of a fan of London and hadn't planned on what to do. Although Phelps had agreed to cover her out of pocket expenses and a little extra, it would still be an expensive week and she just didn't have the money to take in the sights of the city and keep Christopher happy at the same time.

Maria and Phelps discussed the week ahead and arranged to meet that evening to start the second round of tests.

Maria quickly showered and got ready for the day while Christopher lay in the cot playing and cuddling Misty. She washed and changed him and then headed to the restaurant for breakfast.

After last night's ordeal she wasn't hungry, but knew she needed to keep her strength up. She chose a light breakfast of fruit and yoghurt and fed Christopher a mashed banana.

By the time she'd finished breakfast it was only eight forty five. She wasn't looking forward to the rest of the day, partly because she was dreading the evening and partly because she wasn't looking forward to traipsing around London with Christopher in tow.

After breakfast she returned to her room. She'd picked up a complimentary newspaper from reception and turned the television on to occupy Christopher. He happily watched CBeebies as she perused the latest headlines.

She was about to make a cup of coffee when the phone in the corner of the room rang. She quickly turned around as the shrill tone took her by surprise.

"Can I speak to Maria Jameson please?"

"Speaking."

"Good morning, this is Paula in reception, I have some people here who would like to see you."

"Who are they?"

"They want me to keep it as a surprise."

"A surprise?"

"Yes, can you come down to reception please."

Maria put Christopher in his buggy and made her way along the corridor to reception. The area was full of people. Doctors and consultants were busy talking by the coffee machine, nervous looking parents were waiting with their children and a salesman was pacing up and down adjusting his security pass.

She walked over to the desk and asked for Paula, who came from the room behind reception with a pair of reading glasses perched on the end of her nose.

"Hi, I'm Maria, you just called me."

"Ah yes, your visitors. They're waiting for you in the restaurant."

Maria thanked her and made her way back to the restaurant, where she'd been just over an hour earlier.

As she turned the corner she caught sight of a couple who were sitting face to face across a table. One had orange juice and the other had coffee.

"No!" exclaimed Maria under her breath, as her face lit up. Her pace quickened as she made her way towards them.

Christopher, who was trundling along in his buggy, spotted the lady and called out, "Sam".

The couple stood up, stepped away from the table and moved towards Maria.

"What are you doing here?" asked Maria as she threw her arms around Samreen.

"We wanted to surprise you," replied her best friend.

Campbell waited patiently behind Samreen.

Maria kissed Samreen on her cheek, stood back and took a breath. She turned round and faced Campbell and then they held each other in a tight embrace that seemed to go on forever. Samreen was feeling a little awkward, like she was playing gooseberry.

Samreen bent down and picked Christopher out of his buggy and gave him a huge hug.

Eventually Campbell and Maria let go of each other.

"When did you two get here?"

"We pulled into Paddington at eight thirty, jumped on the tube and now here we are!" replied Samreen as she bobbed Christopher up and down in her arms.

"You two have really made my day," said Maria. The expression on her face reflected the happiness she felt.

"It was Samreen's idea," said Campbell.

There were more hugs and kisses and cuddles for Christopher before they left the hospital for a brief tour of London.

"How long are you staying?" asked Maria.

"Just for today," said Campbell.

"I've taken the day off and need to be back for work in the morning, he continued.

"And I'm off to Birmingham tonight as I have to attend a conference at the NEC tomorrow," said Samreen.

They spent the day taking in some of the sights and finished the day with a trip on the London Eye.

They shared a taxi back to the hospital and after hugs and kisses Maria returned to her room. She was exhausted and it was only a quarter past five.

She had forty five minutes until her meeting with Phelps and the next round of tests which were to get underway.

Christopher was sleeping in his buggy and she was tempted to lie on the bed and shut her eyes. She decided against it. She was so tired she would have probably slept until morning.

Instead she jumped in the shower and freshened up. This made her feel better. She looked at the clock and decided what to do for the next thirty minutes. She was hungry after the busy day and decided to head down to the restaurant for a quick snack and something for Christopher, who was still sleeping.

When she got to the restaurant she saw Hudson and Prince having an early evening meal before the night shift began. She hoped they wouldn't see her as she couldn't face sitting with them discussing Christopher's head banging, after all, it was the only thing they had in common.

She chose a panini for her and a children's lunch box for her son. She knew that most of his food would end up being launched from his high chair, but she wasn't clearing up tonight and didn't care.

She struggled to balance her tray of food and push Christopher in his buggy as she made her way to an empty table.

"Hi, Maria, can I give you a hand?" called June Hudson from the other side of the restaurant.

Maria was about to answer, when she just about stopped the tray full of food from slipping onto the floor.

Hudson ran over and got there just in time.

"Mike and I are over there in the corner, would you like to join us?"

Maria hesitated, but knew she couldn't be rude.

"I'd love to," she replied.

Mike Prince pulled up a high chair and Maria strapped Christopher in and laid out a selection of food for him to pick at.

She tucked into her panini and waited for the small talk to begin.

"So, what have you been doing today?" asked Hudson.

Maria told them about her day and that her lovely friends had travelled to London just to be with her.

She did her best to avoid any conversation involving her son, as she really couldn't face talking about the reason why he was in the hospital. She had the next few days ahead of her which would be all about his strange behaviour.

Instead, Maria was able to steer the conversation around to Hudson and Prince. Hudson was divorced and Prince was in a long term relationship. They both lived in London. Prince lived in Tower Hamlets and Hudson in Harlesden. She avoided asking questions about their jobs and whether they enjoyed working at the hospital, as this could easily have brought the conversation round to the subject of Christopher.

Hudson checked the time on her phone and said that it was time for her and Prince to get going. They left Maria to finish her food. Christopher was eating slowly so Maria asked them to tell Phelps she would be a few minutes late.

She got to her room at six fifteen and apologised to Phelps for being late.

"OK Maria, you know the routine. It will be the same as last night. June and Mike will attach the sensors to Christopher when he's sleeping and they'll do their best not to wake him. If tonight is anything like last night we'll hopefully get some good data."

Maria left the experts alone to work whilst she changed Christopher and prepared him for bed in the other room.

Although he'd spent most of the day being pushed around London in his buggy and not had a particularly active day, Christopher was crotchety and ready to sleep. He wriggled and fidgeted as Maria struggled to do up the poppers on his sleep suit.

"Keep still you little….." said Maria, without finishing the sentence.

Eventually she emerged holding her son in a new pale blue towelling sleep suit.

Phelps, Hudson and Prince left Maria on her own with Christopher whilst she sang him a song and kissed him goodnight. Maria lowered the lights and sat on the couch and waited for him to sleep.

Fifteen minutes later he was sound asleep and gently snoring. Maria took a moment alone to watch her son's gentle slumber before the others returned. She knew that before long he would change from a normal, happy little boy into something completely different. She looked at his innocent face with his cheek resting on the pillow and watched his eyes occasionally twitch as he dreamt. She wondered what on earth was going on inside his head. Where in the depths of his young developing brain was he coming up with the strange chants?

Maria was snapped from her thoughts by a gentle knock on the door. Phelps and the technicians were waiting to come in and get the evening underway.

"Is he sleeping?" whispered Phelps.

Maria nodded and let them in.

She hated the next bit, so shut herself in the other room and lay on the bed whilst the technicians and Phelps prepared for the next round of tests.

At twenty past seven Christopher was gently rocking from side to side and groaning. This was how his head banging normally started.

The pens on the printer were twitching as they recorded the increase in his brain activity. Phelps walked over to the printer and looked at the patterns emerging as paper slowly chugged out.

Christopher stopped rolling and started lifting and dropping his head onto the pillow. At first his head banging followed no pattern and was quite random, but after a few minutes he developed a definite five beat sequence which included a 'grunt' each time his head hit the pillow. The grunts developed into words and in less than a minute he was repeating the same five words as he'd done the previous night.

"Free – me – from – this – hell"…. "Free – me – from – this – hell"…. "Free – me – from – this – hell"…. "Free – me – from – this – hell"…. "Free – me – from – this – hell"…. "Free – me – from – this – hell"…. "Free – me – from – this – hell"…. "Free – me – from – this – hell"

Maria lay on the bed in her room. Although she had closed the door, it had swung open allowing her to hear Christopher. She pulled the pillow over her head in an attempt to block out the sound from the other room. And as she listened to her son's mantra she made up her own.

"Make it go away, make it go away, make it go away."

CHAPTER SEVENTY SIX

The Awareness

Ben was awake and was furiously repeating the same five words.
"Free – me – from – this – hell".... "Free – me – from – this – hell".... "Free – me – from – this – hell".... "Free – me – from – this – hell".... "Free – me – from – this – hell".... "Free – me – from – this – hell".... "Free – me – from – this – hell".... "Free – me – from – this – hell"

He could sense the same echo and knew someone was listening to him.

But why was he not getting a reply?

The anger and bitterness which was fuelling him was spiraling out of control. The harder he tried to be heard didn't seem to make any difference.

He paused for reflection. The rancor, bitterness and hate bubbled and stewed until he snapped.

He cleared his thoughts and concentrated on something new and different to say. He wanted to get the attention of whoever it was that was listening to him. But he just couldn't think of what to say. He needed something well-crafted that would be remembered and hopefully be the key to set him free.

The more he focused, the less he could come up with the right words, like a song writer facing a mental block.

As his mind worked overtime his frustration grew and the bitterness and anger increased. And then he took himself by surprise as he spurted out four clear, concise and angry words................

"SOMEBODY FUCKING ANSWER ME!"

CHAPTER SEVENTY SEVEN

The Portland Hospital
7.29pm

Christopher stopped head banging and chanting. Phelps and the technicians looked at each other then walked towards the cot and watched as he peacefully slept.

"What happened?" asked Phelps.

"He just stopped," replied Hudson.

From her room Maria could hear that Christopher had stopped chanting. She stood up and walked to the partially opened door. She opened it further and looked into the other room where she saw Phelps, Hudson and Prince standing over the cot. Phelps was rubbing his chin and the technicians looked concerned. They whispered and they were too quiet for her to hear what they were saying.

She quietly entered the room and stood alongside the other three and looked at her son sleeping soundly in the cot.

"Is everything OK?" she whispered.

"I think so, he just stopped," replied Phelps.

"He doesn't normally just stop like that, he tends to get quieter and then he just peters out."

Christopher wriggled in the cot and kicked his feet. His eyes twitched and he began to screw his face into a distorted grimace like a gargoyle peering down from a church wall. The expression on his face became more intense and he rolled his head from side to side as if he was enduring a terrible pain.

He rolled onto his back and with his eyes wide open he surveyed the room and the four faces looking over him. He turned his gaze to Maria and looked her directly in her eyes. His mouth began to quiver as if he was about to cry. But instead of crying his lips pursed tightly and his head began to shake. He looked away from his mother, rolled his eyes around his head and then refocused his stare directly at her. He drew in a breath, raised his arms above his head and shouted………..

"Somebody fucking answer me!"

Maria held on to the side of the cot, feeling hot and dizzy as a wave of nausea came over her. Her legs gave way and she hit the floor like a sack of coal.

CHAPTER SEVENTY EIGHT

Devon
Sunday 6th May 2012
Eighteen months later

Maria and Campbell were returning from a long weekend in Devon. The Sunday afternoon traffic on the motorway was nose to tail due to an accident on the other carriageway.

"Bloody rubber-neckers," said Campbell in his soft Southern Irish accent

Friday had been a brilliant day. Campbell had done the right thing and even got down on one knee when he presented Maria with a small red box wrapped with a gold ribbon.

She'd said yes without giving it another thought, as he slipped the diamond engagement ring onto her finger.

He'd booked a cottage in the small seaside town of Brixham and arranged for Maria's mother to look after Christopher.

Campbell was working for TM.I.T. He'd left the coffee shop just over a year ago when the I.T. company offered him a position working as a programmer in a small team who were designing an on-line shopping website for a high street supermarket. After finishing his PhD he had been holding out for a position as a Cyber Security Consultant, but decided to take the web design job as a stopgap until the post he really wanted came up.

The last couple of days had been wonderful and it was the first time Maria had been away from her son. She missed him terribly, but embraced the freedom of a couple of days where she and Campbell could do whatever they wanted.

They'd woken early that morning and went for a walk around the town. At eight o'clock they were hand in hand on the harbour wall watching the fisherman prepare the boats to go out to sea. Maria watched as the small town came to life. Shops were opening, the streets were being cleaned and a lorry was slowly making its way up the narrow harbour road with a delivery for a grocery shop.

For a short period of time she was able to forget about Christopher and his strange behaviour.

She huddled against Campbell before getting to her feet to return to the cottage for breakfast.

The traffic on the motorway was slowly beginning to move. Each time their car inched forward she felt the pangs of anxiety return.

Things hadn't ended well between Maria and Peter Phelps. After spending a stressful week in the London hospital, which seemed to have made Christopher's RMD worse, then waiting six months for Phelps to analyse the data, only to be told that he could find no reason why her son was chanting was too much for her.

She'd accused him of being an unprofessional time waster and even suggested that he'd used the grant he'd been awarded to fund his own lavish lifestyle.

Her accusations had been unfounded as Phelps had worked tirelessly to get to the bottom of what was causing Christopher's behaviour, but after six long months and after the grant had been spent he had to admit defeat. He just couldn't find anything wrong with Christopher. He'd applied for additional grant money, but had been turned down.

Phelps was disappointed that his research had yielded no results. It had been a stressful time which had put pressure on his marriage and caused his other work to suffer.

He hoped that someone else could carry on with the work he'd started and was frustrated that it was unlikely to be him who'd find the answer to the strange new abnormal variant of Rhythmic Movement Disorder which affected Christopher Jameson so severely.

Campbell looked at Maria from the corner of his eye and saw that she was crying. He didn't need to ask why, he knew Christopher was on her mind and she was dreading returning home.

He had moved in with her in January and was as affected by Christopher's disorder as much as she. Most nights were made up of interrupted sleep listening to whatever new mantra he would be chanting that week.

Over the past eighteen months Maria and Campbell had written down and recorded over sixty different chants. Most of them were four or five words long and every chant was delivered with the same laborious head banging.

Every chant followed the same theme. It was always a 'cry for help'. Either he was asking to be heard, to be answered or he was pleading to be set free. As Christopher had grown older, the voice he used at night had matured.

During the day he was a different child. He was happy, intelligent and loving. He had accepted Campbell as his father and the two had formed a close bond. Christopher played well with other children and was adored by his friend's parents.

His speech was developing and Maria enjoyed their little chats.

He seemed to be the perfect son, until the evening came.

Having Campbell in her life had been a blessing. She loved him dearly and would not have been able to deal with the horrors of the night without him. He had a calming influence on her. Just having him next to her during Christopher's bouts of RMD reassured her that somehow everything would be alright.

Campbell was a levelheaded and rational man who rarely raised his voice. He complemented Maria's fiery character and provided the antidote she needed to lower her stress levels and reduce her anxieties.

The traffic was now moving and their journey home continued. Maria was in the front passenger seat with her head turned to the left as she watched green fields and farmland pass by. She was quietly weeping and looked away from Campbell so he couldn't see her. Campbell knew she was crying and not just because he happened to see the first tear roll down her cheek. He could sense her body language. The way she held her head as she looked away from him, and her slightly laboured breathing, told him she wasn't happy.

They were fifty miles from Bristol and had about an hour to go until they were home. Campbell saw the sign for the services.

"Do you fancy stretching your legs?" he asked as he gestured to the sign.

Maria shrugged her shoulders.

"I need a comfort break and could do with a drink," said Campbell as he indicated and pulled across to the nearside lane.

He pulled into the service station car park. Maria was still looking out of her window. He put his hand on her shoulder.

"I just can't face the thought of going home," said Maria, who was still looking the other way.

"I know, but we can't stay away forever and despite what he does when he's sleeping, he's your little boy and he needs us."

She turned to him and wiped her tears with her sleeve.

"I know, I'm being stupid."

He stroked her cheek and shook his head.

"No you're not."

Campbell got out of the car and walked round to Maria's side and opened the door for her. They walked slowly hand in hand to the service station building and made their way to the restaurant.

"I don't want anything," said Maria as she sat at the nearest table.

"I need coffee, I'm I was almost falling asleep at the wheel."

She sat and watched him as he ordered his drink. Maria briefly pondered where she would be had she not met him.

He made his way to the table with two coffees on the tray.

"I said I didn't want one."

"I know, but I thought ahh, what the heck," he said as he slid her coffee across the table.

Campbell had something he needed to speak to her about, it was about Christopher and he knew she wasn't going to like it.

Maria didn't want anyone to know about her son. There were a handful of friends, family and doctors who knew about Christopher's sleep talking, and that was the way she wanted it to remain.

Campbell had been talking to a work colleague about Christopher. He hadn't intended to, but the conversation had just steered around to something that he thought could help get to the bottom of what was happening.

"Maria, I think I may have an idea of how we can find out what's happening to Christopher."

She looked up from her coffee and put her cup on the table.

"I think we should consider hypnotherapy."

"No, no, no. He's not being hypnotised. He's not even three for Christ's sake. Anyway you couldn't hypnotise a child."

Samreen had also suggested hypnotherapy and she had dismissed it then, and she was dismissing it again.

"Please hear me out" said Campbell gently.

"I've been talking with Connor in the office……."

"You've been talking to your friends about my son?" said Maria in a raised voice.

"Please listen Maria, let me finish."

Maria pushed away from the table and sat upright with her arms folded. He waited for her to relax before continuing.

"Connor was telling me about his brother who is a professional hypnotherapist and I was asking him about the sort of work he does."

Maria let him continue.

"Connor was telling me about how hypnotherapy works. According to him the subconscious mind does not forget anything at all. It is all stored there, neatly filed away."

Maria said nothing.

"The subconscious mind is far more powerful than the conscious one."

She picked up her cup and took a sip of coffee. Campbell waited for her to speak, but she said nothing.

"I'm just saying, give it some thought."

He'd planted the seed of thought in her mind. He was a clever man and knew when to stop talking. If Maria was going to come around to the idea of letting her son be hypnotised, she'd do it on her own terms.

Campbell had hardly mentioned Christopher to Connor. He had skipped the finer details and brought up that his partner's son had trouble sleeping at night, spoke when he was sleeping and that some of the things he said were unusual.

Connor had given his brother's details to Campbell and suggested he should think about giving him a call.

They finished their drinks and left the restaurant. Maria was quiet and still wasn't in the mood for conversation.

Before leaving the service station Campbell bought a bunch of flowers for Claire to say thank you for looking after Christopher.

It was quarter past five when he parked their car outside the flat. Maria left Campbell to get the cases from the boot whilst she opened the front door.

She turned the key in the lock and could hear Christopher running down the hall shouting, "mummy's home, mummy's home". The door swung open and he was jigging up and down with excitement waving Misty over his head. She bent down to hug him and he jumped into her arms. She gave him the biggest hug she could remember giving anyone.

"I've missed you darling."

Christopher wouldn't stop kissing her.

Campbell struggled with the cases and dropped them with a thud in the hall.

"Daddy!" squealed Christopher as he wriggled down from Maria and ran to cuddle Campbell.

After another long hug, Campbell put him down.

Christopher was jabbering excitedly about all the things he'd been doing with his nanny.

"Nanny got me ice cream and we went to the swings and nanny got me a train and nanny let me play on my bike and……….."

"So you've had a nice time with nanny?"

Christopher stood in the hall nodding his head looking very pleased with himself.

"Daddy can we play?"

"Ooh, let me sort myself out darling, then we can have a little play."

Christopher skipped down the hall and ran to his room.

Claire was standing at the end of the hall with a big smile on her face.

"Welcome home lovebirds."

She hugged Maria and turned to Campbell and kissed him on his cheek. Campbell gave her the flowers and Claire told him how lovely they were and that he shouldn't have.

"Are you guys hungry?" asked Claire, as she walked to the kitchen.

"I've made some sandwiches if you are."

She brought the plate of sandwiches into the lounge and placed them on the table.

Christopher ran into the lounge shouting for sandwiches.

They sat in the lounge and talked about the weekend. Maria stood up and read the engagement cards which were on the table.

Christopher ran out of the lounge and came back seconds later waiving a piece of A4 paper which was covered with random colourful crayon scribbles.

"Card for mummy and daddy," he said as he pushed it in Maria's face.

"Someone's been creative whilst you were away. He wanted to make you both an engagement card."

Claire stayed at the flat until Christopher was in bed. Maria read him a story and Campbell sat in the corner of his bedroom pulling faces behind Maria's back which made the little boy laugh.

"Is daddy being silly?" asked Maria.

"My daddy's funny," replied Christopher.

After the kisses, hugs and tucking in was done they shut his bedroom door and quietly stepped across the hall into the lounge.

"Well, how was he?" asked Maria.

"Same thing," replied Clare.

"I love my grandson so much, he's a wonderful little boy. He's so loving, happy and polite. I can't believe he's the same boy at night."

"I know," nodded Maria.

"Is there nothing else that you can do?"

"Look mum, we've been over this before. It seems that I had the top man in the country on the case and he couldn't work it out, so where else can I turn?"

Campbell stood up and walked to the kitchen as Maria watched him leave the room.

"Push the door shut mum."

Claire lent over and nudged the door with her hand and it slowly swung shut.

"Campbell thinks that we should take him to a hypnotist."

"Surely Christopher is far too young for that hocus pocus?"

"That's what I thought, but apparently he's not."

"And what good would hypnotising him do? It's not like you want him to stop smoking."

"I'm not sure."

Even though they had been speaking quietly, Campbell could hear what they were saying from the kitchen.

He came back to the lounge as Claire was getting ready to leave.

"Thank you Claire, I couldn't have taken Maria away without your help."

He hugged his prospective mother-in-law.

"You're a good man Campbell, and you're good for Maria."

"I know," he replied in his soft southern Irish accent. He smiled at her with a sparkle in his brown eyes.

Claire pushed him away and laughed.

"Campbell, put my mother down, she needs to go home," laughed Maria.

Maria stood at the door and waved to her mother as she drove away. When Claire's car was out of view she closed the door and returned to the lounge. Campbell was unpacking the cases in the bedroom.

"Leave that, I can unpack tomorrow, whispered Maria as she crept into the room. She put her arms around him and pulled him to the bed. He fell on top of her and kissed her on the lips. Maria kicked a small half empty case off the bed as he kissed her neck. She ran her hands under his shirt and held on to his back as his kissing became more loving. Maria was softly moaning with passion……..

"Ughh ughh ughh ughh ughh ughh ughh ughh ughh.

Christopher was chanting again.

"Talk about a passion killer," said Campbell as he rolled onto his back.

Maria lay next to him and stared at the ceiling.

They lay in silence as his chanting formed into words.

"Set me free - set me free - set me free - set me free - set me free - set me free - set me free - set me free - set me free."

"I've not heard that one in a few months," said Campbell in a tired voice.

Maria sighed.

"Set me free - set me free - set me free - set me free - set me free - set me free - set me free - set me free - set me free."

Campbell turned and looked at Maria. The evening sun shone through the window between the slats in the blinds. He admired her beauty in the half light and wondered what was going through her mind as a tear formed in her eye. He was used to seeing tears, and lately there had been more of them.

"Set me free - set me free - set me free - set me free - set me free - set me free - set me free - set me free - set me free."

Maria stared blankly at the ceiling. She drew a breath and turned to him. His face was silhouetted by the sun breaking through the half closed blind. He waited in anticipation for her to say something

"Campbell……."

She paused before continuing, "Call the hypnotist…….and do it tomorrow."

Campbell nodded and Maria closed her eyes.

CHAPTER SEVENTY NINE

Truro, Cornwall
Monday 7th May 2012

Daniel Boyd didn't do heights and hadn't planned on being halfway up a ten metre ladder whilst cleaning the office windows of Cornwall County Council in Truro.

In truth, Boyd hadn't planned anything during the past eighteen months he'd been living in Cornwall. He seemed to have stumbled across jobs that paid just enough to keep him going.

His car washing job came to an abrupt end when the business closed down. There was no big announcement, no discussion, it had just stopped.

One morning Boyd strolled over from the porta cabin that he'd called home for the last three months and saw that Don Mudge had not arrived to open up shop.

Cars were queuing to be washed but there was nothing Boyd could do but apologise. The keys to the cleaning equipment were locked in Mudge's office and Boyd stood around the forecourt looking like a lemon.

After a week it was clear to Boyd that Mudge had upped sticks and fled. Boyd knew that his boss had cash flow problems and assumed he'd fled from his creditors.

Over the months Boyd had picked up and lost many temporary jobs, including labouring, door security, dishwashing and speedboat hire. His favourite work had been during the summer when he'd spent a few months picking fruit. He enjoyed the outdoors and the weather had been particularly good that season.

"Stanley, you've missed a bit," yelled Boyd's latest boss.

His newest employer was an obnoxious man called Tony Dawes. He had a huge head and wore glasses which were so thick they gave the impression that his eyes were floating in the air. He played trumpet for the

Salvation Army and had a permanent red welt on his lips due to his constant trumpet playing.

Boyd stayed clear of the man and only associated with him when he was working. He'd stuck at the job despite loathing Dawes and hating heights, because like all of the other jobs he'd found, it was work that paid him in cash.

As far as the Inland Revenue was concerned, Boyd had disappeared from the face of the earth and had been replaced by the odd job man Stanley Jarrett.

He rented a cheap, grubby bedsit that wasn't much bigger than a cupboard. It boasted a Baby Belling tabletop cooker and a wardrobe. It was better than the porta cabin because it had heating and a bathroom which was only across the hall, as opposed to the other end of the street.

The downside of living there was his neighbour. A Neanderthal of a man called Jon Lightfoot. Lightfoot by name, but definitely not by nature. The bulky bald-headed man never smiled and stomped whenever he walked. Lightfoot's bedsit was the same size as Boyd's, but it sounded like he was permanently on a sponsored walk. Boyd wondered if Lightfoot's bedsit was a Tardis. Bigger on the inside than it was on the outside.

Boyd's neighbour was also fond of nineties indie rave music and let the whole of west Truro know by blasting it out until the small hours. Boyd had once, and only once, knocked on Lightfoot's door to politely ask him if he wouldn't mind turning his music down ever so slightly. Lightfoot's response was to lift Boyd by the neck and carry him back to his room and drop him unceremoniously on the floor. After this Boyd had acquired a pair of ear defenders which he nabbed from a council worker who had stopped digging the high street for his ten thirty tea break.

The ear defenders were an improvement, but they didn't stop the boom boom boom of the bass vibrate his teeth as he lay in bed. Boyd had been late for work on several occasions as the ear defenders blocked out his alarm clock.

Boyd had kept out of trouble and, other than taking the ear defenders, he'd steered clear of crime since moving to Cornwall. He'd hardly given any thought to the violent murder he'd committed nearly two years earlier and lived a remorseless life.

But the night before he'd had a dream. A very vivid and strange dream. He didn't dream very much these days because of the noise coming from the bedsit across the hall, but that night the Neanderthal had not been at home. Boyd assumed he was annoying other people elsewhere in Truro with his late night music.

Boyd had dreamt he was in court and was being tried for the murder of Ben Walker. His dream had been so realistic that he could smell the musky odour of the court room and his back ached as he sat on the hard wooden pew. The judge and the jury were all children. Not one of them had been older than three. Other than him, there were no adults in the court room.

The prosecution, who was a small girl wearing a silk gown with a flap collar and long closed sleeves, called the main witness. The court usher pushed a white Silverline pram to the front of the court. The hood was up so Boyd could not see the infant in the pram, but could see a baby's hand waving a small grey cuddly toy in the style of a cat with floppy legs.

The witness in the pram was sworn in and Boyd was surprised to hear that the baby in the pram had the voice of an adult.

The promise from the witness boomed around the wood clad court room.

"I promise before Almighty God that the evidence which I shall give shall be the truth, the whole truth, and nothing but the truth."

The dream continued with the baby witness detailing what had happened the night of the murder. The baby with the grown up voice recalled everything that happened. Memories that Boyd had forgotten were resurfacing in the strange dream.

The jury were about to deliver their verdict when Boyd was jolted by an abrupt bleeping sound. He opened his eyes as he woke to the sound of his alarm clock.

"Saved by the bell," he whispered, as he reached to switch off the alarm.

He knew it had only been a dream, but it troubled him, and he wondered if it was supposed to signify something.

The following day he'd kept looking over his shoulder and was paranoid about getting caught.

That evening he sat alone in a pub and had a few drinks before returning to his grimy bedsit.

He wasn't looking forward to sleeping as he didn't want the dream to return and to hear the verdict of the jury of children. For the first time he wanted the Neanderthal to play his music in the hope that his sleep would be so light that dreaming would be impossible.

At ten thirty the Neanderthal cranked up his music as Boyd lay on his back and endured the noise. He didn't sleep. Instead he stayed awake the whole night thinking about the dream and what it could possibly mean.

He was almost two hundred miles away from the hill in Badock's Wood but, like Carla Price who was way up in Darlington, there was no escaping from the mystical power of the strange Bronze Age burial mound.

CHAPTER EIGHTY

Thomas Judd's Hypnotherapy Practice
Bristol
Wednesday 9th May

Campbell sat alone in the small office. The bookshelf was neatly packed with books on law, psychology and counselling. He spotted one book which grabbed his attention called Therapists in Court. He was about to walk over to the shelf and take a closer look when Tom Judd entered the room with two mugs of coffee.

Judd was a tall wiry man in his mid-fifties. He had thinning, sandy hair and wore horn rimmed glasses. He oozed confidence and had an ability to put people at ease.

Judd had been fascinated by hypnosis since he was seven. He'd been on holiday with his family in Southport and one evening the family entertainment included a stage hypnotist. The young boy was mesmerised by how volunteers from the audience could be invited up to the stage and within minutes were performing the most ridiculous acts.

From that day Judd read as much as he could on the subject. Being only seven years old, he found a lot of what he read difficult to understand, but by the time he was eight he was able to use the power of suggestion to make his school friends do simple things that amazed them.

This was just the beginning of Judd's future as a hypnotist. By the time he'd left school he already had a reputation as the strange young man who could get you to do anything.

When he was seventeen he'd secured a job as a warm up act at a strip club. The audience would often call for him to return to the stage for an encore. Darren, the club manager had never seen anything like it. Warm up acts were always booed off stage so the leering audience of grubby men could get the girls onto the stage earlier. But Judd was different, the audience seemed to prefer to watch him than see the performing girls. Or perhaps it was that many of the girls Darren employed were past their prime.

Darren took a chance and replaced one of his regular strip nights with Tom Judd's own show. The gamble had paid off and the hypnosis nights were a success. The audience numbers doubled and were no longer ogling men, it consisted of husbands and wives, boys with their girlfriends. It had become a family show.

Word had got around and Tom had requests to perform at other venues around Bristol. Darren stepped in as his manager and was taking a crafty thirty percent of his fee.

It didn't take very long for Tom to work out that he had no need for a manager as the bookings were coming in thick and fast. Darren and Tom had fallen out several times over the amount of fee Darren was taking. Luckily for Tom, no contract had ever been drawn up between them as their agreement had been based upon a handshake.

On Tom Judd's eighteenth birthday he walked away from Darren and swore that he'd never work for anyone other than himself.

He'd spent many years, and had made good money, as a stage hypnotist but there came a time when he became restless and decided to move away from the lighter side of hypnosis and concentrate on using his abilities to help people.

When he was twenty six Judd had qualified as a professional hypnotherapist and had an outstandingly high success rate in curing clients of a list of phobias which included fear of snakes, cockroaches, spiders, flying, dentists, driving, tunnels and speaking in public.

Word of mouth quickly spread and he was helping his clients stop smoking which was ironic as at the time Judd was a heavy smoker, who had no intention of giving up. He was obsessed with smoking and even collected paraphernalia on the habit. He had scrap books of adverts from the nineteen seventies and collected lighters, roll up machines and loved all the different flavoured cigarette papers.

Eventually it dawned on him that smoking was taking over his life and he decided it was time to give up. By using self-hypnosis he'd given up within three days and hadn't touched a cigarette since. A friend had given him a cigarette and a match in a glass fronted wooden box with 'In Case Of Emergency Break Glass' written on it. Judd kept it and placed it on his office wall as a reminder of his smoking days.

In two thousand and nine he qualified as a Forensic and Investigative Hypnotist and was employed by the police to use Forensic Hypnosis as a way to get evidence during hypnosis that could be used and accepted in court.

Campbell thanked Judd for the coffee.

"I would normally charge a consultation fee, but as you know my brother I'll let you have this for free," said Judd with a look which denoted he was the boss.

Campbell wasn't sure whether he liked the man, but as Judd's brother had spoken highly of him and the testimonials on his website were good, he decided to hear the man out.

They discussed Christopher's sleep talking and RMD. Campbell had brought along his laptop to show the videos that he and Maria had made.

Judd watched the videos and Campbell saw the expression on his face change from one of nonchalance to concern.

"Please could I have a copy of these files?" he asked as he lowered the screen of the laptop.

"Why would you need them?"

"They would help me prepare for the hypnotherapy session, which would give me a better chance of curing Christopher in the first batch of sessions."

Campbell nodded reluctantly.

"Just as long as they don't surface on YouTube."

"Of course they wouldn't, besides I have my professional reputation to protect."

Judd fumbled through a draw of odds and ends and found a USB drive. He plugged it into the side of Campbell's laptop and copied the files.

"What Christopher is doing may seem extreme, but at the end of the day he's only talking in his sleep," said Judd as he waited for the video clips to slowly transfer to his USB.

"But why do you think he's coming up with such grown up stuff?"

"I can't answer that, and if your man in London didn't work it out I'm sure I can't either," Judd paused before continuing, "but it's my guess that Christopher has heard things, either on the television, or the radio, or perhaps he's just overheard conversations, and these sentences have lodged in his subconscious."

"So do you think you can help?"

"The mind is a powerful thing and is capable of some amazing stuff. Hypnotism is all about suggestion, and what I can do is place a suggestion in his subconscious which will switch off the sleep talking."

"Would you be able to stop the RMD?"

"Let's take things one step at a time."

Campbell nodded.

Campbell was pleased because at last things were moving forward and there was a glimmer of hope that Christopher's bizarre night time chanting could be a thing of the past.

"But the boy's not even three, is it possible to hypnotise a child?" asked Campbell.

"I've hypnotised children as young as four. Sometimes children are easier to work with than adults."

After the files had finished copying Judd closed the laptop, removed the USB drive and handed the computer to Campbell.

Judd gave him a price list and Campbell gulped when he saw the hourly rate. He shook Judd's hand and said he'd call to book a session.

Judd saw Campbell to the door and wished him goodnight.

When Campbell had gone Judd loaded the videos onto his desk top and watched in amazement as Christopher pleaded and begged to be set free and was shaken when he heard the infant swear like an adult.

He had no idea what was happening to the little boy and wasn't convinced that hypnosis was the answer.

"What the hell am I getting myself into? this kid's possessed by the devil," he said under his breath. He played the clips until he had seen enough.

CHAPTER EIGHTY ONE

University of the Arts
London
9.47pm
Thursday 10th May

Carla Price had achieved great 'A' level results at sixth form in Darlington. She had an unconditional offer from her first choice university in London.

She'd started the BA in Graphic Design last September and had immersed herself in her studies and loved university life. She shared a room with a student called Natasha at Manna Ash House. Manna Ash was close to central London and was a short tube ride from the campus.

She missed her father terribly, although things had never been quite the same since he'd found the sketch she'd made of Markland Garraway nearly two years earlier. They spoke regularly on the phone. She'd tried Skyping him, but he was struggling with the technology, so they had resorted to phone-only conversations. She had last seen him during the Easter vacation and was looking forward to the thirteen week summer break starting next month, after her exams were over.

Tomorrow was an important day as she had a written examination. She was with Natasha, who was facing the same exam at nine thirty the following morning, and they were going over some eleventh hour revision.

Natasha stretched and looked at the clock.

"I'm done in Carla, I don't know about you, but my brain cannot take in any more information."

Carla agreed. Her brain was like a saturated sponge and she was delirious with fatigue.

"I'm so tired I could cry," said Carla.

"Come on girlfriend, we've got a busy day tomorrow, let's get those lights out."

Carla neatly placed her revision in a pile on her bedside cabinet and climbed into bed.

Natasha switched out the light and felt her way across the dark room to her bed which was about ten feet from Carla's.

Carla's brain was spinning as revision notes circled her mind. Even though she was beyond tiredness she couldn't sleep. Natasha was gently snoring and Carla was jealous.

Why is she sleeping while I'm wide awake? she thought.

The room was pitch black other than the faint red glow of her bedside alarm clock. She lay in silence and tried to clear her mind.

Eventually she drifted off and was dreaming.

Back in Bristol the hill was reaching out to her and infiltrating her dreams.

In her dream Carla found herself in a court room. It was the same Crown Court that Daniel Boyd had dreamt of earlier that week. The dream was as realistic as Boyd's had been. She too could smell the muskiness of the wood clad court room and felt the discomfort of the seats.

She looked around and saw that everyone in the court room were children, with the exception of two figures. Alongside her to the left was an adult. His face was obscured as he was wearing a black hoodie, and in the seat behind her was a tall man wearing a suit and tie.

The children were muttering and giggling and the judge, who was also a child, called for silence in court.

Silence fell. Carla could hear the creaking of a wooden pew as a small girl wearing a silk gown with a flap collar and long closed sleeves stood up and spoke. The young girl called the main witness. Carla couldn't make out the name of the witness.

Then, just as in Boyd's dream, a court usher pushed a white Silverline pram to the front of the court. She couldn't see the baby in the pram as it was obscured by the pram's hood, but she could see the same floppy legged grey cuddly toy cat waving in the baby's hand that Boyd had seen in his dream.

The witness in the pram was sworn in and Carla heard the booming voice of an adult come from the pram.

"I promise before Almighty God that the evidence which I shall give shall be the truth, the whole truth, and nothing but the truth."

She looked at the adult to her left who slowly turned to face her. He pulled down the hoody which was covering his face. It was Daniel Boyd, with his pale spotty skin and his dark greasy hair. With a menacing smile he spoke to her.

"Hello Carla, remember me?"

"You're Daniel Boyd," she replied.

"No, I think you must be mistaken. My name's Stanley, Stanley Jarrett and we're going to prison for a very long time."

Carla covered her mouth to stifle a scream. She turned her head to look away and saw the other adult in court. He was behind her and was staring directly at her with a stern look. She recognised him as the man from her dream almost two years ago. The same man who she'd made the sketch of. It was Markland Garraway.

Garraway leant forward and whispered in her ear.

"If you do as I say, there'll be no prison for you Carla."

His Scottish accent was as clear as a bell. She turned back to Boyd who was smiling his evil grin.

"Prison Carla, you and me, we're going to prison."

He held his head back and laughed, which had a rippling effect on the children in the court who giggled along with Boyd.

"Silence in court, silence in court," called the judge, but Boyd and the children continued to laugh and giggle.

Carla awoke and sat up. She was shaking and her forehead was soaked in sweat. She got out of bed and made her way to the bathroom.

Natasha was woken by the sound of Carla crying. She ran in to be with her.

Carla lifted her head and looked at Natasha.

"My God Carla, you look awful, what's the matter with you?"

Carla stood up and made her way back to her bed as Natasha held her arm around her to support her.

"You're shaking."

Natasha sat her on the bed and went back to the bathroom to get her a glass of water.

"Whatever it is, I don't reckon you'll be sitting the exam tomorrow."

Carla took a sip and climbed back into her bed.

The dream had scared her because it was so real. Natasha turned out the light, got into bed and fell straight back to sleep.

Carla lay awake thinking about the dream for almost an hour before drifting off.

The hill had spoken to her.

CHAPTER EIGHTY TWO

Thomas Judd's Hypnotherapy Practice
10.50am
Saturday 12th May

Maria, Campbell and Christopher walked up the garden path which led to Tom Judd's practice. Judd ran the practice from his home and had converted the basement of his three story house into a consulting room, which led into the place he liked to refer to as the 'Quiet Area'.

"What are we doing mummy?"

"We're going to talk to a nice man who will help you sleep better at night," said Maria, as she glanced at Campbell.

"I'm a good sleeper aren't I mummy. I never wake up."

Maria squeezed his hand.

"I know darling, but sometimes when you are asleep you are a bit noisy and you keep me and daddy awake."

"I don't," said Christopher looking up at Maria with his angelic smile.

"If you're a good boy when we see this man we will treat you to something special afterwards."

"Toy, toy, toy, toy," said the excited little boy as he jumped up and down.

Campbell apprehensively pressed the buzzer on the silver intercom.

"Hello," said the voice as it crackled over the speaker.

"Hi Tom, its Campbell for our eleven o'clock."

"OK, the door's open, come on down."

He pushed the door and let Maria and Christopher go ahead of him. The heavy wooden door swung closed behind him.

Maria looked at the row of framed certificates that hung in the hallway. Campbell led the way down to the basement to a half glazed door which opened to the consulting room.

The room was pleasantly decorated and smelt of fresh coffee.

Tom Judd propped his glasses onto his head, stood up from behind his desk and walked over to Maria and Campbell.

"Nice to see you again Campbell," said Judd shaking his hand.

"And you must be Maria, pleased to meet you."

Maria took his hand and shook it whilst trying to portray an air of confidence.

Judd crouched down to Christopher's level and ruffled his hair.

"And who are you?"

"My name is Christopher and my mummy and my daddy they say I sleep funny, but I don't, don't I?"

Judd smiled and whispered in his ear.

"I think you probably sleep very well, but we need to do something today which will prove that you sleep really, really well. Would you like to help me with it?"

Christopher nodded.

"Good, I just need to talk to your mummy and daddy."

Judd stood up. He couldn't understand how this polite and happy little boy was the same one in the video. The same boy who cursed and pleaded for help.

Judd went to his desk and opened a drawer.

"Before I start I need you to sign some forms."

Campbell skim read the paperwork which was basically a list of disclaimers covering Judd if anything went wrong, or if the hypnotherapy didn't work. Maria took the sheet of A4 paper from him and read it.

"Let's just sign it," she whispered.

They handed the signed form back to Judd who made a copy for them and filed the original back in the drawer.

Judd turned to Maria.

"I've watched the videos and I am aware of what Christopher does in his sleep," he said quietly under his breath.

Christopher was oblivious to the fact they were talking about him and was busy spinning on Judd's office chair.

"I've already explained to Campbell what I intend to do, but I will go through it again for you."

Maria listened intently and was clearly nervous about the whole thing.

"The first thing I want to do is reassure you that hypnotherapy is completely safe. What I intend to do, and I may not get this right first time, but my intention is to flick a switch in his mind and turn off the sleep talking."

"Is it as simple as that?" asked Maria.

"Perhaps I've over simplified it, but basically that's what I will do by using the power of suggestion."

"Will it be scary for him when you put him under?"

Judd smiled.

"There's nothing scary about it, children love the experience. Kids have brilliant imaginations and once Christopher works out how to combine relaxation with his imagination, I can then begin to switch off the sleep talking."

Outwardly Judd was oozing confidence, which helped Maria relax, but inside he had no idea how the session would go and was apprehensive.

A few years ago he'd dabbled in regressive hypnosis when a client was convinced he'd been Winston Churchill in a previous life. Judd didn't believe in reincarnation, but there was something about Christopher which made him nervous. He put the thought out of his mind and stood up.

"Shall we," he said gesturing towards the door which led to the Quiet Area'.

Maria took Christopher by his hand and walked him to the other room behind Campbell and Judd.

The room was small and the walls had been painted in plain magnolia. The carpet was thick, which muffled their footsteps as they entered the room.

In the middle of the room were two chairs. One faced the wall and the other faced the side of the first chair. Against the back wall was a small settee.

Maria and Campbell nervously perched on the edge of the settee and held hands.

Judd picked Christopher up and placed him in the chair which faced the wall.

"Christopher, tell me what is your most favourite thing?"

"Meee," replied Christopher.

"Your favourite thing is you?"

"No, silly, Mee, my toy."

Judd looked confused and glanced at Maria.

"He's talking about his toy fluffy cat, he takes it everywhere."

Judd nodded and smiled.

"And do you have Mee with you today?"

Christopher shook his head.

"Sorry, we've left him at home," whispered Campbell.

Judd turned to Christopher and in a gentle voice asked him what else was his most favourite thing.

Christopher put his finger in his mouth and looked to the ceiling.

"Um, umm, umm……trains!"

"You like trains, I love trains," replied Judd.

"I think I've got just the thing."

He walked over to a small cupboard and pulled out a framed picture.

"Do you like that?" he said, showing Christopher a picture of Thomas the Tank Engine.

Christopher nodded enthusiastically.

Judd hung the picture from a hook on the wall directly opposite Christopher.

"What I would like you to do is to look at the picture of Thomas, can you that do for me?"

The little boy nodded happily.

"Good. When you're looking at Thomas I'm going to talk to you and I would like you to listen to what I say……can you do that for me too?"

Christopher nodded again.

Judd sat alongside Christopher and spoke in a quiet and confident voice.

"Now, do you remember what it feels like to go to sleep?"

Christopher nodded.

"Yes, that's right. And it can feel very good to drift off to sleep, can't it? And your body really likes to go to sleep because it feels so good."

He nodded again.

"So, let's think about your toes. Your toes can go to sleep. Your toes know how to go to sleep. Let them go to sleep now and tell me when your toes have gone to sleep."

"My toes are sleepy," said Christopher.

"Good, now your feet…let me know when your feet have gone to sleep."

"My feet are sleeping."

"You're doing very well Christopher. Now let your legs below your knees go to sleep and let me know when they're asleep."

Christopher nodded. "Legs asleep."

"Now let your legs above your knees go to sleep. Sleepy, sleepy legs. Let me know when the top parts of your legs are asleep."

"Legs asleep."

"Now your whole legs are asleep. Very sleepy legs. Nice and heavy………just sink into the chair now."

"Now let your bottom go to sleep. Sleepy, sleepy bottom. Let me know when your bottom has gone to sleep."

Christopher sleepily giggled and squirmed. "Sleepy bottom."

"And your tummy…sleepy, sleepy tummy."

Judd didn't need to carry on, Christopher was under hypnosis. Judd stood up and smiled at Maria and Campbell.

"He's under," whispered Judd, as Christopher slumped comfortably in the chair gently rolling his head from side to side.

CHAPTER EIGHTY THREE

The Awareness

Ben was awake and felt different. He didn't have quite the same urge to be heard and his pent up anger had gone. He almost felt relaxed.

He was recalling a childhood memory of when he was holidaying with his family. He was splashing with his brother on a Dorset beach and was enjoying the memory until something interrupted his train of thought.

His visual memories were distorted by a dim light. The light became intense and soon bleached the images from his memory. The light was swirling as if it was illuminating a churning mist. He could hear his brother's voice and the crashing of the waves, but he couldn't see anything.

And then Ben heard a different voice. It was a voice that he did not recognise.

CHAPTER EIGHTY FOUR

Thomas Judd's Hypnotherapy Practice
11.27am

Thomas Judd sat alongside Christopher, who was slumped in the chair with his eyes closed and gently rolling his head from side to side.

"Hello Christopher, can you hear me? If you can I would like you to say 'yes'."

Christopher stopped rolling his head. He opened his eyes and starred directly at Judd.

CHAPTER EIGHTY FIVE

The Awareness

"Hello Christopher, can you hear me? If you can I would like you to say 'yes'."

Ben was confused. This was not one of his memories. He hadn't just thought those words. He'd actually heard them. He felt the resonance and boom of a man's voice.

The white light had reached a peak and the intensity of the glare was almost painful. Then he heard the words again.

"Christopher, can you hear me? If you can I would like you to say 'yes'."

The words were as clear as a bell. But who was Christopher and to whom did the voice belong?

Ben didn't know how to answer. He'd been used to using his anger and hatred as an energy force to project his thoughts and he was aware that someone had heard him. But this was different. He felt no anger or rage, but was calm and relaxed. If it hadn't been for the intense white light, things would have been tranquil.

"Christopher, can you hear me? Please if you can hear me I would like you to let me know."

Ben focused on the words which were coming from the white misty light. He concentrated on the glaring intense luminosity and prepared his reply.

CHAPTER EIGHTY SIX

Thomas Judd's Hypnotherapy Practice
11.31am

Christopher lay in the chair and, with his eyes fixed on Judd's, he opened his mouth to speak.

Maria was craning her neck so she could see her son and was about to stand up. Campbell motioned for her to stay sitting down.

And then the boy spoke.

"I'm sorry, but who is Christopher?"

The boy's eyes were fixed upon the hypnotist's. Judd had to use all his will power to stay calm.

"You're Christopher, your name is Christopher Jameson," replied Judd in a quiet and reassuring voice.

"I think you're mistaken. My name is Ben."

The voice coming from Christopher was different. It had a different character. It was the same voice he used when he chanted and banged his head.

Maria began to shake. Campbell held her hand tightly.

"Hello Ben, do you have another name…..do you have a surname?"

Christopher nodded and kept his gaze directly on Judd.

"I do have another name, but before I tell you, would you do me a kindness?"

Judd's voice was beginning to waver.

"What would that be Ben?"

"Please could you tell me who you are, where you are and where on earth am I?"

Judd stood up and turned away from Christopher. For the first time in his professional career he didn't know what to do.

Maria was sitting upright on the settee, rocking to and fro. Campbell was pushing his fingers through his dark hair and was looking at Judd.

"Make him stop," whispered Maria.

Judd turned back to Christopher and began to bring him out from his hypnotic state.

"Christopher, I am going to count backward from five and as I do, you will slowly and gently begin to wake up."

"My name is not Christopher and I am not sleeping."

Whoever Judd was speaking with was not letting him talk to Christopher.

"OK Ben, my name is Tom and I need to say some words and I need you to listen very carefully……."

Judd paused and considered what to say next.

"Ben, tell me, is there anything you can see, is there anything on which you can focus."

"Hello Tom, it's nice to talk with you…. this may sound corny, but I am staring into a light."

"Good, that's good. Now I want you to keep looking into the light and concentrate on my voice".

Judd continued to use a similar routine to hypnotise Ben as he did with Christopher.

Within a few minutes Ben had stopped talking. Christopher's eyes were closed and his head was gently rocking from side to side.

Next, Judd brought Christopher out of hypnosis.

Christopher slowly opened his eyes and smiled when he saw Judd.

"I'm sleepy."

He turned in the chair and looked at Maria.

"Was I good mummy, can I have a toy now?"

He jumped down from the chair and, with unsteady legs, he ran to his mother and jumped on her.

"You were brilliant darling, and yes, you can have a toy."

He jumped up and down with excitement.

Judd turned to Campbell,

"We need to speak, come with me."

He followed Judd to the office and gestured to Maria to stay with Christopher.

Campbell shut the office door.

"What just happened?"

Judd shook his head.

"What just happened Tom? Because if you ask me, there is no way that was Christopher you were talking with."

"I'm afraid I can't help you," said Judd. His once confident and booming voice was now shaky and barely louder than a whisper.

"What do you mean, you can't help?"

"I meant what I said, I can't help you. Look, I won't charge for today and I'm sorry I've wasted your time."

"Tom, you've not wasted our time, we've made a breakthrough today."

Judd shook his head.

"I'm out of my depth, I've been doing this for over thirty three years and I've not seen anything like this before."

Judd drew a breath before continuing.

"We've all seen the stage hypnotists, you know, the charlatans, the ones that drag people on stage then put them in a trance and the volunteer claims he was Charles Dickens or someone in a former life."

Campbell nodded.

"Well, I think Christopher really is someone in a former life, or if not a former life, then he's definitely someone else and he's someone called Ben."

Judd sat on the edge of his desk and looked at Campbell.

"And that is why I can't help you……I'm out of my depth, way out."

"What do we do now?" asked Campbell.

Judd shrugged his shoulders.

"I don't know, but I'm sure there are other hypnotists that would be more than happy to take your money."

"But you said it yourself Tom, they're charlatans and you, well, you're the real thing."

"Sorry, but the answer's no."

Campbell went back to the quiet area.

"Come on, we're going."

"What's happening?" asked Maria.

"I'll tell you in the car."

Campbell and Maria walked out of the room. Maria held Christopher in her arms as they passed Judd who was perched on the edge of his desk. He couldn't look at them as they left his office and climbed the stairs.

Tom heard a little voice from behind the door leading up the stairs.

"Thank you Tom, mummy's getting me a new toy, thank you."

Judd heard the front door slam shut. He sat on the edge of his desk and was shaking. He glanced up at the cigarette and match in the little wooden case hanging from the wall and read what was written on the glass.

IN CASE OF EMERGENCY BREAK GLASS

Judd slithered off the edge of his desk and slowly walked to the case. He looked at the cigarette and read the words on the case out loud.

"In Case Of Emergency Break Glass"

He took the case from the wall and smashed it on the edge of his desk. The wooden case splintered and the glass shattered sending shards across the desk and onto the carpet.

The cigarette lay in front of him. It was attached to a piece of card by a tiny spot of glue. He carefully removed the cigarette with unsteady hands, carefully trying not to rip the paper.

Judd bent down and found the match which was resting on a large piece of broken glass.

He put the cigarette to his lips and held the match between his fingers. He looked around for something to strike the match with. On his desk was a pebble which he used as a paperweight. He picked it up and felt its rough surface.

He struck the match against the pebble. It didn't light. A tiny wisp of blue smoke rose from the match and Judd could smell sulphur.

He tried again and this time the match lit. He held the flame up to the end of the cigarette and drew in the smoke. It tasted stale and was at least ten years out of date.

As he inhaled smoke instead of oxygen, he was hit by a wave of dizziness and slumped against the wall.

He inhaled another breath of smoke and began to feel a little calmer. Judd sat on the carpet with his back against the wall and smoked the cigarette to the butt.

He stood up and put what was left of the smouldering cigarette in an empty cup.

Judd propped himself up against his desk with both hands and let out a large sigh. He thought about Christopher and what just happened.

He was certain that it wasn't Christopher who'd spoken. Every word that had come from the boy's mouth was far too mature to have been thought up by an infant. The boy wasn't even three and was speaking like he was thirty three. The subconscious was a powerful thing, but Judd doubted whether it was Christopher's subconscious that was talking.

He thought about the little boy and how happy and excited he had been to be there and how he trusted Campbell and Maria when they let Thomas Judd, a complete stranger, perform the strange act of hypnotism on him.

He thought about his own parents and how he'd trusted them when he was little.

He stood up, brushed the cigarette ash away from his shirt and straightened his tie.

He had made up his mind to help Christopher.

Judd picked up his phone and called Campbell.

CHAPTER EIGHTY SEVEN

Liz Mason's home
Bristol
12.15pm
Saturday 12th May

Liz Mason was lying in her bed in the newly built room which had been designed and paid for by her father Terry.

The room was an extension to the large four bedroom house in the salubrious Sneyd Park area of Bristol. Terry and Anne had wanted a room for their daughter with sleeping quarters for carers who could be with Liz twenty four hours a day, in case there were any complications. Another reason her parents wanted around the clock care for their daughter was because they wanted someone with her at all times in case she awoke from the coma.

Liz's new room was decorated in subtle colours and paintings adorned the walls. On her bedside table were pictures of her family and a few of her friends. Her mother had placed one of Ben Walker next to her bed, but had decided to remove it. She thought it wouldn't be a good idea if Liz awoke from the coma and saw a picture of Ben, only to be told he was dead.

The radio was constantly on throughout the day. Terry had decided that classic FM would be a good thing to have on. Although she was a young girl, Liz loved classical music. Terry had no idea whether she could hear the music, but there was no harm in trying.

Liz had been in a coma for over two and a half years. She'd hardly responded to any stimulation. Apart from the occasional twitch or eye movement below her lids, she had remained in exactly the same state as when she'd been found at the bottom of the hill in Badock's Wood in September 2009.

The carers that her father employed had just finished making Liz comfortable after changing her bed sheets.

Chloe Bryson and David Irvine where two of the six carers that worked shifts looking after Liz.

David was busy preparing Liz's lunch, which was a well-balanced intravenous solution, while Chloe was washing Liz's face with a damp flannel.

They'd been attending to her since February. Terry and Anne Mason had appreciated the care and hard work they'd put into looking after their daughter. Although they were employed by the Masons, the love and attention they paid to Liz made it seem as if they were part of the Mason family.

Chloe felt Liz's forehead as she dried her face with a hand towel. Liz felt hot to the touch and was beginning to show signs of restlessness.

"David, I think something's up."

David put down the solution he was preparing and walked over to the bed.

"Have you taken her temperature?"

"No, not yet, but I'm just about to."

Chloe took Liz's temperature. The readout on the digital thermometer read thirty nine point five.

"Shit," said David as she showed him the digital read out.

Liz became more irritable.

"Let's get that temperature down, I'll get her paracetamol," added David.

"You'd better call Mrs Mason, don't worry her, just tell her that Liz has a slight temperature and we're on the case," said David, as he prepared the paracetamol.

Within half an hour her temperature had dropped a degree, but was still a little high.

Anne Mason was sitting at her daughter's side and was wiping her forehead.

"If Liz gets worse, you must call a doctor," said Anne.

"I will," replied David.

"I'm sure she'll be fine. Don't worry Chloe and I will keep a close eye on her and if anything changes we'll call the GP."

"I know, I expect she's picked something up, Terry had a cold the other day, perhaps Liz caught a germ from her dad," said Anne, as she brushed Liz's hair from her eyes.

"The paracetamol has already begun to work, her temperature should be back to thirty seven before you know it," added Chloe in her best reassuring voice.

What was about to happen to Liz during the next few weeks would need a lot more than paracetamol to cure.

CHAPTER EIGHTY EIGHT

Maria and Campbell's flat
3.18pm

Campbell listened to the voicemail left by Thomas Judd.

"What did he want?" asked Maria, as she unboxed Christopher's new toy.

"He didn't say, he just wants me to call him."

Maria handed Christopher a red remote control Ferrari. He couldn't contain his excitement.

"Thank you mummy, thank you daddy," said Christopher, as he ran to the hall to play with his new car.

Maria was shaking after what had happened that morning and Campbell had poured her a large glass of wine. He had told her what Judd had said about Christopher, and what he thought about Ben being someone from a past life.

She didn't accept what Judd thought, but at the same time she wondered if there was any way that her son could be possessed by something or someone. A paranormal explanation would certainly make what had been happening easier to explain.

"Call him and see what he wants."

Campbell hit Judd's number and waited for it to ring.

"Put it on speaker," said Maria, "I want to hear what he has to say."

The two of them waited silently as they listened to the ringing of Tom Judd's phone. The only other sound was Christopher playing with his new toy in the hallway.

"Hello, Tom Judd speaking."

His voice was weak and tinny over the speaker. He sounded nasally, almost like he had been crying.

"Tom, its Campbell, I'm returning your call."

"Oh, hi Campbell," his despondent tone dropped further when he heard Campbell's voice.

"Campbell, I want to apologise about this morning, I'm sorry, I just wigged out."

"Yeah, we noticed," said Campbell in his calm Irish accent.

"Well, like I said, I'm sorry……I'm sorry and I would like to help."

"What do you propose?" asked Campbell.

"I would like you to bring Christopher back and I'll see if I can recreate what happened this morning………..that is, if you would like me to."

Campbell looked at Maria and she slowly nodded.

"OK Tom, we'll bring Christopher back."

"But I'll only do it if you agree to a few conditions," said Judd.

"What conditions?" asked Campbell cautiously.

"Number one, I want somebody else present, preferably a professional of some kind, you know, a doctor or a policeman. Number two, I insist that everything is recorded, I need audio and video of whatever happens and number three, I'm doing this for free and that's nonnegotiable."

Maria gestured to Campbell to come closer and whispered in his ear. Campbell nodded.

"OK Tom, we'll agree to your conditions, but we would like to add one of our own."

"And what's that?"

"We'll choose the professional person."

Judd paused for a second and then agreed.

Campbell told Judd he'd get back to him after they'd spoken with the professional.

CHAPTER EIGHTY NINE

The Awareness

By seven fifteen Maria had put Christopher to bed and it hadn't taken him long to get to sleep.

As he was sleeping, Ben was waking. Earlier that day Ben had briefly made contact with Tom.

Ben had no idea who Tom was. Ben was confused. Had it been a forgotten memory resurfacing, or had he actually been speaking to a real person? He didn't recognise the voice and he couldn't recall knowing anyone called Tom.

Perhaps his cries for help were working. He was certain that he'd been heard before, but he'd never received a reply until now.

But where was Tom? He was here one minute and gone the next.

Ben fell back on his reserves of pent up anger and loathing for the person who had killed him to create the energy needed to speak. This time he would make a direct request to speak to the only person he knew who could answer him.

"I need to speak to Tom - I need to speak to Tom - I need to speak to Tom - I need to speak to Tom - I need to speak to Tom - I need to speak to Tom - I need to speak to Tom - I need to speak to Tom."

CHAPTER NINETY

Christopher's bedroom
8.21pm
Saturday

"I need to speak to Tom - I need to speak to Tom - I need to speak to Tom - I need to speak to Tom - I need to speak to Tom - I need to speak to Tom - I need to speak to Tom - I need to speak to Tom."

Maria tiptoed into Christopher's room with Campbell close behind. They stood over Christopher as he rolled from side to side and banged his head against the pillow.

"I need to speak to Tom - I need to speak to Tom - I need to speak to Tom - I need to speak to Tom - I need to speak to Tom - I need to speak to Tom - I need to speak to Tom - I need to speak to Tom."

Maria spoke to Campbell in a voice which was barely above a whisper.

"Why don't we try talking to Ben?"

"How?" replied Campbell.

"Just by talking, like we do with normal people every day."

Campbell shrugged his shoulders,

"We could give it a go, I suppose."

Maria knelt down so her head was at Christopher's level.

"Ben, can you hear me?"

Christopher stopped banging his head and lay still with his head to one side. After less than ten seconds he started again.

"I need to speak to Tom - I need to speak to Tom - I need to speak to Tom - I need to speak to Tom - I need to speak to Tom - I need to speak to Tom - I need to speak to Tom - I need to speak to Tom."

Maria tried again.

"Ben, can you hear me? Speak to me if you can hear my voice."

Again Christopher briefly paused, but was soon head banging and chanting.

"I need to speak to Tom - I need to speak to Tom - I need to speak to Tom - I need to speak to Tom - I need to speak to Tom - I need to speak to Tom - I need to speak to Tom - I need to speak to Tom."

Maria stood up and looked at Campbell.

"Nothing's happening, I can't do it, why don't you have a go?"

Campbell leaned over and whispered in his soft voice.

"Hello Ben, my name is Campbell. Can you hear me?"

Christopher didn't stop head hanging or chanting.

"I need to speak to Tom - I need to speak to Tom - I need to speak to Tom - I need to speak to Tom - I need to speak to Tom - I need to speak to Tom - I need to speak to Tom - I need to speak to Tom."

Campbell tried a few more times before giving up.

"We don't have the knack, we need Tom Judd."

Maria nodded.

"You're right. Let's pray that Judd doesn't freak out like he did last time, I think he's our only hope."

CHAPTER NINETY ONE

TM.IT offices
9.15am
Monday 14th May

Campbell, Connor Judd, George Marshall and Toni Dufy were in the boardroom of TM.IT for the Monday morning conflab.

Terry Mason, TM.IT's managing director, insisted on a half hour meeting which each team every Monday morning.

Terry was late and the four members of the web design team were waiting for him to arrive.

Connor leaned towards Campbell and whispered as the other two were talking about the team's latest project.

"I heard you saw my brother over the weekend."

Campbell nodded.

"Why, what did he tell you?"

"He told me nothing, client confidentiality and all that, he just told me that you made the appointment."

"Yeah, we went to see him."

"He sounded pretty shaken when I spoke to him on Saturday."

"I expect he probably did."

Terry Mason entered the boardroom and everyone stopped talking.

"Good morning everyone, sorry to keep you waiting."

Mason dropped a folder and notepad onto the boardroom desk and went to the water dispenser. Campbell watched as he filled a plastic cup, drank the water and threw the cup in the recycling bin. Campbell looked at Mason's tired face and the bags beneath his eyes.

Campbell didn't know much about his boss, but he knew that his daughter was ill and had been in a coma for a long time. According to those who had worked for him over the years, he'd changed and was a different man.

A few years ago he was lighthearted and, even with the pressure of running one of the West Country's most successful IT companies, he had been calm and relaxed and hardly ever raised his voice.

Since Campbell had worked for him, he saw him as a man with a short fuse. Their paths didn't cross very often, but when they did Campbell felt like he was walking on eggshells and was nervous about saying the wrong thing.

Connor, who had worked for Terry Mason for over five years, told Campbell that Mason's change in character could be pinpointed to the time his daughter became ill.

Those who worked closely with Terry were of the opinion that lately he ran the company as a diversion to take his mind away from his daughter and that his heart and soul were no longer in the business.

Although he was the Managing Director, most of the business decisions were instigated by the Sales Director, Carl Cooper. Carl had taken over the running of the company after Terry's daughter had fallen into a coma. Over the following months Terry slowly returned full time, but it was now Carl who many of the staff turned to if they needed guidance or had to discuss important issues.

Terry was about to commence the meeting when his phone rang. He checked who was calling, made his excuses and left the room to take the call.

"He looks like shit this morning," whispered Campbell to Connor.

"You're right. I guess there's trouble at home."

Connor was right, there was trouble. Terry's daughter had picked up an infection and had been running a temperature over the weekend. Terry's wife Anne had called the doctor who prescribed a course of antibiotics. The medicine would take at least four days to clear the infection. Terry was jumpy and was having difficulty thinking about anything other than his daughter. He wanted to stay at home to be with her, but Anne insisted he went to the office. She was right, there was nothing he could do. The two carers looking after his daughter were able to keep a close eye on her condition and would be in contact with the doctor immediately, should things worsen.

Terry Mason came back to the boardroom and went to the water dispenser for another drink.

"Is everything OK?" asked Connor.

"Yeah Connor, things are fine, just a hiccup with the new account with the BBC that Cooper bagged last week. Some contractual bullshit needed sorting. Nothing to worry about."

Mason sat at the table and opened his folder.

"Well, I trust you all had a good weekend and are all refreshed for a new week."

Campbell and the rest of the team nodded enthusiastically.

"Good, let's get going."

Mason turned to Campbell.

"Mr. Broderick, you can start today's meeting. Is there anything you wish to raise?"

Campbell was telling Mason about a coding glitch that had been causing an issue on a website when he became lightheaded and had to stop to take a breath. He rested his head in his hands.

"Are you OK?" asked Connor.

Campbell didn't answer. The colour drained from his face. He could hear a buzzing in his ear which became so intense it blocked out the sound of his colleagues voices. He looked up to see Connor offering him a glass of water.

"Here, have a sip, you look like you've seen a ghost."

Campbell had just experienced a strange sensation. He felt a bonding between him and Terry Mason, and a very strong one. He couldn't pinpoint what it was, but he was sure they had something in common. It was almost as if they were family, but not as brothers or father and son. It was a dark connection which made Campbell uneasy.

The feeling soon past, but it left him feeling unsettled.

"You look like you're about to cry," said Mason in a mocking tone.

Campbell couldn't be there, he had to leave. He stood up, grabbed his papers, apologised, and left the room.

The others sat in a momentary silence.

"It looks like we've lost Mr. Broderick," said Mason.

"Connor, would you like to carry on."

CHAPTER NINETY TWO

Thomas Judd's Hypnotherapy Practice
The Quiet Area
5.15 pm
Friday 18th May

Christopher happily sat in the chair where Tom Judd had hypnotised him the previous Saturday. Misty was wedged under his right arm as he struggled to turn the pages of a comic given to him by Judd. He could hear the grownups talking in the other room but paid no attention to what they were saying.

Maria introduced Esther Hall to Judd as the professional that he'd insisted on being present during the hypnosis.

Maria and Esther hadn't spoken for a long time. She'd been aware that Peter Phelps and Maria had some kind of falling out, but didn't know exactly what had gone wrong between them.

Maria had called Esther at the beginning of the week and told her what had happened when Judd had hypnotised Christopher. Esther wasn't big on hypnotherapy, but was intrigued by what Maria had told her and agreed to be present as she was interested to see for herself and to be there in her professional capacity as Christopher's Child Health Visitor.

The four adults walked into the quiet area where Christopher was happily thumbing through his comic. Misty had fallen onto the floor. Esther bent down and picked up the toy cat and handed it to the little boy.

"You don't remember me, do you?" she asked as he took the grey cat from her.

Christopher nodded, then paused and with a big grin he shook his head.

"I didn't think you would, you were tiny the last time I saw you and now look at you, you're a big boy."

"My mummy and daddy say that I don't sleep very well and Tom is going to make me sleep well."

Esther smiled as she ruffled his hair.

"Mummy is going to get me another toy if I'm a good boy today."

Judd positioned his Olympus digital camera on a tripod and focused it on Christopher. He checked the battery level and selected the movie setting. He zoomed in on Christopher, but not too close, as he wanted to make sure the video included himself. He didn't know how the session would go and wanted to make sure he was captured in the video along with the boy. He pressed the little multi-function switch and the camera began recording.

Judd asked Maria, Campbell and Esther to sit on the settee and not to speak during the session. He took the picture of the train from the cupboard and hung it on the wall. He crouched down to Christopher's level and spoke in his quiet and calming voice.

"Christopher, do you remember last time you came here and I made you feel nice and sleepy?"

Christopher nodded.

"I'm going to do it again today."

"And my mummy will get me another toy."

"That's good. Aren't you a lucky boy?"

Christopher nodded again.

He told Christopher to look at the picture of the train and commenced the routine. Within a few minutes Christopher was gently rolling his head from side to side with his eyes closed.

"Christopher, let me know if you can hear me."

CHAPTER NINETY THREE

The Awareness

Ben immediately saw the strange misty light. It was the same one that accompanied the voice he'd heard before.

He was drawn to the light which swirled and spiraled like a whirlpool. It was hard to work out its colour. It mesmerised him. Ben was compelled to stare at its centre. He became overcome with a feeling of serenity and warmth as if he was enveloped by a hazy fog of love and kindness. He felt happy. And then he heard the voice.

"Christopher, let me know if you can hear me."

Ben could almost see the voice emanating from the light. He focused his attention towards it and replied.

CHAPTER NINETY FOUR

The Quiet Area

Christopher relaxed comfortably in the oversized chair. His eyes were gently closed and his head was slowly rolling from side to side.

Christopher stopped rolling his head, opened his eyes and looked at Judd. His mouth opened as he began to speak.

Judd crouched in anticipation.

"Hello Tom, it's Ben. Who's Christopher?"

Judd had no rehearsed lines and had not planned what to say. He was just going to let the conversation unfold, but was mindful of Christopher's safety and knew he had to bring him out of hypnosis should anything go wrong.

Maria squeezed Campbell's hand as the stranger's voice came from Christopher's mouth. Esther watched in awe.

"Hello Ben, it's Tom again. Let me introduce myself. My name is Thomas Steven Judd. What's your name?"

"I'm Ben Walker, no middle name, just Ben Walker."

Judd looked at Christopher. His eyes had closed again. He looked happy and relaxed and showed no sign of distress. Judd decided it was safe to continue.

"Hello Ben, I think we may have lots of questions for each other, but I don't know whether we'll find all the answers today. Let's just treat this as an opening dialogue."

"OK Tom, I'll go along with that."

Judd drew a breath and began.

"OK Ben, can I ask, where do you think you are?"

"I've no idea, absolutely no idea whatsoever."

"Are you in a room, a garden, or a field?….. tell me what you can see."

"I see nothing, nothing but my memories. Memories are all I have."

"What sort of memories and how far do they go back?"

"It feels like I've been here forever, and the memories, they go back, way back."

Judd looked towards the settee and saw Maria staring intently at Christopher. He gestured to her to make sure she was happy for him to continue. She snapped out of her stupor and Judd gestured again. She nodded. Judd turned back to Christopher.

"OK Ben, what kind of memories do you have?"

"I remember lots of things. My life, my family, my friends...........and............I remember clearly...........I remember very clearly...........my death."

Tom took a while to absorb what he'd just heard. *Death? This person says he's dead.*

Judd was stumped. He had so many questions for Ben. He didn't know what to ask first. He felt stupid. He should have been prepared for something like this. Then Ben spoke again.

"Tom, this is two way thing, isn't it?"

He nodded, then remembered Ben couldn't see him.

"Yes, it's a two way thing."

"Good, then I've some questions for you."

The room was silent. A silence which underwrote the importance of the moment.

"Tom, tell me about you, and also I would like to know where you are and how you found me."

"OK Ben, I'm just going to cut to the chase, things can't get much stranger than they are, so here goes."

Judd's nerves were getting the better of him. His throat was dry and his hands were trembling. He reached for a glass of water, took a large gulp and cleared his throat.

Judd began to answer the questions one by one.

"I am a professional hypnotherapist and as we speak I am in my practice in Bristol."

He briefly paused to consider whether to mention Christopher. After a little deliberation he decided to tell Ben everything.

"I have a little boy sitting in front of me and he's under hypnosis. He's been brought to me because he is restless at night. You see he talks in his sleep. His family wanted me to stop the sleep talking. But now I know it's not the little boy who talks, it's you Ben."

"This little boy, I presume he's Christopher."

"Yes, he is. I need to say something very important, and I hope you will understand. If things start to go wrong with Christopher whilst we are talking, I will need to bring him out of hypnosis, which means I will do what I did before with you. I will need to hypnotise you first."

"Tom that must have been a first. You surely must be the first person to have hypnotised a dead person."

Judd suddenly went cold all over.

"Could you do something for me Ben? I have Christopher's parents nearby and they're listening as you speak, so you've got everyone's attention. His mother's name is Maria and his father's name is Campbell. Please could you stop pleading to be heard. You've been putting Maria and Campbell through a couple of years of hell."

"Tell them I'm sorry, I didn't know."

"Tell us a bit more about you. When were you alive? Did you live to be an old man? And where did you live?"

Ben struggled to answer the first question. He had no concept of times and dates and couldn't work out the year he'd died. Time was something he couldn't comprehend.

"Sorry Tom, I can't work out dates and times, but I know I died young and that's something of which I'm certain. Oh, and were did I live? I lived in Bristol. Bristolian born and bred".

Maria stood up and walked over to Christopher. She looked at her son gently lying in the chair, eyes shut and looking relaxed.

"Tom, it's time to finish now, I don't want this to continue tonight. Give Christopher a rest, please."

Judd nodded and raised his hand and gestured for her to wait a little longer.

"Ben, Christopher's mother is getting concerned for her son, and I hope you can appreciate how she must feel, so I'm going to bring Christopher out of hypnosis very soon, but I have one more question before we finish today."

Christopher lay still for a few seconds and then he began to speak.

"Sorry Tom, I'm beginning to feel tired, I don't think you'll need to hypnotise me, but I'll try to answer. What's your question?"

"You said you remember your death very clearly. How did you die?"

Christopher became restless and Judd was concerned that he was coming out of his hypnotic state.

Christopher opened his mouth and quietly mumbled something which was just about audible.

"I was murdered Tom, somebody killed me."

CHAPTER NINETY FIVE

Truro
Cornwall
5.37pm
Friday 18th May

Boyd was nervously teetering on the eighth rung of the ladder. He'd hoped that his latest job as a window cleaner would have helped overcome his fear of heights, but the phobia was getting worse.

He daren't look down or else he would experience a wave of nausea and dizziness. He had only been on the job for five weeks but already he'd had enough of it. He wasn't lazy, these days he worked very hard to keep his head above water, it was the heights, and he hated them.

If anyone was lazy, it was his boss Tony Dawes. Boyd hated the man and this was the other reason why he wanted to move on.

It was a warm afternoon in May and Boyd had one building to finish before he was done for the day. He should have finished half an hour ago, but he was having a bad day with heights and was taking longer than usual to clean the windows.

Dawes was standing at the bottom of the ladder impatiently waiting for Boyd to hurry along.

"Stanley, what the hell's wrong with you today, speed it up will you."

"Fuckin' idiot," said Boyd under his breath.

Boyd climbed another seven rungs of the ladder to reach the highest window of the three storey house at the end of the leafy road in Truro. He reached for his T bar and gingerly dipped it in the bucket of soapy water which was hanging from the ladder. Hauling that bucket of water up the ladder with one hand whilst holding on with the other made his legs turn to jelly.

Cautiously Boyd reached over to his right and covered the window with suds as water dripped from the T bar to the garden below. The pane was masked with soapy water obscuring the view into the room beyond the window. Boyd tucked the damp T bar back in his tool belt and grabbed a wiper blade to remove the soap from the window. He strained as he reached the far corner and worked back towards the middle of the window.

As he cleared away the soap he saw a figure standing in the window. The figure of a young man was staring at Boyd. Boyd smiled at the man, which was something his boss insisted he did with his customers, but the man didn't smile back. The intensity of the man's stare bothered Boyd. He chose to ignore him and continued to clear the soap from the window. The streaks of water distorted the man's face so Boyd couldn't make him out. As the water evaporated in the warmth of the late afternoon sun, the man's face became clearer. Boyd tried not to stare back and carried on with his work. The weight of the man's stare fell upon Boyd and even without looking he knew the man was watching him.

Eventually Boyd had finished the last window of the house and was about to make his way carefully down the ladder. He looked back to the window and saw that the man was still there, still staring at him. The sun disappeared behind a cloud, taking some of the glare away from the window which made it easier for him to see the person who was watching him. It bothered him why this strange man was so interested in him.

Suddenly Boyd froze with dawning recognition when he realised who the man was. His hands tightly gripped the ladder as he stared back at the man in the window.

The man in the window slowly shook his head with a disapproving look.

Boyd was confused, how could it be. The man moved closer to the window and Boyd could clearly see his face. There was no doubt as to who the man was. Boyd was staring into the eyes of a dead person, it was Ben Walker. Walker looked at him and a menacing grin spread across his face. Ben Walker put his face up to the glass and mouthed four words through the window. Boyd could clearly read Walker's lips.

"I've got you now."

In shock Boyd released his grip from the ladder and fell. He dropped like a stone and fell twenty five feet to the garden below. Luckily he had a soft landing in the hedge which separated the garden from the pavement. He dropped from the hedge and awkwardly landed on the grass, only just avoiding an ornamental sundial.

Boyd lay on the grass as Dawes came running over, almost knocking over the sundial.

"What do you think you're doin' Stanley?" shouted Dawes, showing no concern for Boyd's wellbeing.

Boyd groaned as he turned over in the grass and looked at Dawes.

Dawes was used to seeing Boyd's pale and insipid complexion, but was taken aback when he saw how colourless he looked as he lay face up in the grass. He was whiter than white.

"Good God Stanley, you look awful."

CHAPTER NINETY SIX

Thomas Judd's Hypnotherapy Practice
The Quiet Area
5.42pm

Christopher was rocking in his mother's arms as she sat back on the settee. Other than feeling tired, he showed no ill effects from being hypnotised.

The four adults said nothing as they contemplated what they had just witnessed.

Eventually Judd spoke.

"So what happens next?"

"Nothing, nothing is going to happen next," said Maria, as she nuzzled into Christopher's hair.

"We can't stop now, I've got to hypnotise him again, and the sooner the better."

Judd's shock at what had just happened had turned to excitement. He was desperate to find out more about Ben Walker.

"Leave my son alone."

For Maria the nightmare was getting worse. There was nothing that could have prepared her for what had just happened. The first time he'd been hypnotised had been bad enough. She was hoping that Judd would have been able to use hypnosis to stop the sleep talking, but when this Ben character briefly popped up she had been horrified.

But after speaking with Campbell, it seemed likely that Ben was a figment of her son's imagination which was enhanced by hypnosis. She'd expected today's session to stop the sleep talking and put an end to Christopher's imaginary friend.

But it hadn't. It really seemed that Ben was a real person. There was no way on God's earth that her son could have come out with the things he'd said under hypnosis. He just didn't have that level of vocabulary and understanding of the English language.

"But Maria, this is really important, ground breaking," pleaded Judd.

"I don't care, this isn't what I signed up for." Maria pulled Christopher closer.

Campbell was keeping quiet. While he agreed with Judd and was eager to find out more, he also respected Maria's wish to cease the hypnosis.

"I would like to hear it from Esther's standpoint, I'd appreciate the view from a professional." said Judd.

Esther had been standing with her back against the wall. She moved forward and cleared her throat to speak.

"From my professional position as a Child Health Visitor I have to consider Christopher's welfare and to be honest, I know very little about hypnotherapy, so I agree with Maria that there should be no further hypnosis."

Judd was about to say something, but paused as Esther raised her hand to imply she had not finished.

"But, on the other hand, I have to agree with Tom, something is happening here, something very unusual. Unless Tom is staging an elaborate hoax, and I don't think he is, then I agree that we need to get to the bottom of it. If whatever is going on with Christopher isn't stopped, it may have implications for his health, and I mean from a mental health angle."

Judd nodded. "I agree with Esther."

Maria didn't want to hear any of this. She looked at Christopher, who clearly didn't like the attention he was getting.

"Can I go home mummy?"

Maria nodded.

"We'll be going soon darling," said Maria whilst kissing his head.

Esther continued, "I would like to make some enquiries about the implications of hypnosis and what effect it may have upon Christopher. If there is chance that it could be harmful, then I agree with Maria and the hypnosis should stop……..but, if my enquiries confirm that there will be no ill effects, I think Tom should continue."

Nobody spoke. Christopher was irritable and was getting tired. He hadn't eaten since lunch time and wanted to go.

"I think we're missing an important point," said Judd, as all eyes turned to him.

"This could be considered a murder case, Ben said that he'd been killed by someone."

Maria put Christopher on the settee, stood up and walked over to Judd until she was facing him.

"Can you hear yourself? You're literally accusing my son of murder and that's ridiculous. You clearly have no idea how stupid you sound. In any case, if my son is possessed by the soul of some dead person, if Ben Walker had been a real person, he would have probably been a pirate, or someone from hundreds of years ago, so murder isn't an issue."

She paced the room looking for the words needed to convey her anger.

"Tell me Tom, am I right, whenever you hear of people who are hypnotised and regreviss, regreshiv…." in her anger Maria struggled to find the word.

"Regressive hypnotherapy," offered Judd.

"Yes, regressive hypnotherapy, whenever regressive hypnotherapy is used it always conjures up someone noteworthy like Henry the Eighth, or Joan of Arc or someone famous like the other Joan, Joan Collins."

"Joan Collins isn't dead," said Judd interrupting her flow, which heightened Maria's anger. Her fiery temper was rising.

"You know what I mean, these characters are always someone we've heard of."

"You're confusing hypnotherapy with stage hypnosis. You saw what just happened, I'd hardly had time to hypnotise Christopher before Ben began speaking. Regressive hypnosis takes time and is a laborious task. Play back the video and see for yourself, I didn't set any of this up."

The camera was still on and recording everything. Judd walked over and switched it off.

"And a lot of help you are, I thought you were supposed to be on my side," said Maria to Campbell in an accusatory tone.

"I am on your side, but I have to say that I do agree with both Esther and Judd. If Esther can confirm that none of this will effect Christopher, then I think Judd should continue."

Maria threw her hands in the air.

"Campbell, I'm sorry to have to remind you, he's not your fucking son, he's mine and it's got nothing to do with you or anyone else in the room. Now, if you will excuse me, I'm taking Christopher home."

She picked Christopher up and held him close as she left the Quiet Area, leaving Campbell and the others behind.

They could hear Maria struggling with the door which led out of Judd's office, up the stairs and out of the building.

"Can someone help me with this door please!" shouted Maria.

Esther went to the office and opened the door, allowing Maria to clump up the stairs. Christopher was crying.

They heard the outside door thud as it shut behind her.

"Give her some time and she'll come round to the idea," said Campbell in a calm voice. The others nodded.

Campbell decided to give her some space and not go back to the flat that evening. He sent her a text message to say he was staying at David's house. David was an old friend from the coffee shop and was to be Campbell's best man. In his text message he told Maria to contact him if she needed anything.

That night was the first time since she could remember that Christopher slept without chanting. He banged his head, but he was quiet. He didn't even resort to the old 'ughh ughh ughh' he used to do before the talking started.

Maria lay in bed listening to Christopher gently bang his head and she remembered that the voice purporting to be Ben Walker promised to stop talking when Christopher slept. She dismissed the thought as nonsense and put it down to coincidence.

The next morning, after a bad night's sleep worrying over what had happened, she woke and got Christopher and herself ready for the day.

"Where's daddy?" asked Christopher.

"He's not here at the moment."

"I want daddy."

Maria checked her phone. There were no missed calls or texts, other than the one Campbell had sent from David's.

She could be a stubborn woman and at times held a grudge when it would be better to give in. Many times she had cut off her nose to spite her face. She was adamant not to contact Campbell.

She had planned to meet with Samreen later that day, but after yesterday's events wasn't in the mood to see anyone. She wanted to hide away from the rest of the world and be on her own.

By ten thirty, she was climbing the walls with boredom and had to get out of the house. She strapped Christopher into his buggy and left her flat. Leaving the car parked outside, she decided to walk. She had no idea where she was going and let her feet take her anywhere.

It was a beautiful May morning and the high street was busy. Maria negotiated the pedestrians as she weaved Christopher's buggy in and out of the clusters of old ladies who gathered outside the charity shops which were dotted up and down the high street.

She stopped to look in the window of a clothes shop and caught site of her reflection. In her mirrored image she saw how tired looking she had become. Bags were beginning to form under her eyes and her red hair was starting to show wisps of grey.

"Where are we going mummy?" asked Christopher.

Maria bent down to his level.

"Where would you like to go darling?"

"The park, please mummy."

"Good idea, let's go to the park."

Maria turned around and headed to the large park which was behind the shops on the high street.

The play area in Keynsham Park was quiet. Most children were at school and other than a small group of mums and their young children, the park was empty.

"Swings mummy," called Christopher as he pointed to the row of four empty swings in the corner of the playground.

She placed him on a swing and pushed him as he cheerfully laughed and giggled.

"Higher mummy, higher."

She pushed the swing and became entranced in thought as she recalled what had happened the day before. She'd been thinking about it all night as she had been trying to get to sleep and now, during the day, it was consuming her in her waking hours.

She had been pushing Christopher back and forth on the swing for almost twenty minutes whilst lost in her thoughts. She was brought out of her dreamlike state by the sound of her son, who was close to tears.

"I said I want to get off now mummy."

She snapped out of her brown study to see the group of mothers staring at her as she'd been aggressively pushing the swing back and forth in a robot like manner. Maria slowed it down until it stopped and pulled Christopher out of the swing.

Within seconds he had stopped crying and was running over to the small climbing frame which had been made in the shape of a steam train.

Lazily she followed him and sat on a nearby bench as he clambered upon the frame and made train like noises which were punctuated with cries of 'all aboard' and 'tickets please'.

Maria's phone was buzzing. She'd received a text. She grabbed the phone and opened her messages. She was hoping for a message from Campbell, but was disappointed to see it wasn't from him.

Maria was still angry with Campbell for not siding with her and was holding out for an apology. But no apology was forthcoming. Not even a text to ask her how she was.

She recalled what she had said to him in anger, 'he's not your fucking son.'

No wonder he wasn't contacting her. It had been an awful thing for her to say. The man had stood by her for almost two years and had to endure the strange behaviour of her son. Most men wouldn't have put up with it, but Campbell had, and without any complaints.

He'd bonded with Christopher as if he were his own child and the two of them had become inseparable. She missed him.

The message was from Samreen. She was checking whether they were still on for lunch.

Maria knew that Samreen would be desperate to know how it had gone yesterday and would have expected Maria to have called her as soon as she'd put Christopher to bed. Maria hadn't even called her mother and had ignored three missed calls from her. She hadn't wanted to talk to anyone.

She sat on the bench and watched Christopher playing happily. It was going to be a long day, and keeping her son occupied without going out of her mind would be a challenge, especially after the lack of sleep.

Maria picked up her phone and replied to Samreen's message.

'C U in the coffee shop 12.30. M xxx'

She pressed send and checked the time. It was twenty to twelve. She stood up and called to Christopher.

"Come on, it's time to meet Samreen."

Christopher cheered and hurriedly clambered down from the climbing frame and jumped into his buggy. Maria strapped him in and made her way to Coaster's.

Maria arrived at Coaster's just before twelve thirty, ahead of Samreen. She ordered two cappuccinos and a babyccino for Christopher. She sat at a table with Christopher and looked around the coffee shop. This was the place where she had first set eyes on Campbell. She remembered how she felt when she first saw him and how he had that special something that attracted her to him. She checked her phone again and was disappointed to see still there were no missed calls or texts from him.

Samreen arrived a little late. She was flustered and apologised for not being on time.

Maria told her what had happened at the hypnotherapist, as Samreen listened intently, not speaking until Maria had explained the evening from beginning to end. They spoke in hushed tones as Christopher was sitting alongside and Maria was mindful that he shouldn't know what had happened when he was under hypnosis.

"I'd hate you to think that I'm not on your side, but I think that you should allow Christopher to be hypnotised again, if for nothing else but to get rid of whoever Ben Walker is. I don't think it matters whether Christopher's made him up or if he's real, I think you need to use hypnosis to stop all this from happening."

Maria was considering whether her behaviour last night was over the top. She remained almost certain that she wouldn't allow Christopher back to Tom Judd's place, but there was now a nagging doubt in the back of her mind.

Deep down she knew that Ben Walker must somehow be a real person who was communicating through her son. What else could explain the knowledge and vocabulary he was coming out with. Let alone his expression.

He sounded so different under hypnosis. There was little sign of his still-to-develop infantile voice. Although his voice was clearly childlike, due to his immature vocal cords, there was something about the delivery of his tone whilst he was under hypnosis that made him sound older in years. The manner in which he constructed sentences and answered Tom's questions were way beyond his capability.

Christopher sat on Samreen's lap and excitedly told her about Tom and the toy he'd been given for being a good boy and how Tom made him go to sleep just by talking to him.

Maria listened to him chatting away to her best friend. He certainly seemed unaffected by his ordeal.

They left the coffee shop and strolled around the high street before going their separate ways. It was early afternoon and Maria had nothing planned for the rest of the day.

She checked her phone and saw there was still no attempt by Campbell to contact her.

Slowly she made her way back to the flat. When she turned the corner of her street she was horrified to see that the car had gone from where she'd left it yesterday evening. She quickened her pace as a mild panic set in.

She opened the door and hurriedly manhandled Christopher and the buggy into the hall. She closed the door and saw a note had been put through the letter box and was lying on the floor. She bent down to pick it up, it was from Campbell.

'I called round to see you, but you were out. I needed the car to get to a meeting in Cardiff. I will drop it back later. I hope you are OK.
Love Campbell x x'

She put the note in her pocket and wheeled Christopher into the lounge, undid the straps and he climbed out of the buggy.

"Is my daddy home?"

"Not yet darling, I'll expect you'll see him later."

Maria walked over to the window and gazed down the street, hoping that Campbell would be back early from the meeting. She craned her neck to see whether he was driving down the road.

Maria spent the rest of the afternoon entertaining Christopher. After the previous evening's events, and the bad night's sleep, she was exhausted.

By seven o'clock Christopher was in bed and she was stretched out on her bed longing for sleep. She forced herself to stay awake in case Campbell returned with the car. She was losing the battle with fatigue, and soon she was sleeping.

Campbell returned with the car just after eight. He'd received no text or call from her so he assumed that she wasn't in the mood for talking. He posted the car keys through the letterbox and left a note saying he'd call her after work tomorrow.

He hoped that after two full days of not being with him she'd have calmed down.

At eight twenty five Christopher began to quietly bang his head and rock from side to side. There was no grunting or chanting, he just gently nodded his head into his pillow.

CHAPTER NINETY SEVEN

The Awareness

Ben was awake. He could see no mysterious light and so assumed he would not be speaking with Tom.

He'd contemplated what had happened when he had spoken with him. He was certain they weren't memories as he had no recollection of speaking with Tom when he was alive. The more he thought about his conversation with him, the more things began to make sense.

Somehow, he had ended up within the body of a small boy. Was this reincarnation? Would Christopher grow up and would Ben live on through Christopher's existence? Perhaps, but it didn't feel that way.

Ever since he had died, Ben had a need to be heard. He'd accepted he'd been killed and was now in some kind of afterlife. The longing to be listened to was stronger than ever. He knew what it was he wanted to say, he was desperate to name his killer and get the bastard locked away. Something made him think that his killer had never been caught, it was just a feeling. He also wanted to get a message to Liz to let her know he'd never stopped thinking about her and that the last memory of the two of them was his favourite memory of all.

Ben planned what to say to Tom the next time they spoke. The first thing he intended to do was name the person who killed him. He replayed the memory of just before the rock was slammed into his head, the moment he looked his killer in the eye. He knew that he'd had a connection with the person who'd killed him, he couldn't recall what the connection was, but he was aware that they'd met before.

But what was his name? Ben could not remember his killer's name.

When Ben first developed within Christopher he spent his time collating memories, putting them in order and working out who was who. It wasn't long before he could name close friends, family, work colleagues etc. These had all been people with whom he'd been close. He had difficulty remembering the names of those who had not been so close. As hard as he tried to remember, Ben did not know the name of his killer.

The other thing Ben struggled with was time. He still had no concept of the passing of time and had no idea how long it was since he'd died. He couldn't even remember what time of year he'd been killed. He recalled it being a day of fair weather, but it could have been any season.

He was starting to get angry. What if all of this hard work struggling to be heard was a waste of time and he would end up trapped within Christopher's body forever? And what would happen to him after Christopher eventually died? The anger was building and he needed to get a message out. He needed to speak with Tom again. Tom was the only one he could talk to. Perhaps Tom had the answer.

The anger and hatred towards his killer was building. He'd promised Tom he'd stop making himself heard so Christopher could sleep peacefully, but he was desperate to get another message out.

This time he had a message directly for Christopher's parents. He couldn't recollect the father's name, but he remembered the mother's name, Maria.

He let his hatred and anger rise to boiling point until he had the energy to project his thoughts through Christopher.

"Maria I need to speak to Tom - Maria I need to speak to Tom - Maria I need to speak to Tom - Maria I need to speak to Tom - Maria I need to speak to Tom - Maria I need to speak to Tom."

CHAPTER NINETY EIGHT

Maria's flat
8.31pm

Maria was sleeping lightly when the chanting voice crackled over the baby monitor.

She opened her eyes and sat bolt upright. It was light outside as she checked the time on her bedside alarm clock.

The chanting wasn't as loud as it normally was, this time Christopher's chanting was barely louder than a whisper and she couldn't hear the words.

She got out of bed and cursed under her breath.

"I thought he was going to stop this nonsense."

She opened Christopher's door, crept in and stood over his bed. She was drowsy and couldn't work out what he was chanting. Kneeling down, she put her ear to his mouth.

"Maria I need to speak to Tom - Maria I need to speak to Tom - Maria I need to speak to Tom - Maria I need to speak to Tom - Maria I need to speak to Tom - Maria I need to speak to Tom."

She recoiled when she heard the words.

"Maria I need to speak to Tom - Maria I need to speak to Tom - Maria I need to speak to Tom - Maria I need to speak to Tom - Maria I need to speak to Tom - Maria I need to speak to Tom."

"No, no, stop it, please go away, whoever you are, leave my son alone….please."

She sat on the floor and wept as Christopher banged his head and whispered the new chant. A chant which was addressed to her. The whispered tone made the chanting sound more surreal than before.

She recognised the voice as not being her son's, it was the same voice he'd spoken with when Tom Judd had hypnotised him and it was the same voice he used every time he chanted in his sleep.

Maria edged away from Christopher until her back was against the wall. She banged her head against the wall behind her, and again, and then she did it again until she was thudding the back of her head along with the slow but steady beat drummed by her son.

"Maria I need to speak to Tom - Maria I need to speak to Tom - Maria I need to speak to Tom - Maria I need to speak to Tom - Maria I need to speak to Tom - Maria I need to speak to Tom."

Each time her head thumped against the wall, she let out a pathetic whimper like a puppy dog. The dull pounding was hurting her head, but it didn't bother her, in fact she drew comfort from the dull pain.

"Maria I need to speak to Tom - Maria I need to speak to Tom - Maria I need to speak to Tom - Maria I need to speak to Tom - Maria I need to speak to Tom - Maria I need to speak to Tom."

Time stood still as she sat with her back against the wall, banging her head, trying to block out the words coming from her son.

Maria started her own mantra out of frustration and madness.

"Leave me the fuck alone – leave me the fuck alone - leave me the fuck alone - leave me the fuck alone - leave me the fuck alone - leave me the fuck alone - leave me the fuck alone - leave me the fuck alone."

Campbell hurried as he made his way along the street and back to the flat.

He'd walked over half the way to David's house and stopped dead in his tracks. He couldn't explain why, but he knew something was wrong and had to get to Maria.

He could see the door of the flat just a hundred yards ahead of him and quickened his pace. Stopping at the door he clumsily fumbled for his keys and as his nerves got the better of him. He struggled to get the key into the lock.

The door swung open and he quietly walked into the hall. He looked for Maria. She wasn't in the lounge. He turned and walked towards their bedroom.

He stopped as he passed Christopher's room. He could hear a thumping noise which was accompanied by a voice.

It didn't sound like Christopher's head banging. The door was ajar and he was about to enter, but stopped. He thought it would be better to get Maria first and he assumed that she was sleeping in their bed.

He tiptoed across the hall and into their bedroom. The bed was empty, but he could tell by the untidy duvet that she'd been lying on it.

The monitor was on and he could hear chanting over the speaker. He bent down, picked it up and put it close to his ear. He could hear two distinct faint chants.

He dropped the monitor and ran to Christopher's room. He pushed open the door and as his eyes grew accustomed to the dull light he saw Maria sitting with her back against the wall thudding her head and sobbing. He knelt down and listened to what she was chanting.

"Leave me the fuck alone – leave me the fuck alone - leave me the fuck alone - leave me the fuck alone - leave me the fuck alone - leave me the fuck alone - leave me the fuck alone - leave me the fuck alone."

Christopher was also chanting, he was very quiet and Campbell couldn't make out what he was saying. He moved closer and put his ear to the boy's mouth.

"Maria I need to speak to Tom - Maria I need to speak to Tom - Maria I need to speak to Tom - Maria I need to speak to Tom - Maria I need to speak to Tom - Maria I need to speak to Tom."

My God, Ben's trying to contact Maria, thought Campbell, as he backed away from Christopher.

He stood up and was uncertain what he should do first. Maria seemed to be having a breakdown. He weighed up the situation and decided that the first thing he should do was attend to Maria. He knew that Christopher showed no ill effects from head banging and chanting. It was Maria who needed help.

He walked over and gently held her arm and as he went to speak, he saw an empty vacant look in her eyes.

"Maria, it's me. Can you hear me?"

She continued to thump her head.

"Leave me the fuck alone – leave me the fuck alone - leave me the fuck alone - leave me the fuck alone - leave me the fuck alone - leave me the fuck alone - leave me the fuck alone - leave me the fuck alone."

She stopped, then looked him straight in the eyes and slowly and concisely repeated the five words, but this time they were aimed directly at him.

"Leave ….. me ….. the ….. fuck ….. alone."

CHAPTER NINETY NINE

Maria's flat
10.47pm

Campbell had called the out of hours' surgery. Dr Sullivan arrived just after ten thirty and prescribed a sedative to calm Maria.

She had become violent towards Campbell after he'd attempted to move her from Christopher's room. He gave up trying and left her slumped against the wall, rocking back and forth whilst quietly sobbing.

After she had taken the sedative, Campbell and the doctor slowly walked Maria to her bed, lay her down and Campbell made her comfortable. He didn't undress her and let her sleep wearing her clothes.

"Is she having a breakdown?" asked Campbell trying his best to not sound overly concerned.

"I don't think she's having a breakdown, what is happening is extreme anxiety. From what you have told me she's been through a lot these last few weeks, Maria has been through an awful lot of stress." replied the doctor.

Campbell didn't go into detail about what had happened at Judd's practice, but he did tell the doctor about how Christopher's RMD had got worse and had now developed into sleep talking and how he and Maria had resorted to taking Christopher to a hypnotherapist.

"I remember when Maria brought Christopher to see me about his head banging, it must have been well over a year ago. I can't believe that he's still keeping his mother up at night with RMD, and now he's talking in his sleep."

Campbell nodded.

"It's good to see she has you and doesn't have to face this on her own."

Sullivan said he'd arrange another doctor to visit in the morning and that Maria should not go to work the next day.

Campbell thanked the doctor and saw him to the door.

Christopher had stopped chanting just before the doctor had arrived and was peacefully sleeping. Campbell looked into their bedroom and watched Maria sleep as Claire sat alongside her. The sedative had worked quickly.

Claire had arrived shortly after Campbell had called her and was sitting on the edge of the bed keeping a watchful eye over her daughter.

"How is she?"

"She's sleeping now," replied Claire.

"Would you like me to stay for the night, I could sleep on the couch?"

Campbell considered Claire's offer. He had no idea how Maria would be in the morning and wasn't looking forward to facing her alone.

"Thank you, I think I'll take you up on your offer."

Campbell and Claire shared half a bottle of wine. Both found the scenario awkward. It was the first time the prospective in-laws had been alone together and the reason for spending an evening in each other's company was another cause for them to feel uneasy.

Campbell was surprised when he'd found out that Maria hadn't told her mother exactly what had happened when Christopher had been hypnotised.

Claire found it difficult to comprehend what Campbell had just told her. He watched as the expression on her face turned to one of shock.

"I can see why she didn't want to worry me," said Claire, taking a large swig of wine and putting the empty glass on the table.

"There's another bottle in the fridge," offered Campbell.

Claire waved her empty glass, "go on then, I need another."

"Sorry, but I'd assumed that Maria would have told you about Ben Walker."

"No, she didn't, she only told me that Christopher had been hypnotised but it hadn't worked and she wouldn't be taking him back." Claire filled her glass before continuing.

"Tell me Campbell, you were there. What do you think is happening to my grandson and what do you make of this Ben Walker character?"

He sat back in the chair, shrugged his shoulders and slowly shook his head.

"I really don't know. When he's under hypnosis and when Ben Walker talks, it's like you are hearing a different person. It's just not Christopher who's talking."

"So do you think Ben Walker was murdered and is now inside Christopher?"

"If you don't mind, I'd rather not answer that one."

"But do you think Christopher should be hypnotised again, you know, to get to the bottom of all of this?"

Campbell looked her in the eye and nodded.

"Yes, I do Claire."

Campbell looked at his watch, it was eleven thirty.

"If you don't mind Claire, I need to sleep, I'll get a duvet and pillow so you can sleep on the couch, unless of course you'd rather sleep with Maria?"

"No, that's OK. I think it would send her over the edge if she woke in the morning to find me lying next to her."

Campbell smiled as he went to get the bed covers. He returned with a double duvet and a couple of pillows. He laid the duvet on the couch and plumped up the pillows.

Claire kissed Campbell on the cheek and sensed his embarrassment.

Campbell had an awful night's sleep. His strange dreams were punctuated by Maria as she restlessly tossed and turned. She hadn't woken during the night and by the time Christopher was stirring she was still out for the count.

Campbell knocked on the door of the lounge and quietly tiptoed in. Claire was still sleeping. He gently nudged her.

"Claire, Claire……you need to get up, Christopher's awake."

She slowly opened her eyes and Campbell went to get Christopher.

"Daddy, you're home! shouted Christopher as soon as he saw Campbell.

He leapt out of his bed and into Campbell's arms.

He jumped down and ran into the lounge to find his grandmother on the couch with a duvet wrapped around her.

"Nanny's here, daddy, come and see, nanny's here."

He looked around the lounge.

"Where's mummy?"

Campbell stepped into the lounge.

"Mummy's a bit tired so she's staying in bed."

"Let me wake her, let me wake her."

Campbell grabbed him before he ran in to see his mother.

"Hold your horses little man, let mummy have a lie in."

Christopher huffed and plonked himself next to Claire.

Maria didn't wake until eight thirty. She rubbed her eyes and looked at the clock. Her first thought was that she'd overslept. Then gradually she remembered snippets of what had happened the night before. The memory was vague, but she could remember Christopher had been chanting and that he needed to speak with Tom, or had it been Ben that had needed to speak with Tom?

She could hear voices coming from the lounge. Christopher was giggling and she could hear her mother. Campbell's voice was coming from the kitchen and it sounded as if he was on the telephone.

As she got out of bed her body felt as heavy as a rock, her legs were aching and her head was throbbing. It felt like the worse hangover she'd had in years, yet she couldn't remember drinking last night, in fact, the more she thought about it, she couldn't remember very much about last night at all.

She trudged into the lounge to be greeted by Christopher who was ecstatic to see her. He ran over to her and threw his arms around her. Maria held the palm of her hand to her forehead in a vague attempt to ease her aching head.

She said nothing as she sat down.

Claire looked at her and saw what a mess she was. Mascara had run down and stained her face, her eyes were red and swollen and she had slept in her crumpled clothes.

"Do you want coffee?" asked Claire.

Maria shook her head and in a croaky, dry voice asked for a glass of water.

Claire went to the kitchen and passed Campbell in the hall.

"She's in there," said Claire, pointing to the lounge.

"How is she?"

"She seems pretty rough, and hasn't said much."

"I've called Westhouse and told them she won't be in today."

"What did you say was wrong with her?"

"You know, women's stuff, it seemed to do the trick, the woman on the phone stopped pushing me for details when I told her, I think she felt sorry for me."

Claire smiled.

"I'm getting her a glass of water, why don't you go in and say good morning."

He nodded and with trepidation entered the lounge.

Maria looked miserable. Christopher sat next to her and he was also looking miserable.

"Mummy's not talking to me."

"I know Christopher, mummy's a little unwell this morning."

"I don't want mummy to be unwell."

Campbell hugged him and kissed his head.

Claire brought the water and handed it to Maria. Her hand was unsteady as she took a sip.

"Can you get me some paracetamol please."

Campbell went to the kitchen and came back with two tablets.

"How do you feel?" asked Claire.

Maria shook her head and didn't speak.

"Campbell, I'm due to have Christopher today as Maria would have been working, but I'm worried about leaving her alone, but at the same time

I don't want Christopher bounding around the place, I'm worried that he'll push her over the edge," said Claire barely above a whisper.

"I'll call the office, I'm sure they'll let me have the day off so I can stay with her."

He went to the kitchen and called TM.IT and arranged a day's leave at short notice.

Claire took Christopher to the bathroom and got him washed and dressed. By nine o'clock she had him ready for the day.

She sat next to Maria and held her hand.

"I'm taking Christopher somewhere nice for the day so you can have some time to yourself, and Campbell will stay with you, that's if you would like him to."

Maria didn't respond. Claire squeezed her daughter's hand and looked up at Campbell, who was standing by the settee.

"Come on tiger, how would you like to go to the zoo?" said Claire as she picked Christopher up and held him in her arms.

"Zoo mummy, zoo mummy, nanny's taking me to the zoo."

Maria didn't look up at her son who was flailing around in Claire's arms, instead she vacantly stared at the wall on the other side of the room.

Christopher face dropped when his mother didn't answer. He was upset and had never seen her like this.

"What's wrong with mummy?"

"Mummy's got a headache, that's all, she'll be better soon," said Campbell in his best reassuring voice.

Claire kissed Maria and left the flat with Christopher, who had regained his enthusiasm for a daytrip to the zoo with his grandmother.

Campbell's phone was ringing and he took the call in the kitchen. The call had been from the doctor's surgery to confirm the time of the visit. A home appointment for eleven had been made.

The flat was silent. Neither the television nor the radio were on and Campbell felt like a spare part. He walked around looking for something constructive to do as Maria sat and stared into space.

Eventually he tried talking to her.

"Maria, what do you remember about last night?"

She didn't reply and was holding the glass of water that Claire had given her almost an hour earlier.

"Maria, can you hear me?"

She turned her head slowly, looked at Campbell and then stared back towards the wall.

He went to the kitchen and was in need of coffee. His mouth was dry and he felt desperately tired. He made two drinks, he couldn't be bothered to mess around with the cappuccino machine and made two instants, both with heaped teaspoons of coffee granules.

He brought the drinks into the lounge and put one on the table for Maria.

And then she spoke.

"My son has a dead person inside of him, hasn't he?"

Campbell was uncertain whether he was being asked or told, whatever, he didn't know what to say. He bit his lip, before he attempted to speak.

"Don't worry, you don't have to answer, I already know," said Maria in a lifeless monosyllabic tone.

"Listen Maria, you've a visit from the doctor booked for this morning and I think we need to talk before he turns up. What do you want to say about Christopher?"

"Why should he ask about Christopher?"

"Dr Sullivan was here last night, do you remember?"

Maria shook her head.

"Well, he was, and he gave you something to help you sleep. I'd explained to him the stress you'd been under with Christopher's sleep issues and I told him he'd seen a hypnotherapist, but I mentioned nothing about Ben Walker and I don't think you should mention it either."

Maria nodded.

"I'm sorry about all of this," said Maria attempting a smile.

Campbell took her hand and kissed her on the cheek.

After half an hour she began to drink the coffee, even though she'd let it go cold, it made her feel more awake as the caffeine coursed through her system.

She went to the bathroom and tidied herself up. She removed the mascara stains, but couldn't be bothered to apply new makeup.

Dr Parry had been and gone by eleven forty five and had diagnosed exhaustion which had been brought on by Christopher's RMD and the lack of sleep over the last couple of years. He agreed that the sleep talking would have compounded the issues and prescribed something to allow her to sleep.

Campbell agreed that he would deal with any issues Christopher may have during the night to take the pressure away from Maria.

Dr Parry signed her off work for two weeks and wrote on her fit for work note that she'd suffered nervous exhaustion.

Maria hated the diagnosis as it made it sound as if she'd lost her mind.

Neither of them had eaten and Campbell was feeling shaky. He made some toast. Maria picked at hers whilst he finished his in minutes.

Campbell returned from the kitchen after taking out the plates and he was carrying another two mugs of coffee. This time he'd used the cappuccino machine. The bitter instant coffee had left a nasty taste in his mouth.

"I suppose we should talk about the elephant in the room," said Maria in a quiet voice as she hugged her coffee mug.

Campbell nodded.

"I've been in denial since all of this kicked off, I mean since Ben Walker reared his ugly head."

Campbell said nothing and waited for her to continue.

"At first, I didn't want any more hypnosis because I was worried how it may affect Christopher, but now it's because of me. I'm worried how it will affect me."

She stood up and walked to the window and continued to talk with her back to Campbell.

"I've no idea what's happening to my son and I agree that we need to use Tom Judd to find out what is really going on. Providing Esther doesn't come back with anything which suggests hypnosis could be harmful, then I think Judd should continue."

Campbell nodded again.

"But……." she continued, "I don't want to be there when it happens."

"Why not? I'm sure Christopher won't go ahead with it unless you're there."

"I'll go along, but when Judd hypnotises him, I'd rather wait in the other room."

"OK, well you can always change your mind, it's a woman's prerogative, isn't that what they say?"

Maria smiled.

Campbell called Judd and put the wheels back in motion.

CHAPTER ONE HUNDRED

Liz Mason's home
2.27pm
Monday 21st May

Liz's temperature had been fluctuating for the past week. The medicine had initially worked, but after finishing the course of antibiotics, her temperature was on the up again.

Terry had called the doctor as her carers were concerned.

The doctor arrived midafternoon and spent half an hour examining her.

"I've prescribed another course of stronger antibiotics and I'm confident that this time they will work," said the doctor as he calmly wrote the prescription.

"But, if they don't, I think it would be wise to admit her."

"What, you mean she would need to go to hospital?"

"I think so. You've a great team of carers looking after your daughter, but if things get worse she needs to be somewhere where she can get the best treatment."

Chloe and David, the carers, did their best not to appear offended.

The thought of his daughter going back to hospital left Terry Mason cold. He hated the place, which was one of the driving forces which compelled him and Anne to get Liz home as soon as possible.

Until now there had been no major issues with Liz's health. She'd had the odd cough, cold and stomach upset, but nothing out of the ordinary, and certainly nothing that the carers were not able to handle.

The doctor had not been able to pinpoint the reason for her fever and was concerned that things could become serious.

Terry thanked the doctor for his time and asked David to collect the new course of drugs from the pharmacy.

He sat by his daughter as she lay in the continuous slumber from which she hadn't woken for over two and a half years.

He watched her chest gently rise and fall and thought how serene she appeared. He wondered what, if anything, went through her mind. Did she dream, or was it a constant blackout?

Terry could hear Chloe in the other room. She was sorting some clean bedding for Liz which had just been washed.

His mind began to wander and he recalled the meeting in the boardroom the other week when Campbell Broderick had a funny turn. For reasons he couldn't explain, Terry suddenly became very nervous of Broderick and considered him a threat. Not to him, but a threat to his daughter. He couldn't explain it, but there was something about the young Irishman that he didn't like.

As far as Terry was aware Broderick was a good worker and seemed to be a decent person.

He couldn't put his finger on it, he just had a sense that the man was trouble. He made a mental note to check the man's background and personnel files when he was back in the office.

Just recalling Campbell Broderick's face was starting to make Terry feel uneasy.

CHAPTER ONE HUNDRED AND ONE

Thomas Judd's Practice
7.32pm
Thursday 24th May

Tom Judd had called a meeting to discuss how to proceed with Christopher.

Maria, Campbell and Esther were present, and this time Maria had wanted her mother to be there for moral support.

She was fragile after her mini breakdown and needed her mother to be with her during this difficult time.

Christopher was at home and Samreen had agreed to babysit.

Esther was the first to speak.

"I've been researching the dangers of hypnotherapy, and unlike most other areas of therapy, there doesn't appear to be a governing body which sets the standards to which hypnotherapists should perform. There are organisations to which they may belong, but this is up to the individual hypnotherapist." Esther paused as she turned to Judd.

"I've spoken with the Association for Professional Hypnosis and Psychotherapy and although Mr. Judd has assured us that hypnosis and hypnotherapy are harmless and have no ill effect upon clients, this appears to not be wholly accurate."

Judd shuffled nervously as Esther paused and continued to look at him.

"From what I understand, hypnotherapy is safe, providing the hypnotherapist doesn't suggest things to his client that could cause the client harm. Am I right Mr. Judd?"

Judd nodded.

"But you told me that a person couldn't be hypnotised to do something which they would not normally do when not under hypnosis," said Campbell in a raised voice.

Judd said nothing and Esther continued.

"However, after speaking with the Association for Professional Hypnosis and Psychotherapy, of which Mr. Judd is a fully paid up associate, they have assured me that he is one of their most highly regarded members and have also assured me that he would not do anything below the highest level of professionalism."

"Other than lie to me," said Campbell bluntly.

"It seems to me that Tom and the Association for Professional whatever they're called are in bed together," added Campbell.

Judd shook his head as Esther continued.

"Campbell, I think Judd was doing his best attempt at salesmanship, although I don't condone him for stretching the truth, I have faith in him and don't think he would do anything that would harm young Christopher. Besides, it was his idea to record the hypnotherapy sessions in the first place and I think this should prove he has every intention to perform to the highest level of professionalism to which he claims to adhere."

Judd let out an audible sigh as the others viewed him with suspicion.

"Finally, I would like to add that Tom appears to have the ability to quickly hypnotise Christopher and conjure up, if that is the right word, Ben Walker."

"I can assure you Esther, there is no conjuring involved. Either Ben Walker is, or was, a real person, or he's a character within Christopher's psyche."

Esther apologised for her poor choice of words and continued to speak.

"And in addition, Christopher appears to suffer no ill effect after being hypnotised, in fact, he seems to enjoy it, am I right Maria?"

Maria nodded.

"So I guess I have Esther's stamp of approval." said Judd.

An air of mistrust filled the room and the atmosphere could be cut with a knife.

Next, it was Tom Judd's turn to speak.

"To get to the bottom of what is affecting Christopher we need to ascertain two things. Firstly we need to work out whether Ben Walker is a creation of Christopher's imagination. And assuming he is not, we need to establish when Ben Walker was alive, and considering he says he was killed, we need to know when the murder took place."

Silence filled the room.

"In the heat of the moment, Maria said something the last time we were together, she referred to the notion that Ben Walker may be someone who had lived hundreds of years ago, and if this is the case, I need to find a way of switching him off so he no longer troubles Christopher."

Judd paced the room with his hands in his jacket pockets whilst searching for inspiration for what to say next.

"But……..if we can prove that Ben Walker had been murdered in the recent past I have to consider that we have a murder case on our hands and that puts a whole different angle on the matter."

Campbell stood up from his chair.

"And just how do you propose we prove either of the things you suggest?"

"Well, if Ben is a creation of Christopher's imagination, no matter how well he is able to express himself verbally whilst under hypnosis, the knowledge will have been picked up and stored within his subconscious mind. He would be recalling conversations he'd heard in the past and somehow retained the information, which, when under hypnosis, manifests as an alternate person."

"Do you think my son has a split personality, could he be schizophrenic?" asked Maria.

"No I don't" replied Judd attempting to reassure her.

"It's early days yet, but I don't think your son is suffering from anything as severe as schizophrenia. Anyway, as I was saying, if Christopher has created Ben walker, no matter how real he seems, he'll fail some basic tests."

"What kind of tests?" asked Esther.

"I've not given this much thought yet, but I am thinking along the lines of basic mathematics test, you know, the twelve times table."

"I'd struggle with the twelve times table myself, I don't think that would prove anything," replied Esther.

"Well OK, maybe not the twelve times table, but something a child may not know, like who painted the Mona Lisa, or name some books written by Charles Dickens, that sort of thing."

Everyone agreed that a test like Judd proposed could prove whether or not Ben Walker had been a real person.

"So if we prove that Ben was a real person who is presently residing in Christopher's subconscious, we need to work out when he existed and again this can be done by asking a series of questions."

"Like what year where you born?" asked Claire helpfully.

"Unfortunately not, Ben has already confirmed he can't remember dates and seems to have no concept of the passing of time. I think we need to ask him about the world he remembers. Perhaps we should ask what sort of places are in his memories or who was queen, or king."

The others nodded, other than Campbell who was still trying to work out whether Judd was as squeaky clean as he professed.

"If Ben is someone who died a long, long time ago, and if there is no reason to find anything about who killed him, then I propose, with Maria and Campbell's permission that I use hypnosis to suppress Ben Walker, which should stop him waking when Christopher sleeps."

Judd paused, expecting someone to say something and then continued.

"But if Ben had been murdered and if it took place in the recent past, then we should consider what to do next."

"Tell the police?" suggested Esther.

"If Ben Walker can name his killer, then bingo, tell the police and let them do the rest, and then after the killer's been put away, you can hypnotise Christopher to stop Ben from waking," added Esther.

"You wouldn't even get the chance to be laughed out of court, because it would never get to court," said Campbell.

"Campbell's right, I don't think evidence from a two and a half year old boy under hypnosis would gain a conviction. We could offer what we know to the police, but I wouldn't expect them to do anything with it" said Judd

"You seem to know a lot about the law?" said Maria in an accusatory tone.

"I'm just using common sense Maria, however, I do have some knowledge of how the law works, as I am a trained Forensic and Investigative hypnotist."

"Which means you do what?" asked Esther.

"I use hypnosis to gain information and evidence from witnesses, that they would otherwise not have remembered, and that evidence could be used and accepted in court."

"You kept that quiet," said Campbell.

"If you'd taken the time to read my business card, you would have seen it written on the back."

"There's one more thing I need to mention," added Judd.

"I don't know how long I can speak with Ben Walker until he flakes out. If you remember last time he was only with us for around five minutes before he faded, so we need to draw up a list of questions for him based upon what I've suggested this evening."

The meeting had been heated at times, but eventually it was agreed that Tom Judd should continue to hypnotise Christopher. A date was set for the following Saturday.

CHAPTER ONE HUNDRED AND TWO

Markland Garraway's home
8.15pm
Friday 25th May

Markland Garraway had returned to work just over twenty months earlier after being signed off as unfit for work due to nervous exhaustion and acute arthritis. His mental state of health had improved, but the arthritis was as bad as ever and showed no signs of remission.

He still held the rank of Detective Chief Inspector, but hadn't been an active detective since 2009, when he was removed from Ben Walker's murder case.

He'd spent the last eighteen months running training courses for constabulary staff and had gained the respect of many as a great mentor to new recruits to the force.

Every day was a struggle, his body was riddled with the illness and every joint from his neck down to the soles of his feet hurt. He took Methotrexate daily to ease the pain, but even on a good day the pain was almost unbearable.

Garraway was a fighter and he was determined not to give in to the pain which had got worse over the past few months due to the additional stress he'd been under since his wife, Joan, left him at the end of March.

She could no longer stand being with him. They had become distant since his breakdown and she'd struggled to deal with his mood swings and drinking. He'd been off the bottle for over a year, but the damage had been done and she'd moved out to stay with her sister until she found a place of her own.

Garraway had been married to the role of Detective Chief Inspector and Joan had always played second fiddle. Since she'd left him, and because he was no longer an active detective, he had become a very lonely man.

His part time work as a trainer was all he had and he did his best to make the most of it. But occasionally his pain was so bad he couldn't even dress to go to the office and today was one of those days.

He lay on his bed and called the office to tell them he wouldn't be in. Luckily he had no training sessions booked and it would have been a day of administration, which could wait until the following week. He put the phone on his bedside table and stared at the Artex patterns on the ceiling.

The death of Ben Walker had never left him. The unsolved case was something that had tormented and consumed him and had been the cause of his breakdown. Although mentally he was in a better place, he knew he wouldn't be happy until Walker's killer was found. What's more, he was desperate to be the one to close the case. He had no faith in Colin Matthews, his former partner, and had barely spoken to him in over a year.

Deep down he knew that somehow he would still be involved in solving what had been the most extraordinary murder case of his career.

CHAPTER ONE HUNDRED AND THREE

Thomas Judd's Practice
The Quiet Area
2pm
Saturday 26th May

The entourage had grown to include Samreen, who joined Claire, Esther, Campbell and Maria to be present when Tom Judd hypnotised Christopher. Samreen wasn't just there to witness Christopher's hypnosis, she was there to distract him after he'd been brought around from the trance so the adults could discuss what happened after Judd had hypnotised him.

There was an air of tension in the room, which Christopher could sense and it was making him unhappy. Maria didn't want to be there when he was under hypnosis as it distressed her to hear Ben Walker's mature voice coming from her little boy. She'd asked Esther to step in to stop the process if things got out of hand.

The camera was set and was ready to record the proceedings, but Christopher didn't want to climb onto the hypnotist's chair. Maria couldn't stand to watch her son as his bottom lip began to quiver.

"I don't want to go on the chair again, I don't like it anymore."

He was pulling at Maria's heart strings and she was considering stopping the whole thing before it had even begun.

Samreen walked over to the scared little boy and crouched down to his level.

"What's the matter sweetie? You've done this before."

"There are too many grownups," he said as he hugged Misty.

"You know you'll get another nice toy if you let Tom make you go to sleep."

"I don't want another toy anymore."

"Tell me what you would like and I'll get it for you."

Christopher looked at her with his big blue eyes and sad little face and thought about what he should ask for.

"I want to go to Thomas Land."

"I'll tell you what, if you let Tom make you go to sleep I'll take you to Thomas Land next week, what do you think about that?"

Samreen glanced toward Maria who nodded and smiled.

"OK," replied Christopher in a deflated tone.

Samreen lifted him onto the chair as Tom hung the picture of Thomas the Tank Engine on the wall. He looked at Samreen and mouthed 'thank you', Samreen smiled and walked away from the chair.

Tom pressed the record button on the camera and began to hypnotise Christopher.

CHAPTER ONE HUNDRED AND FOUR

The Awareness

Ben Walker stirred from the state of inactivity in which he spent most of his strange existence and observed the misty whirlpool of light he'd seen before.

He could hear Tom Judd's voice, and as before the voice was coming from the direction of the light.

"Hello Ben, its Tom, can you hear me?"

Ben concentrated his thoughts and focused his attention towards the light and replied.

"Hello Tom, yes I can and it's good to hear you again."

Maria couldn't bear to listen and had retreated to the office while Claire, Samreen, Esther and Campbell stayed with Tom and Christopher in the Quiet Area. All four of them sat in silence as Ben Walker's words came from the little boy's mouth.

Judd was commanding the situation, but he was nervous. He knew that the window of opportunity to talk with Ben was likely to only last for a few minutes before he faded away. In his hand he held a list of prepared test questions to work out whether Ben was the real thing, or something dreamt up by Christopher's subconscious mind.

"Ben, I hope you appreciate that this is a rather unusual situation and I guess this is just as strange for you as it is for me."

"It is strange, and you need to understand what it's like from my point of view, you're the only person I've spoken to since I was killed." Christopher's head gently nodded as he spoke.

Ben Walker was not only controlling the words that came from Christopher's mouth, he was also influencing his body movements.

The gravity of the moment was exerting tremendous pressure on Judd to get things right. It was all about words. It was all about asking the right questions and dealing with the answers appropriately. He didn't want to upset Ben as he didn't know how this may affect Christopher. He needed to tread carefully.

"I guess we're both in the same position," replied Judd.

Samreen was shaking as she sat next to Claire. She felt as if she was taking part in a strange movie scene.

She glanced at Campbell and Esther and wondered how they were able to remain calm. She looked at Claire who attempted to smile, but the smile didn't happen.

If Esther and Campbell looked calm, then it was not how they felt. Campbell was on a knife's edge. The stress of the moment was almost too much for him.

Esther had been in many situations when her professional responsibility had required her to remain in control, especially when she had dealt with distraught parents who were beside themselves with worry over their child's health. She was using her skills to remain level headed as she listened to Judd talk with the stranger whose voice was coming from Christopher.

"I need to be completely honest with you Ben, and I hope you understand the situation from my perspective."

Christopher nodded.

"I need to be sure that you are who you say you are and not a creation of Christopher's subconscious mind."

Christopher nodded again.

"I have a few questions for you and if you answer them correctly I think we can agree that you are real and not a character made up by Christopher."

"I hope I pass the test, as I would hate to think I'm the figment of someone's imagination……….by the way, can I ask, how old is Christopher?"

"He's just over two and half years old."

As Judd replied, he realised that Ben had to be the real deal. There was absolutely no way that a child's mind could create this all on its own. It was just impossible. Judd was now convinced it was more than possible that Ben had been reincarnated and Christopher's body was the host. His mind was made up before he'd asked the questions.

"OK Ben, here goes with the questions, I hope you're good with mathematics because the first one is about multiplication."

Judd adjusted his glasses and read from the sheet of paper.

"Ben, what is eight times twelve?"

"You had to go and choose the twelves, I always struggled with the twelve times table."

The room fell silent, other than the sound of breathing, as Christopher's head moved from side to side. He had a look of concentration and frowned before answering.

Ben hated maths. It was one of the few subjects in which he didn't do well. He'd struggled to get a low grade in his GCSEs at Whitcroft School.

'OK, twelve, twenty four, thirty six, forty eight, um fifty eight......shit, no start again'

Ben worked through the tables and focused his attention away from the swirling light so Tom Judd couldn't hear his thoughts.

He tried again, and this time formed an image of fingers, he needed something to count on.

'Twelve, twenty four, thirty six, forty eight, sixty, seventy two, eighty four, ninety six'.

He focused his thoughts back to the light.

"Ninety six Tom, eight twelves are ninety six."

Campbell was the only one who hadn't been breathing whilst Judd asked the question. Without realising he had been holding his breath in anticipation. As soon as he heard the correct answer he exhaled a lung full of air, which was loud enough to make Esther turn around and glare at him.

"OK, Ben, ninety six is correct, now we're getting somewhere."

The next question that had been agreed upon was based on history. It was a question to which most people, even school children would know the answer.

The problem with a history question was if Ben had died before the historic event had taken place, he wouldn't know the answer. This was a chance they'd decided to take.

Judd lifted the sheet of A4 paper, adjusted his glasses and read the next question.

"Question number two, when was the Battle of Hastings?"

"I'm sorry Tom, I can't do dates, or times. It's something I've lost all concept of. I can't even tell you when I was born, the year I died or how old I was when I was killed, I'm going to have to pass, sorry."

An air of disappointment filled the room. Perhaps the maths question was just luck and Ben really was only a figment.

Christopher lifted his head as Ben began to speak.

"I may not be able to remember the date but history was one of my strong points."

"OK," said Tom, "what do you have for me?"

"The battle was between Duke William of Normandy and King Harold's Anglo Saxon army and the Duke's guys won."

Everyone gasped.

Judd looked at the rest of the questions and was about to ask another.

Esther leaned towards Campbell and whispered in his ear.

"Is it really worth asking any more questions? I don't think Christopher would know anything about the Battle of Hastings, I don't know that much myself."

Campbell waved at Judd to get his attention and mouthed to him 'no more questions'. Judd squinted and mouthed back 'what?'

Campbell repeated, but this time he whispered, just loud enough for Judd to hear him.

"No more questions, I think we know Ben's for real."

Judd looked around the room and the others nodded. They all knew that Ben was genuine. There was just no way Christopher could have answered those questions.

Christopher had been under hypnosis for less than five minutes, but already Ben was losing his focus. The swirling misty light was beginning to fade as his energy drained. He was determined to stay alert and was desperate to be given the chance to tell his story.

He stared into what remained of the fading light and concentrated with all his might to bring it back.

He thought of the story he had to tell and the anger he felt because of his futile death. The anger and rage began to stew and consume him.

The light began to return, it wasn't as intense as it was before, but it was getting clearer and Ben could make out the swirling mists as they grew in strength.

Judd's voice was back and he sounded as clear as a bell, clearer than before.

"OK Ben, I think that's enough of the questions, we're all convinced you're real."

"We? Did you say we? There are others who are with you?"

"Yes, there are."

"Who are the others?" asked Ben curiously.

Judd told Ben who else was in the room and that Christopher's mother was finding the whole thing too hard to deal with and was in another room.

Maria was standing by the door of Judd's office. The door was slightly open and she was listening to what was happening in disbelief. She silently opened the door wide enough to step into the Quiet Area. Nobody saw her enter or noticed her as she stood at the back of the room. Everyone was too consumed with what was happening to pay the slightest bit of attention.

"OK Ben, we would like to know when you lived. We don't know whether your death was in our time, or a long, long time ago, before anyone in this room was born."

"More questions?" asked Ben.

"OK, fire away, but make sure it doesn't take long, I don't know how much longer I can keep going, I'm starting to ebb a little."

Judd looked down at the list of questions that he and the others had come up with to allow them to work out when he had lived and decided to use an idea that Campbell had thought of.

"Ben, when you were alive, did you like sport?"

"I loved sport. I spend a lot of my time remembering the sport I played. Cricket was my speciality, I played for Horfield in Bristol, and I was also a keen rugby player."

"So not a football fan then?" asked Judd.

"Football was my passion, I watched every City home game at Ashton Gate......... but I was a useless player, nobody would have me in their team."

Judd laughed.

"Sorry to hear that. Did you follow the World Cup?"

"You bet, ever since I was a kid. I was never able to fill a complete sticker book though."

Judd was now sure that Ben had been alive in recent times, or at least the last seventy years or so.

"What was the last World Cup you remember, who won?"

Instantly Ben answered.

"Italy beat France. The match finished one all and went to penalties."

"You seem extremely sure about that."

"I was there, I went with my father to Berlin. That year I was confident for England, but it never happened. My dad and I had a brilliant time, one of my favourite memories."

"Is this another memory you replay often?" asked Judd.

Christopher nodded.

Judd looked around the room and saw Maria standing by the door. He smiled at her and she smiled weakly in return.

It was clear to all that Ben had definitely once been alive and furthermore had been alive recently.

Ben was fading and he was fading fast. The light was dimming and he was finding it hard to stay focused. He knew that Judd and the others believed in him and now was his time to make his story known.

Ben had always had a sense that his killer had never been caught and this is what had been his drive, his ambition to be heard. In life Ben hadn't been a quitter and he wasn't going to be one in death either.

"OK Ben, let's find out more about you, and something which everyone in this room wants to know……..how did you die?"

There was no answer.

"Ben, can you hear me, how did you die?"

Christopher rolled his head from side to side as his eyes began to flutter.

"Ben, it's Tom, I need to know how you died, where did it happened and who killed you, concentrate please…….don't fade on me now."

Christopher turned his head to one side and opened his mouth to speak.

The atmosphere was tense and everyone moved nearer to hear what Christopher was about to say.

"Tom, sorry, I…… I …….. can't quite find the………."

"Please Ben, try, please try your hardest."

Christopher nodded.

"I'm trying………I was killed in……..I was killed in the ……..woods."

Christopher's voice was now barely above a whisper.

"Did you say you were killed in the woods?" asked Judd.

Christopher nodded.

"In the woods," whispered Ben.

"Which woods, can you remember the name of the woods?" asked Judd desperately.

Christopher nodded again, but this time he hardly moved his head.

"Badock's………….."

Judd interrupted him, "Badock's Wood, were you killed in Badock's Wood?"

Christopher nodded again and started rolling his head from side to side as his eyes began to open.

"Ben, stay with me, please stay focused….just one more thing and then you can sleep."

Judd reached forward and held Christopher's hand.

"Ben, how did you die, what did the murderer do to kill you? Please Ben."

Christopher started to speak, but his voice was so quiet Judd couldn't make out the words. He leant forward and put his ear to the boy's mouth.

"Ben, say that again, I didn't hear you…..how were you killed?"

Judd closed his eyes and listened to the weak and tired voice with all his powers of concentration and could just make out what Ben was trying to tell him.

"With a rock Tom, ………he killed me with a ………rock."

And then Ben was gone.

CHAPTER ONE HUNDRED AND FIVE

Thomas Judd's Practice
The Quiet Area
2.21pm
Saturday 26th May

Tom brought Christopher out of hypnosis. The little boy looked around the room, rubbed his eyes, saw Maria at the back by the door and smiled at her wearily.

"Did I do well mummy?"

Maria nodded.

"You did very well, you were brilliant."

He clambered down from the chair and ran to her, swinging his toy grey cat by its tail as he went.

"Samreen is taking me to Thomas Land."

"I know darling, you're a very lucky boy. Give me a cuddle."

As the two of them hugged the others looked on in silence. Tom was the only one who had heard what Ben had told him about the murder and where it took place. Christopher had whispered the crucial information and Tom could only just hear the words. But there was no mistaking what Ben had told him. 'He killed me with a rock'.

The others had heard Tom prompt Ben to say Badock's Wood, which meant nothing to them, other than Esther who thought the place sounded familiar.

Maria put Christopher down and ruffled his hair, doing her best not to show her anxieties.

"Samreen's got some nice things for you, why don't you go into the other room with her and play."

Christopher sensed something wasn't right. He could tell there was an atmosphere and the grownups didn't seem very happy. He was worried that he'd done something wrong.

Samreen picked up a carrier bag. In it was some of Christopher's toys, and she had bought him comics, a colouring book and some crayons. She walked over to Christopher, took his hand, led him to Judd's office and shut the door while the others remained in the Quiet Area.

Tom swiveled the camera on the tripod, focused on the others who were congregating around the settee and let the camera continue to film.

The shocked silence was broken by Esther.

"So he was killed in Badock's Wood."

"That's what he told me" replied Judd.

"I've never heard of it, where's Badock's Wood?" asked Campbell.

"It's between Henleaze and Southmead, it's a lovely place," said Judd.

Judd was visibly shaken by what had just happened and reached for a glass of water from the pitcher on the small desk next to the settee.

"Tom, you can't keep us in suspense any longer, how did he die?" asked Esther.

"With a rock, he said he was killed with a rock."

Judd took a sip of water and wiped his forehead.

"The thing is ……. I remember the murder…….I remember it so well."

He trembled as he spoke.

Suddenly, something dawned on Maria. Instantly she was overcome with a wave of nausea. Campbell jumped up and ran over when he saw the colour drain from her face.

"Grab something," he called as he held his arm around her.

Esther picked up the throw which covered the settee and passed it to Campbell. Maria took it from him and was sick, catching the contents of her stomach in the floral throw.

"I'm sorry," said Maria as Campbell sat her down on the settee.

"What is it?" asked Esther.

"It suddenly hit me. I remember seeing the murder on the news. It was all over the papers for a couple of weeks."

She wiped her mouth with a tissue, reached for the water and continued speak.

"I'd just returned home from hospital after having Christopher, I came home on the Monday, but I didn't hear about the murder until a couple of days later. I saw the press conference on the news and worked out that the boy had been killed as I was giving birth to Christopher."

She wiped her mouth again and looked around the room.

"Don't you see what this means?"

Nobody spoke. Maria put her head in her hands and began to cry. Campbell put his arm around her and she rested her head on his shoulder and sobbed. Maria wiped her eyes and continued.

"When Ben Walker died……. when he was murdered…….my son was born."

It was beginning to make sense. The others remained silent as they contemplated the gravitas of what Maria had just said.

"Isn't someone going to say something for fuck's sake?" shouted Maria.

Judd spoke up.

"You mentioned the press conference."

Maria nodded.

"I know the policeman in that conference. Occasionally I work with him."

"How would you know him? You're not in the force."

"He's Detective Chief Inspector Markland Garraway, he was the one heading up the murder case." Judd paused as he took another sip of water to wet his dry mouth,

"You remember I told you that I am a Forensic and Investigative hypnotist?"

Campbell and Esther nodded while Claire and Maria watched motionless.

"Well that's how I know Garraway. He's no longer active as a detective, the Ben Walker case was the last one he was involved with."

"Why, what happened?" asked Esther.

"I'm not exactly sure, I don't know Garraway all that well, but from what I've been told he had a mental breakdown because of the Walker case, somehow it was all too much for him." Judd rubbed his chin and shook his head.

"I didn't put two and two together, I didn't connect the name Ben Walker to the person murdered in the woods, I mean I remember the murder, but not Ben's name."

"Well, it was almost three years ago, none of us remembered it either. So how do you know the detective, what was his name, Callaway?" said Esther.

"No, it's Garraway, his name is Markland Garraway. As I said, he's no longer an active detective, although I understand he still holds the rank of Detective Chief Inspector, but he's now in charge of training."

"Training who?" asked Campbell.

"He mainly trains rooky detectives, and for part of the training he gets me involved. I get up and say my piece about Forensic and Investigative hypnosis. It's one of the many tools that detectives can use to help nail a case."

"So should you tell him about Christopher?" asked Esther.

"Well, I suppose we should tell someone, but I'm not sure that Garraway is the best one to tell. You see he's a bit of a mess these days. Not only did he suffer a breakdown, he can barely walk,………he has terrible arthritis, the poor bastard."

The five of them sat in bewilderment, all completely dumbstruck. Then the sceptic in Campbell spoke up, again doubting Judd's integrity.

"Sorry to bring this up Tom, but I didn't hear Christopher say anything about being killed by a rock, nor did I hear him say Badock's Wood. I heard you prompting him to say Badock's and I heard you telling us that he said he was killed with the rock. You could have easily fabricated this whole thing."

"And why would I have made it up, what's in it for me? I'm not even charging for these sessions."

"Play back the video," suggested Claire helpfully.

"I doubt whether the microphone on the camera would have picked it up. I certainly couldn't hear it and I was only a few feet away," said Campbell.

"Take the film away, get it analysed, do what you want............but I'm not making this stuff up, you need to believe me."

"OK, everyone take a breath," said Esther as she tried her best to calm the situation.

"I think we need to hear what Maria thinks about all of this," she said looking to the frightened redhead who was perched on the edge of the settee.

"I believe it's all real, I think Ben is in Christopher."

Maria spoke in a dull quiet tone. Campbell was worried that she was about to crack up, she had the same look in her eye as she did the night he found her slumped and chanting in Christopher's room.

"OK Campbell," said Esther, "you work for a computer company, surely you know someone who could do something with the sound on that film, you know get it enhanced or what not, so we can all hear what Christopher said and, assuming Judd hasn't fixed all this, what do we do next?"

Another awkward few seconds followed and eventually Tom Judd spoke.

"OK, I'll speak with Garraway, I've got a meeting with him and his people next week, I'll take him to one side and have a quiet word, I just hope he doesn't freak out............oh and Campbell, I agree with Esther, get the audio on the video enhanced, I need Garraway to hear what I heard."

CHAPTER ONE HUNDRED AND SIX

TM.IT boardroom
9.35am
Monday 28th May

Terry Mason entered the boardroom for the team briefing. Campbell was sitting at the table between George Marshall and Toni Dufy whilst Connor Judd was at the far end of the table preparing a slideshow of the team's project.

Mason was bothered by Campbell Broderick, he couldn't put his finger on what it was, but something about the man made him uneasy. It all started a week ago when he had become overwhelmed with a feeling of apprehension towards Campbell, and he sensed it had something to do with Liz.

The previous week he had asked Tracey Grimmer from Personnel to do a bit of searching on Broderick to see if she could find anything about his past that could have caused Mason to feel so uneasy about the man. It was only a gut feeling, but a very strong one, and Mason was sure there was something about the man that was trouble.

But Tracey had turned up nothing. He had no criminal record, not even a speeding ticket. She checked his university background and there was nothing false about the PhD he said he'd been awarded by the University of Hertfordshire.

Mason wasn't satisfied and planned to carry out his own private investigation. He knew certain people who could do a more thorough check than young Tracey. Terry Mason was a member of the Bristol Masonic Society and there were one or two members of the society that sprung to mind, who he was certain could find something about Broderick.

Mason sat at the table and made his usual small talk by asking what everyone had done during the weekend, and when it came to Campbell's turn to chat, he just shrugged his shoulders and said that he'd not done much. Mason knew he was lying.

Connor launched into his presentation and Mason soon found himself immersed in a conversation with his team about their latest project. The only one not engaging was Campbell. He couldn't stop thinking about what had happened on Saturday afternoon at Tom Judd's place. In his tightly clenched fist he held a little USB stick and on it was the file downloaded from Tom Judd's camera. The file which contained the video Tom had made of the hypnosis session. He had arranged to meet with Naomi King at lunchtime to ask her whether she could enhance the sound. He knew her well and could trust her to keep the video of Christopher's hypnosis to herself. Naomi was a computer whiz kid and had a laptop rammed with software. She was an aspiring musician who composed on her computer and had a programme which would easily pick out and enhance what Christopher had whispered on Saturday afternoon.

As the meeting drew to a close Connor ended the presentation and shut the lid on his laptop.

"You were very quiet this morning Mr. Broderick, not much to say?" asked Mason.

"Sorry Terry, I had a bit of busy weekend."

"Well make your mind up young man, just now you told me you'd not done much."

Campbell smiled nervously, he felt like he was being interrogated, as if Mason knew something.

"I didn't do much that would have been of interest to anyone, you know, just stuff that needed to be done."

Connor glanced toward Campbell. He knew there'd been another session at his brother's hypnotherapy practice at the weekend. His brother had been getting tetchy lately and it had started since he'd hypnotised Christopher.

At twelve fifteen Campbell was in the Printer's Devil with Naomi King and was treating her to a ploughman's lunch.

Naomi was a tall girl with peroxide blonde hair, which stood up like Rod Stewart's. The two of them got on well and at one point rumours were abound that they were an item. Even Maria had become suspicious at one point, until she'd met her and found out for herself that she was a person she could trust. Besides, Naomi was totally loved up with her musician husband and had no intention of doing anything untoward.

As Naomi waited for her food she sipped on her diet coke. Campbell handed her the USB stick.

"So what's all this about?" she asked.

"I'd rather not go into too much detail, but when you watch the video you will see something which I would prefer that you keep to yourself, don't even tell your husband."

She looked at him suspiciously.

"What are you playing at?"

"You'll see when you watch the clip."

He handed her a piece of paper with some numbers scribbled on it.

"Those are the two points in the video I need enhancing."

Naomi looked at the numbers. Five minutes, thirteen seconds and six minutes, twenty four seconds.

"I'd prefer it if you could fast forward to those two points and not watch the whole thing, but when you see and hear what I need enhancing, I know you'll want to watch the entire video."

"I must say, I am intrigued………nothing outside the law I hope?"

"Well, nothing outside the law as far as I'm concerned, but if you're able to enhanced the sound enough I'm certain the police will want to know about what's on the video."

"The plot thickens," said Naomi as she slid the USB stick into her purse.

Neither of them had noticed Terry Mason sitting at the table behind reading a copy of the Financial Times. Mason had listened to every word they'd said.

CHAPTER ONE HUNDRED AND SEVEN

Naomi King's flat
8.17pm
Tuesday 29th May

Naomi King had stayed up late the night before, and now she was paying for it. She'd not got to sleep before four in the morning after staying up until after midnight enhancing the sound quality on the video that Campbell had given her earlier that day. She'd clambered into bed after her husband, Josh, grumpily insisted she packed it in for the night.

Initially she respected Campbell's wishes and had advanced the video clip to five minutes, thirteen seconds. The video showed a tall man in his fifties leaning towards a little boy on a chair. She could clearly hear the man, but the boy's voice wasn't clear, it was below a whisper. She replayed the section, which only lasted a couple of seconds, several times to pinpoint the exact time the boy spoke. Campbell hadn't said which words needed enhancing, but Naomi knew which section needed to be heard.

The man's voice was very clear when he said 'which woods, can you remember the name of the woods?'

But the boy's answer wasn't picking up, his whisper was much too quiet.

After the boy had spoken she could clearly hear the man speak, 'Badock's Wood, were you killed in Badock's Wood?'

"What the ....?" she muttered as she started to enhance the sound.

Naomi was intrigued, and wondered what the hell was going on. She spent the next hour processing the sound by balancing the EQ, reducing the background noise and then she pumped the audio as high as it would go before it started to distort.

Eventually she'd cracked it, she could just about pick out the boy's voice, it was faint, but clear.

Next she spliced the man's voice so it was playing back at the unenhanced levels and when the little boy spoke she dropped in the enhanced section, which lasted one and a half seconds after which the sound reverted back to the unenhanced voice of the man.

She exported the section as an MP3 file and played it back.

Man's voice - "Which woods, can you remember the name of the woods?"

Boy's voice enhanced - "Badock's............."

Man's voice - "Badock's Wood, were you killed in Badock's Wood?"

After the man had asked whether it was Badock's Wood the boy clearly nodded his head to confirm that it was.

She replayed it over and over and couldn't believe what she was hearing.

She looked at the man in the video, he looked familiar. She froze a frame which captured a particularly clear image of him.

"I know you," she whispered.

She was intrigued and excited. She moved the virtual slider on her computer to advance the video to six minutes, twenty four seconds as instructed by Campbell, but moved the slider so it stopped a few seconds before the time he asked her to enhance. She pressed play and watched the clip.

"Ben, how did you die, what did the murderer do to kill you? Please Ben."

Naomi saw the little boy's mouth open, but like before, she couldn't make out the words.

Then the man spoke again.

"Ben, say that again, I didn't hear you…..how were you killed?"

The man was clearly concentrating on what the boy was saying but, like before, nothing was picking up on the recording.

"What the fuck is going on? This is some weird shit Campbell," she whispered to herself.

This time it didn't take long to enhance the boy's voice. She had saved the settings on her computer and it was a ten minute job to reload the equalisation and improve the quality and a further fifteen minutes to splice everything back together.

She pressed play and let the short clip run.

Man's voice - "Ben, how did you die, what did the murderer do to kill you? Please Ben."

Boy's Voice enhanced – "He killed me with a rock."

Man's voice - "Ben, say that again, I didn't hear you…..how were you killed?"

Boy's voice enhanced – "With a rock Tom, ………he killed me with a ………rock."

She froze with fear.

"What the hell is Campbell involved with?"

She played the two clips over and over until her husband knocked on the door and told her to come to bed.

Josh saw the look on her face.

"Bloody Hell, what on earth's wrong with you? You look ill."

She closed the lid on her laptop.

"I'm OK, I've finished now, I'll be there soon."

Josh went back to bed while she sat on her own for another few minutes contemplating what she had just seen and heard.

She climbed into bed and lay there for over three hours unable to sleep, with the video clip going over and over in her head until she eventually dozed off.

That was last night. She'd not gone to work today as she was too damned tired. She had called in sick.

"Jeepers Naomi, you sound awful, what's the matter?" asked Jack Allen as he took her call earlier in the day.

She had called Campbell and arranged for him to come to her place just after eight. She had made copies of the video.

Whilst she was waiting for him to arrive she played the entire video with the enhanced edits.

She saw the whole thing from start to finish.

From the little boy being hypnotised, to the change in his voice and the emergence of the mysterious Ben character. She listened to the questions about maths and the Battle of Hastings and the talk of the world cup. She watched it to the very end, right up to the section she'd enhanced.

There was a knock at the door. Naomi stopped the clip and walked to the front door. She peered through the spy hole and saw Campbell with Maria, who she'd met once before.

She let them in and took them to the lounge.

Campbell could tell by the look on her face that she'd seen the whole clip and was clearly shaken.

"What the hell have I just been watching?" asked Naomi in an irate tone.

"Did you manage to make it so Christopher's voice can be heard?" said Campbell, choosing to ignore her question.

"Yes I did……..what the hell's going on? I don't like what I've just seen."

"I'll tell you after I've seen for it myself, a lot hinges upon the words which come out of Christopher's mouth."

"Christopher, he's your son, isn't he?"

"He's Maria's son, but I'm up for the job of being his dad."

"And the man in the video, the hypnotist, that's Connor Judd's brother isn't it?"

Campbell was surprised she knew who he was.

"Yes, it's Tom Judd, how did you know?"

"I met him a couple of times, when Connor was out for drinks after work, he met up with Tom. I remembered how tall he is, he's like a bean pole."

Campbell nodded.

Maria hadn't said a word, she wasn't looking forward to watching the video and was having trouble coping with what was unfolding in her life.

"Follow me," said Naomi as she led them to the spare bedroom which had been converted into a recording studio.

"Where's Josh?" asked Campbell.

"He's rehearsing with his band."

"Has he seen the video?"

"No. Nobody has seen it other than me."

Maria looked around the room which was strewn with guitars, keyboards and a bank of equipment which meant nothing to her.

"Welcome to our little studio."

The three of them squeezed into the small room.

"I'm afraid you'll have to sit on the floor, there's only room for one chair and I need it. I'm knackered and can hardly stand up. I was working on this until gone midnight."

Maria and Campbell huddled together on the floor as Naomi fiddled with the laptop. She angled the screen so they could see it. She had rigged the sound to come from the speakers attached to the wall.

"OK, are you ready?" asked Naomi.

Campbell and Maria nodded simultaneously. They sat on the floor, holding hands as Naomi hit play.

They nervously watched the whole thing. The clip was getting closer to the section they really needed to hear. Maria was holding Campbell's hand so tightly her nails were digging into the palm of his hand. He didn't even notice as he concentrated on the screen and listened intently to the words.

And then they heard it. They heard every word between Judd and Christopher.

"Which woods, can you remember the name of the woods?"
"Badock's………….."
"Badock's Wood, were you killed in Badock's Wood?"

Hearing Christopher's amplified whisper brought Maria out in a cold sweat. She looked away from the screen.

They waited for the final piece of the clip to play, which was only seconds away, but it felt like an age as their anticipation grew.

"Ben, stay with me, please stay focused….just one more thing and then you can sleep."
"Ben, how did you die, what did the murderer do to kill you? Please Ben."
"He killed me with a rock."
"Ben, say that again, I didn't hear you…..how were you killed?"
"With a rock Tom, ………he killed me with a ………rock."

Naomi hit stop and swivelled in her chair to face them.

"So there you have it, now would someone care to tell me what the fuck just happened?"

Campbell filled her in. He explained the events of the last couple of years, and started with Christopher's head banging, to the sleep talking, to the week spent in London with Dr Phelps and he brought her up to date with the hypnosis.

After Campbell had finished, Naomi sat in her chair and stared at him in disbelief.

"I'm so sorry, I had no idea. What are you going to do now?"

"We're not entirely sure. This is why we needed to enhance the audio, we needed to know what Christopher had said, we couldn't just take Tom Judd's word for it, we needed to hear it for ourselves."

"But it's a murder, you need to report it to the police."

Campbell sighed, "do you really think the police would use this as evidence? Anyway, no one's been named as the killer."

"But you need to hypnotise him again, and get Ben Walker to name his killer."

"They wouldn't do a thing with it, Christopher's not even three, and he wasn't even born when the murder happened. The police would just laugh at us."

"That's nonsense, they'd have to listen."

"Well, Tom Judd knows someone in the force who may listen, and that's another reason why I've asked you to improve the sound."

Campbell took the USB and thanked Naomi for what she'd done and made her promise to tell no one, not even her husband. Maria, who'd said nothing since she'd been there, also thanked her and shook her hand.

Naomi saw them to the door and after they'd left she let out one huge sigh.

She went to the kitchen and poured a glass of wine and went back to her computer. She took a large mouthful of Shiraz and began typing.

'Ben Walker murder Badock's Wood'

Google returned the results in seconds and at the top was the press conference. She clicked the link and waited for the video to load.

When it began to play, she listened and watched the Scottish detective appeal for anyone to come forward who could help with their enquiries. She paid little attention to the parents of Ben Walker who were sitting behind the detective or the other man and woman sitting to his right.

When the detective had finished speaking the camera jerkily panned to the right and focused on the girl's parents. As the man stood up to speak, Naomi's heart was beating as if she was having a panic attack.

"No!" she exclaimed as she watched in disbelief.

Terry Mason, her boss, the managing director of TM.IT was speaking at the press conference. In her confused state she paid no attention to what he was saying, she just stared at the screen. She played the video again and this time she listened to what he was saying.

With shaking hands she picked up her phone and called Campbell and waited nervously for him to pick up.

Damned voicemail, he must be driving, she thought.

After the tone she left her message.

"Campbell, it's Naomi…….ring me as soon as you get this message."

CHAPTER ONE HUNDRED AND EIGHT

Avon and Somerset Police
Kenneth Steele House
Meeting room seven
11.50am
Wednesday 30th May

The long and drawn out meeting which had commenced at eight thirty that morning was finally drawing to a close.

Markland Garraway had been asked by Devon and Cornwall Police to provide a training package for their new detectives. Garraway had earned a reputation as an excellent trainer. His coaching of young detectives had proven to be so successful he was sought after by other constabularies around the United Kingdom.

He didn't present the whole training package on his own. He called upon others within and outside the force to add their expertise and they were handsomely rewarded for their efforts. In fact the training he provided was a nice little earner for Avon and Somerset for which other constabularies were happy to pay. In April he'd spent three days with the Greater Manchester Police presenting a bespoke training session.

The meeting had included Kit Langley and Jack Hall from Devon and Cornwall, Forensic Pathologist Jeremy Banting, Criminal Psychologist Paula Murray and Forensic and Investigative hypnotist Tom Judd. Between them they'd spent the morning discussing a training package designed specifically for Devon and Cornwall Police.

Now the meeting was over the six of them were relieved to take a break and stretch their legs. Other than Garraway, who was happy to stay seated and wait for the others to leave. Even getting out of a chair was an effort for him these days and he preferred to do it when the others had left the room.

Garraway looked up after putting his laptop back in its case and saw that Tom Judd was still in the room.

"You're still here Tom, don't you fancy some fresh air? It's a lovely day out there."

Judd smiled nervously. He'd not been looking forward to approaching Garraway, but knew it had to be done. He'd considered speaking with Colin Matthews, Garraway's former partner, but knew by his reputation that he wouldn't entertain what Judd had to say. Garraway was the one he needed to speak with.

"Markland, I need to talk with you."

Garraway saw a look in Judd's eye that concerned him.

"What's the problem, you look worried?"

"It's something which concerns both of us, and quite a few others. Is there somewhere we can go, somewhere quiet where we can speak alone?"

"We could sit in my car," replied Garraway, "but it would take me about half an hour to get there."

Judd saw Garraway's crutches in the corner and had fleetingly forgotten about his disability.

"This meeting room's ours until one o'clock, we could do it here if you want. What's it all about?"

Judd reached for the pitcher on the table in front of him and poured himself a glass of water. He was normally a confident man, but Garraway could sense his nervousness.

"I need to talk with you about the case of Ben Walker's murder."

CHAPTER ONE HUNDRED AND NINE

TM.IT
12.01pm
Wednesday 30th May

Campbell walked across the car park and headed for the sandwich shop on the other side of the road from where he worked.

"Campbell, wait up."

He turned around to see Naomi King running after him. The tall athletic girl didn't take long to catch him?

"Why didn't you return my call?"

Campbell looked puzzled.

"I left you a message, I rang as soon as you and Maria left last night."

He looked at his phone and saw that he'd had several missed calls. *Shit, I'd left the thing on mute,* he thought as he put the phone back in his pocket.

"Sorry, I didn't get your message, what's going on?"

"This Ben Walker thing, if it's not weird enough already, it's just got a whole lot weirder."

She explained what she'd discovered last night and told him all about the press conference and their boss Terry Mason.

Campbell stood rooted to the ground in the middle of the car park considering the consequences of what he'd just been told. He was brought out of his stupor by the honking of a car's horn to get him to move out of the way.

"I'll walk with you to the sandwich shop," said Naomi.

"I've lost my appetite," he replied in a confused and perplexed tone.

From his office window, Terry Mason saw the two of them talking. He was becoming paranoid and didn't trust Campbell or the girl. It took him a few seconds to remember her name.

"Naomi King," he quietly said to himself.

He made a mental note to ask Tracy Grimmer to check into her background.

Paranoia and distrust were beginning to ruin him. As far as he was concerned, they were both an existential threat to his daughter.

And he wasn't wrong.

CHAPTER ONE HUNDRED AND TEN

Kenneth Steele House
Meeting room seven
12.07pm
Wednesday 30th May

"I don't think I'm the best person to talk to about Ben Walker, I was removed from the case, you need to speak with Colin Matthews," said Garraway.

"I'm aware of that, however, I don't think what I am about to say will impress Matthews."

"Why's that?"

Judd drew in a breath and considered where to begin.

"Well Markland, it's all very strange, and I mean very strange, so please hear me out, no matter how weird this gets".

"If you're talking about the Ben Walker murder case, then weird wouldn't surprise me."

"Oh, why's that?"

"Never mind, just tell me what you need to say."

Judd stood up and walked to the window of the meeting room then swung around to face Garraway.

"I've been speaking with Ben Walker, we last spoke on Saturday."

Garraway looked at Judd nonchalantly.

"And just how did you manage that?"

"Remember that I said that things might get weird? Well here goes."

Judd sat down and moved his chair close to Garraway's.

"I've been helping a couple, they have a little boy who talks in his sleep, well it's not talking, it's more like chanting. He comes up with all sorts of strange things."

"What kind of strange things?"

"Loads of things, but there's a common theme running through his chanting, one of the first things he came out with was 'please hear my voice'."

Garraway looked at Judd.

"What did you just say?"

"I said there's a common….."

Garraway interrupted him.

"No, no tell me what the boy said, when he chanted."

"Please hear my voice……..why, does that mean something to you?"

"Maybe, maybe not,…….. carry on."

This meant an awful lot to Garraway, it was the four words that came to him when he had been alone on the hill way back in October 2009. The first contact Ben had made with the world of the living.

Judd continued.

"There is a common theme, the chanting is always about wanting to be heard, to be set free from some kind of prison, it's all very distressing."

Garraway nodded.

"It does sounds distressing."

Judd continued.

"They brought him to me to see whether I could use hypnosis to stop the sleep talking and chanting. It should have been a fairly easy thing to do, I've done it before, not with children as young this little boy, but it was something which I should not have had a problem with."

Judd paused and Garraway waited silently for him to continue.

"But this is when it began to get peculiar."

Garraway shuffled uncomfortably in his seat as his arthritis made him wince.

"Are you OK Markland, do you want me to continue?"

Garraway nodded his head.

"As I said, this is when it gets strange. When the boy was hypnotised, it should have been a straightforward enough process for me to place a suggestion in his subconscious which should have stopped the chanting, but instead……but instead….."

Judd hesitated before continuing, and was interrupted by Garraway.

"But instead you woke the sleeping ghost of Ben Walker."

"Look Markland, I'm serious about this, but yes, that's pretty much what I did."

"I don't disbelieve you, carry on."

Judd retraced his thoughts to where Garraway had interrupted him and then continued.

"As I said, please hear me out. But yes, instead of talking to the young boy, whose name is Christopher, I was having a conversation with a person calling himself Ben."

"How did you know it was Ben Walker?"

"I didn't, not at first. The first time I spoke with Ben it was very fleeting, a very short conversation which lasted no more than a minute. At this point I wigged out a bit and ended the hypnosis."

Garraway could sense Judd's nervousness. He was good at reading body language and could tell by the way he was behaving, and by the beads of perspiration forming on his brow that he was not making this up.

"I presume you were able to hypnotise Christopher again?"

"Yes, a week or so later, and this time I recorded it. I was worried about what might happen, so I videoed the whole thing."

Garraway's expression changed when he heard that it had it had been recorded.

"The second time, I was able to quickly hypnotise Christopher and speak with Ben. This was when he told me his full name, and this was the time he told me that he'd been murdered."

"Did you believe he'd been murdered?" asked Garraway.

"To be honest I didn't know what to believe, I wasn't sure, you see I needed more proof. It wasn't until the third time I hypnotised Christopher and spoke with Ben that things really began to heat up."

Garraway was doing his best to remain calm, but could feel twinges of anxiety returning as the conversation continued.

"Was the third time you hypnotised the boy the last time you spoke with Ben?"

"Yes, and it was on Saturday. This time he told me he was murdered in Badock's wood and that he's been killed with a rock."

"But, with no disrespect Mr. Judd, all of this information about how and where Ben Walker was murdered is common knowledge. It was all over the papers and on the television. How do I know any of this is true?"

Judd pulled a USB memory stick from his pocket and on it was the video clip that Campbell had sent him the evening before from his TM.IT email address. Judd had added the first video clip, the one which had captured the second time Judd had spoken with Ben.

He waived the USB in Garraway's face.

"See for yourself, it's all on here."

He passed the memory stick to Garraway who held it in his twisted hand.

"Play it, play it now," said Judd pointing to Garraway's laptop, which was in a case beside him on the floor.

"If you don't mind, I'd rather watch it when I'm alone."

"Please Markland, I need you to see it, and I want to be with you when you do."

Garraway looked at the memory stick as he held it between his fingers and, as he did, a familiar wave of nausea washed over him.

CHAPTER ONE HUNDRED AND ELEVEN

TM.IT
12.27pm

Terry Mason had been watching Campbell Broderick and Naomi King in the car park for over twenty minutes. From the window of his third floor office he couldn't hear what they were saying, but he knew that they were talking about him and his daughter Liz.

The once rational and composed man was becoming paranoid and suspicious. Carl Cooper, TM.IT's sales director, and Mason's right hand man, had noticed a dramatic change in him over the last week and was concerned about his wellbeing. Carl had seen Terry make some unusual business decisions recently and was keeping a close eye on him.

Terry's phone rang, which snapped him out of his dreamlike state. It was Anne, his wife.

"Terry, you need to come home, Liz isn't well. Chloe has called the doctor and he's on his way."

"What's the matter, what's wrong with her?"

"I don't know, but it's her breathing, it's all wrong."

"I'm on my way."

Mason put the phone in his pocket, grabbed his keys and quickly left his office. He hurried past Sally, his secretary, without saying a word and slammed the office door behind him.

Within fifteen minutes he was at his daughter's bedside. The doctor was examining her.

"We need to get her to hospital, it looks like Liz has developed pneumonia."

CHAPTER ONE HUNDRED AND TWELVE

Kenneth Steele House
Meeting room seven
12.52pm
Wednesday 30th May

Garraway finished watching both video clips and had heard the voice pertaining to be Ben Walker saying he'd been killed by a rock in Badock's Wood.

He took a moment to think about what he'd just seen and what Tom Judd had been telling him.

"I understand what you're proposing," said Garraway.

Judd looked at him with an inquisitive glance.

"You're hoping to hypnotise Christopher and get Ben to name his killer."

"I know it's something that wouldn't stand up in court on its own, it could never be used as evidence."

"You're right, but perhaps Ben could tell us something that we don't already know, something which could give us a helping hand."

Judd nodded enthusiastically.

"The problem is, and we've already discussed this, but it isn't my case anymore, it belongs to Collin Matthews and he won't touch any of this with a barge pole, it's just not his thing."

"Ben Walker is bound to have more to tell, I think I should hypnotise Christopher again and I think you should be there."

All of this was making Garraway feel very uneasy. The ghosts of the past couple of years were beginning to reappear.

"You may or may not know, but Ben Walker's murder case made me very ill, it virtually ruined my life. Even now I sometimes lie in bed and think about the case, and I don't sleep because of it. I won't bore you with what happened, but the whole thing had a profound effect upon me."

"I'd heard something about that," said Judd.

"I expect you did. I have somewhat of a reputation around here of being a bit, well let's just say, a bit different."

Judd nodded.

"However, as much as I agree that useful information could be garnered by speaking with Ben through Christopher, I need to think about whether I should be involved. It's taken me a long time to recover and get to where I am today, and I wouldn't want to be back to square one,...... to where I was a couple of years ago."

Judd looked at him and saw a tired and tense man. He looked different to the person he was talking to twenty minutes earlier. He noticed how Garraway had not baulked when he had told him about the hypnosis of Christopher. It was almost as if he accepted it as something which was quite normal.

"Can I keep this?" asked Garraway as he motioned towards the memory stick.

Judd nodded.

Garraway took the little grey USB stick and slipped it in his pocket.

"Give me some time to think and I'll get back to you."

CHAPTER ONE HUNDRED AND THIRTEEN

Southmead Hospital
8.48pm
Wednesday 30th May

Liz Mason lay in a hospital bed, only a few wards away from where she had been when admitted to intensive care back in September 2009.

Her parents were by her bed. Terry hated hospitals and was longing for his daughter to come home. She'd not even been in hospital for twelve hours.

Her symptoms were too severe for her to be treated at home and the added complications due to her being in a coma had meant that hospital was the best place for her. Antibiotics and fluids were given to her intravenously and she had an oxygen mask covering her face to help with her breathing.

Anne held Liz's hand and was fighting back tears. She had not spoken to her daughter for over two and half years and to all intents and purposes Liz may as well be dead, other than for the desperate hope that sometime soon she would awake from her coma and talk to her parents again.

That day would happen, and was about to happen very soon.

CHAPTER ONE HUNDRED AND FOURTEEN

Markland Garraway's home
9.15pm
Wednesday 30th May

Markland Garraway was tired. Just leaving his house, going to the office and coming home had exhausted him. But the meeting he had with Tom Judd had taken the wind out of his sails. The thought that Ben Walker was still in his life scared him, but he also had a need to be involved. He had a gut feeling that if the killer was caught and brought to justice then he would find some kind of peace in his life.

Supporting himself with his crutches, he slowly made his way to the bottom of the stairs. He rested the crutches against the wall and climbed aboard the stair lift. He strapped himself in, held his laptop close to his chest and pressed the switch and ascended the stairs. It took another five minutes to get off the stair lift and walk to his bedroom using another pair of crutches he kept on the landing. He collapsed on his bed and sighed.

Rolling over onto his left hand side he switched on his laptop and loaded the two videos that Judd had given to him earlier. He watched them several times and was convinced they were genuine. Unless the video clips had been tampered with, how else could the young boy's voice have sounded so mature? Garraway was astounded by the way the boy spoke, the tone of his voice and the way he confidently interacted with Tom Judd.

And what about those four words that Judd said Christopher had spoken. The first four words he'd chanted during his sleep. The same four words that Garraway had heard the time he was alone on the hill.

PLEASE – HEAR – MY – VOICE.

After playing both clips another five or six times he lay on the bed and looked through the open window. He watched as a gentle wind blew the nets and the soft breeze wafted over his face. The cooling effect of the lightly moving air was relaxing and soon it had coaxed him into a deep sleep.

While deep in slumber, in the depths of sleep where most people are beyond dreaming, the hill was reaching out to him and it was planting a seed which would flourish into a vision. A vision which would influence his decision to help Ben Walker.

As he lay on his bed and slept, he dreamt of a girl. It was the same girl he had dreamt of once before on the anniversary of Ben Walker's brutal murder. The last time she'd appeared in his dream he knew she had been in the woods when Ben had been murdered. He'd never seen or met her before, but he knew she was the link. She was the missing link in the chain to put an end to all of this turmoil and sadness.

The hill had sent him an ember of a thought that burned and glowed brightly into a clear and distinct image. The image hung lifelessly, as if it were in suspended animation.

The image was of Carla's face. It was motionless yet full of life, like a photograph imprinted in his subconscious.

While in a state of deep, deep sleep he climbed out of his bed and stood tall. None of the symptoms of his crippling illness were affecting him as he confidently walked out of his bedroom and down stairs towards the lounge. His eyes were tightly shut during his somnambulistic journey, and the vision of Carla was clear in his mind's eye.

He opened the door to his lounge and walked to the book shelf and laid his hand on a paperback copy of 'Notes from Under the Floorboards' by Dostoevsky, the same book he'd fallen asleep with in his hand the first time he'd dreamt of Carla. The same book he'd used to write down the description of the girl in his dream and the attack in the woods.

He opened a drawer and picked up a pen and on the page opposite to the notes he'd made of the girl's appearance, he sketched a detailed and perfect image of her. Garraway wasn't an artist, he could just about draw a stick man, but in his sleep the hill had guided him to produce a perfect likeness of the girl. He finished the sketch and placed the book face down and open on the table with the picture of Carla Price ready for him to find in the morning. He put the pen back in the draw and climbed the stairs back to his bedroom. The image of Carla faded from a dream he would never remember and for the rest of the night he enjoyed the longest uninterrupted and dreamless sleep he'd had in a long time.

Garraway was woken by the eight o'clock alarm. It took him a few minutes to come around as his eyes became accustomed to the sunlight pouring in through the open window. His laptop was next to him and he was disgusted to find he'd slept through the whole night wearing the clothes he had been wearing the day before. Even his tie was loosely and sloppily hanging around his neck.

He didn't have to be in work until ten, but he needed two full hours to get himself washed, dressed, fed and watered. Working the part-time reduced hours that had been written into his contract since he'd returned to work afforded him the luxury of time he required to be in work by ten 'o' clock.

For the first time in a long time he felt refreshed after his long and uninterrupted sleep. His body still hurt, but his mind was clearer than it had been in months. He swivelled his body around and hung his legs over the edge of his bed and with one great heave he pulled himself up. Reaching for the crutches he kept by the side of his bed he slowly made his way to the stair lift. He glanced at the bathroom and considered having a wash before breakfast, but decided against it. This morning he was starving and had made up his mind to eat first and spruce himself up later.

He strapped himself into the stair lift, pressed the button and the lift quietly creaked and whirred as it slowly descended.

He stepped down from the stair lift and, supporting himself on the banister, he reached for the crutches and made his way to the kitchen. After making coffee he walked to the lounge, trying his best not to spill the hot drink.

He saw a book on the table and eyed it suspiciously. He couldn't remember seeing it there the night before. It was a book he'd finished reading over a year ago. It had been a struggle for him to read, but he'd been determined to see it through to the end, after it had been recommended to him by a friend.

But how did it get there? Nothing else in the house appeared to have been disturbed, the doors were all locked and he hadn't heard any noises during the night.

He moved towards the table and set the coffee down on a coaster. The book had been placed in the middle of the table and he struggled to reach it as the pain in his arm was close to being unbearable.

He used one of his crutches to reach the book and slide it nearer to him over the surface of the wooden table. His clumsy and crippled hand awkwardly pulled the book too far and it fell to the floor by his feet.

He sat on a chair and leaned forward. He could just about reach it. He picked it up and placed it in front of him on the table.

Thumbing through the book he wasn't sure what he was looking for, but was hoping to find a reason why the thing had appeared on the table. He thumbed to last page of the story and was about to put it down when he remembered the notes he had made at the back of the book describing the attack in the woods and the girl he'd dreamt about on the first anniversary of Ben Walker's death.

He turned the page to his notes and on the opposite side he saw a drawing. It was a pen sketch of a young girl and it was a very good one. The girl looked familiar. His eyes danced between the sketch and the description of the girl in his dream until he realised that they were one and the same.

He laid the book on the table and looked at the girl.

What on earth, who could have done this? He thought.

The girl's youthful appearance was tarnished by a look of sadness. She had an expression which made him think she had a secret to tell.

He sat back in his chair and tried to think if he'd let anyone borrow the book. He was certain he hadn't and was sure the thing had never left his house.

He didn't get very many visitors these days, and certainly none that he knew were talented enough to draw as well as this.

He looked at the girl and reread his description and, as he did, he was overcome by the familiar feeling of nausea that he'd come to expect when dealing with the events which had happened on the hill. The bitter taste of bile rose in his throat. He reached for his coffee and slurped a mouthful and burnt his tongue. The feeling of sickness soon went, but was replaced by the pain left behind by the scolding hot coffee.

Whether he liked it or not, he was still embroiled in Ben's murder and there was no escaping the fact.

All of the strange things were happening for a reason. From the visions on the hill, to the suicide of Polly to be with her lover Sarah, to the chanting of the little boy and right up to the drawing of the girl he'd just found in the book.

Ben's murderer had to be found and he knew that Colin Matthews wouldn't be revisiting the case anytime soon. It would be down to Markland Garraway to do what he did best.

He picked up his phone and called Tom Judd.

"Hi, Tom, it's Markland. I've made up my mind…….count me in."

CHAPTER ONE HUNDRED AND FIFTEEN

The Fox and Goose
Barrow Gurney, near Bristol
12.15pm
Thursday 31st May

Don Hodges was at a window seat in the picturesque country pub waiting for Terry Mason who was at the bar ordering drinks.

The well-built, middle aged man was a private investigator. He had worked for Mason once before back in two thousand and eight, when he had been employed to discretely investigate two of TM.IT's employees who Carl Cooper and Mason had been certain were stealing customer account information and selling it to one of their main competitors in London. Their hunch had been right and the two employees were prosecuted and removed from their well-paid positions.

Mason had been introduced to Hodges by a fellow member of the Bristol Masonic Society.

Hodges watched Mason as he waited to be served and noticed how his appearance had changed since he'd last seen him. He needed a shave, his hair was a mess and his shirt was hanging out. Hodges remembered him as being an immaculately dressed man. Even when he was casually dressed he looked smart. Hodges was aware that there had been some dramatic changes in the man's life which had affected him and assumed this was likely to be the cause of the change in his appearance.

Mason's hands were shaking as he put the two pints of bitter on the table and sat across from Hodges.

They exchanged small talk for several minutes, but it became apparent to Hodges that he had no interest in talking and wanted to get down to business.

Mason pulled two folders from his brown briefcase and slid them across the table to Hodges.

Hodges opened the first folder which had several pages of notes, a printout from TM.IT's personnel files and a black and white photograph of an attractive girl in her late twenties. He turned the folder over and looked at the name written on the front in bold black marker pen: **'Naomi King'**.

He put the folder down and picked up the other one. He looked at the name on the folder, which was also written with a black marker pen and in the same handwriting as the other one: **'Campbell Broderick'**.

"What is it you would like me to find out?" asked Hodges.

Mason shifted uncomfortably in his seat.

"Whatever you can."

"Can you be more specific?"

Mason looked awkward and perturbed.

"Terry, why is it you need me to investigate these two, what have they done?"

"It's my daughter," replied Mason.

"What about your daughter?"

"They're both a threat to her and I need to stop them from whatever they're planning on doing?"

"What kind of threat? You need to tell me more if you want me to help."

Mason wasn't making any sense and Hodges was becoming impatient. Although he knew Terry Mason could afford him, he needed more information and if Terry Mason wasn't going to tell him what all this was about in the next few minutes Hodges would walk.

"My daughter was attacked and left for dead a few years ago, and she's been in a coma ever since."

Hodges looked up from his drink and saw a tear in Mason's eye.

"Do you think that these two were involved in the attack?"

"I don't know, I mean, I don't think so. The police haven't arrested anyone, they've given up. Her boyfriend was murdered in the attack."

"But do you think that these two were involved?"

"No, I don't think I do, but there is a connection between them and my daughter, especially between Broderick and my daughter."

"Sorry Terry, I know this must be difficult for you, but I really don't understand what I am supposed to do for you."

"Don, do you ever get a gut feeling about something, do you ever work on a hunch, you know, like instinct?"

"Of course I do, it's a sixth sense we private investigators have, well, at least the good ones."

"Good, well then you'll understand when I tell you what I have is a hunch…..a gut feeling…….instinct, it's all of those things. I just know that something bad is going to happen to my daughter and that man and that woman have something to do with it."

Mason was trembling and Hodges knew he was sincere.

"I do understand, but isn't there anything else, anything at all that you can give me to go on? Have you heard these two talking, is there anything written down and why would they wish to harm your daughter, what's in it for them?"

"NO, I DON'T HAVE ANYTHING!" shouted Mason, he apologised, took a sip of bitter to calm his nerves and continued.

"No, I don't have anything written down but I did hear them discuss something. They talked about a video and I just know it's something to do with my daughter. He gave her a USB stick which must have contained the video………..but this gut feeling I have, it's been nagging me for a while………even before I heard them talking."

Hodges said nothing as an awkward moment prevailed.

"I just know something bad will happen to my daughter and it has something to do with whatever is on that video."

"OK, now I have something to go on, you should have told me about the video in the beginning."

Mason shrugged his shoulders.

"I still don't have much, but it's a start. I'll get my hands on the video and we'll take it from there."

Hodges stood up, swigged the last mouthful of bitter, put the files under his arm and turned to leave the building. Hodges stopped and turned back to Mason.

"Look if there is something you're hiding, something you're not telling me……..anything at all, you really need to let on, it would make my job a hell of a lot easier you know."

Mason merely nodded.

Hodges sighed and left the pub. He was sure Mason wasn't telling him the whole story.

CHAPTER ONE HUNDRED AND SIXTEEN

Markland Garraway's house
7.30pm
Friday 1st June

Garraway hadn't witnessed this many people in his house for years. Maria, Claire and Esther were sitting next to each other on the settee. Tom Judd was standing by the window and Campbell was in the kitchen making coffee. The only one who wasn't present was Samreen who was looking after Christopher.

Garraway had phoned Tom Judd early on Wednesday morning and told him to call a meeting with everyone who had been there when Christopher had been hypnotised. He'd asked Judd to arrange the meeting to take place at his house.

Garraway waited for Campbell to bring in the drinks before starting. He was nervous and the anxieties he'd experienced in the past had returned. He had to be strong and overcome his personal demons which were back and trying to break him down.

Campbell handed out the coffees and Garraway cleared his throat and began.

"Thank you for agreeing to meet this evening and thank you also for agreeing to have the meeting at my house. As you can see, I don't get around too well these days and it's easier for me to speak to you all from here."

Everyone nodded.

"As most of you may know by now, I was the original detective inspector, assigned to investigate the murder of Ben Walker. It is a case which, from the very beginning, has been strange."

He paused for reflection and then continued.

"Ben Walker was brutally murdered on the sixth of September two thousand and nine. His head was smashed in with a rock and his friend, Liz

Mason, was left for dead. Ben's body was found early the following morning. The person who'd discovered them thought Liz was also dead and it wasn't until the emergency services had arrived that it was found she was alive, but only just, had she been found later she probably would also have died. Unfortunately she fell into a coma, from which, as far as I am aware, she has never woken."

Campbell was having difficulty appreciating that the girl was his boss's daughter.

"The murderer, or murderers, as we know there was more than one assailant, have never been caught. We have DNA on record, which we are certain is from the murderer, or someone who was there during the attack, but unfortunately the DNA doesn't match anyone on the police database."

Garraway sat silently in an effort to compose himself for what he was about to say next.

"From a personal perspective, this is the strangest inquiry I have ever encountered. It's been a case which from the very beginning has been fraught with strange happenings and it has made me very ill. I could tell you all about the peculiar things that have happened to me during the investigation, but to be honest, at this particular time, I would prefer not to. However, suffice to say, it didn't come as a great surprise when I heard from Mr Judd about Christopher and what'd happened to him whilst under hypnosis. So what I propose to do today is to discuss how to move forward, and how we can use anything Christopher can tell us about what happened to close the Ben Walker murder case."

"Don't you mean use anything that *Ben* can tell us about what happened to close the Ben Walker murder case?" suggested Judd.

Garraway nodded.

"How would you go about doing that?" asked Maria, who was concerned that Christopher would have to undergo further hypnosis sessions, of which he was already becoming increasingly unhappy.

"I suggest that we treat Ben as if he were any other witness……."

"Other than the fact that he's not like any other witness," interrupted Campbell.

"This is true, but he could provide information detailing what happened that night….. perhaps a description, what his attackers looked like, what they were wearing, he may even remember how they sounded………if I'm really lucky, he could even give me some names."

"Should you tell Ben about the girl, Liz?" asked Esther.

"I'm not certain about that, he's bound to ask…….."

"I think you need to tell him, you need to brutally honest with him about everything," interrupted Esther.

Garraway nodded.

"What I would like is a description from Christopher, sorry, I mean Ben, of what Liz Mason looks like and perhaps if she has any identifying marks on her body that proves he knew her, or knows her even."

The strange scenario was causing Garraway to mix his tenses. It wasn't every day he referred to a dead person in the present tense as if that person was still alive.

"Why would you need to ask questions about Liz?" asked Judd.

"With no disrespect to your good self Mr. Judd, and I don't believe that any of what I've been told isn't true, but it would satisfy me if I could ask a question or two of my own, just to convince myself that all of this is definitely happening."

Garraway asked Campbell, who was standing near the bookcase, if he could find a novel on the shelf by a writer called Dostoevsky. Campbell looked through the varied collection of books until he found 'Notes from Under the Floorboards'.

"Is this the one?" asked Campbell waving the paperback with a puzzled expression on his face.

"Yes it is. Please could you turn to the page on the back inside cover and show everyone in the room what you see."

Campbell did as Garraway asked and found the sketch of the girl. He held the book up and showed it around the room.

"Who's the girl?" asked Maria.

"I don't know her name, but I believe she was there at the time of the murder."

"How did you come by the picture?" asked Campbell.

"I've absolutely no idea, it just appeared in the book."

"When?" asked Esther.

"A couple of days ago."

Blank expressions filled the room. Campbell looked again at the sketch and saw the notes on the opposite page. He read the scribbled comments Garraway had made of his dream and also the description of the girl. Beneath the description was written a date. Sixth September two thousand and ten.

"What's this? It looks like a description of Ben's murder, and the girl, you've written a description which matches her perfectly," said Campbell.

"I know, and if you look at the date, I wrote it a year to the day of the murder."

"It's a pretty detailed description of what happened, like you were there at the time."

"It came to me in a dream, and I jotted it all down, and a description of the girl before my memory of the whole thing faded," said Garraway.

"And you've no idea who did the drawing?" said Esther.

Garraway shook his head.

"As I've said, I came downstairs and there it was, on the table ready for me to find."

Campbell passed the book around so everyone could read what he'd written and get a closer look at the sketch of the girl.

"There is one thing of which I am certain," added Garraway, "the girl in the picture is the person who can bring this whole thing together. I'm sure she's out there somewhere and can tell me what happened and who was there on the night of the murder………..it's all to do with the hill in Badock's Wood, where Ben was murdered."

"What do you mean?" asked Esther.

"There's something about that hill, it's a Bronze Age burial mound, and it reaches out and it gets to you, it gets to your very core…..it communicates with you."

Everything connected to the murder of Ben Walker was so surreal, that no one in the room questioned what Garraway had just said. It had almost become that 'strange was the new normal'.

"So what's next, I hypnotise Christopher and you ask him a list of questions?" asked Judd.

Garraway nodded.

"Hold on, hold on just one second, aren't you forgetting someone? Someone who is crucial to this whole thing and someone to whom none of you seem to have given a second thought," said Maria.

"If it wasn't for my Christopher, none of you would be here today. But what if he doesn't want to be hypnotised anymore? You can't force him and between you and me, the bribes of toys and trips to Thomas Land are beginning to lose their appeal. I'm not sure whether he wants to be part of this anymore."

Maria was right. Everyone was assuming that Christopher could just be plonked in the chair and would happily slip into Ben's character like a performing animal. Other than Maria, no one had given much thought to what Christopher felt about what was happening. He wasn't even three years old and it was an awful lot to expect of the little boy. Even Campbell was getting so carried away with the whole thing that he was forgetting about Christopher.

"Does he still bang his head and chant?" asked Judd.

"He's a little better, but he is still doing it," replied Maria.

"Until we satisfy Ben that we will catch his killer, I think your son will continue to keep you awake. Ben now knows about us, and he won't let go until his killer is caught. It's almost as if he wants to be part of the team, he wants to be involved as if he is working on the case." said Judd.

Suddenly a light bulb shone over Garraway's head.

"That's it Tom, you're right……it's all making sense."

"Why, what is it?" asked Judd looking puzzled.

"What you just said about Ben wanting to be involved in the case."

Garraway shuffled in his chair and was agitated with excitement.

"Ben Walker was a policeman, well he would have been if he'd lived another day. Had he not been murdered, he would have started his first day of work as a police officer on the 7th September. He had been a PCSO for a couple of years, and was about to become the real thing."

"What's a PCSO?" asked Claire, speaking for the first time since the meeting had begun.

"A Police Community Support Officer, he was like an unpaid policeman."

Claire nodded.

"That's correct, one thing I know about Ben is that he was obsessed with police work, and ultimately he wanted to be a detective. It must be hardwired into him to make sure his killer is caught."

"Or killers," added Campbell.

"So what you're suggesting is that if we use Ben to catch his own killer, he will leave Christopher in peace and everyone will live happily ever after?" asked Maria.

"Or die happily ever after," suggested Judd.

"Yes I do, I really do," said Garraway excitedly.

"But why do you think this is happening? There must have been lots of similar instances when police have been murdered, and you don't hear of any others coming back from the afterlife to hunt down their murderer," asked Esther.

Garraway paused and looked at everyone who was in the room.

"It's because Ben was murdered at the hill, the hill in Badock's Wood."

CHAPTER ONE HUNDRED AND SEVENTEEN

Don Hodges' office
8.07pm
Friday 1st June

Hodges poured himself a beer and looked through the manila files Terry Mason had given him. It wasn't his kind of thing. He specialised in industrial sabotage and had become a very wealthy man because of it.

He was an American, born in New England. Hodges had worked for the FBI for many years before moving to Britain ten years ago. Disheartened by the direction the Bureau was taking, he quit his job and turned his back on his country.

He didn't want to take on Terry Mason's case, but as he'd worked for him before, and they were both members of the Bristol Masonic Society, he was doing it as a favour. He had told himself that he wouldn't get too involved, just find the video, get a copy of it to Mason and that would be it. Job done.

Finding the video wouldn't be a problem. He knew it had been on a USB memory stick which meant at some point the file had been, and probably still was, on Campbell Broderick's and Naomi King's computers. Child's play for a man like Hodges, who'd spent years hacking into some of the most complex and secure systems in the world to locate files which had brought down industrial pirates whose intentions had been to get their hands on intellectual property and sell it to the highest bidder.

And it was to be even easier than that. Mason had provided him with personnel files on the two, which included both their TM.IT company email addresses and their private ones. Knowing this information and by hacking into their email accounts Hodges would have access to the IP addresses of both King's and Broderick's computers. With this information, whilst in the comfort of his office, he could easily get into their computers, silently take over and control them and search for the most recently added mpeg or mp4 video files and copy them.

For such an established and respected IT company, Hodges found it almost laughable how appallingly low TM.IT's security was. Within minutes he was reading Naomi King's emails. He had easily found his way into her account, n.king@tmit.co.uk. He didn't want to spend too much time on this job as he had far too much other work to be getting on with. Now he was into her account he looked to see whether she'd emailed Broderick the video file. He scrolled through the emails she had sent since Tuesday, which was the day Mason told him she'd been given the memory stick. He couldn't see any correspondence between her and Broderick. He pondered that perhaps they'd agreed not to communicate by email. Before he spent too much time breaking into her personal computer, he decided to get into Campbell's account, c.broderick@tmit.co.uk, and check whether there were any clues.

He pushed back his chair and with a smile on his smug face shouted 'bingo' when he saw an email had been sent to one Thomas Judd. The email had a video attachment and the subject of the email was the biggest give away, which was 'Enhanced Video'.

Hodges laughed as he downloaded the file. Although he considered this a favour to Terry Mason, he would still charge him for what had been less than twenty minutes work. He considered a figure of around two thousand pounds should be fair. Hodges had the business philosophy that every deal should stand on its own two feet and make a profit and this was exactly what he would do with Mason. He knew the man could afford it and had seemed so desperate to get the video he would probably pay twice that amount.

When the video had finished downloading Hodges opened the file to see what the whole thing was about. He was sure that it had to be the video that Mason had become so paranoid over, and was curious to see what had been affecting the man so seriously.

As the clip loaded, Hodges poured another drink.

He took a slug of beer and grabbed a handful of Nachos as the video began to play.

He saw a tall man talking to a little boy in a chair. The lighting was poor, but he could easily make out what was happening. He put down his drink and moved closer to the screen.

"Hello Ben, its Tom, can you hear me?"
"Hello Tom, yes I can and it's good to hear you again".

"Ben, I hope you appreciate that this is a rather unusual situation and I guess this is just as strange for you as it is for me."

"It is strange, and you need to understand what it's like from my point of view, you're the only person I've spoken with since I was killed."

"I guess we're both in the same position."

"I need to be completely honest with you Ben, and I hope you understand the situation from my perspective, I need to be sure that you are who you say you are and not a creation of Christopher's subconscious mind."

"I have a few questions for you and if you answer them correctly I think we can agree that you are real and not a character made up by Christopher."

"I hope I pass the test, as I would hate to think I'm the figment of someone's imagination……….by the way, can I ask, how old is Christopher?"

"He's just over two and half years old."

"OK Ben, here goes with the questions, I hope you're good with mathematics because the first one is about multiplication. Ben, what is eight times twelve?"

"You had to go and choose the twelves, I always struggled with the twelve times table…………………………….. ninety six Tom, eight twelves are ninety six."

"OK, Ben, ninety six is correct, now we're getting somewhere."

"Question number two, when was the Battle of Hastings?"

"I'm sorry Tom, I can't do dates, or times. It's something I've lost all concept of. I can't even tell you when I was born, the year I died or how old I was when I was killed, I'm going to have to pass, sorry."

"I may not be able remember the date, but history was one of my strong points."

"OK, what do you have for me?"

"The battle was between Duke William of Normandy and King Harold's Anglo Saxon army and the Duke's guys won."

"OK Ben, I think that's enough of the questions, we're all convinced you're real."

"We? Did you say we? There are others who are with you?"

"Yes there are."

"Who are the others?"

"OK Ben, in the room with me are Christopher's mother and grandmother, Christopher's mother's fiancé, Christopher's health visitor and a friend of the family, so as you can imagine, we're all on the edges of our seats."

"OK Ben, we would like to know when you lived. We don't know whether your death was in our time, or a long, long time ago, before anyone in this room was born."

"More questions? OK, fire away, but make sure it doesn't take long, I don't know how much longer I can keep going, I'm starting to ebb a little."

"Ben, when you were alive, did you like sport?"

"I loved sport. I spend a lot of my time remembering the sport I played. Cricket was my speciality, I played for Horfield in Bristol and I was also a keen rugby player."

"So not a football fan then?"

"Football was my passion, I watched every City home game at Ashton Gate………. but I was a useless player, nobody would have me in their team."

"Sorry to hear that. Did you follow the World Cup?"

"You bet, ever since I was a kid. I was never able to fill a complete sticker book though."

"What was the last World Cup you remember, who won?"

"Italy beat France. The match finished one all and went to penalties."

"You seem extremely sure about that."

"I was there, I went with my father to Berlin. That year I was confident for England, but it never happened. My dad and I had a brilliant time, one of my favourite memories."

"Is this another memory you replay often?"

"OK Ben, let's find out more about you and something which everyone in this room wants to know……..how did you die?"

"Ben, can you hear me, how did you die? …………………………..Ben, it's Tom, I need to know how you died, where did it happen and who killed you? Concentrate please…….don't fade on me now."

"Tom, sorry, I…… I …….. can't quite find the………."

"Please Ben, try, please try your hardest."

"I'm trying……….I was killed in……..I was killed in the ……..woods."

"Did you say you were killed in the woods?"

"In the woods?"

"Which woods, can you remember the name of the woods?"

"Badock's………….."

"Badock's Wood, were you killed in Badock's Wood?"

"Ben, stay with me, please stay focused….just one more thing and then you can sleep."

"Ben, how did you die, what did the murderer do to kill you? Please Ben."

"He killed me with a rock."

"Ben, say that again, I didn't hear you…..how were you killed?"

"With a rock Tom, ………he killed me with a ………rock."

Don Hodges stared blankly at the screen, his hand gripping his glass of beer tightly.

"What the fuck was that?" he said out loud.

He replayed the clip. Watching it for the second time, it had lost none of its impact, in fact it was even creepier.

He could hear the two sections of the clip which Naomi King had enhanced, and the way in which the boy's voice suddenly increased and became clear made the whole clip sound surreal.

It hadn't taken Hodges long before he'd worked out that the little boy was under hypnosis and was speaking the voice of someone who was dead.

"Reincarnation," he whispered to himself.

Hodges was wondering what the connection was between Mason's daughter and the video. Then he remembered what the boy had said, he told the hypnotist Tom, that he'd been killed in Badock's Wood.

He brought up Google and feverishly typed 'Liz Mason Badock's Wood'.

Up came the results. He clicked on the press conference link and saw Garraway heading up the conference, he sat in awe as Terry Mason made an appeal for anyone who could provide useful information to come forward to the police.

Mason was right thought Hodges. He could see there was something on the video which affected his daughter. Whether it was a direct threat upon her life or not, he could not tell.

He loaded the clip onto a memory stick and put it in an envelope.

He picked up his phone and called Mason.

"Terry, it's Don………I have the video, meet me tonight. Come to the The Fox and Goose, be there by ten."

CHAPTER ONE HUNDRED AND EIGHTEEN

Daniel Boyd's bedsit
Truro, Cornwall
8.46pm
Friday 1st June

Boyd was lying in bed. His painful ankle had kept him away from his cash in hand window cleaning job for the past two weeks. While Boyd wasn't working he wasn't getting any money and he was praying that his ankle would soon be well enough to allow him to work.

He'd not seen a doctor about the injury. He hadn't even registered with the local practice as he was worried that by giving either his real name, or his alias, it would allow the police in Bristol to trace him to Truro in Cornwall.

During the past two weeks he'd spent a lot of time thinking about the person he saw looking at him through the window, the person who had frightened the life out of him and caused him to fall from the ladder. He'd also had time to consider how alone he was. He hadn't received any calls or visitors. No one had contacted him to see how he was. He had left the house just twice in the last fortnight and that was to stock up on cigarettes, Special Brew and a few basics to keep in the fridge.

Each day since falling from the ladder had been a miserable existence of moping around the flat, watching pornography on his second hand laptop, smoking, drinking and being kept awake for most of the night by the deafening music coming from his Neanderthal neighbour's bedsit.

Is that all there is to my life? Thought Boyd as he drew on a Benson's and took another swig of Special Brew. He had purposely alienated himself from people since he'd murdered Ben Walker. He'd become paranoid about making friends on the off chance that he might say the wrong thing to the wrong person and end up raising suspicions which could ultimately lead to his arrest and conviction for the murder he'd committed over two years ago.

On occasions like this, when he became very low, he often thought about handing himself over to the law. At least he could rest easily without spending the remainder of his futile existence looking over his shoulder.

His mind wandered back to the person he'd seen in the window. Could that have really been Ben Walker? From what Boyd could remember, it certainly looked like him. He recalled the words the person had silently mouthed at him through the window.

'I've got you now'

It can't have been Walker he thought. *I killed him over two years ago.*

Boyd pondered. Possibly the person in the window just bore a striking resemblance to Walker and perhaps he hadn't mouthed the words 'I've got you now', maybe it was something completely different. Boyd knew he had become paranoid and wondered if he'd twisted things in his mind. The memory of the strange person wouldn't leave him and it was clear as the day he'd seen it two weeks earlier.

Since he'd bought the second hand laptop three months ago, which was the first computer he had ever owned, he'd spent most of his time searching for pictures and videos of pornography. But he'd also found another use for it. He could use search engines to find almost anything he needed to know. He'd searched for Jarrett's, the company where he used to work in Bristol and found a picture of Stanley, the man he'd enjoyed working with. The only person he had ever considered to be a real friend. It had been Stanley's name he'd used as an alternative persona in Cornwall.

He'd used the computer to find out what had happened to some of the kids from Whitcroft School and had found a number of pictures of the ones he used to beat up and terrorise. They seemed to be doing well in the world. Some of them had been to university and appeared to have well paid jobs. A few of them kept cropping up on something called LinkedIn, whatever that was.

Then Boyd had an idea. Perhaps there was a picture on the internet of Ben Walker. His murder had made the headlines and was probably archived on a local news website.

He got off the bed and hobbled over to the little table where his laptop was charging. The computer was so old that the battery would only hold about forty five minutes of life before Boyd had to plug it in to the mains.

He lifted the lid and the clapped out machine slowly whirred into life.

Boyd shuffled to the bathroom which was at the end of the corridor to relieve himself after drinking two cans of Special Brew. It took him a good couple of minutes to slowly limp back to the room, holding on to the wall for support and by the time he'd got back to his room the laptop had only just started to show signs of life. He lit another cigarette and waited impatiently. After another four or five minutes the half a dozen or so little desktop icons had appeared and the thing was ready for use.

He fired up Google and typed 'Ben Walker murder Badock's Wood, Bristol'.

Google returned result after result. There were links from many news websites, it was like Ben Walker had been some kind of national hero. There were images of him on nearly every website that carried a report of his murder.

Boyd found one particularly good image, which was fairly large, as many of them weren't much bigger than the size of a postage stamp.

He looked at the picture of Walker and saw that the resemblance to the person he'd seen in the window was identical. It had to have been Walker……..but how?

He sat down on his bed and finished the cigarette. Some of the links in his search were video clips. He hobbled back to the laptop and searched for a clip.

He'd never given much thought to what had happened after Ben's body had been found. It had never really occurred to him that there had been a murder investigation, or that devastated families and friends would have been affected by his actions that September evening in two thousand and nine. He'd never given any consideration to the poor woman who had stumbled across Ben Walker's mutilated corpse the following morning. The woman who had found Ben and Liz had to attend counselling sessions to help her come to terms with what she'd discovered at the bottom of the hill in the woods. He'd not given a moment's thought to the thousands of people that had been affected in some way or another by the murder and the viscous and brutal attack that had resulted in Liz Mason being in a coma. He'd spent the last two years and eight months in denial.

He found the press conference and clicked play and watched the seven minute thirty eight second clip. He listened to the Scottish detective talk about how Ben had been found in the woods and how brutally he had been murdered. He listened to what was said about the girl who'd been left for dead. Boyd could barely remember the girl even being there. He had been so intent on revenge, he'd blinkered out what was going on around him.

And then he watched the girl's father stand up to speak and appeal to members of the public to come forward if they had any information……the same man to whom he'd delivered breeze blocks with Stanley back in October 2010.

Boyd felt a tear well in his eye. He wiped his hand across his eye to stop the tear before it had a chance to properly form and roll down his cheek.

He closed the lid on the computer, hopped back to the bed and lay there. He lit another cigarette and tried to block out the memory of the video he'd just watched.

A shiver went down his body.

He recalled the man in the window, the man who was definitely Ben Walker.

Boyd had an unsettling feeling that his past was catching up with him, and it was catching up rather quickly.

CHAPTER ONE HUNDRED AND NINETEEN

The Fox and Goose
10.07pm
Friday 1st June

Terry Mason sat alone in the pub with a soft drink. He was at the same table where he'd been the day before when he'd pleaded with Don Hodges to help him find something on Campbell Broderick and Naomi King. He needed something to confirm that they were a threat to his daughter. He wasn't so sure about King, he didn't have a strong feeling towards her and perhaps she was only involved by association. It was Broderick that concerned him the most. It was an odd gut feeling that came from nowhere and it had happened just over a week ago. In the short space of time the gut feeling had developed into something more. It had grown into an obsession that had taken control over Terry Mason's life.

The once rational and level headed man was now an illogical nervous wreck. He hadn't washed or shaved for the past three days. His friends and work colleagues were concerned for him. His wife, Anne, was particularly perturbed as the man she once relied upon as her rock was crumbling like sandstone in front of her very eyes.

It hadn't occurred to Mason how unreasonable he'd become over the past few days. But perhaps things weren't as illogical as they seemed. He was sure that there would be something on the video he'd heard Broderick and King discussing in the pub that would incriminate Broderick. He was certain it would contain something that would prove to him that Broderick was some kind of threat to his beautiful daughter.

The call he had received from Hodges just over an hour ago must have proved he was right. Why else would he have called so soon after yesterday's meeting?

Mason was rudely whisked away from his deep thoughts by Don Hodges, who was standing over him.

"Sorry I'm late Terry……..there was an accident on the other side of Barrow Gurney. The police have blocked the road and I had to go the long way round."

Terry looked up and saw Hodges but hadn't heard a word he had said.

Hodges looked into his empty eyes.

"I said sorry I'm late."

"Oh, that's OK, I was miles away, I didn't notice what time it was…………can I buy you a drink?"

"No thanks Terry, I just want to keep this brief."

Hodges pulled up a chair and sat beside Mason.

"I've got your video," said Hodges as he put his hand in his jacket pocket and pulled out a brown envelope which he handed to Mason.

"…..And, was I right?" asked Mason.

"I don't know what Broderick has to do with what's in the video, but it definitely concerns your daughter, but it's more to do with her past than her present."

Mason looked at him with a puzzled expression.

"Why?"

"Just watch it and see for yourself. As far as I'm concerned there's some strange shit going on, which I don't want to be part of."

Mason picked up the envelope and viewed it with suspicion.

"The memory stick is in there and I've printed the email to which the video clip was attached, the email was sent to someone called Tom Judd."

"Judd…..Judd, I know that name," said Mason in low voice.

Mason was trying to work out why the name sounded so familiar, then he remembered Connor, Connor Judd the man he employed to head up the team which Broderick was part of.

His paranoid mind was beginning to consider that another member of his company was a threat to his daughter.

"Oh, and there's this," said Hodges handing Mason another envelope.

"What's this?"

"It's an invoice."

Mason took the envelope and put it in his pocket.

"I'll send you a cheque," said Mason, without even bothering to look at it.

"Terry, whatever all this is about, be careful," said Hodges as he stood up to leave.

Mason said nothing as Hodges walked out of the building.

A few minutes later, Mason put down his unfinished drink and left the building. He held the brown envelope tightly as he walked to his car. His black Audi TT was parked in the corner of the car park. He looked around to make sure he wasn't being followed before getting into the car.

He put on his seatbelt and before starting the engine he opened the brown envelope and took out the memory stick and the copy of the email between Broderick and Tom Judd. After placing the memory stick on the passenger seat he unfolded the piece of A4 paper and read the email.

Subject - Enhanced Video
Dear Tom,
I've managed to get the video of Christopher enhanced and have attached it to this email.
It's now clear that Ben's words were just as you said.
Sorry for doubting you.
See you soon,
Campbell

Mason read the short message twice and wondered what it could mean. Who was Christopher and Ben? He needed to watch the video for it to make any sense.

He drove fast through the country lanes, forgetting what Hodges had told him about the accident which had resulted in the road through Barrow Gurney being closed. He slammed on the brakes as he turned a bend in the road. He saw an upturned car. The fire brigade were cutting the door to free the driver from the wreck.

A policeman slowly strolled over to Mason's car.

"In rather a hurry sir?" asked the policeman as he spoke to Mason through the open window of the driver's door.

"I'm rather keen to get home officer, my daughter is in intensive care at Southmead and I've been with her for most of the day," lied Mason.

Mason spotted the memory stick which was on the passenger seat and was worried that the police officer would start asking questions about it. The officer didn't even notice it, but in Mason's current state of mind anything could happen.

The officer was concerned that such a dishevelled looking man was driving a brand new Audi TT. The TT was one of six cars owned by Mason. He was going to drive his Porsche Boxster, but it was too much of a faff getting it out of the garage, so opted for the TT which was in his driveway.

"Can I see your driving license please sir?" asked the officer.

Mason fumbled in his wallet and handed over the license.

The officer examined the license and saw Mason's vague resemblance to the man in the photograph. He spotted his luxurious Sneyd Park address. It was an area he knew well as he'd been called out on several occasions to deal with burglaries in the location. He knew that Mason could well afford the Audi if he could afford to live at the address on his driving license.

"What's the matter with your daughter, if you don't mind me asking?" enquired the officer.

Mason's sad eyes met with the policeman's.

"She has pneumonia and she's also in a coma."

"I'm sorry to hear that sir. What happened, was she involved in an accident?"

"No, she was attacked and left for dead over two years ago, you may remember the incident, her friend was murdered in the attack."

"Did it happen in Badock's Wood?" asked the officer.

Mason nodded.

"I do remember it," said the officer.

He'd been one of the foot soldiers looking for evidence in the woods and remembered it well. Now he appreciated why Mason looked the way he did. *The poor man must have the weight of the world on his shoulders* thought the officer.

"OK Mr Mason, you'd better be on your way, please drive carefully sir."

Mason nodded, turned the car around and headed home the long way round.

By eleven o'clock Mason was sitting in the snug at his home. It was his little office where he could keep himself to himself when he needed a little quiet time away from the worries in his world. Anne, his wife, was upstairs and already in bed.

He poured himself a glass of 16 year old Lagavulin whisky and took the memory stick from his pocket. His computer was already turned on, he'd left the thing in a rush to get to the meeting with Hodges.

He plugged the memory stick in and waited for the drive to open.

When the folder opened he hovered his mouse over the file icon and waited in anticipation as he wondered what could be on the video. He double clicked the icon and impatiently tapped his fingers on the desk as the video loaded.

The clip started playing and Mason squinted his eyes to make out what was happening.

He watched the clip that Hodges, Judd, King, Garraway and Broderick had all watched earlier.

The whole thing made no sense. He couldn't understand why a little boy was recalling the events of Ben Walker's death, and was talking as though it had happened to him. He was tired and stressed and his brain couldn't compute what he was seeing.

The snug was hot, which was making him feel weary. He stood up and opened a window to let some air circulate around the small room. He sat back down and was about to take a sip of whisky, but instead he pushed the glass away.

He got up again and walked out of the snug and across to the downstairs bathroom. He ran the water until it was as cold as it could get and scooped a handful as it surged from the faucet and threw it over his face in an attempt to lessen his tiredness. After wiping his face with a hand towel he returned to the snug to watch the clip again.

He felt a little more awake and hit the replay icon.

Terry Mason had met Ben Walker several times and had liked the boy. He seemed a kind and honest person. Mason had found out that Ben would have become a police officer had he lived to see the next day. He knew Liz liked him a lot, she'd never actually told her parents, but it was her body language that gave her away. Liz was always laughing and giggling, but when she was around Ben she laughed and giggled even more. Terry Mason liked Ben because he made his daughter happy and he had secretly hoped that they would become boyfriend and girlfriend and so did Anne.

He played the clip again and this time he was more alert.

That little boy has been hypnotised he thought as he watched the video for a second time.

He listened closely to the boy's voice and in particular he paid close attention as the little boy stated that he'd been killed.

"It is strange, and you need to understand what it's like from my point of view, you're the only person I've spoken with since I was killed."

He moved the slider on his screen back several frames and played it again.

"It is strange, and you need to understand what it's like from my point of view, you're the only person I've spoken with since I was killed."

He moved closer to the speaker on his computer and played the section a third time.

"It is strange, and you need to understand what it's like from my point of view, you're the only person I've spoken with since I was killed."

"That's Ben Walker's voice," said Mason out loud, in fact he was so loud, he gave himself a fright.

He turned around to make sure he was still on his own, he was worried that he'd woken his wife, although the bedroom was up on the next floor.

He let the video clip continue until the end and listened closely to the enhanced section, the section for which he knew Naomi King had been responsible.

"OK Ben, let's find out more about you and something which everyone in this room wants to know……..how did you die?"

"Ben, can you hear me, how did you die? ………………………….Ben, it's Tom, I need to know how you died, where did it happen and who killed you, concentrate please…….don't fade on me now."

"Tom, sorry, I…… I …….. can't quite find the………."

"Please Ben, try, please try your hardest."

"I'm trying………I was killed in……..I was killed in the ……..woods."

"Did you say you were killed in the woods?"

"In the woods."

"Which woods, can you remember the name of the woods?"

"Badock's………….."

"Badock's Wood, were you killed in Badock's Wood?"

"Ben, stay with me, please stay focused….just one more thing and then you can sleep."

"Ben, how did you die, what did the murderer do to kill you? Please Ben."

"He killed me with a rock."

"Ben, say that again, I didn't hear you…..how were you killed?"

"With a rock Tom ………he killed me with a ………rock."

As Mason listened to the enhanced sections, especially the very last line, "With a rock Tom ………he killed me with a ………rock." he froze.

The first time he'd listened to it, his tiredness had prevented the significance of what he'd heard from registering in his fatigued mind.

But this time he was alert and the enormity of what he was watching became apparent.

It was clear to Mason that the hypnotist had somehow found a way to speak with Ben Walker, but what he couldn't understand was why the hypnotist would have gone out of his way to do such a thing?

Walker was dead and that was that. As horrific and upsetting as it had been, there was nothing that could be done to bring the young man back.

His mind was swimming in Confusion Lake. The video was clearly showing it was possible to communicate with the dead, and the hypnotist, Tom, who he assumed was the brother of Connor Judd, had the means to do such a thing.

He needed to clear his mind, consider the content of the video, link it to the people around him and figure out the threat to his daughter.

He ejected the memory stick, turned off the computer, left the untouched whisky and walked out of the snug.

He wearily climbed the stairs to his bedroom, passing his daughter's old bedroom on the way. The one in which she'd spent most of her years since she was a little girl. He opened the door and looked in. He turned up the dimmer switch so her bedroom was illuminated in a half light. He looked at her bed and her posters on the walls. There were get well soon cards on the top of her chest of drawers that had been there since she'd returned home from hospital over two years ago. He walked over and opened one of the drawers and took out a T-shirt. It was white with the Tae-Kwon-Do emblem on the back. He held it to his face and breathed in. He could smell a faint fragrance, a smell which reminded him of her at a time in her life when she was happy, full of youth and with the rest of her life ahead of her. Now she was alone in intensive care at Southmead Hospital. He desperately wanted her back in the house, just so he could sit beside her, talk to her and hold her hand.

He had barely set foot in Liz's bedroom since she had been moved to the newly built extension in late two thousand and ten.

Her bed was made and the duvet cover lay neatly on top. It looked ready for her to walk right in and climb into for a good night's sleep. But sleeping was about all she had been doing since she was attacked.

On her pillow was a fluffy toy dog. She'd had it since she was a baby. Terry walked over to her bed and picked up the toy. Memories of her childhood came flooding back and when they did a floodgate opened as his emotions spilled over. He dropped onto her bed, clutching her toy dog close to his chest and cried.

Eventually the crying stopped and he lay in the half-light still holding the fluffy yellow dog. He was tired, but too tired to sleep.

It was late and he didn't want to disturb Anne by climbing into their double bed. She'd been through as much as he had and needed as much rest as possible. He decided to sleep on Liz's bed. Just being in her room, on her bed, brought him closer to her.

He thought about the video and considered its significance and the potential threat that he was certain it had upon his beautiful daughter. Whoever was behind all of this clearly needed to know something about Ben Walker. Perhaps when Ben had been alive he'd known something about someone, or had some information which was important to these people. Perhaps this was the reason why he'd been murdered. If his memory served him well, nothing had been taken from Ben, his wallet, watch and phone had been found on him.

The more he thought about things, the more he was certain that the same people would come after his daughter. Perhaps she also had access to some crucial information that they needed, and if they couldn't extract it from the small boy whilst he was under hypnosis, then surely the next thing would happen is that they'd come after her.

Then he thought about Campbell Broderick. He knew he was heavily involved. He wasn't in the video, the edited section Mason has seen only showed the hypnotist and the boy. Mason considered the fact that Broderick must have infiltrated TM.IT to get close to him and then move on to his daughter.

Mason knew it was up to him to put an end to all of this. He had to stop Broderick, stop the hypnotist, stop the little boy and stop anyone else who was involved in whatever was happening.

Eventually tiredness enveloped him and he slept soundly until the sun shone through the open window at six fifteen the following morning.

Terry Mason awoke and felt a little better after having five hours of continuous sleep. It had been the longest uninterrupted rest he'd had in weeks. He was still clutching the fluffy toy dog. Quietly and calmly he got out of bed and walked downstairs to the kitchen. As he prepared himself a cooked breakfast he instigated his plan.

He sat at his breakfast bar and ate the plate of bacon, eggs, fried bread and hash browns. He washed the food down with a glass of fresh orange juice, rinsed the dishes and loaded them into the dishwasher.

He casually strolled outside and onto his driveway and looked at the TT he'd driven the night before. He turned to face one of the two double garages and flicked a remote which was in his pocket. The large garage door slowly opened revealing a gold Porsche Boxter and a silver E-Type. He looked at both cars and then slowly walked towards the Porsche.

He climbed in, started the car and inched it onto the driveway. He shut off the engine and walked back to the garage, returning with a bucket of soapy water and a bag containing a sponge, polish and a chamois leather.

He spent the next hour cleaning the car and polishing it by hand until it looked as if it had just been driven out of a showroom.

He locked the car and closed the garage and went back to the house. After a shower and a close shave, he trimmed his unkempt hair with a number two razor.

He looked at himself in the mirror as he cleaned his teeth.

Mason crept into his bedroom, Anne was still sleeping. He opened the walk-in wardrobe and looked for a suit. He hadn't worn one for over two weeks and had been lulling around in untidy jeans and T-shirts. He rifled through his selection and carefully removed a grey Italian William Fioravanti. Next, he walked over to the chest of drawers and chose a light blue shirt and a grey tie. He dressed in front of the full length mirror and after straightening his tie he walked over to Anne who was sleeping, bent forward and kissed her on her forehead.

Quietly, he tiptoed downstairs and into the kitchen where he picked up a six inch kitchen knife, ran it under the tap and then dried it in a tea towel. He wrapped the blade in a few sheets of kitchen roll and slipped it into the inside pocket of his two thousand pound suit jacket.

He walked to the hallway and then to the front door, he turned around and glanced at the staircase and up towards the bedroom where Anne was still sleeping. He picked up duplicates of the files he'd given to Don Hodges the night before, put on dark glasses and left the house.

The Boxter looked immaculate as it shone in the early summer sun. There wasn't a blemish on it. Mason climbed in, buckled his seatbelt and entered Campbell Broderick's postcode into the satnav.

He started the engine which roared into life and pulled out of his driveway and headed towards Keynsham on the other side of the city.

He tapped along on the steering as he listened to The Four Seasons by Vivaldi blasting from the sound system.

Twenty two minutes later he pulled into Campbell Broderick's road and slowly crawled the street looking for number twenty seven.

He spotted the terraced house and parked directly opposite. He pulled the kitchen knife from his pocket and removed the kitchen roll. It was so shiny, he could see the reflection of his dark glasses in the metal blade.

He replaced the knife in his pocket, shut off the engine and got out. Adjusting his cufflinks he slowly walked toward the house were Campbell Broderick, Maria Jameson and her son Christopher called home.

CHAPTER ONE HUNDRED AND TWENTY

Maria and Campbell's flat
10.57am
Saturday 2nd June

Maria was cutting stems from a bouquet of beautiful flowers and was lovingly placing each flower into a heavy glass vase.

Today was not a day to which either she or her mother were looking forward to. It was the fourth anniversary of her father, Christopher Jameson's death.

Claire had been due at eleven o'clock and the two of them were to visit his grave, place some flowers, say some words and probably shed quite a few tears. Following the visit to his grave, they had planned on meeting with Campbell who would bring Christopher, Samreen and a few of Claire's friends to raise a toast and remember Christopher senior at the Talbot Inn.

Claire had called to say she was running late, but would be there by eleven fifteen.

Things had become a little more relaxed over the past week or so. Although he still banged his head at night, Christopher had stopped chanting and other than the occasional grunts and moans he made no noise whenever his Rhythmic Movement Disorder happened. Cleary Ben Walker had been true to his word and had stopped calling out to be heard.

Maria's hands were unsteady as she arranged the flowers. The very thought that Ben Walker was somewhere within the flesh and blood of her son scared her. It had frightened her to the degree that she felt distant from him. When she picked him up to cuddle him she felt she was cuddling two people, both Christopher and Ben.

She was desperate for Markland Garraway to find Ben's killer as she was holding on to the hope that if and when the murderer was convicted, then Ben would pass over to the place in which he rightfully belonged and sever his ties with the world of the living.

It had been arranged that Christopher would be hypnotised the next day, this time in the presence of Markland Garraway. Everyone was hoping that Garraway could garner some useful information to help convict whoever had killed Ben.

Maria had been praying that Garraway would only need Christopher to be hypnotised one final time in order to put an end to all of the troubles which had been ongoing for the past few years.

She was brought out of her thoughts by the throaty sound of a high performance car turning into her road. She turned and looked out of the window and saw a gold coloured car slowly making its way along the road. She was surprised to see it park opposite her flat.

She watched as the driver sat for a few minutes with the engine running, an engine so loud that even when idling it made the windows of her lounge shake.

The engine stopped and the driver got out of. He was wearing a grey suit and dark glasses and had closely cut hair.

She was surprised when he crossed the road, walked up to her door and rang the bell. Christopher was playing on his own in his bedroom, whilst Campbell was in the kitchen, clearing away the breakfast dishes.

Maria put down the scissors she'd been using to cut the stems and nervously walked to the door. She opened it wide enough for her and the stranger to see each other's faces.

"Can I help you?" asked Maria.

"Yes, please may I speak with Campbell Broderick?"

"May I ask who you are?"

"My name's Terry, Terry Mason……don't worry, he knows who I am."

Maria asked him to wait outside while she went to get Campbell. Maria recognised the name. She knew that Terry Mason was the managing director of TM.IT.

Maria pushed open the kitchen door as Campbell was putting away the dishes.

"I heard the door, is it your mother?" asked Campbell.

"No, it isn't," replied Maria, and then in a whisper she added, "It's Terry Mason."

"Terry Mason?" mouthed Campbell,

Maria nodded.

"What does he want?"

Maria shrugged her shoulders.

Campbell put down the plate and walked along the hallway and opened the front door.

"Hello Terry, this is unexpected, what can I do for you?"

"May I come in? We need to talk."

Campbell invited him in and showed him to the lounge where Maria was arranging the flowers.

He was surprised by the visit from his boss, so much so that he'd forgotten to shut the door of the flat which swung closed, but remained slightly ajar.

"Can I get you something, a coffee perhaps?" asked Campbell nervously.

"No thank you. I need to ask you something and I'll come straight to the point."

He took off his dark glasses and placed them on the table alongside the cut flower stems.

"What is it you want with my daughter?" demanded Mason in an intimidating tone.

Maria looked up and dropped the flower she was about to place in the vase.

"I don't understand…..I …don't want anything….." Campbell paused to compose himself, he wasn't going to be threatened by anyone.

"Mr Mason, what's all this about and why do you think I want anything to do with your daughter?"

"Don't fucking lie to me, I've seen the video, I watched it last night."

Campbell was confused, to which video was he referring? Surely not the one of Tom Judd and Christopher.

"Which video?"

"The one in the hypnotist's room, the one you gave to Naomi King."

Campbell was lost for words. His mind was in a muddle. How on earth could Terry Mason have got a copy of the video? As far as he knew it had only been handled by Naomi, Tom Judd, Markland Garraway and himself.

Mason took a step closer until his face was inches away from Campbell's. They were similar in height and build. Maria froze with fear as she watched the menacing man stand face to face with her fiancé.

"I said, don't lie to me Broderick, I need to know what it is you want with my daughter?....and I am deadly serious."

"There's nothing I want with your daughter, and I'm also deadly serious. Now back away from me or I will remove you from my house….I don't care who you are, I will not allow you to come to my home and intimidate me in front of my family."

Mason but his hand in his jacket pocket and quickly pulled out the knife and pressed it against Campbell's Adam's apple.

"This is the last time I'm going to ask you, what is it you want with my daughter?"

Campbell was about to open his mouth when Christopher came running into the lounge and saw the stranger holding a knife to the man he considered to be his father.

"Daddy!" shouted Christopher.

Mason was fleetingly distracted by Christopher and instantly recognised him as the boy in the video.

Campbell took advantage of Mason's brief distraction and swung his right leg forward. With one swift move, he swept his leg catching the back of Mason's knee joint with his foot, causing Mason to lose his balance and fall to the floor. As he dropped to the floor, the knife sliced into Campbell's bicep, cutting his skin. Campbell instinctively put his hand over the wound as Mason struggled to get back to his feet.

Maria picked up the heavy glass vase and quickly stepped forward and brought the vase crashing down upon Mason's head rendering him unconscious.

Christopher screamed as he watched his mother smash the glass over the stranger's head and he screamed again when he saw blood running from his father's arm.

Campbell got down on the floor and checked whether Mason was alive.

"He's still breathing," announced Campbell, relieved that Maria hadn't killed him

"Grab me those tie backs," shouted Campbell as he pointed to the curtains.

Maria quickly pulled the two heavy rope curtain tie backs and threw them to Campbell.

Whilst bearing the pain from the cut, he turned Mason over, yanked his arms behind his back and tied his hands together. With Mason lying on his front with his hands tied behind him, Campbell pulled his boss's legs so his feet were against his buttocks and with the other tie back he secured his feet tightly together.

Campbell pulled the belt from his trousers and used it to secure Mason's feet to his hands.

He had secured Terry Mason and had made the situation safe within a minute of the man hitting the ground.

Christopher was beside himself and was crying his eyes out just as Claire walked into the lounge. The front door had been left open and she could hear the disturbance so let herself in.

She stood with her mouth open trying to make sense of the carnage. She saw the blood seeping from Campbell's arm, the unconscious man on the floor lying amongst a scattered bouquet of flowers, an upside down vase and a kitchen knife which was under the lounge table.

And then there was Christopher. She instinctively picked up and hugged the scared little boy.

Campbell grabbed a shirt which was hanging from the back of one of the chairs and made a tourniquet to reduce the flow of blood from the cut to his arm.

"Call the police," shouted Maria.

"No, no don't," said Campbell.

"When he comes around, he won't be going anywhere in a hurry and I need to talk to him and find out what the hell's going on."

Claire took Christopher to his bedroom and Maria followed behind.

"What's just happened?" asked Claire.

"I'm not entirely sure……..that man is Campbell's boss. He came here to confront Campbell and attacked him with a knife……...something to do with his daughter."

"His daughter?"

"That's what he said, he's got a copy of the video, you know, the one from Tom Judd's place."

Claire rocked and hugged the scared little boy whilst she sat with him on the edge of his bed.

"Listen mum, I think the plan to visit dad's grave today will have to be cancelled."

Claire nodded.

"I don't think it's a good idea to have 'you know who' present when Terry Mason comes around," said Maria pointing to Christopher.

"Is there any chance you could take him somewhere for a couple of hours?"

"Don't worry, I'll find somewhere nice to take him……..make sure you're careful, I'm worried about you and Campbell."

"Don't worry about us, the way Campbell has trussed the man up, he won't be going anywhere in a hurry."

Claire left the house holding Christopher's hand. Christopher was holding on tightly to his little grey toy cat.

Maria and Campbell waited in their lounge for Mason to wake up. After three quarters of an hour he began to moan.

"Get him a couple of pain killers, I think he's going to need them," said Maria.

Mason wriggled on the floor but was unable to get up.

"Get me up," demanded Mason in a weary voice.

"I don't think so……...you have some explaining to do," said Campbell.

"Here have two of these."

Campbell forced a couple of paracetamol tablets into Mason's mouth.

"Don't worry, they're pain killers, for your own good."

Mason struggled to swallow the tablets, he tried to muster up some saliva, but his mouth was so dry he coughed and the half dissolved tablets dropped from his mouth and on to the carpet.

"I'll make sure you won't be working for TM.IT after today."

"That's your privilege Mr Mason, but to be honest that's the least of my worries. And I think you should be more concerned about what the police will have to say when they arrive."

"You've called the police?"

"We're just about to, but before we do, why don't you tell me what the hell's going on?"

Mason struggled to free himself from the ropes.

"I've got all the time in the world, and the more you struggle, the tighter I'll tie those knots."

Mason slumped forward. His wrists ached from the rope and he had cramp in his legs.

"I'll tell you what Terry, I'll make Maria and myself a nice cup of coffee and you lie there and think about things."

While Campbell went to the kitchen Maria stood over Mason with the knife in her hand.

"I think you really should tell us what all this is about," said Maria as she inspected the sharp knife which had traces of Campbell's blood on it.

Mason went to open his mouth.

"Don't bother now, wait for Campbell to come back," said Maria.

Campbell returned from the kitchen with coffee for Maria and himself. Maria was impressed by how calm her fiancé was, but noticed how much his hands were shaking as he handed over her coffee.

Terry Mason considered his options, and he figured he didn't have very many. He lay on his front and wondered why he was so sure that Campbell Broderick was a threat to his daughter. He had no rational reason why he should suspect him, but he had a strong instinct that the man was harmful. He knew his instinct had been right, the video clip had proved it.

Mason thought hard about how he could put into words the gut feeling, that little voice in his head that was telling him something wasn't right, and that something had a lot to do with Campbell Broderick. How stupid was he going to sound when he told him all of this when he didn't have a scrap of evidence to prove Campbell was really a threat to Liz? But there was the video, surely that meant something. It linked Campbell Broderick with the murder of Ben Walker, and the attack on his daughter.

"OK, if you untie the ropes and let me sit down I'll tell you," said Mason.

"How do I know you're not going to attack me again?"

"I guess you don't, you're just going to have to take my word."

"I'll tell you what, I'll untie you and you can sit down, but I'm tying you back up as soon as you're on that chair. Don't forget, we've got your knife and we have that very heavy glass vase. Maria merely knocked you unconscious with it, but me, well I promise I can do a lot more damage."

Campbell undid the leather belt that tied his feet to his hands. Mason let out a sigh of relief as he was able to straighten his legs. His feet and hands were still tightly bound with the rope so Campbell had to help him up, and onto the wooden chair.

Maria stood over Mason with the vase raised in readiness should he try anything stupid. Mason had already made his mind up that he had no intention of escaping.

Mason sat on the chair, his hands still tied behind his back. Campbell positioned his arms so they were behind the back of the chair. With the leather belt he secured Mason's feet to the legs of the chair.

Once Campbell was sure Mason was secure he stood back and wiped his brow. Adrenalin had made him briefly forget about the pain in his arm, but know he was beginning to relax he could feel the wound throb beneath the tourniquet.

"I could do with those pain killers now please."

Maria went to the kitchen and returned with a glass of water and two more paracetamol. Campbell put the tablets in Mason's mouth and held the glass to his lips.

"What can I say Broderick, other than I know you're trouble and I know you have something on my daughter, something worth killing for. The video proves you're involved with the killing of that poor boy Ben Walker, and now you're out to get my daughter, for whatever reason."

"Is that it, is that why you came here and attacked me because you've seen the video of Christopher under hypnosis?"

Mason said nothing.

"What led you to believe that I had anything to do with your daughter, which may I add, I don't?"

"Something told me, it came to me that I shouldn't trust you."

"What do you mean, something told you? What something?"

Mason sat on the chair and lowered his head as if in shame. He didn't have the vocabulary to explain how he knew, but he just did.

"I think I know what he's talking about," said Maria.

Both Mason and Campbell looked at her.

"It's the hill, it's been reaching out to him, in the same way it reached out to Markland Garraway in his dreams."

"What hill?" asked Mason.

"The hill in Badock's Wood, it seems to have a tendency to drive people crazy. It's already had me in its grip, but thanks to Campbell I've escaped lightly."

She was referring to the night when Campbell had resorted to calling Dr Sullivan.

"Maria's talking about the hill in the Woods where Ben and Liz were found," added Campbell.

Terry Mason remembered the hill clearly. He could see it in his mind's eye festooned with flowers which had been left by well-wishers.

"For some reason the hill is trying to tell you something……..something about your daughter. It's clearly trying to forewarn you of something and it's linking your daughter with Campbell, but I assure you…….I promise you……. that no one intends to cause any harm to your daughter."

Mason's head throbbed as he tried to take on board what Maria had just told him.

"But what about the video, explain to me what's going on?"

Campbell sighed. He'd been through this before and he really wasn't in the mood for going over it again.

"Don't worry, I'll explain," said Maria.

She pulled up a chair and sat alongside him and explained the entire thing from the very beginning until the present day. Terry Mason listened as she told him about the time her son was born which was the exact moment Ben Walker's life had ended. She told him about her son's RMD and how it had developed into chanting, which was Ben Walker pleading to be heard. She went into detail about the hypnotherapy sessions with Tom Judd.

"So you see Mr. Mason, neither Campbell nor any of us have any harmful intentions towards your daughter."

"But I don't understand, there is definitely something to do with your son and Ben Walker which will affect my daughter, and not in a good way."

"Perhaps you're right, but I don't see how."

"Do you remember Markland Garraway?" asked Campbell.

Mason nodded.

"He was the detective who was in charge of the murder enquiry," said Mason.

"That's right, he *was* in charge, but he's no longer fit for duty, the hill got to him too. The poor man had a breakdown over the whole thing."

"I'd heard something about that."

"Well, he's back on the case now, in an unofficial kind of way."

"What do you mean?"

"Tomorrow, Tom Judd is going to hypnotise Christopher again, hopefully for the final time, and Garraway will be there to ask Ben Walker what really happened."

"Like Ben will be a witness to his own death, and give evidence."

"Exactly, and hopefully he can tell Garraway something which will lead the police to Ben's killer and also to whoever attacked your daughter."

Maria and Campbell let Terry Mason take on board everything he'd just been told.

"Can't you see how the hill works? It finds people and it brings them together. The hill is powerful, but it's also benign," said Maria.

"It brought Campbell and me together, it brought Campbell to you, it brought Tom Judd to us and most importantly it's brought Markland Garraway to all of us. It can't all be coincidence."

For the first time in weeks Terry Mason felt relaxed. It did make sense and he believed everything he'd just been told. It was hard to comprehend, but he did believe.

"I owe you both an apology," said Terry Mason.

Campbell believed him when he said he was sorry.

"OK Terry, I think I trust you. I am going to untie you, but any stupid moves and that vase will be crashing down on your head again."

Campbell untied the knots and unbuckled the belt. Mason slowly stood up and rubbed his hands, then felt the bump on the back of his head.

"Can I ask you something, and I won't be surprised if your answer's no?" said Mason.

Campbell and Maria looked at him without speaking.

"Tomorrow, you said Tom Judd is going to hypnotise your son and let Ben Walker speak with Markland Garraway?"

Maria and Campbell nodded.

"With your permission, I'd like to be there."

After Terry Mason had left the flat, Maria and Campbell's day continued with no further events. The cut to Campbell's arm was nothing more than a flesh wound, albeit a painful one. Maria eventually met up with her mother and laid flowers at her father's grave followed by a late lunch at the Talbot Inn with family and friends.

Maria put Christopher to bed early that evening. Tomorrow was to be a busy day and the evening would be spent at Tom Judd's for what Maria hoped would be the last time.

Christopher hadn't chanted since the night Ben repeatedly called 'Maria I need to speak to Tom'. Since then Christopher had occasionally banged his head against his pillow or rocked from side to side, but there was no more disturbing chanting. Ben had kept his promise.

As Christopher slept, he gently rocked from side to side.

Ben was awake. He no longer needed to shout to be heard because he knew Tom Judd was out there and was on his side. Ben had faith in Tom and was certain that somehow he would find a way to help him.

Ben was wallowing in memories, both good and bad. Memories of his childhood, memories of his family and friends but most of all memories of his beloved Liz. He wondered what she was doing now. It was something he thought about and it was something he intended to ask Tom the next time they spoke.

He thought about Christopher, the little boy whose nocturnal life he'd taken over and how much stress and anxiety must have been inflicted upon his parents.

His memories returned to those of Liz, his beautiful Liz. If only that night in the woods had ended differently then perhaps they would have ended up together, perhaps they would have married and started a family. That's what Ben would have wished for.

He longed to see her again. Just to hear her voice would be something.

And then something happened.

Ben was distracted from his memories and thoughts, by a voice. A voice he knew well.

"Ben, when it's time, meet me at the hill………..and don't be late"

It was Liz, Liz had spoken. He instinctively called her name, but she didn't answer.

No one in the flat heard Christopher as he lifted his head and called Liz's name. His head dropped back down on his pillow and he slept soundly until the morning came.

CHAPTER ONE HUNDRED AND TWENTY ONE

Thomas Judd's Hypnotherapy Practice
The Quiet Area
4.50pm
Sunday 3rd June

The entourage which had gathered to watch Christopher as Tom Judd hypnotised him had grown. The small room which Judd referred to as the Quiet Area, where he would relax his clients and hypnotise them, was barely large enough to fit everyone. All who were there were talking in hushed tones, but together the hushed tones amounted to what sounded like a monosyllabic din.

Maria, Claire and Esther were squished together on the little settee which had been designed to fit two people. Campbell stood alongside Markland Garraway and Terry Mason with their backs pressed against the wall. Samreen was in the corner kneeling down with Christopher and Tom Judd was preparing his camera to make sure whatever happened was captured on video.

It had taken Garraway ten painful minutes to edge cautiously down the staircase and into the basement of Tom Judd's house. Tom had considered carrying out the evening's session upstairs in his lounge as it would have made things easier for Garraway, but had decided against it as he didn't want to break the routine to which Christopher had become used to. He knew that Christopher was becoming weary of being hypnotised and all the attention he was getting, so Judd didn't want to risk things going wrong.

Christopher had learnt to play a game with the adults. If he didn't get something out of being hypnotised, he wouldn't be climbing up onto Tom's big chair. So far he'd got a remote control car, a toy fire engine and a trip to Thomas Land. This time he'd planned to ask for something really big.

After Tom had set the camera he raised his hands in the air and asked for silence. The atmosphere in the room suddenly changed.

If things went well and if Markland Garraway asked the right questions, then hopefully the name of the person who had slammed the rock into Ben's head would be revealed.

Samreen lifted Christopher onto the chair and stroked his cheek.

"But I don't want to do it, I'm tired, tell mummy I'm tired," said Christopher as he wriggled to get down from the big chair.

"Come on sweetie, do this for your mummy and daddy."

"But I don't want to."

Christopher knew what was coming next.

"Listen, if you do this, just one more time, you'll get another nice treat."

Christopher sat still in the chair and thought.

"Can I have………can I have……...can I have………"

He looked at Samreen, with a finger in his mouth and a cheeky grin across his face, "I want a ride in a real steam train."

Samreen looked around the room and everyone nodded.

"OK Christopher, we'll get you a ride on a real steam train."

Tom found it particularly easy to hypnotise Christopher. The first time it had taken him two or three minutes to run through the routine, but since then he could hypnotise him in under a minute. He wished that some of his other clients would be as easy as Christopher.

Christopher concentrated on the train on the wall and in no time at all he'd been hypnotised. Tom Judd beckoned to Garraway to come over and stand beside him.

Ben could see the familiar vision of misty swirling light and knew that the next thing he would hear would be Tom Judd's voice. This time Ben decided to make the first move.

"Hello Tom, how are you?"

Although he had watched the video of Christopher under hypnosis, seeing and hearing it first-hand took Markland Garraway's breath away.

He watched in amazement as the voice he recognised as Ben Walker's was coming out of the little boy's mouth. It wasn't exactly the same as Ben's due to Christopher's undeveloped vocal cords, but he immediately recognised Ben's intonation and accent. Garraway had heard Ben's voice before when he was actively on the case as he'd watched family videos which may have provided information which could help find his murderer.

"Hi Ben, I'm fine, thanks for asking," replied Judd.

"Ben, today is an important day and I know you can get tired and so time is of the essence. So I would like to get going straight away and introduce you to a man who was the Detective Chief Inspector in charge of your murder case."

"Wow, are you kidding me?"

"No, I wouldn't joke, especially not today, we don't have that kind of time. Standing to my left is DCI Markland Garraway. He will be asking some questions and hopefully the answers you give will lead to the arrest of your killer. There is a chance that when he talks you may not hear his voice, and if that happens, I will ask the questions on his behalf."

Garraway moved forward and took a pad and pen from his pocket. Nervously he started to speak.

"Hello Ben, this is Markland, can you hear my voice?"

As Ben concentrated on the swirling misty vision of light Garraway's Scottish accent came through loud and clear.

"Hello Ben, this is Markland, can you hear my voice?"

Ben was surprised how clear Garraway's voice sounded.

Christopher moved his head in the direction of Garraway as Ben replied.

"Yes, I can hear you, I can hear you very well."

Garraway was tense. It had been a long time since he'd interviewed a witness to a murder, and this was the first time he, or probably anyone else, had interviewed a witness to their own killing.

"OK Ben, I need to satisfy myself that what I am seeing and hearing today is real, so I want to ask you something which will remove any doubt in my mind that you are who you say you are."

Christopher nodded his head.

"Ben Walker was not alone the night he was murdered. If you are Ben Walker you should be able to tell me the name of the person you were with that night."

"That would be Liz Mason, the most wonderful human being I'd ever known."

Terry Mason gasped. He felt he should say something and went to move forward. Campbell held his arm to stop him.

"Can you identify Liz? I need a description of what she looks like".

"She's around five foot seven, the last time I was with her she wore her brunette hair in a bob."

"OK, good, but is there anything else, anything that would really prove you knew her well?"

Ben shuffled through the most recent memories of Liz, right up to the evening he was killed.

"There are a couple of things. Her upper lip, she has a tiny scar on her top lip, which I always thought was cute, and the other thing is something I noticed the day I died, she has a little tattoo on her back."

"A tattoo of what?"

"A butterfly, a little blue butterfly."

Terry Mason stood routed to the spot, he couldn't believe what he was hearing.

Garraway looked in his direction for confirmation of Ben's description. Mason nodded.

This made Garraway's job a little easier. Had Terry Mason not been present to confirm what Ben was saying was true, then Garraway would have had to access the case files of Ben's murder and check whether the description of Liz matched what Ben had just told him.

"Thank you Ben, I think I can safely say that I'm convinced."

All the extraordinary things that had happened to him since he'd taken on Ben's murder case were making sense. The supernatural power of the hill had chosen him to be the one in charge of the case. It should had been Detective Inspector Tom Strawbridge's case, but he was mysteriously taken ill just after Ben had been killed. Whatever, or whoever was controlling the hill knew that Garraway was the man for the job and had cast a spell to make sure no one else would be in charge.

But there had been so many things getting in the way. Sergeant Colin Matthews for one was a major obstacle, Garraway's mental breakdown and his crippling arthritis were another two reasons why he could have given up, but hadn't. Deep down he knew the case was his to solve and always would be.

He considered that the hill must have a darker side, an evil side which was hell bent on stopping him.

"Ben, I'm going to cut straight to the chase………..do you know who killed you……..what was the name of your murderer?"

Christopher paused for a few seconds and the atmosphere in the room was electric. Then he spoke.

"I'm sorry, I don't know his name……….I knew him from somewhere,…….but from where, I cannot remember."

Garraway's heart sank. He had hoped it would have been as easy as that. If Ben could have named the person who had killed him, Garraway could have fabricated a reason to bring him in and once a DNA sample had been taken and matched against the blood found on the rock that was used to murder Ben, then it would have been all done and dusted.

"OK Ben, so let's go back a little, what happened before you died, tell me about the time leading up to the attack."

Ben had been through these memories over and over time and time again and was able to recall them step by step.

"Liz and I were walking in the woods. We were fooling around and I chased her up the hill. She tripped, fell back and landed on me."

Christopher paused and Garraway worried that he was losing Ben.

"What happened next?"

"What happened next was probably the best thing ever to happen to me……..we kissed……..we lay at the bottom of the hill and we kissed."

Terry Mason wiped his eyes. The room was silent as everyone waited to hear what was to come next.

Judd glanced at the camera to check the red recording light was definitely on.

"And then the moment was shattered, my beautiful moment with Liz was over. It was like from one extreme to another."

"Is that when you were murdered, just after you kissed Liz?"

"No, that happened later. The person who murdered me started off by wanting to fight, I didn't want to, I had no reason. By now Liz and I were standing up. The next thing that happened was that he hit Liz…for no reason he just punched her………but Liz threw him to the ground……….she was an amazing martial arts expert……my murderer wouldn't have known this and it took him completely by surprise."

"So was there just the one person in the woods? because the evidence suggests that there were a number of people present when you were murdered," asked Garraway.

"That's right, and I'll come to that next. I jumped on him and pinned him to the ground…….but he called for help and before I knew what was happening I was being attacked by three or four youths, young boys. I didn't know who any of them were."

Garraway was feverishly taking notes. His pen began to dry up and he hurriedly searched his pockets for another, ignoring the agonising pain in his hand.

Ben continued.

"The next thing I remember was one boy, all on his own, as if he was separate to the others, and he was kicking Liz. He was just kicking her over and over and over again and there was absolutely nothing I could do to help. I was weak, I should have been there for her…….but I couldn't."

Garraway saw a tear form in Christopher's eye. It rolled down his cheek.

"Then I remember seeing a rock held above me, and it came crashing down. The first time, I managed to block it with my arm. My killer picked the rock up and he slammed it down on me a second time……….and that was the last thing I remember."

Garraway looked around the room, Maria, Esther and Claire were holding back tears, whilst Terry Mason was letting his flow.

"Ben, I know this must be difficult for you, but you must try your best to remember. Can you tell me what your killer looked like?"

"He was a vile looking bastard. You know, the look of someone who is undernourished, drinks too much and doesn't look after himself?"

Garraway took down a detailed description of Daniel Boyd, from the clothes he wore, to his ghostlike pallor, to his greasy hair. Ben had even described the way the killer had smelt. Cigarettes and sweat, he told Garraway.

Judd could tell by the way Christopher was talking that Ben was beginning to fade.

"Markland, don't stop, I don't think we have much time left, Ben's starting to get tired," said Judd in a whispered, but urgent voice.

Garraway nodded and turned his attention back to Christopher.

"Tom's right, I'm finding it hard to concentrate," said Ben.

"There something I need to tell you, something which may be important………..I heard Liz's voice…….she spoke to me and she said something and I need to tell you what she said."

"Tell me quickly Ben, we don't have much time."

"She said to me 'Ben, when it's time, meet me at the hill………..and don't be late'."

Terry Mason stared intently at Christopher as he listened to the words spoken by the little boy.

"OK Ben, I've noted what you've told me………" said Garraway, but was interrupted by Ben.

"Markland, what happened to Liz? I mean after we were attacked, is she OK?"

Garraway was quiet, he didn't plan for this question, although it had been brought up at the meeting in his house on Friday, he wasn't sure exactly what to say. He looked toward Esther who was vying to get his attention.

"You must tell him, he needs to know the truth," she whispered.

Terry Mason nodded in agreement.

"Tell him Mr Garraway."

"OK Ben, Liz survived the attack, but………but she's been in a coma ever since."

"When you say ever since, is ever since a long time?"

Garraway wasn't sure how to answer Ben's question. He knew that Ben had lost the concept of time and found it impossible to measure.

"She's been unconscious for a while, but everyone is hoping she'll wake up soon."

Garraway hoped his answer wouldn't overly upset Ben, as from a selfish point of view, he needed Ben to remain focused so he could answer the next question before fading away.

"Now this will probably be the last question and it's an important one………other than your murderer, the boys who were attacking you and the boy who was attacking Liz, was there anybody else present,………perhaps a girl, an onlooker, someone not getting involved?"

He was hoping that Ben would remember the girl that had come to him in his strange dream, the same girl whose picture had appeared in the back of the book earlier in the week.

"I don't remem………..I don't…………"

"Are you saying there was or wasn't a girl amongst the attackers……..please Ben, I just need a simple yes or no answer…… was there a girl, about fourteen years old, short dark hair and brown eyes?……….just answer yes or no."

Christopher's head began to rock from side to side.

"He's waking up," said Judd.

"Ben, please try and answer me, yes or no."

"…………..no………..sorry, no girl."

And then Ben was gone.

Garraway was exhausted, both physically and mentally. His body ached more than ever and he was utterly drained. He was also disappointed. He was certain that the girl in his dream would have been there when Ben was murdered, there was no shadow of a doubt. He was sure that the hill had reached out to him and let him know she was there, and that she was the key to unlock the mystery.

Terry Mason stood forward.

"What did he mean? What was it he just said about my Liz? 'Ben, when it's time, meet me at the hill………..and don't be late'…….what the hell does that mean?"

"What does any of it mean?" said Judd.

"I'm serious, he said about Liz meeting with Ben at the hill, you must get Ben back now and find out what he means."

"I'm afraid that won't be happening today, Ben's gone now and I don't think we'll be hearing from him again…….I've promised Maria," said Judd.

Christopher was crying, he was tired and upset.

"I've got to get my little boy home, this is just too much to ask…….I don't think he can go through this anymore."

Maria was right. The attention that Christopher was getting was too much for a boy of his age. He no longer liked to be hypnotised and he didn't like all the strangers being there.

"You've got what you came for Mr. Garraway, now it's up to you to use what you have to find Ben's killer, but please leave us alone now, there is nothing else we can do for you……..please leave my family alone."

Maria picked up Christopher and nodded to Campbell indicating that it was time for them to leave.

Campbell turned to Judd and Garraway.

"I'm sorry, but Maria is right. I don't think there is any more information you will get from Ben and this is getting too much for Christopher. Ben said that he can't remember his killer's name, but he gave you a pretty good description and also what happened that night, so use the information he's given you as best as you can………..and let me know what happens."

Campbell followed Maria and Christopher out of the Quiet Area, up the stairs and out of the building. Samreen chased after them calling for them to come back, and then she was also gone.

Judd, Garraway, Mason and Esther sat in the Quiet Area. Nobody spoke.

Terry Mason was trying to deal with what he'd just witnessed and was staring into space.

Garraway was exhausted and disappointed, he'd hoped to get more from Ben. He knew it was a longshot, but he'd wished that Ben had known the person who had killed him.

"So what happens next?" asked Judd.

Garraway didn't answer. He sat on the settee, rubbing his chin.

"You've got a good description, why can't you get a photofit or an E-Fit made, or whatever they're called these days and get it out there," asked Mason in a demanding manner.

"It's not as simple as that," replied Garraway.

"Why not?"

"You try convincing my Detective Superintendent…….my boss, that we put out a picture asking for the public to be on the lookout for Ben Walker's murderer…….and that the description came to me by way a two year old boy, who wasn't even born when the murder took place…….it'll never happen."

"Lie then, tell him you got the description from someone else."

"Like who, I can't just make this stuff up. Whatever is used has to stand up in a court of law."

"Well, what was the point in all of this, if none of what Ben, or Christopher, or whoever the fuck was supposed to be speaking, would stand up in court?"

Garraway knew that Mason was right. The whole thing had probably been a complete waste of everybody's time.

What Garraway had wanted, other than finding out the name of the killer, was to find out more about the girl he'd dreamt about. He was certain that she'd been there.

"I'm sorry Mr Mason, I am just as confused by the situation as you are……..I've never done anything like this before, and there is no blueprint, there's nothing for me to follow, I've just got to go with this and hope something will come up."

Terry Mason was struggling with the whole thing. He'd just heard the voice of his daughter's friend. The voice had given a detailed description of Liz, right down to the scar on her lip and the tattoo on her back. What scared Mason the most was what Ben had said about hearing Liz's words, 'Ben, when it's time, meet me at the hill………..and don't be late'.

He didn't know what it meant and he didn't like the sound of it. It was clearly very important and that scared him.

Mason stood up, grabbed his jacket and announced he was leaving.

"If you need me for anything, you know where to contact me."

Mason slammed the door behind him, climbed the stairs to the ground floor and left the building.

Esther, Garraway and Judd sat quietly. Now that Terry Mason had left, the three of them felt more comfortable discussing what had just happened. Mason was an emotional wreck and just being in the room with him felt awkward.

"So where do we go from here?" asked Judd.

Maria had made it very clear that Christopher was not to be hypnotised and Judd and Markland had to respect her wishes. In Christopher's best interest Esther agreed with Maria.

"I don't really know," replied Garraway.

"Even if I was to speak with Ben again, I don't think he would tell me anything else."

An atmosphere of despondency filled the room.

"If you don't mind I would like to go home now," said Garraway.

"It's going to take me a good fifteen minutes to climb your stairs Mr. Judd, so I'd better get a move on."

Judd helped Garraway up from the settee and passed his crutches. Garraway said he didn't need any help climbing the stairs. Judd and Esther waited at the bottom until he had made it to the top step. They followed him to the ground level where Judd opened the door.

"If any of you get any bright ideas, let me know……….I'm not giving up, not yet, but I could do with as much help as I can get," said Garraway before bidding Esther and Judd farewell.

They watched as he drove away.

"Don't worry Tom, we've got this far…….I'm sure Markland will find a way around all of this. He's a clever man."

CHAPTER ONE HUNDRED AND TWENTY TWO

Markland Garraway's home
11.16pm
Sunday 3rd June

Garraway lay in bed and thought about what had happened that day. Despite all the strange things that went hand in hand with Ben Walker's case, he found what had happened unbelievable. He'd actually spoken to someone who was dead. The implications were immense. It proved with no shadow of a doubt that there was life after death. Sure there were many reports, stories of reincarnation, sightings of ghosts, but none of them were ever tangible. This was different. Ben had said things about his past that no one else could have known, and the fact his conduit was a two year old boy made the entire thing even more amazing.

If this was ever reported on television, or in the newspapers then people would be talking about it for years to come, he thought.

The implications on mankind would be colossal.

And then it came to him.

As he lay in the dark an idea formed. He smiled as the germ of a plan started to evolve in his tired and overworked brain.

He picked up a notepad by his bed and jotted down four words to remind him what to do in the morning.

'Flush out the girl'.

CHAPTER ONE HUNDRED AND TWENTY THREE

Avon and Somerset Police
Kenneth Steele House
10.18am
Monday 4th June

Garraway had woken early. The events of the previous day had resulted in a restless night's sleep. His dreams had been punctuated by the plan he'd thought of the night before. For the first time in a long time he was excited. He had woken with something to look forward to. Had it not been for his arthritis, he would have jumped out of bed with a spring in his step. The notepad was where he had left it and it was the first thing he saw when he woke. He read the note he had scribbled on the pad.

'Flush out the girl'

The plan he had formulated had lost none of its lustre. In fact it seemed to make more sense than it did when he'd been lying in bed last night.

What Garraway had in mind was as crazy as the whole Ben Walker case had proven to be. Before he could get the ball rolling he had to speak with Colin Matthews. Matthews had worked with him closely and since Garraway's breakdown had taken over the case.

There was no love lost between Garraway and Matthews. Garraway thought Matthews to be slovenly, considered him a sloppy worker and he was frustrated because he wouldn't deviate from the rule book.

At times Matthews found Garraway to be patronising and sarcastic. He didn't like the way he treated him as if he was a mere boy, despite being in his mid-thirties. But what Matthews really thought about Garraway he had kept to himself. He considered the man to be an idiot and all the nonsense that he had come out with about the supernatural powers of Badock's Wood had proved this.

Since Matthews had taken over the case, things had ground to a halt. In Matthews' defense, there was little to go on. There was just not enough evidence to pinpoint anyone present at the time of the murder. As time went on, his caseload increased and with Garraway being signed off as unfit for work, all detectives were picking up the slack and taking on more work than they could cope with.

Although he'd never let it be known, Matthews was pleased when Garraway had been signed off. As far as work was concerned, with Garraway being off the scene, Matthews had a new lease of life. He no longer felt as if he was playing second fiddle to the Scottish detective and was free to make his own decisions.

There had been times when they had bumped into each other in the canteen or in corridors and things had been awkward. After a couple of minutes of small talk any conversation was over.

They knew how they felt about each other, and it was no secret around the force that they disliked one another. This in itself wasn't unusual. The place was a melting pot of diverse and disparate characters, some of whom just didn't fit in. There was jealousy, rivalry, competition and at times the force could be a very unharmonious place to work.

Matthews was relieved when he'd found out that Garraway wouldn't be coming back to work as a detective after his return to the force. He found it laughable that he was able to retain the title of Detective Chief Inspector, and yet have nothing to do with the role. He had heard that Garraway had found a new position as a trainer and had turned out to be excellent at coaching rooky detectives.

It had come as a surprise to Matthews when out of the blue he'd received a call from Garraway suggesting that they should meet as he had new information on the Walker case. Information that Garraway knew would be of interest to him.

Garraway had told Matthews that he wanted to meet in private and not in the general office area, which was full of other detectives and administration staff. He told him he wanted to meet somewhere quiet and suggested meeting room three, which by chance was available that morning and also happened to be the last room along the corridor, which meant it had very few passers-by.

Matthews had agreed to meet Garraway at ten thirty.

Garraway was already in the room when Matthews knocked on the door.

"Come in," called Garraway, smiling at Matthews as he shut the door behind him. Matthews viewed Garraway's smile cautiously. He thought the man looked demented. On the table in front of Garraway was his mobile phone and two cups of coffee.

"White with no sugar, if I remember correctly," he said as he passed one of the cups to Matthews.

"Thank you, sir," replied Matthews, instantly regretting that he'd just referred to him as sir.

Old habits are hard to break thought Matthews.

"How are you Colin, I've not seen you in ages, I trust you're keeping busy?"

"Very busy, as always it's nonstop."

"Have you found yourself a woman yet?"

"No, I'm a bit like you sir, you know, married to the job."

Garraway knew that Matthews was making an underhanded remark referring to the fact that his wife had recently left him.

Garraway nodded and mentally brushed the glib comment to one side.

"I understand you wanted to see me about the Ben Walker case sir, you said that you had some new information?"

Matthews cringed as he heard himself refer to Garraway as sir again.

As Garraway began to speak, Matthews saw how old looking his ex-work colleague had become. He had developed bags beneath his eyes large enough to carry a week's worth of shopping, his skin was lined with cracks and his thinning hair was showing signs of grey. He looked pitiful as he hobbled around the building struggling on his crutches.

"Yes, I do Colin, I have something I think you'll find very interesting and I'm sure the case will spring to life after what I am about to tell you."

Matthews took a sip of coffee and waited for Garraway to continue.

"I have a full description of the murderer and a picture of someone who was there and witnessed the whole thing. Unfortunately I don't have any names to put to the faces, but I think it's a step in the right direction, don't you?"

"How did you come by this new information?" asked Matthews.

"Don't worry about that right now, I'll tell you later."

Garraway pulled the notebook from his jacket pocket, the same notebook he'd jotted down the description Ben had given him the day before.

"Now, you might want to write this down," said Garraway as he began to describe the person who murdered Ben Walker.

"Hang on, hang on a minute," said Matthews holding a hand in the air.

"Who gave you this description?"

"I'll come to that in minute……..why aren't you writing this down, you'll need to write it down?"

Matthews saw a glint in his eye and something about his smile that made the man appear deranged.

"OK, OK I'll write it down."

Garraway read the description again as Matthews reluctantly wrote it down.

"And that's not all," added Garraway after he'd finished describing the killer.

"Look at this," Garraway took the Dostoevsky novel from his case, opened it to the back inside cover and showed Matthews the sketch of the girl.

"Who's she?"

"She is the one I just told you about. She's our key witness. If you can trace her, she'll tell you what happened that night……..she'll tell you the whole thing."

Matthews looked at the girl and looked to the opposite page and read the notes Garraway had made of the dream he'd had on the first anniversary of Ben Walker's murder.

"And what's this all about?" asked Matthews as he pointed to the notes written by Garraway.

"Oh, that's nothing, that's just some stuff I jotted down about what happened the night of the murder."

Matthews was confused. He couldn't understand how Garraway had suddenly come across this new information. If it was valid, then Garraway was right, this was a massive step in the right direction and could breathe life back into the dormant case.

"OK Markland, you have my full attention. I need to know who gave you this information and why they didn't come straight to me……..after all, you've not been an active detective for quite some time."

"I'll tell you who gave me the description, and you're going to love this bit, you really are."

Matthews waited for Garraway to continue and as he did he saw a look upon his face which reminded him of Jack Nicholson in 'The Shining'. He looked insane.

"Ben Walker gave it to me."

"Ben Walker gave what to you?"

"The description, he gave me a really good description of the person who killed him?"

"Sorry Markland, what the fuck are you talking about?"

"Ben Walker told me…….."

"Just hold on a minute, how did Ben Walker tell you?"

"Welllllll, he told me last night. He talks to me through a two year old boy under hypnosis. He's been kind of reincarnated you see."

Matthews suddenly stood up and knocked over what was left of his coffee.

"You're mad, you've really, really lost it, you're just wasting my time."

"Wait, don't you want to find out how I got the information on the girl?"

Matthews decided to let him continue, if for no other reason, just to humour the poor man. He'd known Garraway had suffered mental health issues as a result of the Ben Walker case, but had been told that he'd made a good recovery. From Matthews' standpoint Garraway was still suffering delusions.

"OK Markland, tell me about the girl."

Matthews sat back down, leant back, crossed his arms and let Garraway continue.

"Well, it was the first anniversary of the murder and I was in bed……..and what happened on the night of the murder came to me in a dream, it was so realistic. And there was a young girl ……I know she wasn't meant to be there, she was in the wrong place at the wrong time and if it wasn't for her, then Liz Mason would have ended up dead too. She's the one who stopped the attack."

Matthews looked at Garraway with a blank expression.

"So, as soon as I awoke from the dream I wrote everything I remembered in the back of this book," added Garraway waving the book in Matthews' face.

"And I suppose you sketched the girl while she was still fresh in your mind?" said Matthews with an air of sarcasm.

"Don't be stupid Colin,………I can't draw for toffee……No, what happened there was really strange. I came down the other morning, the book was open on the table and the picture of the girl was there. I didn't draw it."

"Well, who do you suppose did?" asked Matthews.

Garraway shrugged his shoulders and pulled a 'how am I supposed to know' face.

"It just appeared."

Matthews rubbed his face and sighed.

"Markland, with all due respect, you're a fucking idiot. You've lost it, you've really lost it."

"But this stuff's gold dust, its evidence you can't ignore," said Garraway pointing towards the novel.

"And the description I gave you of the killer, it came from the person who he killed…….how often to you get that kind of information."

"I've had enough, said Matthews, standing up to leave.

"Aren't you going to use any of this?" asked Garraway.

Matthews stood by the door, looked at him with pity and shook his head.

"Well if you're not going to use it, then I'm not letting this kind of evidence go to waste."

"What do you mean, let it go to waste?"

"If you're not going to do anything with it, then I am."

"What are you going to do with it?"

"Oh, I don't know, perhaps take it to the papers, or get it shown on TV. It'll get a lot of attention and surely it would jog someone's memory."

"How could you get something like this on the television? It's a drawing in a book, a couple of paragraphs about a dream and a description of someone, that in your confused state of mind, came from a dead man…..Just tell me how that will end up in the news?"

"Because it will. I'm a respected detective and I know the right people."

Matthews was about to explode. Garraway watched as his face turned red with rage.

"Listen, you do whatever you want, but just don't involve me……and don't forget, you signed a confidentiality agreement when you became a defective, so don't come crying to me when you're being prosecuted and you're out of a job."

"So are you giving me permission to take this to the press?"

"As I said, you do whatever you want, just keep me out of it………for your sake I hope they find you insane, because if they do, it'll explain why you've wasted everybody's time…….Just do whatever you bloody well please."

And with that, Matthews left meeting room three, slamming the door behind him.

"Perfect. Hook, line and sinker," said Garraway under his breath as he turned off the voice recorder app on his smart phone.

CHAPTER ONE HUNDRED AND TWENTY FOUR

Markland Garraway's home
7.49pm
Monday 4th June

Garraway finally put his phone down after a marathon session of two hours of calls.

First of all he'd called Maria Jameson, followed by Terry Mason, Tom Judd and lastly Esther Hall. All of them agreed, at least in principle, to his idea. Maria wasn't happy with the general public knowing about her son, but Garraway had assured her that his identity would not be revealed.

Tomorrow he intended to meet with Ben Walker's parents with the harrowing task of telling them about Christopher Jameson and what happened when he had been hypnotised. He needed to ask their permission to use his totally unorthodox plan to catch their son's killer. He hadn't spoken with them since he was removed from the murder case.

CHAPTER ONE HUNDRED AND TWENTY FIVE

The Turnpike
Bristol
9.22pm
Monday 4th June

Colin Matthews sat alone in the beer garden of The Turnpike. He'd finished a meal with a couple of work colleagues. He'd considered asking their opinion on what had happened between him and Garraway that morning but decided against it.

Now they'd gone he sat quietly with time to think about his meeting with Garraway earlier that day. The man was clearly insane and how on earth he was allowed to go within fifty feet of the Kenneth Steele building, let alone work there, was beyond Matthews.

On one hand he felt sorry for the man. After all, he'd been through an awful lot over the last couple of years and was clearly nowhere near recovered, but on the other hand Matthews was angry with him. The idea of him touting his ridiculous story to the press irked him. He considered speaking with Detective Superintendent Munroe, but knew that as soon as Munroe knew of Garraway's ludicrous intention he'd make sure that Garraway would be out of a job, and to Matthews that just didn't seem fair. As crazy as Garraway had become, his current job within the force was surely helping him by adding structure to his life.

Matthews decided not to tell anyone about the meeting as he was certain that no one in the media would waste their time on such a story. He doubted if the story would even make the pages of the Fortean Times.

He finished his drink and walked home, pulling his jacket tightly around him to keep him warm on the particularly chilly June evening.

CHAPTER ONE HUNDRED AND TWENTY SIX

Sophie and James Walker's home
7.48pm
Thursday 7th June

Garraway sat in Ben's parent's back garden. It had been a warm day, warmer than the day before. The sun was getting lower, casting long shadows across the garden.

Sophie appeared from the back door of the house carrying a tray with three lemonades which were precariously balanced. Garraway looked round when he heard the chinking of ice cubes bobbing around in the tall glasses. James stood up and took the tray from his wife and placed it on the patio table. Sophie adjusted the patio umbrella to prevent the sun from getting in Garraway's eyes.

"I understand that you have some information which could help find our son's murderer?" said James Walker in a quiet voice.

Garraway nodded as he took a sip of cold lemonade.

"I understood that you were no longer on the case," continued James.

"That's correct, I was removed from your son's case because I suffered a nervous breakdown," confirmed Garraway.

"So why have you come here today, if you're no longer involved?" asked Sophie in a puzzled voice.

"It's a long story, well perhaps not long, let me rephrase that, it's an unusual story, a very, very unusual story. You will probably find what I am about to tell you upsetting, and I know that you will be angry with me, and I appreciate how you will feel, but however upset you get, please hear me out, please let me tell you the whole thing from beginning to end."

Garraway had brought his laptop and had the video of Christopher Jameson loaded and ready to show them if needs be.

It took him over an hour and a half to explain what had happened when Christopher had been hypnotised for the first time and the subsequent sessions which had led to the interview between him and Ben.

He told them about the strange properties of the hill in Badock's Wood and how it had connected Polly Ellis to her beloved Sarah. He told them about the many people who were certain that the hill had supernatural qualities which could not be explained.

By a nine thirty five the sun was dipping behind the neighbouring houses and the evening was becoming chilly.

"Well Mr. Garraway, you certainly have a tale to tell, and as you requested, my wife and I have let you speak to the end of your story, but to be perfectly frank with you, I wish you hadn't come to our house tonight," said James.

"I don't know whether you've lost children, but Sophie and I have lost two. Our first son, Michael, died of cancer when he was a little boy and now that we've lost Ben we have no children," he added as tears began to flow.

"James and I have only recently come to terms with the loss of Ben and we don't appreciate you bringing back the terrible memories of what happened to our son that night in the woods," said Sophie, with more than a hint of anger in her voice.

This is exactly the response that Garraway had expected. He thought about the video clips which were ready to be played on his lap top. He hadn't told them that Tom Judd had recorded the hypnosis sessions and was considering whether he should show them now or wait until another day. There was a high probability that he would not be allowed back to their house and therefore miss the chance of speaking with them again about their son.

Garraway cleared his throat as he removed his laptop from its case.

"What if I was to tell you I can prove everything I've told you and you can see and hear it for yourself?"

Sophie and James viewed him with suspicion.

"Tom Judd recorded all the hypnosis sessions on video.......please would you take the time to view them and after you have seen them I would be grateful if you then make your minds up as to whether what I have told you is true."

"Is this a joke?" demanded James.

"Absolutely not, far from it. Everything I have told you has happened............ I can't even begin to comprehend how difficult this is for you, but I believe there is enough in these videos to make a conviction. The way I intend to use them is let's say, well, it's not down the normal police route of enquiry, but I am positive good will come of it."

James and Sophie held hands tightly as Garraway lifted the lid of his lap top and showed the videos in chronological order.

As soon as Christopher began talking and Ben's childlike tone crackled over the speakers of the laptop both parents recognised their son's voice. Tears gushed from James's eyes and Sophie ran her finger over the screen of the computer, as if she was touching her son.

James was transfixed as he heard the little boy in the hypnotist's chair recall when he and Ben had spent two weeks in Berlin for the two thousand and six world cup.

Garraway paused the video, he could tell by their reactions that they believed what they were watching to be true.

"Do you want me to continue?" asked Garraway.

"In the next few minutes Ben describes in detail what happened the night he died and I'll understand if you don't wish to see it."

"Let it play, we'll watch it to the end," said James as Sophie nodded in agreement.

Garraway let the clips run as the parents watched, unable to hold back their emotions. After the videos had finished Garraway closed the lid on the laptop and put it back in its case.

Garraway didn't speak as he let the enormity of what the couple had just witnessed slowly sink in.

"Can I give you a day or so to think about things before you give me your response?" asked Garraway.

"Response?" enquired James, wiping his face with his handkerchief.

"I need your permission to allow me to go ahead with my intended use of these clips."

"Do you really think you can use them to find Ben's murderer?" asked Sophie.

Garraway nodded.

"In that case you must do what you have to do," said James.

CHAPTER ONE HUNDRED AND TWENTY SEVEN

Darlington Railway Station
5.14pm
Friday 8th June

Carla Price stepped off the two thirty five from Kings Cross. It had been a long journey. She was tired from the hypnotic lull of the train as it made its way across the country. The trip home for the summer vacation had gone without a hitch and the train had pulled into Darlington station exactly on time.

She sat in the waiting room. She'd arranged for her father to pick her up from the station. She had sent him a text to let him know that the train was on time and he'd replied to tell her the Friday rush hour traffic was bad and he would be there in around twenty minutes.

She was tired from the journey and was finding it difficult to keep her eyes open as she waited for her father to arrive. Her eyes slowly opened and closed as she fought the urge to sleep whilst sitting on the uncomfortable plastic chair. Suddenly she noticed the man on the opposite side of the waiting room. She instantly recognised him. He looked older than she remembered, his hair was thinning and was showing signs of turning grey. His faced looked lined and craggy. She was surprised to see that he had crutches on the floor in front of him as he sat in the waiting room. But it was definitely him. Her pulse quickened. *Why is he here, why is he in Darlington?* she thought as she looked at the man sitting less than twenty five feet away from her.

As the man gazed around the room his eyes met with hers and a look of recognition appeared on his face. When he saw her he smiled. It wasn't a friendly smile, but more of a smile of satisfaction, a smile which signified he'd found what he'd been looking for.

He opened his mouth and said her name.

"Carla."

Although he was on the far side of the room, his voice sounded as if he was right next to her.

"Carla, wake up."

She opened her eyes, as Richard, her father, put his hand on her shoulder.

Carla awoke with a jolt. She looked at her father, stood up and threw her arms around him.

"I'm sorry I'm late darling, how was the journey?"

She looked across the waiting room to where the detective was sitting and was shocked to see he was still there.

It's Markland Garraway, he really is here, she thought as she stared over her father's shoulder at the man. As the feeling of drowsiness slowly left her, she looked again at the detective on the plastic chair and instead of Garraway, she saw a disheveled homeless man with a pair of crutches by his feet. He was smiling at her. She turned her face away from him and nuzzled into her father's shoulder.

"Take me home daddy."

Richard picked up his daughter's case and held her hand as he walked with her out of the station and to his car. The homeless man watched as she left the waiting room. Carla could feel the man's eyes burning into the back of her neck which made her flesh crawl.

CHAPTER ONE HUNDRED AND TWENTY EIGHT

> The Bristol Post
> Temple way
> Ian Lester's office
> 11.07pm
> Monday 11th June

Markland Garraway sat in the busy offices of The Bristol Post as Ian Lester brought over two plastic cups of coffee.

Lester was a young reporter who had worked for the Bristol Post for just over two years. He had briefly met Garraway once before when they'd discussed the possibility of Lester being involved in Garraway's training programmes to give new detectives a view of things from the perspective of the press.

He was the journalist at the Post that the Police Department's News and Information team made contact with when it came to making announcements in the local press. Garraway knew that Lester was a bright and ambitious reporter who was desperate to get his hands on a big story that would make a difference to his career and move him a rung or two up the ladder of success. Garraway had something to share with him of which he was certain would bring the attention of Bristol, if not the rest of the country, and maybe even the world to Ian Lester.

Lester placed the coffee on the table, sat down and turned his chair to face Garraway.

Word of Markland Garraway's mental breakdown and eventual return to work was known to Ian. There wasn't much he didn't know. His mind was like a sponge, it soaked up information, but unlike a sponge, which emptied when saturated, Ian Lester's brain always found space to store something new. Garraway had called him on Friday Morning to arrange a meeting and in between then and now, he had taken the time to find out as much about Garraway as he could.

He knew that the Scot had been a long serving detective with the Avon and Somerset Constabulary. His success rate was outstanding and until the Ben Walker murder case his career had been one of success. He had met Garraway before and had liked the man, and he particularly liked the attitude he took towards his work. He understood that several of his peers disapproved of some of the techniques he used when solving cases, and this was something that Lester liked about him.

"OK, you've got forty five minutes of my time, and then I'm out of here," said Lester looking at his watch.

"Is there somewhere we can talk that is a little more private?" asked Garraway as he looked around the open plan office.

Lester checked his computer and searched for an available meeting room.

"OK, follow me."

Lester jumped up, picked up his coffee and quickly made his way through the main doors of the office and along a corridor. He stopped outside an empty office and turned to talk to Garraway.

"Where the hell?" he said under his breath when he saw that Garraway was nowhere to be seen.

He walked back along the corridor and into the open plan office where he saw him slowly getting to his feet and putting the strap of his laptop case over his shoulder.

"I'm sorry Ian, you'll have to bear with me, I'm not so fast on my feet these days."

Lester apologised and walked alongside as Garraway struggled with his crutches.

Lester opened the door to the small office and held it for him. He shut it behind him and pulled the blinds.

Garraway slumped onto an office chair, dropped his laptop case to the floor, smiled and let out a heavy sigh.

"Thank you for seeing me Ian, I appreciate how busy you are."

Lester smiled.

"What is it I can do for you?"

"Well it's something that we can do for each other."

Lester looked at Garraway with a slightly raised eyebrow.

"I have something for you and it's something I think you would want to report in your newspaper."

"And…..?"

"I was heading up a murder case several years ago, it was the last case I was working on until all this started to happen," said Garraway pointing to his crutches.

"You may remember it? The murder of a young man which took place in Badock's Wood and his girlfriend was left for dead."

"Yes……..if my memory serves me well it happened back in autumn two thousand and nine……..that was before I worked at the Post, but I do remember it, and I remember the press conference at the time."

Lester's memory was impeccable. He could clearly recall Garraway asking for anyone to come forward who could help the police with their enquiries.

"The murderer was never caught if I remember correctly."

"You're right, he's still at large."

Garraway filled Lester in on the basics of the case. He told him of the DNA on the police database, and that there was no one that they were able to match it with. He told him about Liz Mason and how she'd remained in a coma since the attack. Lester was sad to hear that Liz was back in hospital and her health was in decline.

"So what can I report about this case? It seems as if the trail went cold a long time ago," asked Lester.

"Well, there have been developments, fairly significant ones, but the issue is that the detective who is now assigned to the case won't touch the latest evidence with a dirty pole."

"Why not? Surely evidence is evidence, no matter how it's presented."

"I know, that would have been my attitude, but Colin Matthews, who worked with me on the case, and is now in charge of it, agrees to differ with me."

Lester was becoming interested.

"How is it that I can help? You know there is a limit to what I am allowed to report on an ongoing case."

"I know, and this is where I would like to think you would be willing to take a risk, which if it worked in your favour, and the favour of the family of Ben Walker, would forward your career as a journalist many years."

"When you say take a risk, I assume that if things worked against me, things could go tits up in major way."

"Well, yes, possibly…..in theory," replied Garraway in a cagey manner.

Garraway had Lester's full attention.

"OK, what have you got?"

Garraway repeated the story from beginning to end, which like Campbell and Tom Judd before him he was beginning to feel he was just going through the motions. But Lester was a different kind of listener. He showed no sign of cynicism and didn't seem to doubt what he was being told. In fact he had so many questions for Garraway it was refreshing for him to relay what had happened to an audience that seemed to believe what he was saying.

Lester wanted to know everything that had happened to Garraway at the hill and about Polly Ellis, her suicide and the note she'd left with Sarah's unexplained handwriting. He was enthralled by the girl in his dream and was fascinated by how the sketch of the same girl appeared mysteriously in the back pages of the book.

"Wasn't there somewhere you needed to be?" asked Garraway as he pointed to the clock on the wall.

"Shit," said Lester. It was quarter past twelve. He had a meeting at twelve and had been so intrigued with Garraway's story he had lost track of time. He grabbed his phone and made a call.

"Hi Emily, it's Ian, I'm sorry, something's come up, we're going to have to rearrange."

"I hate cancelling on people, but I'm sure Emily will understand when I get this story to print."

Garraway was relieved that he believed him. Lester was as open minded as Garraway, and was always on the lookout for a story with a difference.

"When you say that you're going to print this story, would it also go on the internet?"

"Yeah, it will go to print and also be on the Bristol Post website."

"So, you could show video clips on your website?"

"Video clips?" asked Lester curiously.

"Hypnosis, all the sessions of the little boy under hypnosis."

"Why didn't you tell me?"

"Do you want to see them now?"

"God yes, this is getting better."

Garraway took his laptop from its case and Ian Lester looked like a kid in a toy shop. Garraway started the videos, swiveled the computer around to face Lester and sat back with his arms folded as he watched the look on the young journalist's face.

After he'd watched the clips he asked whether he could get his hands on them. Garraway reached into his jacket pocket, pulled out a memory stick and tossed it over to Lester.

"You'll need to pixelate the little boy's face, we need to protect his identity."

Lester nodded.

"But I think his voice sounds so different, you can keep it as it is."

"I'm going to need something in writing from all who are concerned with this story to confirm that they are happy for me to go ahead."

"I've spoken to the parents of the boy, the hypnotist and both Liz Mason's and Ben Walker's family and they've all said yes, and don't worry, I'll get it in writing."

"Good, leave it with me and I'll get started……although I will need something from you, an interview and an appeal would be great."

"Just let me know when you need me," replied Garraway.

Garraway closed the computer, slowly stood up, shook Lester's hand and made his way home.

CHAPTER ONE HUNDRED AND TWENTY NINE

Tom Judd's home
7.18pm
Friday 15th June

Ian Lester, Markland Garraway, Terry Mason, Esther Hall, Maria, Claire and Campbell where shoe horned into Judd's lounge.

Lester had handed out copies of what he proposed to print in Monday's edition of the Bristol Post.

They were pouring over the news item Lester had written, whilst he sat patiently awaiting their criticisms. Normally he wouldn't be overly concerned about what people thought about his work. He had his critics, but rarely took on board their comments.

But this was different. He had to get it right and he wanted everyone who had been directly affected by the events which had happened since September 2009 to approve of what he intended to print.

The room was silent as everyone read his report.

Two year old boy recalls death of man who died at the time of his birth

By Ian Lester

A two year old Bristol boy, who underwent hypnotherapy as a last ditch attempt to stop Rhythmic Movement Disorder has recalled details of how a man was murdered at the precise time the boy was born.

The boy, who cannot be named, underwent hypnotherapy at a Bristol practice by local hypnotherapist Mr. Tom Judd.

Ben Walker, was 21 years old when he was brutally and fatally attacked in Badock's Wood in the Henleaze/Southmead area of the city, whilst walking with his girlfriend, Liz Mason. Miss Mason was left in a coma, from which she has never awoken. The murderer was never found.

Mr Judd has told The Post how the boy recalled the exact details of how Mr Walker was murdered.

"The boy's parents approached me as they wanted to try hypnotherapy to stop their son's severe Rhythmic Movement Disorder. I was able to hypnotise him easily. As soon as he had been hypnotised he was referring to himself as Ben and was speaking like an adult. I brought him out of hypnosis as both his parents and I were concerned for his safety. His parents agreed that he should be hypnotised a second time to find out more about Ben. The second and subsequent times I put the boy under hypnosis he described, in the words of Ben Walker, how he was murdered in Badock's Wood in Bristol.

I contacted Detective Markland Garraway who was in charge of the murder case at the time. Detective Garraway was present during the last time the boy was hypnotised and spoke with the character pertaining to be Ben Walker who was able to provide a detailed account of how he was murdered."

Detective Chief Inspector Garraway has spoken with The Post and has described what happened when he talked to the boy who was under hypnosis.

"I've never seen or heard anything like it. The boy was able to provide details of the murder of Ben Walker, which would only have been known by Mr Walker or his killer. He was able to provide a detailed description of his murderer."

When asked whether it could be an elaborate hoax, DCI Garraway said,

"Unless the boy was prompted to say the words by someone who was there when Ben Walker was murdered, then no. It's not only what the boy says when under hypnosis, it's also how he talks. When he speaks as Ben Walker, his voice changes and takes on the characteristics of Mr. Walker."

DCI Garraway would like to speak to a girl who he believes can help the police with their enquiries. A drawing of the girl is shown below. If anyone knows the whereabouts of the girl matching the picture below, please contact DCI Garraway via Ian Lester at The Bristol Post. Anyone who contacts The Post will be dealt with in the strictest confidence.

When asked, DCI Garraway said that he was unable to say who provided the information of the girl in the picture.

(Picture to go here)

To see a video of the boy whilst under hypnosis and speaking as Ben Walker go to The Post's website at: (URL to go here).

"Short and sweet, not really front page material," said Campbell.

"It won't be going on the front page," replied Lester.

"Why ever not, it's such a short story, it could get overlooked if it's lost somewhere in the middle of the newspaper," added Esther.

"I need to sneak the story in without bringing it to the attention of my editors."

Lester stood up and walked towards the window and turned around before continuing.

"I'm on dodgy ground with this story. It's reporting unofficial information on an ongoing police investigation. I'm including a picture of a girl, who quite frankly no one knows where it came from and there will be video clips on the website of Christopher under hypnosis giving details of the murder of Ben Walker. If I pushed for it to hit the front pages it wouldn't even make it to print. I'm hoping it will bypass the editors if I slip the story between pages five and eight."

"And what if your editor eventually finds it?" asked Terry Mason.

"Then I'll have a lot of explaining to do, but hopefully before then, enough people will have read the story and watched the clips on-line, and with luck on our side, someone will recognise the girl in the picture and Mr. Garraway can bring her in............"

"At which point I'll have no option but to pass her over to Colin Matthews to interview and hopefully she'll name Ben's murderer," interrupted Garraway.

"Why should she name him, it will place her as an accessory to murder?" asked Maria.

"I'm convinced this girl was at the wrong place at the wrong time. I believe she had somehow got mixed up with the wrong crowd of people. In my dream, she is the one who ended the fighting and if it wasn't for her I am sure that Liz would have also died that night."

"I still think it should go on the front page," mumbled Esther quietly.

"OK, so if nobody has anything else to add I'll get this in Monday's edition of The Post.........if anyone does have any last minute suggestions, they'll need to let me know by close of business tomorrow," said Lester.

Tom Judd stood up, walked over to Lester and was about to shake his hand and thank him when Terry Mason's phone rang.

"Hello, yes this is Mason....................sorry, can you say that again please."

Mason's knees buckled and he dropped to the floor holding the phone tightly in his hand.

Campbell rushed over and could hear a voice speaking over Mason's phone.

"Mr Mason, are you OK, can you hear me?"

Mason dropped the phone, looked towards Campbell and with an unsteady voice he spoke.

"It's the hospital..............Liz is awake.......and she's talking."

CHAPTER ONE HUNDRED AND THIRTY

Southmead Hospital
8.50am
Sunday 17th June

Liz had woken from the coma just over thirty six hours ago. She was very weak and to complicate matters she was still affected by the pneumonia she had contracted at the end of May.

She had been speaking, although her voice was shaky and feeble and she was finding it difficult to get her words out. Terry and Anne where beside themselves with joy.

The word had spread that she was awake and the visitors who had initially called to see her when she was first taken to Southmead almost three years ago were clambering over each other to be the first to see her now she was conscious.

Terry and Anne had requested that their daughter received no callers, at least not for the time being. The medical staff at the hospital agreed. Liz should not be put through any undue stress at this time. She needed to come to terms with what had happened and to be gently eased back to the land of the living.

She had a long way to go. The treatment ahead would aim to improve function, prevent further complications and rehabilitate her and her family both physically and emotionally. Her muscles had deteriorated meaning she would need to undergo physiotherapy so she could build up strength to allow her to walk.

Although the pneumonia was improving, and she had been off the ventilator since the end of last week, the doctors were still concerned and were monitoring her very closely.

"Hello Mummy," said Liz, as Anne Mason held her daughter's hand.

Anne leant forward and kissed her forehead and stroked her hair.

Anne had to keep her ear close to Liz's mouth to understand what she was saying. She hadn't said much since she'd woken.

Doctors had advised her parents not to encourage her to talk too much in the early days of recovery and to let Liz come around at her own pace.

Detective Colin Matthews had been notified that Liz was awake and he was keen to speak with her as soon as possible. Other than Garraway's ridiculous and unsubstantiated new evidence the other day, Liz was the only person who could provide positive information which could lead to the arrest of Ben Walker's killer and anyone else who had been involved in the attack.

Matthews had been advised by the medical staff not to speak to her just yet. He would need to wait a few days until she was strong enough to be interviewed.

He didn't want to risk the chance of Liz slipping back into a coma, or the pneumonia worsening and preventing her from giving vital information. He pleaded with the doctors, but his request had been denied.

Liz looked around the hospital ward and saw the get well cards festooned around her bed. Since she'd woken the cards had arrived by the dozen and not all of them could be displayed.

Anne read the messages from her friends. Liz was having difficulty in remembering who all the well-wishers were. She remembered a few of the names, but struggled to think who most of them were.

"What do you remember?" asked Terry as he held her hand.

"I remember you and mummy," replied Liz in a dry and croaky voice.

"I know darling, but what can you remember before you became ill, what's the last thing you recall?"

Liz lay quietly holding her father's hand as she thought hard about what had happened to her. Terry didn't speak. He wanted to give her time to gather her thoughts and recall something of the night she was attacked.

A minute passed, which to Terry seemed an awfully long time, and then she spoke.

"I remember Ben. I remember we were walking together. He took me somewhere nice."

"You're right, you were with Ben. The two of you were out walking in the woods."

Liz smiled as she recalled the handsome young man who she'd fallen in love with. No time seemed to have passed since she last saw him, but at the same time it seemed a lifetime ago.

"He's dead isn't he daddy?"

Terry was taken aback by what she said and didn't know how to reply.

"How do you know that?" asked Anne.

"I just do, I've known for a long time."

Terry and Anne looked at each other with a puzzled look.

Liz was becoming tired and closed her eyes.

Dr Edison walked over to Liz's bed.

"Let her rest now. It doesn't take much to tire her."

Terry nodded.

"Just wait there and be with her. She'll probably be awake again in an hour or so."

"She told me that she knew that Ben Walker was dead, how could she possibly know?"

Dr Edison shrugged his shoulders.

"She's probably a little delirious and making no sense. Don't worry, her mind will eventually clear. We just need to give her time."

Terry and Anne went for a walk around the hospital grounds hand in hand. Anne turned to her husband and threw her arms around him and sobbed uncontrollably onto his shoulder.

"Our daughter's back, she's with us again, I can't believe it," said Anne, her voice was muffled by her husband's shoulder as he held her close and rubbed his hand across her back.

Terry didn't feel as ecstatic as Anne. It was the best news that he could have hoped for, but the words that Ben said, which had come from Liz, still haunted him. He recalled them in his mind.

Ben, when it's time, meet me at the hill………..and don't be late.

Terry had been concerned about Liz's wellbeing, not only because she'd been in a coma for almost three years, it was also because of the gut feeling he'd had when he'd been convinced that Campbell Broderick was a threat to her.

Now he understood that Campbell had no malicious intentions towards Liz, but he was still troubled. He was certain that there was something or someone lurking in the shadows, who would drag his daughter into the supernatural abyss of the Bronze Age burial mound in Badock's Wood.

Terry Mason was frightened of no man, but the hill scared the daylights out of him because it was something he didn't understand or have any control over.

He considered contacting Maria Jameson to beg that her son be hypnotised one more time so he could speak with Ben Walker and find out what he meant by those words.

Even if Maria granted another hypnotherapy session it would have yielded no useful information, as Ben Walker had no idea of the meaning of the words he'd heard from Liz. They meant nothing to him and he had hoped that Markland could have shed some light on their meaning.

"I think we should call Markland. We need to keep him up to date on Liz," said Anne.

Terry hadn't spoken to Garraway since the last time they were together on Friday at Judd's place.

"I don't want him talking to her, I'd prefer it if we leave it to Matthews to interview her. I'm worried that Garraway would upset her."

"You're right, but I think we have a duty to let him know, after all he's been through."

Terry agreed. Anne was right. It would be unfair not to keep him updated on this significant step forward in the whole series of events which surrounded the hill.

Terry called Garraway and huffed as his phone diverted to voicemail.

"Hi Markland, its Terry Mason. This is just a quick call to update you on our daughter……. as you know, Liz has woken. She's not saying much just yet, and doesn't seem to remember anything about the attack. I understand Matthews will be in to interview her in the next few days, when she's had a chance to come to terms with what she's been through, so…….what I'm trying to say, with all due respect, is that we think it's best that Matthews speaks to her and not you, at least for the time being……….oh and one more thing, she seems to know that Ben is dead, she said she's known for a long time, I just thought you should know. Ring me when you get this message."

Terry slipped his phone back into his pocket and smiled at Anne. They hugged again and this time it was Terry who was crying. Tears of joy, tears of confusion and tears of concern.

The mid-morning sun warmed them as they stood in the gardens of the hospital, holding each other tightly.

"Soon Liz will feel the sun on her face again," said Anne as she nuzzled into her husband. He kissed her on the neck and held her close.

"Let's go back to the ward, she may be waking soon," said Terry.

Anne nodded and they walked slowly back to see Liz.

When they returned she was still sleeping.

"Is she OK?" asked Anne.

Nurse Taylor nodded.

Terry and Anne looked as their daughter's eyes twitched beneath her closed lids.

"She's dreaming," said the nurse.

Her parents hadn't seen this happen when she was in the coma.

"I wonder what she's dreaming?" said Anne.

Terry shook his head. In his mind the words Ben Walker had said kept going around his head.

'Ben, when it's time, meet me at the hill………...and don't be late'

His thoughts were interrupted by the ringing of his phone. It was Garraway returning his call. Terry stepped out of the ward to take the call.

"Thanks for calling me, how is she?" asked Garraway.

"She's sleeping at the moment, Anne and I are waiting for her to wake up…..she's dreaming right now. I was just wondering what could be going through her mind."

Garraway instantly sensed concern in Terry's voice. He knew that he was still worried about his daughter. Not because he was concerned about her recovery after the coma, he could tell by the tone of his voice that something else was bothering him.

"I've listened to your voicemail and appreciate you don't want me speaking with Liz just yet and I understand that Matthews should be the one to interview her when she's ready and not me."

"Thank you for understanding," said Terry, "I'm worried that if you start telling her about all the crazy things that have been happening it might upset her."

"Between you and me, after Ian Lester's story is printed tomorrow, I really believe things will begin to move forward and we won't need to rely upon Liz for evidence."

Terry told him he'd keep him updated on any developments and ended the call.

Terry made his way back to Liz's hospital bed to find her awake. The nurses were propping her up with pillows which were supporting her head.

She smiled when she saw her father. Anne was wiping tears from her eyes.

"How are you?" asked Terry.

"Much the same as when you asked me earlier," replied Liz quietly and with a weak smile.

She turned to face Anne.

"So tell me mum, what has been happening since I've been away?"

Anne and Terry filled Liz in on what had been happening with the Mason family over the last couple of years. They told her about cousins who'd had babies. Liz was sad to hear that her great grandmother had passed away, but was pleased to hear she'd made it to one hundred and one.

Liz suddenly stopped talking and raised her hand and pushed it against her head. Her face screwed up as she winced with pain.

"What's the matter?" asked her mother with concern.

"Oooh, it's OK, it's gone now."

"What has?"

"I just had a sharp pain in my head, it's gone away now."

"Terry, call the nurse" said Anne sounding urgent.

He stood up to find the nurse.

"No mum, I'm fine, it's probably nothing…….remember I've been out of it for almost three years, I'm bound to have a few niggles."

Terry sat back down.

"You're probably right, but let us know if it happens again."

Liz nodded and smiled weakly again.

"Have any more memories returned.......memories of being in the woods with Ben?" asked Terry.

Liz shook her head and then looked at her father.

"I can't remember a thing..........what happened dad?"

Terry turned to Anne who slowly nodded.

"She needs to know," said Anne.

Terry held Liz's hand and moved closer.

"That evening you were in the woods with Ben.......you were......it seems you were both attacked."

Liz said nothing as she gazed beyond her father and towards the ceiling.

"Do you not remember?"

She shook her head.

"I do remember we were messing around on a hill and we kissed.......we kissed at the bottom of a hill."

"That's right, you and Ben kissed each other."

Anne shot a glance and Terry realised he was saying too much. There was no way he could have known about the kiss, unless he'd been told by someone who was there, and that person was Ben.

"How did you know we kissed?" asked Liz curiously.

Terry struggled to find a believable answer, but thinking on his feet he told her that her lipstick had been found on Ben's clothing. Liz wasn't convinced.

She looked at her father and saw how he'd aged since she'd last seen him. His hair was receding and turning grey. He looked about a stone lighter and his faced was lined. She couldn't imagine what the past few years must have been like for her parents. Then her thoughts turned to Ben.

Terry was surprised when Liz didn't seem shaken when he'd told her that she'd been attacked and he wondered about something she'd said earlier that morning.

"Liz, what did you mean when you said that you knew Ben was dead? You told me you'd known for a long time. What did you mean by that?"

She turned away from him and didn't speak.

Anne shot a second glance at him and shook her head.

Liz looked back towards him and then to her mother.

"Ben was killed in the attack, wasn't he?"

They both nodded and saw tears well in her eyes.

"They don't know who did it do they? I mean, the police, they've never caught anyone."

Anne shook her head.

"How did you know?"

"I don't know, just a feeling."

Terry was about to ask another question when Dr Edison walked in.

"Try not to get Liz to speak too much just yet, she's very tired. Remember she's only been awake for just over a day."

Terry and Anne sat up and instinctively edged away from Liz.

"It's OK, you won't break her," laughed the doctor, "just don't ask her too many things right now. There'll be plenty of time for that over the next few weeks."

Terry stood up and took Dr Edison to one side.

"The police want to speak with her, when is that likely to happen?"

"Not for a number of days, her memory should soon begin to return, but I'm concerned that too much attention won't do her any good right now."

"Liz just had shooting pains in her head, is that normal?"

"It's probably fine, but we'll run some tests later. Don't forget, when she was attacked she suffered traumatic brain injury, she may have headaches for a long time, in some cases they may continue for years……..but don't worry about that now."

Dr Edison explained what would be happening over the next few weeks.

"There's a fair bit of work to be done, but with your support and the support of the team here at the hospital I'm confident she'll make a good recovery."

Terry sat back down with Liz and Anne, and made the most of the time he had with the two ladies that meant the most to him. Despite what the doctor had just told him, he had nagging doubts about the immediate future for his daughter. He couldn't put his finger on what it was, he had a feeling from deep within his gut that something wasn't right.

CHAPTER ONE HUNDRED AND THIRTY ONE

Saltford, near Bristol
11.35am
Monday 18th June

Beverly Turner sat in her favourite chair and let out a well earned sigh. She'd had a busy morning getting her eight year old twin daughters to school and her four year old son to nursery. She'd just returned from the supermarket after completing the weekly shop. The groceries had been put away and now it was time to sit down and take a breath.

Sometimes she was envious of her husband, who in her eyes, had a cushy desk job and spent the day drinking milky coffee whilst watching his computer crunch numbers. She, on the other hand, ran the house by moving at the pace of a whirlwind just to keep on top of everything.

But now there was a bit of *me time* for Beverly. She attempted to turn on the television and catch the news channel.

"Bloody thing," she said to herself as she struggled with the remote. No matter how hard she prodded the buttons on the thing, the television wouldn't come on. She got up and walked over to it, flipped down the little plastic cover on the side of the TV and pressed the buttons which were hidden underneath. But still the thing would not switch on.

"Bollocks," she muttered as she sat back down.

The thing had been on the blink for the past week and she'd been onto her husband to get a new one since Friday. "Give it a few more days, and I'll get it looked at," he'd told her. But now the thing had packed up altogether.

She reached under the settee and pulled out the laptop. The kids used it more than she did and she was disgusted because the keyboard was covered in their dirty finger prints. There was what looked like dry yoghurt stains over the screen and something horrible was making the spacebar stick to the 'B' key. She grabbed a damp cloth and cleaned the thing before turning it on.

She'd had a busy weekend and hadn't caught site of the news since Saturday evening and she was desperate to know what was going on in the world and more importantly to her, the world close to home.

She brought up the Bristol Post website. She'd stopped buying newspapers a long time ago, and now relied upon the television or the internet to tell her what was happening in the world.

She trawled through some of the headlines and ended up finding a fairly mundane report about the top ten richest women in the world. She half read it and moved on to the next stories.

She read a sad story of a man who had been killed by a forklift truck, which had happened on an industrial estate less than a mile from where her husband worked.

Another story caught her eye.

Police discover £350,000 worth of cannabis plants being grown in the Bristol area.

And then she saw a story with a headline that made no sense.

Two year old boy recalls death of man who died at the time of his birth

By Ian Lester

She reread it and wondered what on earth it could mean.

'Two year old boy recalls death of man who died at the time of his birth'

Beverly read the story twice and found it hard to comprehend what the report was describing. It seemed to be saying that a two year old, when being treated for a condition, of which she'd never heard, by hypnotherapy had started talking as an adult who'd been murdered at the time the little boy had been born.

She glanced at the picture of the girl the who police were looking for and then hovered her mouse over the link to open the video clip.

She sat on her settee with the laptop propped on her knees as she watched the video of Christopher Jameson under hypnosis speaking as the deceased Ben Walker.

Christopher's face had been pixelated so he could not be recognised. All the videos made by Tom Judd had been cleverly edited together so they ran seamlessly from one into the other, with a date and time fade in, which indicated when the hypnotherapy sessions had taken place.

In the bottom right hand corner of the video was a static image of the girl Garraway had dreamt of. The image remained in place during the entire eleven minutes of video footage.

After the clip had finished Beverly sat motionless holding the laptop in place on her knees. She replayed the clip and listened carefully to the boy's voice.

There's no way that's a little boy talking she thought.

It was the sort of thing the media would do as an April Fools gag. She slumped into the settee and cast her mind back. She could definitely recall a story of a man killed in Badock's Wood. She opened a new tab on her browser and searched the internet for the murder of Ben Walker. It came up immediately showing a link to Garraway's press conference. She watched the conference and Terry Mason's heartfelt appeal for information from the public. She watched DCI Garraway as he spoke in his calm and commanding Scottish accent.

"Shit, this must be the real deal," she said under her breath.

Beverly returned to the on-line news story and watched the video a third time. Each time she watched it the impact of the video was greater than before. She glanced at her watch and realised she'd been watching the clip and reading the story for almost forty five minutes. It was time to get moving. She had loads of things to be getting on with before she picked her son up from nursery at two o'clock.

Before she closed the lid on her laptop she saw two little icons below the story allowing it to be shared on Facebook and Twitter. She clicked one, shared it on her Facebook page and then closed the computer and got on with the rest of her day.

Beverly wasn't the only person to have been astounded as she watched the video. At roughly the same time she'd been watching it, another three and half thousand people in the West Country alone had also seen it, with just over half of them sharing it on Facebook. Add to that, the twenty nine thousand people who would also buy the Bristol Post newspaper that day, and the large percentage of those who would go on-line to watch the clip and then share it on Facebook and Twitter.

Within seven and a half hours of being available on the internet, the eleven minute twenty seven second video of Christopher Jameson under hypnosis and talking the words of the deceased Ben Walker had been viewed over one and a quarter million times.

It had gone viral.

CHAPTER ONE HUNDRED AND THIRTY TWO

Richard Price's office
CKT Ltd, Darlington
6.35pm
Monday 18th June

Richard Price had just been promoted to a management position. It was a brilliant step in the right direction. He'd had a good pay increase, but the downside was that he was putting in more hours. As a manager he was expected to stay until the work was done, and unlike before he had gained the promotion, there was no overtime. His forty nine thousand pound salary put the end to any extra pay for staying late, or working over the weekend.

He wasn't particularly bothered about working late, as long as it wasn't on a Tuesday or a Thursday. Tuesday was pub quiz and Thursday was skittles. That was about the extent of his social life in Darlington. He hadn't found a lady since moving from Bristol and wasn't worried either way. He enjoyed his own company and was quite happy living a quiet life on his own. Although one or two of the girls at CKT thought he was quite handsome for an oldie.

Richard was reading and amending a report on waste management when there was a knock on his office door.

Barry Partridge was looking at him with his mouth squashed up against the window of the door, puffing his cheeks in and out like a goldfish. He stopped and stared at Richard with a cheeky grin. Richard beckoned him in.

"Barry, you old git, what can I do for you?"

Barry liked Richard and he loved his West Country accent which stood out like a sore thumb in Darlington.

"Roight me luvver," said Barry, taking the micky out of Richard's accent.

Richard smiled.

"This better be important," said Richard waving the report under Barry's nose.

"Some of us are here to work, not just use this place as an excuse to stay away from the wife and kids."

Barry put on a childlike *'I'm upset'* face.

Barry was either loved or hated by his peers. The man acted like a kid. He was always clowning around, taking the piss, hiding behind doors and jumping out. The other week he'd brought in a remote control fart machine and had his work mates in the open plan office rolling with laughter, until Chris Kingston, the Managing Director walked in wondering what the hell was going on. Barry had already received a warning from his line manager, but nothing seem to stop the man from acting the fool.

"OK kiddo, what's it all about?" asked Richard.

"Have you been on Facebook?"

"No Barry, funnily enough I haven't. If I had time to mess around on Facebook, I wouldn't be stuck in this shit tip at half past six, I would be at home with my feet up having a cold beer."

"Whatever Mr Dick for Brains, take a look at this."

Barry was prodding Richard's computer monitor with his finger.

"Get Facebook up, you're gonna love this."

Richard sighed and opened up his Facebook account.

Richard hardly ever looked at his account. He only had about forty friends and found the whole thing a waste of time.

"OK, what is it I'm looking for?"

"Oh, let me do it," said Barry as he grabbed Richard's mouse and scrolled through his Facebook page.

"There," said Barry pointing at the link he'd shared.

"You've really got to watch this, you'll be amazed……it's freaky man…. wait 'til you see the girl……."

"It's not one of your usual smutty things is it, like that last thing you shared with those two ugly tarts fighting in jelly?"

Barry tutted.

"What me, no, I've moved on now, I've matured," said Barry whilst looking at Richard with a stupid crossed eyed look on his face.

Even though Richard found him highly annoying at times, he did like the man. He reminded him of an irritating version of Arthur Askey.

Barry clicked the link which opened a new tab in Richard's browser showing a story from the Bristol Post. Before Richard had a chance to read the news story Barry clicked the icon for the video clip which accompanied the story. He clicked the icon so the video went full screen and took up the whole of Richard's monitor.

Richard watched the video as a boy in a chair was talking to a man. At first he didn't noticed the static image of the girl in the bottom right of the video. He was trying to concentrate on what he was watching, but found it hard to make out what was going on due to Barry's incessant chattering.

"What's going on, what's this supposed to be about?" asked Richard.

"Oh, I don't know, I've not really paid any attention, anyway, it's not about the video, look at the drawing of that girl in the corner."

Richard looked at the picture of the girl, which on his screen was about the same size as a three inch square sticky Post It note. He strained to see and reached for his glasses to get a clearer view.

"See what I mean," said Barry excitedly.

Richard was confused. Barry reached over and picked up a framed photograph which Richard kept alongside his desk organiser. The picture was of himself and his eighteen year old daughter Carla, which had been taken earlier in the year. Richard kept it close to remind him of her when she was far away in London studying at the University of the Arts.

"Look, that girl in the video, she's a dead ringer for your Carla."

Barry had met Carla last Easter when he'd been to Richard's house to borrow his power drill. She was home for the university Easter vacation and the pretty teenager had left a lasting impression on him.

Richard took the photograph from him and held it up against the picture on his computer. Barry was right, they looked identical. It was as though his daughter had sat for an artist who had done a sketch of her in pen. Everything about the picture was accurate, from the style of her hair, which she'd not changed in years, the shape of her nose to the dimple on her chin. The sketch also showed the same freckles that Carla had on her cheeks all year round.

"So what's this video supposed to be?" asked Richard a second time.

"I don't really know, I've not watched it properly. Everyone's watching it, it's something to do with a reincarnated dead bloke, from your neck of the woods I think."

Richard hit pause on the video and looked at the sketch again. He hit the back button on the browser which took him to the news story from the Bristol Post. He skim read the item, without taking in the full story. As he did there were two things that jumped out at him. One was 'Badock's Wood' and the other was 'Detective Chief Inspector Garraway'.

"Markland Garraway," said Richard under his breath.

He felt faint as a buzzing sound started deep within his ears which got louder and louder.

"Sheesh man, what's wrong with you," said Barry as Richard lurched towards his desk.

Richard looked at Barry, who was shocked to see all the colour had drained from his face.

"You look awful man!"

Richard took a sip of water, sat back, and reached a tissue to wipe the beads of perspiration from his forehead.

Barry watched as Richard stood up on shaky legs. He grabbed his keys from the desk and walked out of the office. Walking like a drunken man, he was bouncing off desks and knocking into filing cabinets as he made his way out of the building. He left his computer turned on and his office door unlocked.

Barry was bewildered by what he'd just seen.

He ran after him calling his name.

Other than the two of them, the office complex was empty. No one heard Barry as he called after Richard. Not even Richard heard him as he swiped his staff card to open the secure doors which let him out of the building and into the car park. The buzzing in his ears was preventing him from hearing what was going on around him.

Barry looked from the window and watched him struggle to open his car door. Eventually he got in and slammed it shut. The car lurched forward and made a left turn out of the car park.

"What the……..." said Barry as he watched Richard's car disappear from view.

CHAPTER ONE HUNDRED AND THIRTY THREE

William IV
Truro, Cornwall
6.49pm
Monday 18th June

Daniel Boyd sat on his own in the family pub in Truro. It was the first time he'd visited a pub since he'd hurt his foot almost three weeks ago. He finished his pint, stood up and hobbled to the bar to buy another. He stood in the queue behind an excited group of young men who were talking over each other.

Although he'd lived in Cornwall for almost two years he'd not got used to the Cornish accent. He was subconsciously listening to what the men were talking about whilst waiting to be served.

One of the men had his smart phone and was scrolling through a website.

"You gotta see it,...... it's the freakiest thing," said the shortest of the group of six men standing at the bar, whilst he was desperately trying to find something to show his friends.

"I've already seen it, I watched it this morning," said his well-built closely shaven friend.

"What's it all about?" said another of the group as he paid for the round of drinks.

"Hang on and I'll show you," said the short man as he struggled to find the website. While he was looking, the closely shaven man started to explain to the other four what the short man was looking for.

"I'm surprised you guys haven't already seen it.......it's the strangest thing......this kid's been hypnotised or something and he's talking in his sleep or something and this Bristol bloke's been murdered and........."

"Shut up, you'll spoil it," said the short man as he eventually found what it was he'd been looking for. He propped his phone on the bar and played the video clip.

It was Monday evening and the pub was quiet. The six men said nothing as they watched the video clip of Christopher Jameson on the man's phone.

Boyd stood behind them and couldn't see what they were watching, but he could clearly hear the dialogue.

He could hear reference to Badock's Wood in Bristol, murder and Ben Walker.

Boyd dropped his empty pint glass when he heard those three key things. The six men turned around and saw Boyd nervously picking up the broken glass as his shaking hands placed the shards on the bar.

"Good job it was an empty one," said the short man.

"What are you watching?" asked Boyd apprehensively.

"It's a strange video that's doing the rounds" replied the short man.

"What's it about?"

"You need to see it, everyone's watching it."

"Why?"

"A fella who was murdered up in Bristol a few years ago, he's come back to life......he talks through a little boy who's been hypnotised. He tells the hypnotist and a policeman all about his murder and the person who killed him. It's probably a hoax......but if it is, it's been done really well."

"Where was the murder?"

"In some woods in Bristol, Babcock Woods, I think."

"No, it was Badock's Wood," said the closely shaven man.

"Do they say who the murderer was?" asked Boyd who was by now sounding extremely anxious.

"No, but the kid gives a pretty good description, and the cops are looking for a girl."

The short man picked up his phone and handed it to Boyd. He looked at the sketch of the girl and recognised her straight away. He handed the phone back to the man and walked out of the bar without speaking.

"Strange boy," said the closely shaven man.

Boyd struggled to get the key in the lock as he desperately tried to open his door. He limped up the stairs as fast as his painful ankle would allow, opened the door to his bedsit and switched on his dilapidated computer. The thing was taking ages to come on. It always did and Boyd was desperate to see for himself what the men in the pub had shown him.

He lay on his bed waiting for it to come to life and as he did, he thought about what he'd just been told in the pub.

Eventually the computer was ready and he searched for the Bristol Post website. Had it not been for the lads in the pub he would never have known about the news item.

The Bristol Post website finally cranked up and Boyd saw that he could search the site. He typed in 'murder Badock's Wood' and the story came up on his decrepit and ancient computer.

He read the story before playing the video clip. He was a bag of nerves and none of it made any sense. Although the man in the pub had told him what it was about, he was having difficulty comprehending what he was reading. He read it again and saw that Garraway was searching for the girl in the picture.

He played the video all the way through and shuddered when he heard the boy in the hypnotist's chair say the words, "With a rock Tom, ………he killed me with a ………rock."

He watched Markland Garraway as he interviewed the boy but was speaking with Ben Walker. Boyd immediately recognised Walker's calm voice, even though it was coming from a two year old boy.

He played the video a further five times and after an hour lay on his bed. He felt nervous, exhausted and confused. Oddly, the fact that Ben Walker was communicating by means of a two year old boy did not seem strange to him. Strange things had happened since the murder, including peculiar dreams. He recalled the one of the court room when the baby in the pram was giving evidence against him. Was that dream trying to tell him something?

And what about the vision of Ben Walker in the window of the house, the day he fell of the ladder? There had certainly been enough unusual things going on lately to make the video seem believable.

The description given by Ben of Boyd was spot on. Ben had even described the clothes he'd been wearing that night in the woods. That bothered him immensely, but what was unsettling him the most was the picture of the girl. He knew exactly who she was, but he'd never got to know her. He couldn't even remember her name. She just used to hang around with the gang from time to time because she was friends with Charlotte, who was Greeny's girlfriend. One thing he did remember was that it was she who had ended the fighting, by saying she'd seen the police. Boyd knew she'd not seen any police, otherwise they would be everywhere and Boyd would have been arrested and charged that very night.

If she were to come forward, or if someone was call the police and name her it would be game over. He didn't trust her.

He lit a cigarette and lay on his bed. He needed to come up with something. He clicked his jaw and blew smoke rings as his troubled mind thought of what to do next. He struggled to think of anything other than one desperate and impulsive plan.

Boyd sat up and hobbled over to the corner of his bedsit where he prepared his meals, which mainly consisted of microwave dinners and toast.

He rifled through a drawer and found a sharp kitchen knife and put it in his rucksack.

He reached under his bed for a polythene bag in which he kept a few tools. He removed a long screwdriver and a hammer and put them alongside the knife in the rucksack. He grabbed his keys and wallet and left his bedsit and headed to Truro bus station.

Few people saw the pathetic sight of Daniel Boyd hobbling the one mile trek to the bus station with his rucksack swinging from side to side from his shoulder. Twenty minutes later he was checking the coach departure times.

"Shit," he said under his breath. The last coach to Bristol had just left and the next one wasn't due to leave until stupid o'clock the next morning.

He decided not to return to his miserable bedsit and instead, sleep on one of the chairs in the station waiting room. He would probably get a better night's sleep there than putting up with the deafening music that emanated from his selfish neighbour's bedsit, but more importantly he didn't want to miss the early bus. He needed to be in Bristol as soon as possible.

By nine forty five it was dark and street lights illuminated the road outside as he looked through the bus station window. The darker it became the clearer he could see his reflection in the glass. He was looking at the reflection of a killer.

Boyd had devised a plan, and if the outcome was as he intended, it would result in the number of murders he had committed increasing twofold.

CHAPTER ONE HUNDRED AND THIRTY FOUR

> Richard and Carla Price's home
> Darlington
> 9.50pm
> Monday 18th June

Richard Price sat alone. The house was dark. He'd been sitting motionless in the lounge since just before eight o'clock. The sun had gone down, but he hadn't noticed. He was waiting for Carla to return from her evening job in the centre of Darlington.

He had arrived home at seven and had gone straight to his computer, read the news story from the Bristol Post and watched the video again and again. He had printed the picture of the girl and was holding it in his hand.

Everything now seemed to be making sense and things were slotting into place. Ben Walker had been murdered early in September 2009, which was the same time Carla's personality had changed. The same time the happy and carefree teenager had turned into a quiet and reclusive character. The story she'd told him about the sketch she'd done of Garraway had never really sat easily with him. There was something about it that just didn't seem right.

The story in the Bristol Post told of a man who had been murdered and of a girl who had been left for dead. The police were looking for someone who looked uncannily like his daughter. Richard was contemplating whether Carla could be a killer. Surely not? But it seemed that she had been involved. His body was shaking as he considered what he should say to her. Perhaps she had also seen the video and if so, she would have seen her likeness to the girl in the picture. But it was more than just a mere likeness, it was identical. It was Carla and there was no question about it.

He was shaken from his thoughts by the clunk of Carla opening the front door. He heard her call 'hello' and by the cheery sound of her voice he assumed that she had not seen the video.

She turned on the light in the hall. Walking into the lounge she was surprised to find her father in the darkened room. She turned on the standard lamp in the corner, which partially illuminated the room. She smiled at him but felt uneasy when he didn't smile back. He looked at her with tired eyes and without speaking handed her the picture he'd been holding tightly in his hand. It had become crumpled. Carla looked at him with a puzzled stare and held the picture under the lampshade. The paper was too creased for her to make out exactly who the person in the sketch was. She placed it on the dining table and flattened it with her hand and then took it back to the lamp. It only took seconds for her to work out who the girl in the picture was.

"Wow, that's brilliant dad, where did you get it from?"

Richard didn't answer.

"Who did it dad? It looks like one of my sketches, I didn't draw it did I?"

Richard remained silent. The look in his eyes was starting to make her feel anxious. He looked like someone who'd just received some awful news. News which was life changing, like he'd been told someone had died.

"What's the matter dad, you're scaring me?"

Richard didn't know what to say. He'd been waiting for her to come home and dreading the moment when she did. And now she was here, standing in front of him, he didn't know where to begin.

"So you're sure that's a picture of you, are you?" said Richard when he eventually spoke.

She looked at the sketch again, saw the dimples on her chin, the freckles on her cheeks and the way her fringe fell over her forehead. It was like she was seeing herself in a mirror.

She wasn't sure whether agreeing was a good or a bad thing. Her father seemed concerned by the picture, but she didn't know why.

He asked her again.

"Is that you?"

"I does look like me doesn't it?" she nervously replied.

"That's because it is you," he said gravely.

Carla was now officially scared.

"Please tell me what this is all about, you're scaring me."

"I'm scaring you, am I? Well I think you're going to be a little more scared when I show you this."

He passed her his laptop which was in standby mode.

She took the computer, placed it on the table and pressed the enter key. The screen lit up as it displayed the story which everyone seemed to have been talking about, other than her.

Carla took her time to read the report and as she did she began to feel clammy. Her mouth was dry as she read the brief story. Scrolling down, she came to the end of the report and saw the picture of the girl, the same picture she was holding in her hand. She looked at the paper again, almost as if to check whether it was different to the one on the computer. She turned back to the screen and read the story again. She was confused, very very confused. Markland Garraway was looking for her. But how did he know of her and why now, why all of a sudden now?

Everyone else who had read the story had been completely amazed and awestruck that a dead man was communicating through a two year old boy. It had confirmed that there was life after death. A few readers thought the story was a hoax, a lie or perhaps some kind of cruel prank. But the majority of those who'd read it believed in it one hundred percent. But Carla wasn't amazed or shocked by the story, it didn't register as being strange. Because her mind was consumed, consumed by the fact that Garraway was looking for her. He clearly didn't know her name, otherwise it would have been in the story, but he obviously knew what she looked like.

"Now you've read the book, why don't you watch the movie?" said her father in a flat tone of voice.

She looked back at the screen and saw the video link. Her heart was in her mouth as she moved the cursor and hovered it over the link. She read the words which came before the video link.

Click here to see a video of the boy whilst under hypnosis and speaking as Ben Walker.

She swallowed hard and then clicked on the link.

Just over eleven minutes later she muttered under her breath, "what the……....?"

Her father looked at her with soulless eyes, almost like some dead thing. And then he spoke, "Would you like to tell me what all of this is about?"

No matter how she dressed up what had happened, her father would never understand the full extent of what she had been through. Not only had she witnessed a murder, she had been affected by something supernatural. Since the murder she'd been plagued with visions and strange dreams. Like the night she dreamt about Garraway, a year to the day Ben had been killed, and the sketch she had made of him when she awoke. Carla stood up, and holding the picture she ran to her bedroom slamming the door behind her.

Richard didn't go after her. He didn't have the strength to stand up. Carla left him waiting in the lounge for over an hour before she came back downstairs.

He heard his daughter's footsteps as she reluctantly made her way down the stairs and watched as the lounge door slowly opened. She was silhouetted by the light in the hall as she stood in the doorway. He turned his head and his eyes followed her into the room. She stood with her back resting against the table, cleared her throat and then spoke.

She started at the very beginning. She described how she, Charlotte and the boys had climbed into the car which had been driven by Daniel Boyd. She told her father of how they ended up in the woods. Every few seconds she emphasized that she should never have been there and only went along because of Charlotte. She described what happened when Boyd saw Ben Walker kissing the girl and how Boyd had confronted him. Carla had never heard the conversation between Boyd and Walker so never knew why the fight had started.

Her father was horrified when she told him how the boys began attacking Walker and that this was the point which she had tried to break things up.

He listened without talking when she told him how the girl, Liz, had thrown her to the floor. Carla assumed that Liz thought that she had meant trouble, but she hadn't, she wanted the whole thing to end there and then. But it hadn't ended, things became worse, much worse. Richard winced when she told him in detail of John, the quiet and odd youth, and the way he relentlessly kicked the girl. She recalled how his large booted feet kicked her all over her body and her head.

Tears rolled down her face as she told her father how she remembered the dull thud of the rock cracking Ben Walker's skull, killing him instantly.

Finally he heard the part where she shouted 'police' and how everyone ran into the woods.

Ultimately she had saved Liz Mason's life.

"I know I should have told you, I know I should have gone straight to the police, but I was scared, I was so, so scared."

Her father looked at her in silence. Carla felt compelled to keep talking. It was like a deluge of emotions that had been pent up since the murder were allowed to overflow, like someone had opened the floodgates which had been holding back her emotions.

She cried uncontrollably as she tried to explain the strange things that had happened since the attack, but by now she was making no sense.

Richard had heard enough and raised his hand for her to stop talking.

"Are you going to turn me in?" asked Carla as she looked at her father through swollen red eyes.

Richard looked at his daughter, the girl he'd brought up, the girl who he'd tried his best to instil the essence of decent moral fibre. He couldn't believe what he'd just heard.

What had happened to the beautiful and innocent young girl she used to be?

Now it was Richard's turn to cry. The two of them cried together. At times they cried in unison, howling and wailing like banshees. They cried so loud, they could be heard by the neighbours in their houses across the road.

By midnight their tears were subsiding. The emotion of sorrow had changed to that of fear. Carla was scared, scared for her future.

"Tell me dad, what are you going to do? Are you going to turn me in?"

CHAPTER ONE HUNDRED AND THIRTY FIVE

The Offices of The Bristol Post
Temple Way
7.58am
Tuesday 19th June

Ian Lester waltzed into the open plan office complex like the cat that had swallowed the canary. He had written what was probably the most talked about story in the history of the Bristol Post.

Since the video had gone online, just under twenty four hours earlier, it had been viewed around the world over seven and a half million times. The Bristol Post had received over sixty messages from readers who either thought they knew the girl in the picture, or the killer based upon Ben's description. But none of those who'd contacted the newspaper had named either Carla Price or Daniel Boyd.

Lester slung his jacket on the back of his chair and sat at his desk.

Martha Ward, the journalist he sat closest to, popped her head over the partition which divided his work space from hers.

"Forster's gunning for you mate, she wants you in her office right away, and she's not looking happy."

Lester couldn't understand why Jennifer Forster, the managing director of West Media and News, the company which owned The Bristol Post, would be unhappy with him. The sales of the paper must have gone through the roof and as the story would unfold it would surely guarantee an increase in turnover. And what about the Post's website? Businesses would be clambering over each other to advertise on it.

He knocked on her office door which slowly swung open.

Forster was a short, slim woman in her mid-forties. She wore her dark hair in a ponytail and always had a pair of glasses propped on the top of her head, which she never seemed to use for reading. Lester wondered if she wore them purely as a fashion accessory.

As the door opened he could see she was on the phone. She glanced up at him, ended the telephone conversation and pointed to one of the seats in front of her desk. He entered her office, closed the door behind him and sat down.

"What the fuck to you think you're playing at?" said Forster in her East London accent.

Lester decided not to answer, not just yet. He was sure she had more to say and he thought it best for her to get everything off her chest before he said anything.

"I've just found out from Fin Saunders that we've been approached by Trinity Mirror, DMG Media, News UK to name a few, who all want to buy your story."

Lester was confused, surely this was a good thing.

"When I asked Martin Fergusson, your Chief Editor, in case you'd forgotten who he is, he'd no idea the story had even been printed."

She paused as she stood up. Lester had never seen Forster turn such a shade of red. He must have really upset her.

"You've taken it upon yourself to write a story and somehow sneak it in through the back door whilst not getting the authority of any of the editors. You may as well have written a story about aliens landing on College Green and snuck that one through as far as I'm concerned."

Lester opened his mouth to speak, but Forster got in first.

"Whatever possessed you to write such a ridiculous story, about an ongoing unsolved murder case without consulting either the Editor in Chief, or the police?"

Lester tried to speak again, but Forster raised her hand to stop him.

"I understand Munroe from Avon and Somerset has been shouting at Fergusson, wanting to know what the fuck's going on."

Lester attempted to talk again, and this time she let him.

"It's all true, everything I've written is true. None of it was fabricated. The video proves that."

"The video's been pulled," interrupted Forster.

"You've pulled the video? No, you mustn't."

"Whatever possessed you to print a story like this without consulting with anyone, not even the tea lady?"

"Because……..because no one would have allowed it to be printed," replied Lester confidently.

She stared at him in silence and cocked her head to one side. She looked like a confused puppy dog.

"You're right, it wouldn't have been printed……..for one of our top journalists you've just made a very serious mistake…….one which has cost you your job……….and unless he's very lucky, you've probably cost Fergusson his job too."

Lester said nothing as he sat in front of Forster, looking like a boy who had been sent to the headmistress.

"I've no option Ian, other than to relieve you of your position at this newspaper. And I won't be surprised if the police will be next in line to talk to you."

Ian shifted uncomfortably in his chair.

"Do I have the chance to explain myself?"

"You do, I suppose, for what it's worth……..but nothing's going to change……..you no longer work for me."

Lester took the opportunity to explain why he had done what he'd done. He knew he had to choose his words carefully, as he would have just the one chance to convince his boss that he should keep his job.

After he'd explained everything and told her of the importance of finding the girl whom Markland Garraway had dreamt about, the same girl who'd appeared in the back pages of the novel, Forster still hadn't changed her mind.

Lester accepted the fact that he was out of a job. He made one final plea to her, not that he was trying to get his job back, but because there was something he needed her to allow him to do.

"OK, I understand the position I have put you and Fergusson in, and I appreciate that you don't want me to work for you……but can I ask one thing……a favour?"

Forster's expression was one of anger.

"Favours, you want favours?"

"Not favours, just one, just the one favour."

Forster folded her arms and reluctantly let him continue.

"Please can you let me stay at my desk, just until say……Friday, the end of the week?"

"I told you that you're fired."

"I know, I won't be here to work and I won't expect you to pay me…..I just need to be in the office, by my phone."

Forster looked puzzled.

"I am certain that within the next few days, or maybe even by today, the girl in the picture will be identified and whoever it is that knows her will contact me at the Post. You see I need to be by my phone."

"And what happens if this dream girl turns up, what are you going to do then?"

"Tell Garraway, he's the first person who needs to know."

"But he's off the case, and from what I've been told, he's a mad man."

Lester ignored her comment.

"After Garraway's spoken with her, he will contact Colin Matthews, the detective whose case it is now, then Matthews will do what he has to do."

"Why wouldn't you contact Matthews first, after all, like you say, it's his case?"

"Because Matthews wouldn't understand, he's not been as involved in the case as much as Garraway, even though Garraway's been officially off the case for years."

"You really believe in all this hypnotism, reincarnation and all the other strange shit you say has been happening?" asked Forster with just a hint of empathy.

Lester nodded.

"OK, you can have access to your phone…..and your computer……and that's it, nothing else, not even the coffee machine."

"Thank you," said Lester after letting out a long sigh.

"Can I ask you something else?"

Forster looked at him with an expression of irritability.

"What if everything works out, you know, I get the girl and she names the killer and the case is closed…….do I get my job back?"

"Don't push your luck," replied Forster as she pointed to the door.

"Now get out and do what it is you have to do."

Lester left her office and closed the door behind him.

Jennifer Forster smiled as she sat alone in her office.

CHAPTER ONE HUNDRED AND THIRTY SIX

M32 motorway, approaching Bristol
10.37am
Tuesday 19th June

Richard Price and his daughter set off from Darlington at six o'clock that morning and had driven without stopping.

After last night's emotional set to, Carla and her father eventually spoke until the early hours. Richard had convinced her that going to the police was the right thing to do. If what she'd told him was true, then she'd have nothing to worry about. She'd done nothing other than withholding information from the police. Richard was sure, considering the circumstances, that the police would overlook this.

Eventually Carla saw sense and agreed with her father, with one caveat. Instead of going to the police, she would go straight to the newspaper, straight to the person who wrote the story and demand to speak with Markland Garraway.

Richard had agreed, although he didn't think she was in much of a position to demand anything, considering the secret she'd been keeping for almost three years.

The motorway ended and Richard was on Newfoundland Road, leading to the centre of Bristol. He took a left and headed towards the offices of The Bristol Post.

CHAPTER ONE HUNDRED AND THIRTY SEVEN

Bristol Bus Station
10.40am
Tuesday 19th June

Daniel John Boyd had travelled to Bristol on the early coach. He'd hung around Truro bus station all night waiting for the five thirty to Bristol.

During the marathon nonstop five hour journey he'd dozed in and out of sleep and in the few hours when he was awake he'd considered his options once he'd arrived in Bristol.

His plan was to stop the girl from talking. He had to get to her before she got to the police.

He wasn't sure how to find her, he couldn't remember her name and wasn't sure whether he had even known it in the first place.

He decided to head straight to Paul 'Greeny' Green's place and assuming he still lived at the same address, he intended to find out where Greeny's girlfriend Charlotte lived. The girl he was looking for had been Charlotte's best friend and he would *encourage her* to tell him where he could find her. He had enough tools in his rucksack to convince her not to go to the police. A sharp kitchen knife, a screwdriver and a hammer were more than enough to silence her forever.

He had picked up a copy of yesterday's Bristol Post which he'd found crumpled in the corner of the bus station when he stepped of the coach at Bristol. He ripped out page six and crammed it into the back pocket of the jeans he'd been wearing for the last three weeks.

The long journey had tired him and he headed toward the Galleries Shopping Centre in search of strong coffee to help sharpen his mind and allow him to focus on what he'd come here to do. After his brief break in the café he intended to get the number forty two bus and head over to Greeny's in the east of the city. As he sipped the bitter espresso, clarity suddenly gripped him. He pulled the creased newspaper page from his pocket, flattened it out on the table, avoiding the coffee which he'd spilt and read the story, the same story he'd seen on-line last night. Then it occurred to him where he should be heading, and it wasn't to Paul Green's house.

The final paragraph of the story, the one just above the picture of the girl, told him where he should be going.

DCI Garraway would like to speak to a girl who he believes can help the police with their enquiries. A drawing of the girl is shown below. If anyone knows the whereabouts of a girl matching the picture below, please contact DCI Garraway via Ian Lester at The Bristol Post. Anyone who contacts The Post will be dealt with in the strictest confidence.

Boyd needed to be at the offices of The Bristol Post. He knew that the sneaky goody two shoes bitch would cave in under pressure and hand herself in to the police and that she would follow the instructions in the news story. He knew she would turn up at the newspaper's offices in Temple Way and turn herself in. All he had to do was wait outside the offices and stop her.

But what if she'd already handed herself over? What would he do then? It was a chance he had to take. He hadn't seen the story on-line until yesterday evening and he was hoping that she wouldn't have either. He trusted his instincts and that she wouldn't have made an instant decision to go the paper. He was sure that she would have spent the night fretting over what she should do and then give herself up today.

He downed the last of his coffee and headed out of the shopping mall, across Castle Park and took the ten minute walk to the office complex on Temple Way.

By ten past eleven he was waiting by the side of the Stag and Hounds on the corner of Old Market Street and Temple Way, just fifty metres from the entrance to the offices. With his hoodie pulled over his head he stood menacingly in the shadow of the pub with a crystal clear view of everyone who went in and out of the building.

CHAPTER ONE HUNDRED AND THIRTY EIGHT

Temple Meads Railway Station car park
11.11am
Tuesday 19th June

Richard Price locked his Renault Megane and checked that the windows had been wound up. What he'd remembered about the car parks in Bristol meant that he was taking no chances with opportunistic thieves.

He held his daughter's hand and started the five minute walk to the head office of The Bristol Post.

Carla was shaking as she reluctantly made her way alongside Richard. She stopped in her tracks and turned to her father.

"But what shall I say?"

"Carla, we've discussed this over and over.......just tell them exactly what happened, tell them everything you told me last night."

At the age of just nineteen, Carla knew the life of freedom she'd become accustomed to was about to end, no matter how hard her father tried to convince her otherwise, she was certain she was going to prison.

Then she remembered that strange and eerie dream she'd had just over a month ago, the one just before her exams. In the dream she'd been in a court room and it had been the trial of Daniel Boyd for the murder of Ben Walker. Boyd had turned to her and told her she was going to prison for a very long time. But his name was different. He wasn't Daniel Boyd. She tried hard to remember what he said his name was. And then it came to her. He told her his name was Stanley, Stanley Jarrett.

Then she remembered how Garraway had also been in the dream. He had turned to her and said something, something reassuring. It was something to prepare her for now. She began to feel calmer as the words he'd said in her dream echoed in her ears.

"If you do as I say, there'll be no prison for you Carla."

She quickened her pace and turned to her father.

"Come on dad, let's get this over and done with."

Together, hand in hand, Richard and Carla approached the office building and were twenty five metres from the main entrance when Carla was overcome with a tremendous feeling of fear. She wasn't scared about what she was about to do, something else was scaring her. She felt an evil presence and whatever the presence was, it was very close, very close indeed.

Along with the evil presence, she sensed something else, something real, something tangible, something perceptible. It was a smell. She could smell an odour and it was foul. It smelt musty and of sweat, cigarettes, alcohol and old clothes. She'd smelt it before and she knew exactly when and where. It was the stale smell of Daniel Boyd.

"Dad, he's nearby," said Carla.

"He's nearby and he means me harm."

"Who is?"

"Daniel Boyd, the one who killed Ben Walker, he's coming to get me."

Richard tightened his grip on his daughter's hand as they continued towards the entrance of the building.

"Don't worry," said her father.

"If he's here I'll look after you," he added as the two of them tailgated a group of businessmen as they entered the offices of The Bristol Post.

CHAPTER ONE HUNDRED AND THIRTY NINE

Outside the Stag and Hounds
Temple Way, Bristol
11.18am
Tuesday 19th June

Boyd walked away from the side of the pub. He needed to get closer to the entrance of the offices. If he was going to get a clear view of the girl, he needed to be nearer.

He knew that when he saw her, he wouldn't have much time. Temple Way was a busy part of Bristol on a dual carriageway which was one of the main arteries in and out of the city centre. He had one shot at getting things right. He would distract her, grab her and pull her around the back of the building where there was a quiet lane, in which he could make sure she wouldn't repeat a word of what happened that night in Badock's Wood.

He edged closer to the offices, with his hood over his head. He had to be sure no one recognised him, as the description given by his murdered victim was spot on. It was so accurate that Boyd was nervous of anyone who glanced in his direction.

As he got nearer to the offices he saw a group of suits. Five stereotypical business types, carrying briefcases and computer bags slung over their shoulders.

Then he spotted the couple walking a few feet behind them.

He stopped in his tracks.

He was less that fifteen metres away and he recognised her in an instant. She looked exactly the same as she did the day he last saw her in the woods and she looked identical to the picture in the newspaper.

Now was the time, the time to carry out his plan. But she was with someone. He strained his eyes to see who it could be. It couldn't be a boyfriend, he looked far too old.

"Shit, that must her father," he said under his breath.

There was no way he could carry out his plan, no way at all. He stopped feet away from the revolving doors as the suits entered the building, directly followed by Carla and her father.

"Shit, fuck....shit, shit," he cursed to himself. Everything had gone exactly to plan, until now. He couldn't stick around. He had to get away. He needed a friend, someone who could keep him safe, someone who could hide him until things calmed down.

He knew exactly where to go. He turned back towards the Stag and Hounds and ran awkwardly towards Old Market Street and a rank of bus stops.

He didn't have to wait long until the number forty nine pulled up. He jumped aboard, paid the fare and sat at the back of the bus.

He was heading to Jarrett's Builders Merchants, the last place he'd worked before he'd upped sticks and disappeared to Cornwall. He desperately hoped that Stanley, the only man who ever seemed to care about him, still worked there.

CHAPTER ONE HUNDRED AND FORTY

The Bristol Post reception
11.23am
Tuesday 19th June

Carla and Richard had been patiently waiting whilst the flustered receptionist dealt with the short tempered business man who was clearly the man in charge of the other four men standing behind him.

"The meeting was definitely arranged for eleven thirty," argued the bald-headed fifty something man wearing a smart pinstriped suit.

The receptionist dialled another number and looked perplexed.

"We wouldn't have taken the train all the way from London for the fun of it now, would we?"

Richard felt sorry for the girl who was trying her best to help the man.

Eventually she replaced the receiver.

"Mr Dreyfuss is definitely not here sir, he's in a meeting all day. He's away in London."

"London…..London," shouted the bald man, "….what the hell is he doing in London, when he is supposed to be meeting with us?"

"I'll find out for you sir."

The receptionist was back on the phone asking more questions.

"He has a meeting with Lloyds Bank at eleven thirty…..sir," the receptionist told him nervously.

"Lloyds Bank……London?" the bald man was now shouting at the top of his voice and his angry words echoed around the marble walls of the reception area.

He abruptly turned to one of his 'yes' men and demanded that he checked his diary.

The 'yes' man pulled out his smart phone and started poking frantically at the screen. He looked red faced at the bald man and nervously spoke.

"Your online diary says the meeting was booked to take place at Lloyds sir, Threadneedle Street, in your office....sir."

"You mean to say we've traipsed all the way to Bristol when the meeting was in London, in my bloody office?"

The 'yes' man nodded nervously. The bald man looked embarrassed. The mix up had clearly been his fault.

He looked at the girl, smiled and appeared humiliated at the same time.

"Well I guess these things happen from time to time, we'd better be on our way."

The bald man scurried away along with his colleagues. The receptionist let out a sigh of relief as the last of the five men disappeared through the revolving doors and back towards the train station.

"Can I help you?" asked the girl as she looked at Richard who had just stepped up to the desk.

He was about to speak when the girl looked at Carla. The colour drained from her face when she saw his daughter standing alongside him.

She seemed more flustered now than when she did with the angry bankers.

Her voice was unsteady as she spoke.

"You've come to see Ian Lester," said the girl, not asking, but making a statement of fact.

Both Richard and Carla nodded.

Like the others who'd either read the story in the newspaper, or had viewed the video online, she'd seen the picture of Carla's face. In her case she'd seen it only thirty minutes earlier when she had read the story in yesterday's paper which had been lying around reception. She'd heard about the story the day before, but her computer went offline last night so she was unable to watch the clips. After seeing the report so recently the picture of the girl was fresh in her mind.

She grappled with her phone and at the same time looked up Lester's number on The Post's internal directory.

The receptionist turned away from Richard and Carla as she held her hand over the receiver and spoke quietly so as not to be heard. She replaced the phone and turned back to the father and daughter and told them to take a seat as Ian would be down shortly.

Richard and Carla hardly had a chance to sit down before Ian Lester walked out of the lift and hurriedly made his way to where they were sitting.

"Hi, I'm Ian Lester," he said as he offered his hand, first to the man and then to the teenaged girl.

When he looked at Carla it was as if he was seeing a ghost. She was the part of the puzzle which he'd been determined to help solve. He knew it was the same girl who'd been in the picture, the one that had mysteriously appeared in the back of Markland Garraway's novel.

Lester felt the hair stand up on the back of his neck as his hand made contact with the girl's. He shuddered as they shook hands and she could sense his nervousness. He let go of her clammy hand.

Ian Lester wasn't usually a man who was lost for words, but this morning he was flustered and wasn't sure what to say.

It was Richard who spoke first.

"We've travelled from Darlington, we left first thing, so on top of everything else, you can imagine both my daughter and I are rather tired."

"Sorry, how rude of me, can I get you something, a coffee or a tea?"

"A coffee would be great," said Richard and Carla nodded.

Lester jumped up and trotted over to the receptionist and asked her to organise some drinks for his guests.

As Lester was organising refreshments Carla had an impulsive urge to run away.

Lester returned and sat opposite them. He pulled a note pad and pen from his bag which was slung over his shoulder.

"Can I take your names, please?"

Richard and Carla told Lester who they were as he wrote down their names on his pad. He was trying to remain calm, but his shaking hand made his handwriting look like a spider had run across the page after dragging itself through a blot of wet ink.

"You've driven down from Darlington?" asked Lester, as he tapped his pen against his chin.

"Yes, we moved there a few years ago. My job required us to relocate," replied Richard.

"Just your job……..nothing else?" asked Lester.

Richard shook his head.

"OK, well first of all, thank you for contacting me, but as this is a police matter I need to let them know you are here. I will speak with Detective Matthews later, he's the one heading the murder case, but first of all I would like you to speak with someone else."

There was an awkward silence as Lester made a phone call. He stood up and walked towards the revolving doors as he waited for his call to be answered.

"Hi, it's Lester………..yes. She's here, the girl is here in reception with her father. He's driven her down from Darlington………..yes that's right Darlington. Her name is Carla Price……….and that's all I've asked. When can you get here? ……….Oh, OK. Yes I can bring them to you. Where are you, at work or at home? ………..OK, we'll be there soon."

Lester ended the call and walked back to the Carla and her father.

"I've just spoken with DCI Garraway, I'm sure you know who he is. He would like to speak with you, he'd prefer to meet you here……….. but he's unable to come to us, so I need to take you to him."

"To Markland Garraway?" asked Carla.

"Yes, he would like to meet you here, but unfortunately........."

"Unfortunately he doesn't walk well, he's on crutches," interrupted Carla.

"Yes..........how do you know?"

"I just do," she replied, shrugging her shoulders.

Carla recalled the vision of him. The one she'd seen in Darlington Railway Station earlier in the month.

"If you'd both like to follow me, my car isn't far away."

Carla and Richard stood up and followed Lester to his car.

There was silence as the three of them made their way to the car park. Lester's car was parked just feet away from Richard's.

Richard sat in the back, next to Carla as Ian drove to Markland Garraway's home.

Fifteen minutes later Lester was knocking on Garraway's door.

Carla could see a man through the frosted glass of the front door, slowly making his way along the hall. The door opened and Garraway stood hunched in the doorway. Carla's eyes met with his. Richard and Lester watched as tears welled in both the young girl's and the detective's eyes. Carla moved towards him and instinctively threw her arms around him and cried. Garraway winced with pain as the young girl held onto him. He patted her on the back in a reassuring manner. Carla stood back from Garraway and apologised.

"Please come in," said Garraway as he stood to one side to let the three of them into his house.

The four of them sat in his lounge.

"I've been waiting a long time to speak to you Carla," said Garraway.

"I know..........I should have come forward straight away..........but I was scared. You know, I should never have been there that night. I should have stayed at home."

"But if you did stay at home, that young woman would have probably died too..........it was you that saved her life."

"How do you know?"

"I know, because I saw what you did that night, how you stopped that fight..........and the good news is, Liz Mason woke up recently..........she's out of the coma."

Carla began to cry. Her father put his arm around her, then looked at Garraway.

"If you know so much about what happened that night, why haven't you caught the killer?"

"That's a very good question Mr Price, and it's something which is difficult to explain, but in a nutshell it all came to me in a dream."

Richard looked at him warily.

"The same kind of dreams I imagine your daughter has been having," he added.

Carla looked at her father and feigned a smile.

"Carla, I think you should tell me everything that's happened. Everything from the very beginning until the moment Ben Walker died. And then, I need you to tell me what happened after that night. I'd like to know what happened to you……….I think we have a lot in common."

Carla asked for a glass of water, cleared her throat and began. Ian Lester was poised with his pen ready to write down everything. He needn't bother, as Garraway had the voice recorder app running on his phone, ready to record everything Carla was about to say.

CHAPTER ONE HUNDRED AND FORTY ONE

Jarrett's Builders Merchants
12.05pm
Tuesday 19th June

Daniel Boyd stood across the road from the customer entrance of Jarrett's Builders Merchants. He knew Stanley was still working there as his red Volkswagen Golf was parked outside. The car was almost twenty five years old, but looked as though it was brand new. Stanley took immense pride in his car and cleaned and polished it three times a week.

Stanley was a creature of habit, and if nothing had changed since the last time Boyd saw him, Stanley would be taking a twelve o'clock lunch. He always did, providing he wasn't delivering. And when he did take lunch he would always sit on his own, in his car, eating his sandwiches and reading the Daily Mirror which he would buy from the newsagent across the way.

Boyd could see that all three of Jarrett's Hiabs and the flatbed were parked in the yard, so Stanley had to be around. Then he heard a familiar sound. He turned around to catch sight of him coming out of the newsagents with a paper in one hand and a sandwich in the other. Stanley was whistling Jerusalem. He always whistled that tune, especially at lunchtime. He'd told Boyd it was his favourite piece of music. Boyd watched as he walked over to his car and sat in the front passenger seat.

Boyd hurriedly crossed the road and tapped on the window. Stanley screwed his face as he tried to work out who was knocking on his window. Boyd indicated for him to wind it down.

"Stanley, it's me Daniel, Daniel Boyd..........how are you mate?"

Stanley nearly choked on his sandwich.

"What the hell, what happened to you? Everyone thought you'd died."

"Sorry, look it's a long story and I'll explain later. I've been working down south for the past few years, but as I said, I'll tell you about it later..........right now, I'm in a spot of bother and need somewhere to stay for a couple of days and wondered..........and wondered if I could stay at yours..........just for two or three days, and then I will be gone."

"What sort of bother are we talking about?" asked Stanley, sounding concerned.

"Nothing terrible, I've just upset someone, and I just need to lie low for a bit, until things blow over?"

"Is it drugs again?"

"Kind of."

Stanley sat quietly and contemplated what he should do.

CHAPTER ONE HUNDRED AND FORTY TWO

Markland Garraway's house
12.17pm
Tuesday 19th June

Carla took a large gulp of water and began to tell Markland Garraway everything that happened the night of Sunday the sixth September two thousand and nine. Garraway remained calm on the outside, but inside he was a bundle of nervous excitement.

"It all started when I was hanging around with Charlotte Williams……….she was my best friend. She was Paul Green's girlfriend. I started to hang around with Paul Green and his mates, as otherwise I wouldn't see very much of Charlotte."

"Was it Paul Green who murdered Ben Walker?" asked Garraway.

Carla shook her head and continued.

"We were hanging around the Foundation, with Greeny and his mates, Seb, Mossy and someone called………., what was his name? ……….John, his name was John……….do you know the Foundation?"

Garraway nodded.

"Who are Seb, Mossy and John, what are their surnames?"

"Oh, Mossy is Stuart Moss and Seb is……….., I don't know what Seb's surname is."

"How about John, what's his surname?"

Carla shook her head. "I never got to know him. He was an odd character. I think he fancied me, but he was odd, very odd."

"Was it one of these boys who killed Ben?"

"No, the one who killed him was called Daniel……….Daniel Boyd. And like I said just now, I should never have been involved with him."

Lester wrote in his notepad and underlined the name Daniel Boyd. Carla continued.

"Danny Boy turned up at the Foundation in a stolen car."

"Danny Boy?" asked Garraway.

"Yes, he liked to be called Danny Boy, but its Daniel Boyd I'm talking about."

Garraway nodded and asked her to carry on.

"He turned up in this big vehicle, it was obvious he'd stolen it, there was no way he could have owned it."

"What kind of car was it?"

"I don't know, I don't know very much about cars……….it was silver and big enough for all of us……….and more. It was really big."

Garraway mentally matched the people carrier she was describing with the stolen Toyota Previa found on the edge of Badock's Wood, the one that was reported stolen the night of Ben's murder.

"We all climbed in and Boyd drove us across the city. He was looking for trouble, he liked to fight……….I really wish I hadn't been there, it was horrible."

Carla was crying. Richard hugged his daughter to comfort her. Lester looked at Garraway and saw that he was holding back tears.

Carla took another mouthful of water, wiped her eyes and continued. Her voice was trembling as she described what happened next.

"I followed the boys into the woods, I was walking with Charlotte and John was behind us, he was always lagging behind……….Boyd was at the front, and we all trailed behind."

She stopped and gazed into the middle distance and then in a hushed, but defined tone of voice continued.

"And then it all began to happen."

"How did it start?" asked Garraway.

"Boyd saw the two kissing at the bottom of the hill on the edge of Badock's Wood."

Just hearing her say *'the hill on the edge of Badock's Wood'* made Garraway shudder and feel nauseous.

"Boyd was intent on causing trouble, he wanted to fight the boy……….Ben. He walked over to the boy on his own, the others stayed back. They spoke, I didn't hear what they were saying and then the next thing I saw was Boyd hitting the girl ……….Liz, but she hit him harder and he fell to the ground."

Carla stopped again and drank the last of her water, Richard went to the kitchen and refilled the glass. She waited for her father to return before she continued.

"Now, Boyd and the boy, Ben, where fighting and Ben was on top of Boyd, but then Greeny, Mossy and Seb came over and started kicking the shit out of Ben."

She glanced at her father and apologised for swearing.

"This is when I wanted everything to stop, I ran over to the girl and I wanted me and her to intervene, somehow I thought the two of us could stop everything."

"Where was your friend, Charlotte, when this was going on?" asked Garraway,

She shook her head.

"I don't remember, she must have stayed out of the way, I think she may have been with John."

"So John wasn't attacking Ben?"

Carla shook her head.

"No, he didn't touch Ben."

She started to cry again, but quickly composed herself.

"I started shouting at Liz, trying to get her attention so we could do something together and stop the fight, but she must have misunderstood and she threw me to the ground..........and then..........and then that's when John started attacking her."

"Why do you think he did that?"

"I think he fancied me, perhaps he was trying to protect me, but he was relentless, he just wouldn't stop kicking her. He kicked her over and over again, I thought he would never stop, it was horrible, I couldn't bear to watch..........and then I looked at Ben..........I saw Boyd, with a rock, holding it over his head..........and then..........and then."

Carla could no longer speak, she couldn't compose herself this time, she was crying uncontrollably. She was crying more than she had done last night when she had told her father what had happened. Perhaps it was because Garraway was there, the whole thing seemed clearer, as if it had happened the day before, everything seemed so fresh in her mind. Garraway was next to speak.

"This is when you shouted 'police', when you made everyone one run, they ran into the woods didn't they?"

Carla's tears briefly subsided, which gave her an opportunity to speak.

"Yes, how did you know?"

"So it was too late for Ben, Daniel Boyd had killed him, but when you shouted 'police', and there were no police, everyone stopped what they were doing and ran, and this is what, I think, saved Liz's life."

Carla nodded and then said something which took Garraway, Lester and Richard by surprise.

"It may have saved Liz's life, but that doesn't mean much now. I don't think she'll be alive for very much longer."

"Why, why would you think that?"

"Mr Garraway, I think you know as well as I do, there is something about all of this that gives you some kind of sixth sense, you see things, you know things are going to happen."

"It's the hill," replied Garraway.

"There's something about the hill in the woods, it has immense power and it's what's drawn you to me and it's what's drawn the soul, or the spirit or whatever is left of Ben Walker to the little boy in the hypnotist's chair."

Richard stood up and spoke.

"Please can you give Carla a break, she's told you everything she knows."

"For now," replied Garraway, "but I'm afraid she's going to have to go over everything again……….you see I'm no longer in charge of the case."

"Why not?" asked Richard.

"It made me ill, very ill. You see me now, bent over and walking on crutches. I wasn't like this until I headed up Ben's murder case. I've had a nervous breakdown and I am now unfit to be a detective."

"So my daughter needs to do this again?"

Garraway nodded.

"Detective Matthews, who is now in charge of the case will need to speak with her, this is unofficial, with him it will be official………..but before he becomes involved I need to speak with your daughter a little more. There are things we both need to discuss, if not for any other reason than to confirm that neither of us have gone insane."

Carla looked at Garraway and nodded.

CHAPTER ONE HUNDRED AND FORTY THREE

Southmead Hospital
12.50pm
Tuesday 19th June

Anne Mason pressed the orange call button by the side of her daughter's bed as Liz screamed. She was holding her head with both hands and screaming in pain.

Two nurses quickly came over and Anne stood to one side.

"She's in pain, she's says it's her head," said Anne frantically.

Liz was rolling from side to side in her hospital bed, holding her head and screaming at the top of her voice. The nurses were trying to talk to her, but Liz didn't even seem to know they were there.

Dr Edison came running over.

"She needs a sedative, and quickly," he said authoritatively.

One of the nurses went away and quickly returned with a syringe and a phial, which she handed to the doctor. He injected the solution and waited for her to calm down.

"What's wrong, what's the matter with her?" demanded Anne.

"It's probably just an after effect of her brain injury. But I think we should arrange an MRI scan, just to be sure."

"Why, what could it be?" cried Anne.

"Please, please calm down Mrs. Mason, your daughter has suffered a traumatic brain injury, this is why she's been in a coma for so long. The MRI scan will show whether there is anything we've not picked up, you know, belts and braces, just to be sure."

Anne held her daughter's hand as she lay calmly and slept peacefully.

CHAPTER ONE HUNDRED AND FORTY FOUR

Stanley Brown's house
12.55pm
Tuesday 19th June

"Here's the spare key. Let yourself in, make yourself a brew, put the television on, but don't touch anything else," said Stanley as he let Daniel into his house.

Stanley lived alone, his wife had died seven years ago. His two children were grown up and had children of their own. They both lived in London.

"Thank you, thank you, thank you, thank you," said Boyd.

"I need to go, otherwise I'll be late……….remember don't touch anything."

Boyd nodded and thanked him again. He watched him get into his Golf and drive away. He closed the door and slumped into Stanley's easy chair.

"What the fuck am I going to do?"

CHAPTER ONE HUNDRED AND FORTY FIVE

Markland Garraway's house
1.01pm
Tuesday 19th June

Garraway let out a big sigh as Carla dried her eyes.

"How did you know about me, where did you get that picture from?" asked Carla.

"This is what I wanted to speak to you about," replied Garraway.

He asked Lester to hand him the Dostoevsky novel from the shelf. He turned it to the back page, the blank page onto which he'd written the details of the dream he'd had a year to the day that Ben was murdered. He flattened the page and passed the book to Carla.

"Read that, and tell me what you think."

She saw the sketch of her on the opposite page, and resisted the urge to look at it. Carla read the account of the events on the night of the murder and also the description of her.

"Did you write this?"

Garraway nodded.

"And did you draw this?" said Carla, pointing to the sketch.

Garraway looked at her with a blank expression.

"I've absolutely no idea, I can't see how I did, I can't draw."

"This description, it's pretty much as it happened on the night, how did you know?"

"It came to me in a dream, a year to the very day Ben was murdered."

Carla placed the book on the table and stared blankly into space, then turned to Garraway.

"That was the night I dreamt of you, I dreamt that you were in the woods, at the time of the attack."

"That sounds about right," said Garraway in a nonchalant tone of voice.

"So how did the picture of me get there, if you didn't do it?"

Garraway explained to Carla how he came to find the book, on the table with the sketch of her ready for him to see.

She examined the picture and ran her fingers over the pen marks, following the flow of the lines that made up the exact likeness of her.

"I think I know who drew this."

No one spoke as she gazed at the picture.

"I think I drew it," she said as she placed the book on the table.

"What do you mean?" asked her father.

She picked the book up and handed it to him.

"See for yourself, that's one of mine."

Richard looked at it. He didn't want to admit it, but he had to agree, it was exactly like one of her sketches, it was the same style, the way the pen had danced, almost carelessly across the paper. It was Carla's style without a doubt.

"Mr Garraway, I don't know how, but I think I was trying to lead you to me."

Lester had stopped writing and watched in awe as Carla and Garraway spoke, he quickly snapped out of it and scribbled what had just been said.

Garraway and Carla spent the next five minutes comparing the strange things that had happened to them since the night of the murder.

"So what about the little boy, the one in the video, how did he get mixed up in all of this?" asked Carla.

"Well, he's the key to it all. He was born at the precise moment that rock came crashing down on Ben's head. The second he died, was the time Christopher Jameson, the little boy in the video, was born."

"How can you prove that, you can't know the time Ben was killed?"

"We can, and we do. His watch broke at the time the rock smashed down upon him. We know he was hit several times with that rock, and his watch broke just before he died, it must have smashed when he was hit before the final blow."

Carla shuddered.

"So Ben's been waiting patiently inside the little boy, waiting for the chance to be heard?"

"That's the way I see it."

She grabbed another tissue, wiped her eyes and shook her head.

Garraway took hold of his crutches and stood up. What he was about to announce, he needed to say with an air of authority. He didn't think that sitting, crumpled in a chair made him look as though he was in charge.

"Carla, I think you know what's coming next."

She nodded.

"I am going to call Colin Matthews. The two of us don't see eye to eye and I think he's going to be more than a little surprised when I tell him you're here, and I don't think he'll be very happy about the circumstances which have lead you to me."

He picked up his phone from the table, still with the voice recorder app running, and called Matthews's mobile number.

"Colin, its Markland."

"You bastard Garraway, what the hell do you think you're playing at? ………. I've spent the last hour in Munroe's office because of you……….and he's after you sunshine, he's really after your guts."

"That doesn't surprise me……….any way, I have something useful for you, something a little more, let's say real."

"What is it, the rotting corpse of Ben Walker, telling you how he died?"

"No, not quite Colin."

Matthews cringed as he heard Garraway's patronising tone, which was something about him he'd always disliked.

"Do you remember the girl in the picture, well I'm sure you do, she's famous now……….well she's as real as you and I, and what's more she's here with me, in my house………."

"You've lost it big time, you really fucking have."

"Would you like to speak with her?"

"What?"

"I said would you like to speak to her, she's here in my lounge."

Garraway passed the phone to Carla who reluctantly took it and placed it to her ear.

"Hello?"

"Who's this?"

"My name's Carla, Carla Price……….and I'm ……….I'm the girl in the picture."

Matthews listened to the frail voice of the young girl and could sense how uneasy she was.

"I was there, in the woods, I was there the night that Ben Walker died……….and I know……….."

She paused to compose herself.

"And I know who killed him."

"Pass the phone back to Garraway," shouted Matthews.

Carla handed the phone back to him.

"I don't know what you're up to now, but you're in the shit even deeper and Munroe's going to ………."

"Shut the fuck up and listen to me," interrupted Garraway.

"I suggest you send a car around to my place right now, Carla's giving herself over to you of her own accord, and I suggest that you come too."

Matthews sensed by the tone in Garraway's voice that he was deadly serious. Even if the girl wasn't who she said she was, both she and Garraway could be arrested for wasting police time. He grunted an inaudible retort and ended the call.

"I told you he wouldn't be happy."
Carla looked at Garraway. She was tired and scared.
"What's going to happen?"
"Matthews will interview you."
"Will I go to prison?" she asked in a trembling voice.
"No, I really don't think you will."
"Why?" asked Lester and Richard in unison.
"Because I will refer Matthews to Section 71 of the Serious Organised Crime and Police Act."
Carla looked at Garraway and he continued to explain.
"As you will be assisting the police as an offender, Matthews can exercise immunity from prosecution."
The room fell silent.
"Basically, you can't give evidence which could lead to the conviction of a criminal, and be prosecuted at the same time."
"Would anyone fancy a coffee whilst we wait for the boys in blue?" said Garraway as he hobbled towards the kitchen.

Fifteen minutes later two police cars and a silver Audi A6 pulled up outside Garraway's house. Two police officers got out of each of the marked cars and Colin Matthews hauled himself from the Audi. Garraway watched from the window and noticed how much extra baggage Matthews seemed to be carrying, more so than when he saw him earlier in the month.

Ian Lester opened the door as the four officers and Matthews made their way along Garraway's driveway.

Matthews was furious and his erratic driving to Garraway's house had reflected his frame of mind. Garraway had gone too far this time, he had no idea what kind of elaborate hoax he was up to, but clearly the man was completely deranged. Not only had he somehow managed to get the local paper to print a fabricated story, he'd also somehow convinced someone to pretend to be the dream girl.

Matthews pushed in front of the officers and was the first to enter Garraway's house. He walked into the lounge and saw the scared teenager who was sitting next to the table amongst a pile of used tissues. Next to her was a man, in his forties, he had his arm around her and appeared to be comforting her. The man had clearly been crying as his eyes were bloodshot.

"Hello Colin, I'm glad you could join us. Let me introduce you to a few people."

He lifted his hand and motioned to Carla.

"This is Carla Price, you spoke to her earlier and beside her is her father Richard, they've driven down from Darlington this morning, and this is Ian Lester, he's the journalist from The Bristol Post who wrote the story."

Matthews recognised the young reporter.

"Aren't you the journalist the News and Information Team use?"

Lester nodded.

"That's right, I deal with your guys and a lot of your press."

Suddenly things seemed real. Matthews looked at the girl, her father and the journalist. Something about the set up appeared to be genuine. He wasn't sure whether it was the atmosphere in the room, or the look upon the girl's face or something else.

"So you're Carla Price and you were there at the time Ben Walker was murdered?"

Carla nodded.

"And you say that you know who killed him?"

She nodded again.

"Why have you left it so long until you called the police?"

"I was scared, I've been scared of what would happen to me ever since Ben was murdered."

"She didn't call the police, we went straight to the newspaper," said her father.

"OK, you need to come with me, I'm arresting you for Impeding a Police Investigation……….You have the right to remain silent. Should you, however, refuse this right, anything you say can and will be used against you in a court of law. You have the right to an attorney. If you cannot afford an attorney, one will be provided to you by the court. Do you understand what I have just said to you?"

Carla nodded, stood up and was lead to one of the marked police cars by two of the officers. Her father followed behind.

Matthew's looked at Garraway and said nothing as he turned to leave the house.

"Colin, remember Assisting Offender under Section 71 of the Serious Organised Crime and Police Act 2005," said Garraway tapping the side of his head with his finger, like a school teacher who was reminding a pupil of something.

Mathews turned to him and looked at him blankly.

"Use your discretion, immunity from prosecution and all that."

Colin Matthews didn't reply. He turned around, shook his head and walked away.

CHAPTER ONE HUNDRED AND FORTY SIX

Trinity Road Police Station
Bristol
8.38pm
Tuesday 19th June

Carla sat alone and scared on the mattress in Custody Cell number eight. It had been a long day and she was tired and exhausted. Her body was so tense it ached. She thought about all the events that had happened in less than twenty four hours and started to sob again. She had done an awful lot of crying since last night.

She had told Detective Matthews everything that had happened in the woods. She named Paul Green and Stuart Moss who were already known to the police because, since the murder of Ben Walker, they had both been arrested for minor drug offences and theft. Later that day they were arrested and would also be questioned by Matthews.

Matthews hadn't been interested in hearing any of Carla's dreams, or anything of a supernatural nature. He only wanted to hear what he considered tangible information. He needed solid concrete evidence which would lead to the arrest of Ben's killer.

Carla also named Charlotte Williams and gave Matthews her address.

She provided enough information in her description of Daniel Boyd to produce an e-fit image. Carla was staggered with how well it came out. The image was just as she remembered him, which was just how he looked today.

She described Seb and John, but her memory of them wasn't so good and she wasn't sure whether the e-fit images were very accurate. It had been almost three years since she'd seen them and her mind was fogged by the passing of time.

Carla had given enough detailed information to convince Matthews that she'd been there when Ben Walker had been murdered. He had put the supernatural mumbo jumbo to one side and concentrated on the information she had provided.

He had arranged for the News and Information Team to get the e-fit and Daniel Boyd's details on evening regional news. He'd been too late to get a slot on the early news programme, but would have a slot on the ten pm BBC Points West news.

Carla lay on the mattress and pulled the blanket over her. Although it was June, the cell was cold. She shivered and tried to make herself comfortable on the lumpy plastic bed. As unpleasant and uncomfortable as it was, within two minutes of covering herself with the blanket Carla was in a deep sleep.

CHAPTER ONE HUNDRED AND FORTY SEVEN

Stanley Brown's house
10.04pm
Tuesday 19th June

Stanley and Boyd sat next to each other on the settee in Stanley's small lounge. He had cooked a meal for Boyd, which was gratefully received. Stanley had asked Boyd to make a pot of tea whilst he searched for something to watch on television before it was time for bed.

During the meal Stanley had asked where he'd been hiding. Boyd was cagey and Stanley sensed he didn't wish to discuss his recent past. Boyd told Stanley he'd been doing odd jobs down south and Stanley didn't ask any further questions.

Boyd came in from the kitchen holding a tray on which was a pot of tea, two mugs, a jug of milk and a saucer of biscuits. He almost tripped over his rucksack which was on the floor by the side of the settee.

Stanley put on the BBC news as Boyd yawned.

"Not a fan of the news I suppose?" asked Stanley.

"Not really, I never really watch it. I read a paper now and again, you know, The Sport."

Stanley laughed.

"That's not a real newspaper, that's all titillation, you know, boobs and bums. You need to find out what's really going on."

Boyd yawned again.

"The word news comes from North, East, West and South, it means information from everywhere…….., you should watch it more often and then you might learn a thing or two about the world."

Boyd laughed as he dunked a hobnob into his tea.

Boyd froze as he watched the anchor man announce the details of the next story.

"Police are looking for someone who is wanted for the murder of a man in Bristol back in September two thousand and nine."

"The attack happened in Badock's Wood, near the Doncaster Road entrance. Ben Walker, who was twenty one at the time, was brutally attacked and killed, and his girlfriend, Elizabeth Mason, was also attacked but was discovered to be alive the following morning by a passer by. Miss Mason had remained in a coma until recently."

"A witness has come forward and provided new evidence and details of a man who is wanted by the police."

The e-fit image, based on Carla's description appeared on the television screen.

As the announcer continued Boyd put down his mug and slipped his hand inside his rucksack which was on the floor beside the settee.

He looked at Stanley who was watching the report intently but as yet hadn't realised the e-fit was of Daniel Boyd.

Boyd rummaged around in his rucksack and felt the handle of the long screwdriver he'd put there the day before.

"The wanted man is Daniel John Boyd, and police are advising the public not to approach him, but to contact the police with any information which could lead to his arrest."

It took a couple of seconds for Stanley to comprehend what he had just seen and heard. Boyd pulled the screwdriver from the rucksack and before Stanley knew what was happening Boyd had plunged the tool deep into the man's chest.

He felt Stanley's ribs crack as the screwdriver crunched into his chest.

Stanley recoiled and yelled as Boyd pulled the screwdriver out of his bleeding chest and rammed it in a second time. He repeated the attack seven times until he punctured his heart.

Within twenty five seconds of hearing Daniel Boyd's name announced on television, Stanley Maurice Brown, aged sixty two lay dead, slumped on his settee, with a spilt mug of tea on his lap and a screwdriver protruding from his chest.

Blood was everywhere. Over the floor, over the settee and over Boyd.

Boyd panicked and stood up holding his hands against the side of his head. He hadn't planned to murder Stanley, the only man that had ever seemed to care for him, it had been an instinct, an instant reaction to protect himself.

He spotted Stanley's keys on the sideboard, which included the key to his beloved Golf. Boyd hobbled over, picked up the keys and fled the house.

He scurried across the road to where Stanley had parked the car, unlocked it, struggled clumsily to release the crook lock, started the car and drove away into the night.

CHAPTER ONE HUNDRED AND FORTY EIGHT

Southmead Hospital
10.19pm
Tuesday 19th June

Dr David Edison was reviewing the results of Liz Mason's MRI scan. She had been scanned earlier that day after complaining about excruciating pains in her head. She had been given a sedative but after it had worn off she had awoken and again she had been rolling around her bed in agony.

Edison was shocked when he saw the images from the scan.

There was a tumour in Liz's head which was huge. He couldn't understand why she'd only just begun to feel the pain since she'd woken from the coma on Friday.

He knew it was malignant due to its irregular border which was invading the normal tissue around it with finger like projections. Edison was sure it would be difficult, if not impossible to remove.

He sat back in his chair, took off his glasses and rubbed his eyes. He pondered how Liz and her family would take the news. He would speak to them in the morning after consulting with his peers.

Again, he looked at the image of the intimidating white blob standing out against the grey of her brain and knew she didn't have very long to live.

CHAPTER ONE HUNDRED AND FORTY NINE

East Bristol
10.24pm
Tuesday 19th June

Boyd was driving erratically through the streets of Bristol. It was almost half past ten, and he was driving with no lights. His mind was a maze of confusion and panic and he'd not thought about turning them on.

He didn't have a licence as he'd never taken a driving test. He hadn't even taken a lesson and had taught himself to drive in stolen vehicles shortly after being expelled from school years earlier. His driving was awful. He'd not sat behind the wheel of a car since the night he stole Paul Jackson's Previa, the night he'd murdered Ben.

He was heading for the M32 motorway and out of Bristol. He had no idea where he should go. Back to Cornwall? Wales? Or perhaps somewhere totally different? Then he decided that he would aim the car north on the M5 and just drive. He looked at the petrol gauge and saw he had a full tank. If he was lucky he had enough fuel to get him as far as Scotland. Surely he'd be far enough away if he made it there.

He headed towards Junction two of the M32 where he would join the motorway to start his new life as far away as Stanley's Golf would get him.

He was driving at just over forty miles an hour when he sped through red lights outside the Queens Head Pub and as he did, he was broadsided by a Ford Mondeo coming from his left. The Golf skidded sideways and stopped on the opposite side of the road causing oncoming traffic to screech to a halt. The crash was witnessed by over twenty people who were enjoying a beer on benches outside the pub overlooking the main road.

Boyd staggered from the car. He was dazed and had a deep cut on his forehead. Blood ran into his eyes making it difficult to see where he was going. He lurched onto the pavement. The blood from his cut was running down the side of his face and onto his T-shirt mixing with Stanley's.

Although he was confused, he could make out the entrance to Eastville Park, which was twenty feet from where he was desperately flailing. He swayed from side to side as he staggered towards the entrance of the park.

Jason Anderson and his group of friends saw the crash as they sat outside the pub. There was a lot of shouting and confusion as the accident happened. Within seconds the driver of the blue Mondeo was hauled from his car by two men just before it burst into flames.

Anderson spotted the tall and wiry frame of Boyd as he disappeared into the darkness of the park. He jumped up, along with two others, sprinted over the road and chased after Boyd, who was awkwardly running away from the scene of a crime.

There were no lights in the park and Boyd was nowhere to be seen. Anderson and his friends stopped in their tracks.

"He can't be far away," whispered Anderson.

He was right, Boyd had entered the park barely fifteen seconds earlier. He was hurt and disoriented, but the park was so dark it was difficult to see anything other than the trunks of the tall trees and the bushes which lined the edges.

Martin Williams, who was standing next to Anderson opened his mouth to speak, but Anderson raised his hand to stop him.

"Listen," said Anderson and his two friends strained to hear to what he was referring.

A desperate panting could be heard coming from their right, it wasn't much louder than a whisper, but they could all hear it.

"Over there," whispered Williams as the three of them crept towards the bottom of a large horse chestnut tree.

The sight was pitiful. Boyd was crouched against the tree. Blood ran down his face and he looked terrified.

Anderson turned on the torch app on his phone and shone it in Boyd's face. He covered his eyes with his bloodied hand to shield himself from the light.

"Don't hurt me, please don't hurt me," whimpered the pathetic young man.

Anderson and Williams hauled him up and marched him across the road to the pub.

Boyd's ears were buzzing and his head was aching as he could hear the distant sound of police sirens.

Boyd's past had finally caught up with him.

CHAPTER ONE HUNDRED AND FIFTY

Southmead Hospital
3.29pm
Wednesday 20th June

Dr David Edison had the unenviable duty of advising Anne and Terry Mason of the brain tumour which had been revealed by yesterday's MRI scan.

Earlier that day he had consulted with oncology specialist, Dr Dwivedi, who confirmed that Liz Mason's tumour was inoperable and her life expectancy, although he could not be wholly accurate, would be more likely to be weeks rather than months, and possibly days.

He had just given the solemn news to Liz's parents who were understandably beside themselves with grief.

"Why, why, why?" repeated Anne as she cried uncontrollably into a handkerchief.

Dr Edison had delivered news like this on numerous occasions, but the gravity of the grief made it hard for him to deal with, and he was finding it hard not show his emotions.

"Are you sure there's nothing that can be done?" asked Terry.

Edison slowly shook his head.

There was no way of dressing things up to make the news any easier to deliver. It was his professional obligation to give the facts as they were.

He passed a plastic cup of water to Anne. Her grief overwhelmed her so, that she didn't see him pass it to her.

Later he would speak to them again to discuss the fundamentals of what would happen over the coming weeks, but for now he needed to let the news sink in.

Liz had only been awake for around thirty minutes and had drifted back to sleep and was oblivious to the unwelcome news that Edison had delivered to her parents.

"Do you think we should tell her?" asked Anne.

Edison paused before he spoke, he needed to choose his words carefully.

"You don't, but I have an obligation to do so."

"But if she's not got long left, why should she need to know, you said it could be just a matter of weeks..........couldn't those last few weeks be as happy as possible for her, without her having to know?"

Edison chose not to reply. He'd noticed how little Liz had been awake today. By now it was mid-afternoon and she'd been awake for less than an hour. He wouldn't be surprised if she would spend less and less time conscious and coherent and the need to actually tell her may never arise.

At times like this David Edison hated his Job

.

CHAPTER ONE HUNDRED AND FIFTY ONE

Markland Garraway's home
7.07pm
Wednesday 20th June

Garraway reached for the remote and turned off the television. He had just watched the regional news, and although he already knew about the arrest of Daniel Boyd, the news provided the confirmation he needed.

Watching the reporter describe the accident involving the stolen Volkswagen Golf and how Boyd had been apprehended by members of the public made the hard work of the last few weeks seem worthwhile. His only grudge was that he wasn't there to see him hauled in.

His body ached as he reached for his mug of tea, but he noticed the arthritis in his wrist seemed a little less agonising than normal.

He finished his drink and saw the Dostoevsky novel on the sideboard. He slowly got up, walked over to the book and picked it up to put it back on the shelf. He turned to the back pages of the book, where the picture of the girl and the description of his dream were and read the words again. If he'd read them once, he must have read them fifty times. He looked at the picture of Carla which had mysteriously appeared. He'd probably never know how it got there. The accuracy of the sketch was amazing. It was spot on. Each pen stroke had captured every detail of the girl's face, right down to the look of sadness in her eyes.

Then he spotted something he'd not noticed before. About an inch below the sketch, in the bottom right hand corner of the page, was a small ink mark, at first he thought it was a squiggle. He reached for his glasses for a clearer view. He held the book close to his face, until he could focus on it. It was something other than a random blob of ink, or a misguided pen stroke, although he couldn't quite make out what it was.

He opened a drawer in the sideboard and searched for a magnifying glass. He found it wedged at the back of the drawer and pulled it out.

He looked again as the glass magnified the pen stroke.

He concentrated and then it became clear what it was. It wasn't one pen mark, it was two. It was two letters. C and P.

"They're initials," he said to himself.

He looked again and spoke the two letters out loud.

"C and P."

He thought about what they could stand for.

And then it came to him as he said to himself.

"Carla Price."

He put the book down and smiled.

CHAPTER ONE HUNDRED AND FIFTY TWO

The Custody Cells
7.34pm
Wednesday 19th June

Daniel John Boyd sat in the corner of the cell alone and scared. He had spent the day being interrogated by Colin Matthews.

At first he denied any involvement with the murder of Ben Walker, but could not explain how traces of his blood had ended up on the rock which had been used to kill Ben, nor could he explain how saliva, matching his DNA ended up in the hair of the dead man.

He shivered as he thought about his wasted life. Stanley had once told him that a person makes their own luck happen. Perhaps this was true. Most of what had happened to Daniel Boyd was of his own making. Until now, his life hadn't been great and from what he could imagine, the rest of it wasn't going to be much better.

He sometimes thought that if it wasn't for bad luck, he would have no luck at all.

Just after midday on Wednesday nineteenth of June, two thousand and twelve, Daniel Boyd was charged with the murder of Ben Walker.

The following day he would also be charged with the murder of Stanley Maurice Brown.

CHAPTER ONE HUNDRED AND FIFTY THREE

Maria and Campbell's flat
10.07am
Saturday 23rd June

Maria and Campbell were relaxing in their lounge, each with a cup of coffee as Christopher sat in his highchair and was slowly demolishing a rusk whilst watching Balamory on children's TV.

The events of the week had not quite sunk in. Things had happened so fast. From the report of their son in The Bristol Post, to the girl in the picture coming forward and to the arrest of Ben's murderer the following day.

Maria was mortified to hear of the death of the old man, Stanley, and felt partly responsible as it seemed to be connected with the events leading up to Daniel Boyd's arrest.

"Well I guess we should be getting on with things," said Campbell as he stood up and carried his mug to the kitchen.

Maria sighed.

"To be honest, I could sit here all day long."

Christopher giggled at what he was watching on the television.

Ben Walker felt a strange sensation, one he'd not experienced first-hand since before he had died. At first it scared him and then it excited him. It was taste. He was experiencing the sensation of taste, and not just a memory of it.

There was no misty swirling light, so he wasn't expecting to hear Tom Judd's booming voice coming through the haze. But he could hear something. Voices, he could hear lots of voices. Scottish accents and people singing. Ben was confused.

All of a sudden there were images, he could see all around. He couldn't work out where they were coming from. They were moving, the images were moving. But they weren't his memories, they meant nothing to him.

He could see a room, a neatly decorated room which looked like somebody's home. There were pictures on the wall, and magazines on the floor. He attempted to change the angle of his view and found he was able to look up. He could see the ceiling. He looked a little to the right and saw a window and the light coming through was illuminating the room.

He turned the view to the left and saw there was a television. The Scottish voices were coming from the television.

Shit, this is real time, he thought.

He looked down and saw a plastic tray, which was covered in soggy bread and stains. There was a blue plastic child's beaker on the tray. He looked downward a little further and saw a small hand holding a partially eaten biscuit.

He looked across to his right where he could see a lady in her late twenties and she was looking towards the window.

He heard a voice, a man's voice, with a soft Southern Irish accent. His voice was friendly and it was coming from behind.

"Maria, how about hauling your lazy arse off the settee and getting Christopher ready and I'll crack on with clearing the kitchen?"

"OK, OK, give me another couple of minutes."

Ben looked down at the tray and then at the hand. The biscuit dropped onto the plastic tray. He stared at the soggy mess and found he was able to move the hand up and down and from left to right. He pushed out the forefinger and poked it into the partially eaten gooey rusk on the tray.

He could feel the sensation of touch as the finger rubbed against the plastic. He looked for the other hand, but couldn't see it. He strained to the right and looked down and saw a shoulder. He followed it down to an arm, which disappeared under the plastic tray of the highchair. Ben yanked the arm up from beneath the tray and held it high. He examined the small hand and swivelled it to look at the palm.

Shit! he thought as he was suddenly struck by what was happening.

I'm looking through the boy's eyes, I'm controlling Christopher.

Ben was frightened and didn't know why this was happening. Then it occurred to him. It must be reincarnation. This must be what happens when a person dies and becomes reincarnated in the next life.

This wasn't what he wanted. He didn't want to spend another life living like this, with the mind and memories of an adult whilst cocooned in a growing child.

The adults, they had to be Christopher's parents.

Then he heard more talking.

"How many years do you think he'll get?" said the woman.

"I don't know, it's double murder, he'll get life for sure," replied the Irishman.

"What about the girl, Carla, do you think she'll go to prison?"

"Perhaps? Perhaps not. If it wasn't for her, Liz Mason would almost certainly have been killed along with Ben."

Ben heard the words, this could only mean one thing, his murderer had been caught.

But why was this happening, why had he suddenly become Christopher?

He decided to try something and just the thought of doing it terrified him. He looked around the room and again towards the woman. He looked back at the television and watched as the titles came up on the screen. The programme had just ended. He focused on the television and concentrated with all his might and then he did it. He made an audible noise through Christopher's mouth. He had coughed, he had purposely coughed.

Ben was surprised how easy it was to do it, so he did it again, and again, and again and then the woman stood up. He heard her call in an urgent tone.

"Campbell, quick, I think Christopher's choking on something."

She stood over him and looked directly into his face. Ben tried to stop coughing, but once he'd started he found it difficult to stop.

"Campbell, hurry up."

Ben heard the sound of feet racing in from behind and saw the face of a man. He had dark hair and a warm face. He had full view of both of the boy's parents. He saw Maria's pretty face and red hair.

Then the coughing stopped. He felt the sensation as the woman, Maria, rubbed her hand between his shoulders.

Ben really did have full control over Christopher's body. For some reason he had taken it over.

This must be happening for a reason thought Ben.

So his murderer had been caught. He'd achieved what he had set out to accomplish. His hard work making himself heard had paid off.

So why was this happening? He had no reason to be Christopher.

Then he was overcome with a feeling that something was about to happen. Something that would be monumental to him. With everything going on around him it was hard to focus his mind.

And then it came to him. The words he'd heard from Liz.

"Ben, when it's time, meet me at the hill………..and don't be late."

This was something to do with Liz. He had to be with her. He knew that she needed him and she needed him now.

He knew that what he was about to do would push Maria and the man, Campbell, to the edge. But it had to be done. He was certain that if he didn't he would remain trapped in Christopher's body until the boy grew up and eventually died.

He turned to the woman who was standing to his right and pushing her hands through her mane of red hair and he spoke, he looked up at her face from the high chair and spoke five words.

Maria was relieved that Christopher had stopped coughing.

"He probably had a bit of rusk jammed in his throat, he's OK now," said Campbell as he walked back to the kitchen.

"I know, but it sounded nasty, his cough sounded very throaty," replied Maria.

She knelt forward and looked at her son. His face was red after the coughing fit, but he looked different. His expression was somber, like something was troubling him.

And then it happened.

"Maria, this is Ben speaking."

Maria recoiled and fell onto the coffee table which was behind her and then slumped to the floor. She tried to call for Campbell, but couldn't speak. The shock had frozen her.

Ben tried again.

"Maria, don't be scared………..I don't intend any harm to you or Christopher."

Maria panted as she snapped out of her temporary paralysis and made her way across the floor towards the hallway.

Campbell came out of the kitchen to see Maria on the floor, crawling. She was half in the hall and half in the lounge and the look on her face told him something was wrong, very, very wrong.

CHAPTER ONE HUNDRED AND FIFTY FOUR

Southmead Hospital
10.21am
Saturday 23rd June

Liz hadn't woken since Wednesday and when she had, she only spoke for a few moments. She had asked for a sip of water. The pain in her head seemed to have subsided, but she was too weak to say very much. Within half an hour she had fallen back to unconsciousness.

That was almost three days ago. Liz and Terry had been by her bedside ever since, taking it in turns to sleep in the large chair by the side of her bed.

They wanted to stay with her for as long as possible as they knew that her next breath could be her last. Dr Edison had shown them the MRI images and they were shocked by the size of the tumour which was taking over their daughter's brain.

Terry noticed how different Liz seemed. When she was in the coma, he sometimes felt there was a feeling of serenity and also hope that at some point she would wake and they could, as a family, move forward. But now things had changed. As she lay on the bed, with her eyes closed, there was something about Liz that reflected the mood of the moment. Almost as if she knew that her time was short. Her breathing was rapid and laboured. She lay heavy in the hospital bed as if the world was weighing her down.

Anne and Terry's tears had flowed freely since Dr Edison had told them about Liz's tumour, but right now there was no more crying to be done, at least for the time being.

The talking was done and the grieving husband and wife sat in silence. There was a glimmer of hope that Liz would wake and say something, something positive. Perhaps she would say that the pain in her head had stopped. Anne had prayed hard that the cancer would go away, but it would take more than a miracle for that to happen. The tumour was huge and wasn't going anywhere soon. It was here to stay.

Terry glanced at the clock on the wall. It told him it was ten thirty. But was it ten thirty in the morning or the evening? He had no idea and had lost all track of time. He walked out from behind the curtains which gave his daughter privacy and saw the light from the windows streaming in and illuminating the ward.

It must be morning he thought.

He stretched his legs and walked the length of the ward and then back to where his daughter lay.

He stepped back behind the curtain and saw his wife silently sleeping in the chair. He sat back down and placed his hand on Liz's and looked at her.

Her eyes were open.

Terry jumped up and moved closer to her pillow. Her eyes followed him as he moved towards her.

"Are you awake?"

Liz weakly nodded her head.

Terry gently prodded his wife until she woke.

"Anne, Anne wake up………..Liz is awake."

Anne sat up quickly and without thinking straightened her hair. She stood up and walked around to the other side of the bed so they could both be close to her. She felt groggy after being unexpectedly woken by her husband.

She stroked Liz's cheek.

"Hi sweetie, can you hear me?"

Liz nodded.

"How are you feeling?"

"I'm OK mummy, I'm sleepy."

Liz and Terry where thinking the same thing. Should they tell her about the tumor?

"Is there anything you need?" asked Terry.

She shook her head, but lifted her hand to beckon for them both to move even closer. And then she spoke.

"You have to get me out of here."

It wasn't much above a whisper. Terry had heard what she said, but Anne, because she was still sleepy, didn't hear her.

"You need to stay where you are Liz, you're too weak to go anywhere right now," said Terry.

"Listen dad, it's important………..I need to get out, I need to be somewhere else."

Anne stroked her face as she spoke.

"Sorry Liz, your dad's right, you need to stay in bed."

Liz was becoming frustrated and struggled to raise her voice.

"You don't understand, there is somewhere I really, really need to be and I need to get there soon, before………..before it's too late."

Terry went along with the conversation, without meaning to sound patronising, but he found it hard not to. It was clear, even to Liz, that he was humouring her.

"Where do you need to be?"

"The hill dad, I need you to take me to the hill where Ben died."

Terry looked at Anne, who was having difficulty in hearing what Liz was saying.

"She wants us to take her to the hill."

"Why, why do you need to be at the hill?" said her mother.

Liz didn't answer, not straight away. Her eyes looked around as if she was searching for what to say next.

"I need to be with Ben, and I need to be there soon before it's too late."

"She's probably delirious," whispered Anne.

"I am not bloody delirious and I need to get to the hill."

Anne sat back when she heard the determination in her daughter's voice.

"Listen, I don't know if you know, but I am dying. I'm sorry to break it to you, but I don't have long. I know where I am and I know you can get me to the hill in less than ten minutes. I need to be there to be with Ben………..and I can't be late."

The conviction in her voice was staggering. She certainly didn't seem delirious. In fact for the first time since she'd woken from the coma she sounded completely compos mentis.

"Listen, I have complete control of my mind and I know exactly what I am asking of you. I know it won't be easy to wheel me out of here, but I beg you to try your best………..and if you don't, I will get up and walk of my own accord, and I doubt if you'd want that."

Terry and Anne knew she wasn't bluffing. She reminded them of how she was before she was attacked. Stubborn, determined and sometimes pigheaded.

"But why do you need to be with Ben ………..you know he's no longer with us?" asked Anne.

"He's no longer with you, but he can still be with me."

They looked at her quizzically.

"I can't really explain, not right now, but please just do exactly as I say, and do it now. Drive me to the hill, the hill in Badock's Wood."

CHAPTER ONE HUNDRED AND FIFTY FIVE

Maria and Campbell's flat
10.35am
Saturday 23rd June

"Ben's back!" called Maria. She was so shaken she could hardly make herself heard and was lying on her front after tumbling over the coffee table.

"Ben's back where?" asked Campbell, clearly sensing Maria was frightened.

She motioned with her hand and pointed to the lounge.

"In there."

Campbell threw down the tea towel and rushed into the lounge to find Christopher in the highchair. He looked different. Campbell could tell by the expression on his face and the glint in his eye that it wasn't Christopher.

"Sorry for scaring Maria," said Ben.

"What do you want, I thought that you'd agreed not to bother Christopher anymore."

"I'm sorry, I hadn't planned to do this, it just happened."

"Why, what do you want, why are you back?"

Ben was about to answer, when Maria came back into the lounge.

"Make him go away, please tell him to leave us alone," shouted Maria.

"Sorry, this is not my doing………..but I do need your help, and then I promise………..I promise that I'll never bother Christopher again."

Maria covered her ears with her hands and repeated, "Make him go away - Make him go away - Make him go away - Make him go away."

Campbell stepped over to her and held her by her arms.

"Listen to me, stop it and listen to me."

Maria stopped shouting and stared at him. Campbell could see the look in her eye had returned. It was the same look she'd had when she'd lost it completely in Christopher's bedroom the previous month.

"Maria, I can't just make him go away, I can't just pick Christopher up by his ankles and shake him until Ben disappears."

Maria didn't speak and continued to stare manically.

"Ben needs us to do something and we need to listen to him."

Campbell led her by the hand and walked her over to Christopher. He looked up at Maria.

"I'm sorry to put you through this………."

"Just tell us what we need to do to put an end to all of this?" interrupted Campbell.

Christopher's eyes looked at Campbell, then to Maria and then back to Campbell, but it wasn't Christopher's eyes that were looking, it was Ben's.

"I need to be at the hill, the hill where I was murdered."

CHAPTER ONE HUNDRED AND FIFTY SIX

Southmead Hospital
10.43am
Saturday 23rd June

Terry and Anne were trusting their instincts. Neither of them were sure why Liz was so determined to be with Ben, but something about the urgency of the way she had spoken had convinced them to do as she said.

Terry had found a wheelchair and had brought it behind the curtains. He struggled as he opened it, the same way he struggled to put up a deck chair. After a couple of minutes he had clicked it into place and it was ready for Liz to climb into.

Anne pulled back the sheets and noticed the catheter tube under her bedclothes. Terry turned the other way as Anne removed the tube. Liz winced with pain as she did it.

Terry hauled her into an upright position. For a girl whose muscles had wasted over the years and who weighed less than seven and half stone, she was a heavy lump to move. She was floppy like a huge rag doll.

He propped her up as Anne swivelled her around and let her legs hang down over the side of the bed. Liz was helpless and needed her parents to do all the work. She could barely lift her arms and had no strength in her lower body to allow her to climb down from the bed.

Anne wheeled the chair as close as it would go. They struggled to haul her down from the hospital bed.

"The things too damned high," cursed Terry.

"Then lower it," suggested Liz in a pathetically weak voice.

He grabbed the electronic adjuster and fiddled with the buttons until the bed began to lower to the level of the wheelchair.

"Stop, that should be low enough," said Anne.

They slowly lugged her off the bed until she dropped onto the wheelchair. Her limp body skewed to one side.

Liz motioned to the bowl on her bedside table with her other hand over her mouth. Her blood pressure had dropped and she was feeling dizzy and nauseous. Terry got the bowl to her just in time as Liz began to vomit.

"We don't have to do this, why don't you get back into bed?" said her mother.

Liz shook her head.

"I'm OK, let's get on with it," she whispered.

Terry poked his head around the curtain and looked up and down the ward.

"The coast is clear," he whispered.

The insanity of what they were about to do did not occur to any of them. Compared to the strange events of the last few weeks, what they were about to do seemed relatively normal.

Liz's bed was near the top of the ward, about fifty feet away from the reception area, where there were always one or two nurses poking away at computers and making notes.

"How are we going to get past the nurses?" whispered Anne.

"We need to create a distraction," said Terry.

Liz was beginning to fade in and out of consciousness.

"I've an idea, give me a couple of minutes," said Anne as she disappeared along the ward and to the reception area.

Anne walked up to the nurses and asked whether the toilets were vacant.

"What does the sign say?" asked one of the nurses abruptly.

"I'm sorry, I've left my glasses by my daughter's bedside," replied Anne sheepishly.

The nurse popped her head up and looked at the door of the ladies toilets which were opposite reception.

"It's green, they're empty".

Anne thanked her, went into the cubical and locked the door. After a couple of minutes she started knocking and calling for help.

"Can anyone hear me? I've locked myself in and I can't get out. Help, can anybody hear me?"

Terry could hear the commotion and got ready to wheel Liz along the ward.

"Hello, can anyone hear me?" Anne called again.

Both nurses made their way to the toilet door.

"What's wrong?" asked one of the nurses.

"The door won't open," was Anne's muffled reply.

"OK, hold on," called the nurse as she went back to the reception desk to find a screwdriver.

A minute later she had returned.

"Don't worry, these doors can be opened from the outside, we'll have you out in a jiffy."

As the two nurses busied themselves opening the toilet door, Terry quietly wheeled Liz past them and out of the ward and into the corridor.

Seconds later Anne was free. She apologised for causing trouble, looked down the ward and could see that Liz's curtain had been pulled back and she was no longer there.

She hurried out of the ward and caught up with Liz and Terry who were approaching the exit of the main hospital wards.

No one paid the slightest bit of attention to the innocent looking parents taking their poorly daughter for trip around the hospital gardens to breathe in the glorious midmorning air of the magnificent June day. Luckily, even less attention was paid when Liz was bundled into the back seat of Anne's car in the visitor's car park.

Terry took the wheel as the silver Mercedes sped out of the car park and towards the Monks Park Avenue exit of Southmead Hospital, with the sound of the wheelchair sliding from side to side in the boot.

Anne sat next to Liz and propped herself against her daughter's limp body as she listed from side to side as Terry took each turning and roundabout.

He had been driving a little too fast for some of the corners, but was mindful not to go over thirty miles an hour as he didn't want to raise the interest of any passing police officers.

In less than ten minutes they had pulled up at the Doncaster Road entrance of Badock's Wood.

Terry lugged the wheelchair from the boot and wheeled it alongside the nearside rear passenger door. He opened it and reached in to release Liz's seatbelt.

It was a struggle and took several minutes to gently pull Liz from the car. Although she was conscious again, she was of no use. She had little control over her weak and limp frame, apart from being able to hold onto her father's shoulders as he pulled her onto the wheelchair.

Nobody spoke as Terry wheeled Liz towards the woods with Anne walking a couple of paces behind. As they veered to the right along the footpath Liz could see the hill coming into view, where Ben had lost his life that fateful September evening.

Terry and Anne shuddered in unison when they saw it. It was the first time they'd been there since the attack on Ben and Liz.

Liz smiled contently as she approached the exact spot where she and Ben had kissed the night he'd died.

"Ben, promise me you won't be late, I've waited so long for you," she whispered to herself.

CHAPTER ONE HUNDRED AND FIFTY SEVEN

Outside Maria and Campbell's flat
10.35am
Saturday 23rd June

Ben had eventually convinced Maria and Campbell to drive him to the woods. Maria was strapping him into the child seat as Campbell started the car.

"Garraway needs to be there," said Ben.

"Why?" demanded Maria.

"Just because he does, sorry, I should have mentioned it earlier………..call him and tell him to get to the hill now."

Campbell pulled his phone from his pocket and searched for the number.

"Markland, its Campbell………..listen, I can't speak for long. Please stop whatever you are doing and get to Badock's Wood as fast as you can."

Maria strapped herself in as she listened to his side of the telephone conversation.

"I can't really explain why, but Ben's awake………..no he isn't hypnotised, he's just………..he's just awake and he's demanding we take him to the hill and he wants you to be there too."

Campbell paused as Garraway spoke.

"Don't worry, if it means you turn up wearing your dressing gown, just get there as fast as you can."

Campbell ended the call and turned to Maria.

"He's still in bed, I woke him up………..but he said he'll be there."

Campbell turned to Ben in the child seat.

"Garraway says he'll be there."

"Yes, I heard you the first time, now please drive."

Campbell headed towards Southmead. Neither he nor Maria had been to Badock's Wood. It was somewhere she had vowed never to go and it certainly was somewhere she'd never wished her son to visit. But this was different, it was Ben who was going and not Christopher.

Fifteen minutes later they were driving along the main Southmead Road.

"I don't know which way," said Campbell.

Ben was peering out of the window. He knew exactly where he was and which way to go.

"Keep going and I'll tell you when to turn, you'll need to take a left soon," said the voice from the back of the car.

Maria shuddered as Ben spoke.

For just over a minute there was silence in the car, until Ben gave directions.

"Turn left at these lights."

Campbell caught the lights on amber and almost lost control as he took the left turn too fast. He struggled to keep the car on his side of the road and heard the horn of an angry driver.

"OK, this is Doncaster Road, we're nearly there, slow down a little."

Campbell slowed down as they passed the adventure playground.

"It's just here, pull over," demanded Ben.

Campbell brought the car to a halt and parked behind Anne Mason's Mercedes.

Maria unbuckled Ben from the child seat.

"Can you walk or would you like me to carry you?"

Ben tried a few unsteady steps and then fell to the floor.

"Sorry Maria, I've not mastered walking yet, you'll need to carry me."

She lifted him into her arms. It was the strangest thing she would ever do in her life. She carried Christopher, her two year old son, fully aware it wasn't him who was in her arms.

Ben directed Maria into the woods and towards the hill.

"Look!" shouted Campbell as he pointed to the hill.

"She's there," said Ben.

The hill was two hundred metres away and Liz, Anne and Terry could be seen waiting at the bottom.

Terry's jaw dropped when he saw Campbell with Maria, who was carrying Christopher and walking towards them.

"What is it daddy?" asked Liz.

"I'm not sure, hang on, I'll find out what's happening."

Terry walked with a purposeful stride towards them as they approached the hill.

"What are you doing here?"

Campbell was about to speak, but Ben spoke first.

"Because I told them to bring me," said Ben.

Terry stopped in his tracks.

"Ben?" said Terry quizzically with a look of disbelief on his face.

Campbell and Maria nodded.

"He said he had to be here," added Maria.

"I promised Liz I'd be here for her. She asked me to meet her at the hill."

"But why, why now?" demanded Terry.

Ben didn't answer. He knew that Terry understood exactly why he needed to be with Liz.

Maria, Campbell and Ben continued towards the hill, with Terry walking behind.

Ben caught site of Liz. His heart was in his throat. It was the first time he'd seen her in almost three years. As Maria got closer, with Ben in her arms, he began to cry. He could see her in the wheelchair, with her eyes shut and her head tilted forward.

In the short space of time her father had walked over to Ben, Liz had lost consciousness.

Maria placed Ben on the ground and he sat upright and looked up at Liz.

"How long has she been unconscious?" asked Ben.

Anne tried to reply but couldn't. She knew it was Ben who was talking and not the little boy she could see in front of her.

"She was awake just now, she must have only just lost consciousness," replied Terry.

The moment was interrupted by the sound of Campbell's phone ringing.

"Don't answer it, not now," demanded Maria.

"I have to, it's Garraway."

"Campbell, I need a bit of help. I'm here, but I can't make it all the way to the hill………..if you look behind, you'll see me."

Campbell turned around and saw Garraway in the clearing about two hundred metres away. He was propping himself up with his crutches and struggling to walk to the hill.

Campbell looked at Liz slumped in the wheelchair.

"Terry, Garraway is here, but he can't make it to the hill, it's his arthritis, he can't walk very far," said Campbell, as he gestured toward the wheelchair.

Terry and Campbell gently lifted Liz from the wheelchair and laid her on the grass at the bottom of the hill. Anne adjusted her hospital gown to cover her up.

Terry and Campbell walked together as Terry pushed the empty wheelchair to Garraway, who was leaning against a tree.

"Thank you," said Garraway as he flopped into the chair.

Campbell pushed him towards the hill and Terry walked alongside.

"What's happening?" asked Garraway.

"No one's really sure," replied Campbell. "It seems that both Liz and Ben have a reason to be here. They were adamant that they should be at the hill together, and Ben insisted that you should also be here."

In the short space of time it had taken Campbell to wheel Garraway to the hill, Liz had regained consciousness and was looking at Christopher sitting on the grass.

The little boy was wearing the same clothes he had been wearing back at the flat. He had rusk and raspberry stains down the front of his top and his face was dirty. In the rush to get Ben to the hill Maria hadn't had time to change his clothes, or clean his face. She grabbed a wet wipe from her bag and tidied him up.

"Thank you," said Ben.

Liz was lying on her side at the exact spot where she and Ben had their first kiss at the base of the hill. Ben climbed to his feet, and Christopher's shaky legs walked him closer to her. He stumbled in front of her, fell onto the soft grass and crawled the last few inches to be next to her.

Ben lifted Christopher's small hand and placed it in Liz's.

The second their hands touched their worlds changed.

They were alone in the woods, just the two of them. Liz looked at the handsome brave young man she'd fallen in love with and Ben saw the beautiful, funny girl who he'd set his heart on years before.

They smiled without speaking and looked into each other's eyes. Ben ran his finger along her cheek and stopped at her beautiful red lips. She kissed his finger as a tear fell from her eye.

"I've been waiting for you Ben Walker," said Liz in a soft voice.

"I know you have ……….I'm sorry you've had to wait so long."

They got to their feet and climbed the hill. Ben was behind her, and just like the time before, he saw the little tattoo of the butterfly poking out from the top of her shorts as her T-shirt rose up.

They stood together at the top, hand in hand and facing each other. He was a little taller than her and looked down into her beautiful dark eyes. Liz moved forward and kissed him on the lips. He could taste her lipstick.

Ben put his arms around her and felt the warmth of her soft skin and could smell her sweet perfume. Liz enjoyed the feel of his skin against hers as they embraced upon the hill.

Ben could feel a tugging at his shirt and looked down to see a small boy.

"Michael!" exclaimed Ben.

"I've been waiting for you, for a very long time."

Ben turned back to Liz.

"It's my brother, Michael……….., Michael this is Liz."

"I know who she is," replied the boy.

Liz looked down towards the bottom of the hill and saw her mother and father, Campbell and Maria, and her limp and lifeless body holding the hand of a scared looking little boy.

She began to cry as she called to her parents.

"Mum, Dad, don't leave me."

"Sorry Liz, it's you who are leaving them, it's time for you to let go, they'll understand," said Michael.

"No!" she cried as she turned to climb back down the hill. Ben stopped her.

"It's over, but it's not the end………..…..it's our time to move on and be together."

CHAPTER ONE HUNDRED AND FIFTY EIGHT

The Hill
Badock's Wood
11.07am
Saturday 23rd June

"Mummy mummy," cried Christopher Jameson, as he struggled to pull his hand away from Liz's.

She lay still, with her head to one side and her eyes fixed, staring at the top of the hill.

Christopher freed his hand from hers, stood up and unsteadily ran to his mother crying. She bent down and picked him up and he buried his head into her shoulder.

"Home mummy, take me home."

Garraway stood up and calmly strolled over to Liz, held his finger against her neck and patiently waited. After thirty seconds he closed her eyes with the palm of his hand.

He quietly sighed, stood up and turned to Terry and Anne who were holding each other.

"I'm sorry," said Garraway as he walked away from Liz's body.

He glanced at his watch and made a note of the time of her death. And then the crying began. He slowly walked to Maria and Campbell.

"Come on, they need to be alone."

They walked to a bench and sat in silence whilst Terry and Anne emptied their hearts.

"Markland, look at you………..you're walking without your crutches," said Campbell.

Garraway looked down at his legs. He stretched his arms and wriggled his fingers. He rotated his head and rubbed the back of his neck.

"The pain, it's gone."

He stood up and walked around the bench.

"It has………..it's gone, the pain has left me."

Campbell didn't answer. As far as he was concerned, it was just another one of those things that had happened because of the hill.

Christopher looked at his mother with tired eyes.

"Mummy, can we go home now."

CHAPTER ONE HUNDRED AND FIFTY NINE

The Turnpike
7.19pm
Thursday 6th September
Ten weeks later

Colin Matthews watched as Markland Garraway stood at the bar waiting to be served. They had decided to meet up in honour of Ben on the third anniversary of his death and raise a glass to the remarkable young man.

Garraway walked back to the table where Matthews was sitting, weaving his way between tables and other drinkers who were blocking his way.

"So what's the boggle with your arthritis?" asked Matthews.

"It went………..like wham kabam, it just disappeared. My consultant can't explain it. He says I'm a marvel of medical science. He, nor anyone of which he's aware, has ever seen anything like it before."

"And how do you feel?"

"Brilliant Colin, I feel just brilliant."

They discussed Ben Walker's case and other things and buried the hatchet. They agreed that they would never see eye to eye, but from now on, things would be a lot more harmonious between the two men.

"Here's to you………..for finally catching the bad guys," said Garraway raising his pint glass.

"No, here's to us. Without you and your crazy ideas Daniel Boyd would still be at large…………thank you Markland," replied Matthews, as he clinked his glass against Garraway's.

"So what are your intentions?" asked Matthews.

Garraway looked up from his pint glass with froth covering his top lip.

"My intentions?" he replied, wiping his mouth with a tissue.

"Yes, you're fit for work and Munroe considers you to be a hero, would you think about returning to detective work?"

"No, no…………not now. I like what I'm doing."

"Are you telling me, you would rather train detectives, than be one?"

"Yes, yes I would. There's a lot less pressure, and I'm getting too old. I think I'll leave it to the young blood. There's a lot of good new detectives on the scene. I'll leave it to those guys."

Matthews looked at Garraway, and in a slightly sheepish tone, asked him a question.

"Sir, I'm working on a case............and one of the witnesses says that she is certain that she knows who the killer is."

"That's good," replied Garraway.

"I know, but the thing is, she's blind and wasn't anywhere nearby when the murder took place............it seems she had some sort of vision............like a premonition of what happened sir."

Garraway nodded as he listened.

"The thing is sir, a lot of what she says ties in with things we know............and I was wondering, I was wondering, with your experience in this sort of thing, would you consider helping me with this case?"

Garraway smiled.

"Mr Matthews, yes............ I'd love to."

EPILOGUE

After the trial was over and the jury had considered its verdict the sentences were handed out.

Daniel John Boyd was sent to prison for life for the murder of Ben Walker and Stanley Brown.

Paul Green, Stuart Moss and Sebastian Townsend where given long custodial sentences for the brutal attack on Ben Walker. Charlotte Williams was sentenced for a lesser period for withholding information from the police.

John, the young man who viciously attacked Liz Mason, was never found. Police are still looking for him. None of the others involved in the murder of Ben Walker knew much about him. No one knew where he lived or even his surname. He'd just disappeared from the face of the earth.

Carla Price was granted immunity from prosecution under Section 71 of the Serious Organised Crime and Police Act 2005.

The hill became popular with visitors. Many had travelled from around the world to see where the murder had taken place and more importantly to a place which had such mystical qualities.

Some believed what happened to Ben Walker to have been a hoax. Something fabricated to sell newspapers. But most believed it to be true.

The events surrounding the hill had a profound effect on many people, as it proved, without a shadow of doubt, that there was life after death.

When news of what had happened eventually filtered around the world, it was reported that Atheists and Agnostics turned to religion and similarly, those, who before reading about the case had strong religious beliefs, had since found their faith had been turned upside down and inside out.

The identity of Christopher Jameson remained anonymous. The Rhythmic Movement Disorder from which he'd suffered since he was a baby had completely stopped after Liz Mason passed away. He remembered little of what took place and had no recollection of any of the hypnotherapy sessions with Tom Judd.

Tom Judd wrote a bestselling book based upon his experiences.

Maria and Campbell married the following year and Maria gave birth to a daughter shortly after.

Terry Mason retired from TM.IT in two thousand and thirteen.

He and Campbell are now very good friends.

Markland Garraway continued working for the Avon and Somerset Constabulary as did Colin Matthews who was eventually promoted to Detective Chief Inspector.

The mystical power of the Bronze Age burial mound continues to affect people and occasionally weaves its magic by giving hope to some and closure to others.

Many people will attempt to understand its power, but all of those who strive to comprehend the mysterious and supernatural qualities will never learn the secrets of the hill.

Forever, The Hill will remain an impenetrable mystery.

MESSAGE FROM THE AUTHOR

Thank you for reading The Hill and I hope you enjoyed it.

I am a self-publishing author and The Hill is my first book

I would be grateful if you could write a review which would be available to visitors to the Amazon website.

If you would like to contact me with your thoughts on The Hill, feel free to email me at:

andy@andystaffordbooks.co.uk

or visit my website at:

andystaffordbooks.co.uk

Made in the USA
Charleston, SC
30 January 2015